"DAMN LITTLE HELLCAT!"

He reached for her angrily and pulled her struggling body under him, bringing his weight down on her and pinning his hands on either side of her head with his own.

"Now, little virgin," he looked down at her, his face unreadable in the darkness. "Are you going to make this difficult for yourself? Or are you going to be a good girl and let me take you like a gentleman?"

He lowered his mouth to hers, gently parting her trembling lips and teasing with his tongue, tasting the freshness of her and probing the soft contours of her mouth. He smiled knowingly as he moved his body against hers.

"Don't!" she begged. He ignored her, and again his warm mouth came down on hers, not gently, as before, but plundering, demanding. Her breath came in ragged gasps as his lips moved to trace a fiery path down her throat.

"What are you doing?" she asked in a frightened voice.

"Making you my own," he whispered. "My very own."

*　　　　*　　　　*

The Devil's Darling

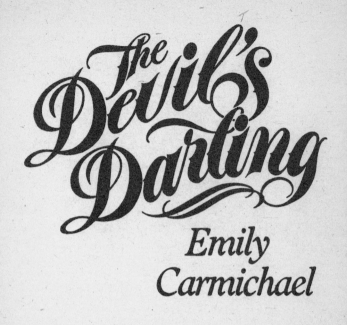

The Devil's Darling

Emily Carmichael

WARNER BOOKS

A Warner Communications Company

WARNER BOOKS EDITION

Copyright © 1987 by Emily Carmichael

Warner Books, Inc.
666 Fifth Avenue
New York, N.Y. 10103

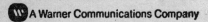 A Warner Communications Company

Printed in the United States of America

First Printing: January, 1987

10 9 8 7 6 5 4 3 2 1

CHAPTER ONE

India Catherine Carey sat in the parlor of Hillcrest House, dutifully stitching on the nightrail that would be a part of the trousseau for her coming wedding. She formed a demure picture of maidenly industry, her dark, glossy head bent dutifully over her work and her graceful fingers plying the needle with energy. A closer look would dispel this sedate picture, though, for her long, tapered fingers jerked the needle and thread in and out as if the nightrail were some detested enemy to be slain. Her finely molded lips were pressed into a tight line of displeasure, and her eyes, usually the blue of a deep, calm lake, were slate-gray and smoking with anger.

"Oh! A pox on it!" she cried indelicately as the needle slipped and a bright blossom of crimson grew on the tip of her finger.

Helen Atkins, her plump body perched a few feet away on the window seat, regarded her friend and mistress with alarm. "India!" she scowled. "I vow you've taken leave of

1

your senses!'' She looked over India's shoulder at the night-rail and declared, ''Why, you've absolutely ruined your embroidery! You silly twit! You'll have to redo the entire thing!''

''A pox on the embroidery, a pox on the nightrail, and don't call me a silly twit!'' India stood with offended dignity. ''I have reason to be upset, as well you know!''

She tossed the nightrail aside and moved to stand at the window, gazing with sadness at the late-summer finery displayed in the formal gardens behind the great house.

''Why must I marry, anyway? Why can't I stay at Hillcrest and be a spinster like old Miss Adams?''

Helen regarded her mistress with sympathy tainted by a hint of envy. It seemed to her that India had positively everything a young lady of fashion could hope for. Thick, glossy black hair, fine white skin, and startlingly blue almond-shaped eyes gave her an exotic look that almost matched her name, which was given her by an overly romantic mother enamored of exotic lands. Her uncommonly lovely features and her figure, though somewhat more slender than fashion would dictate, had made her the envy of every fashionable young woman in the county. Even though her martinet father, Sir William, had never allowed India to journey to London to make the customary rounds of plays, assemblies, and balls, that had not kept the smitten swains from the Hillcrest door. For the past three years, ever since the black-haired beauty turned fifteen, they had besieged the estate with a persistence that left India bemused and Sir William exasperated. The man whose suit Sir William had finally accepted was the cause of India's distress, but Helen failed to perceive what it was about Lord Marlowe that was the source of her friend's dismay.

''India, dear,'' she addressed the agitated girl, ''I'm afraid I still cannot understand how your father's choice has caused this most astonishing rebelliousness in your behavior.''

India fixed her with a perturbed stare that made Helen uncomfortably aware of the boldness of her comment. As the daughter of a poor curate taken into the Carey household as paid companion to the daughter of the house, she really had no place debating such things. But in spite of the sparks igniting in those alarmingly blue eyes, Helen continued.

"Lord Marlowe seems a very amiable gentleman to me, and certainly as suitable a match as any girl could hope for."

"Bah!" India returned with disgust. "I'd like to know what is so suitable about a man whose only thought is of his next card game at Almack's, and whose major concern in life is the cut of his coat!"

"But I hear all the London gentlemen of fashion live in that manner," Helen replied sagely.

"Indeed! But how would you like to spend your life with someone who resembles a peacock more than a man?"

Helen sighed enviously. "I should be glad to live with such a one if it meant traveling about London in a coach and six, having a fine town house with servants at my beck and call, and attending the opera or assemblies every evening."

Perceiving the distress in her friend's sigh, India momentarily forgot her anger and was all sympathy.

"Oh, Helen! Dear Helen! What a selfish pig I'm being! Here I am complaining about marrying and leaving Hillcrest, and you're about to be turned out of your very home!" She grew thoughtful for a time, then tossed her ebony curls defiantly. "You will have to come with me when I marry! That's all there is to it!"

Helen smiled with genuine fondness for her friend's quicksilver moods. "Now you are being a goose!" she chided. "A married lady has no need of a female companion in her husband's house! Besides," she continued with a reassuring smile, "I do believe I shall be quite well off when you leave, dear, for your stepmama's footman, George, has been casting many a sweet smile in my direction. Unless I am mistaken and setting myself too high in his regard, I believe he may very shortly declare himself."

In reality, George had cast a good deal more than smiles in her direction, but Helen had no wish to shock India's delicate sensibilities. In truth, those pampered sensibilities were not quite as delicate as some might wish.

"George is a very fine fellow." India frowned, regarding

her companion with eyes now sparkling with mischief. "But if you marry him, you'd best make him leave my stepmother's service. She'll have him in her bed before you're married a fortnight. I would be surprised if she hasn't already, the witch!"

Helen's eyes went round with horror. "India Catherine!" she exclaimed. "Wherever did you learn such lowbred conversation? I vow if Lord Marlowe ever heard such words come from your mouth he'd believe he'd engaged himself to a maidservant!"

"Do you think I know nothing of what goes on between a man and a woman?" India replied with impudently flashing eyes. "Just because I have not traveled to London does not mean I am simple!" Her brows drew together in a frown as she grew more serious. "My father's wife is a slut, and the whole county knows it!"

Helen threw up her pudgy arms in exasperation. "Such words!" she declared. "One would think you were some low creature born in a ditch, the way you speak! But you truly show your ignorance of the world by your words, for married ladies of fashion may frequently dabble here and there without losing too much in the opinion of the world. And men also. My cousin from London assures me it is so!"

"But I don't wish to have a marriage of that sort!" India answered stubbornly. "And I don't wish to marry Lord Harold Marlowe!"

Helen sighed and shook her head sadly. "You're foolish to carry on so, India. You should accept the world as it is. Besides," she continued practically, "you know you will marry Lord Marlowe simply because your father insists. You can pout all you wish, and talk about what you want and don't want, but I've never known you to completely defy Sir William's will. Come now!" she urged. "Admit it! Am I not right?"

India stood at the window and watched the setting sun paint the garden red and orange. She felt her spirits dying along with the day, for she recognized the truth of Helen's words. She did lack the courage to stand against Sir William's wishes. She knew that open defiance of her father's will would further alienate the affection of that cold man, and above all she had always longed for that affection, going to great lengths in her attempts to win it. But Sir William had been impervious to the pleading eyes of a small girl, so as she grew India had resorted to mischievous pranks and unladylike escapades to draw his attention. Her father's anger, she had reasoned, was better than his cold indifference. But it wouldn't do to let Helen know how right she was, so she turned and answered brightly with an impish smile covering her distress.

"What do you know, you silly goose! Can't I pull a long face without you getting so serious?" Then she picked up the mangled nightrail and regarded her handiwork with regret. "Ah, well." She sighed. "Tomorrow is another day."

Half an hour later India sat at her dressing table, critically regarding her reflection in the mirror. Twit! she admonished herself. She wished she hadn't displayed so childish a temper in the parlor below. Tantrums would do her no good, and only make her the object of poor Helen's sympathy. At this point, she reflected bitterly, probably nothing could do her any good. She might as well accept her future life with as good a grace as she could muster.

Actually, she had to admit, Lord Marlowe was not a bad sort, if one could ignore the frivolity of his character. She supposed that if she'd been part of the social whirl that usually attended young women of quality—the balls, assemblies, playhouses, operas, and promenades—then she might think him quite amiable. But she'd been bred to appreciate more rural pleasures—a solitary ride through the early-morning dew-laden fields, a rainy day spent reading by the huge fireplace, a peaceful summer evening's walk through the Hillcrest gardens. Of late, Sir William and Lady Carey were often in London, and, far from being lonely, India had come to treasure the privacy granted by the peaceful countryside. Hillcrest had become more than a home. It was her sanctuary, and the thought of leaving tore at her heart.

India wound her thick black hair around her hand, then

experimentally piled the shining tresses atop her head,
letting a few naturally wavy ringlets escape to frame her
oval face. Then she sighed and let the heavy mass fall again
around her shoulders. She was not in a mood to dress and
go downstairs to dine with her father and Lady Carey. She
wondered if she should send Mollie, her serving maid, to
announce that she had a headache and would take a solitary
meal in her room tonight. Her stepmother would suspect her
of pouting, but in truth her head pounded more painfully
every time she thought of Lord Marlowe and the inevitabili-
ty of her forthcoming marriage. The more she thought on
the idea of staying in her room, the more appealing it
seemed. Once she was Lord Marlowe's wife, India reasoned, she would be required to sacrifice most of her
evenings to the company of people she found dull. Even her
bedchamber she would be forced to share with someone
else. She shuddered at the unwelcome thought. That was all
the more reason she should take time to herself while
she still could. She smiled as she pulled the bell cord
summoning her maid, then picked up a volume of Shake-
spearian sonnets from her dressing table and curled contentedly on her bed for an evening of peace.

India woke with the first faint glow of dawn in the
morning sky. Instead of snuggling farther down into the bed
as most were wont to do at this house of the morn, she flung
off the warm covers and padded barefoot to the window, her
toes curling in objection to the frigid oak floor beneath her
feet. She smiled with pleasure as she opened the window
and the cool, sweet-smelling September air flooded into the
room, carrying with it a few tentative notes of early-
morning birdsong.

Her pensive mood of the previous night was gone, and
the idea struck her that this was a perfect morning for a ride
on Brandywine, the five-year-old mare she had hand-raised
from a foal. The household would not be awake for hours,
so she need not even observe proper decorum.

India's dark blue eyes gleamed with mischief as she dug
to the very bottom of her wardrobe to retrieve the stable-

boy's breeches and coarse shirt she'd filched five years before, when she was thirteen. Since her stepmother's arrival in her life three years ago, India had only been able to ride astride, in breeches, when her parents were away and Lady Carey's watchful eyes were not following her every move. But this early morning her rebellious nature won over her good sense. She donned her less than fashionable riding costume and surveyed herself in the mirror, observing that the fit was not quite what it had been several years earlier. The breeches pulled tight over her well-rounded little behind and clung snugly to her firm thighs. And the feminine curves of her breasts were more emphasized than hidden by the soft, clinging shirt.

India examined her reflection with dismay, thinking that this business of being a woman was becoming more and more inconvenient. In spite of her small stature, she could no longer be mistaken for a young stableboy. She grimaced at the woman in the mirror. There was no one to see her in any case, she reasoned, and she was not about to ruin a good morning's ride by wearing heavy skirts and riding sidesaddle! With that thought firmly in mind, she coiled her heavy hair into a tight chignon, pulled on stockings and heavy leather boots, and slipped quietly out into the cool morning.

The sun had risen quite a bit higher in the morning sky as India guided the chestnut mare across a quietly flowing stream and into the secluded meadow she thought of as her own private retreat. The soft breeze that caressed her face smelled of moist earth, and dew still sparkled on the grass that was shaded from the warming sun. The only sounds that broke the peaceful silence were the clear notes of birds and the faint rustle of the breeze through the trees.

India breathed deeply of the clear morning air and flung her arms wide to embrace the whole scene.

"What an absolutely perfect morning, in an absolutely perfect place!" she exclaimed to Brandywine, who flicked an ear and turned her head to regard her mistress quizzically. "And what a shame we have to return before the house arises!" she continued on a sadder note. She felt relatively safe, though, since Lady Carey seldom arose much before noon, and her father was not likely to note her absence.

India flung an agile leg over Brandywine's back and jumped to the ground. She deftly lifted the saddle and bridle from the mare and patted her broad rump.

"Go on!" she urged with a smile. "Go on and have fun. You won't get many more chances, you know!"

She laughed as the chestnut mare galloped to the center of the meadow, tossing her head and bucking like a foal every few strides. Then she turned and galloped at India full speed, stopping only about ten feet in front of her with a loud snort. Tossing her head in invitation, she eyed her mistress wistfully.

India laughed at the mare's antics. "You go on and play by yourself." She smiled, lifting her nose in mock haughtiness. "I'm a grown woman now and don't play such silly games."

Brandywine whuffed in obvious contempt, then turned and trotted off. India turned in the other direction, confident that the mare would not stray far from her presence. She wandered idly along the grassy bank of the stream at the meadow's edge, finally sitting in a sunny spot, stripping off her boots and stockings, and dabbling her bare feet and calves in the cold water. Sighing contentedly, she let her mind drift with the slow-moving current.

She would sorely miss the freedom of this life, she thought, though, in truth, it had not been so free since her father had taken a second wife. Before then she had been mostly free to come and go as she liked, since her father was not overly concerned with her comings and goings and took no pains to ensure she was well supervised. So she had roamed the green hills surrounding the great house with a freedom no other female of her station enjoyed, riding astride in breeches and even managing to blackmail a young gentleman neighbor to teach her elementary swordplay.

But when the new Lady Carey arrived, she had insisted that her stepdaughter concentrate on womanly pursuits, lest she cast disgrace on her family when she married. She had even put an end to those happy sessions with the curate,

Helen's father, where India had learned Latin and Greek and sampled both ancient and modern literature. Instead, she had been required to sit for hours with spinsterish Miss Leonora Adams, who labored to teach her the arts of needlework, etiquette, and household management. Seldom in the last three years had she been able to sneak out and ride without the restraints of female attire and female deportment.

"Ah, well," India murmured to a sparrow who perched on a branch above the water. "I suppose it is quite time I grew up."

Marriage might not be so bad, after all. At least she would escape the boring lessons with Miss Adams and discover once and for all the mysteries that married ladies only hinted at in the presence of curious maidens. In spite of her bold words of the previous day, spoken mostly to shock the ever-faithful Helen, India did not really know much about what went on between men and women. Out of unladylike curiosity when she was ten, she had followed a stablehand and kitchenmaid into the bushes one summer's evening. Unfortunately, the little she'd been able to see from her hiding place had been just enough to shock, confuse, and embarrass her and not nearly enough to educate her. Since that time, she'd been content to be ignorant.

Still, there must be something to this man-woman thing, she thought. Though she'd never yet met a boy who could spark her interest, if she let her thoughts wander into forbidden fantasies, she could imagine that somewhere there might be a man—tall, handsome, tender, and adoring— whose embraces might, just might, be acceptable. Unfortunately, Lord Marlowe hardly came close to fitting that fantasy picture.

Slightly embarrassed by the direction her thoughts were taking, India lifted her numbed feet from the stream and rubbed them briskly with her stockings. She spread the stockings over the grass to dry, then leaned back in the grass to enjoy the sun's warmth on her face and legs. I really must be getting back soon, she thought. But it was so pleasant to lie there in the warm sun, with the sweet fresh smell of the grass surrounding her. She closed her eyes for just a moment, then a moment more, and a moment more. . . .

The sun was past its zenith when India was startled awake by the whuff of Brandywine's soft nose in her face.

"Stupid horse!" she complained, raising a hand to push her away. "What do you . . ."

She then noticed she was no longer alone. Her private meadow had been invaded. Not ten feet away, regarding her with mixed dismay and disbelief, stood none other than her father and Lord Marlowe, her betrothed.

India's heart stopped. What wretched luck! To be caught acting the hoyden by the two people in the world least likely to forgive her. Anger at this unexpected betrayal of her private sanctuary warred with acute embarrassment over her dismaying state of dishabille. She supposed the only course open to her was to put on a bold face and brazen the scene out.

Sir William's face reddened with rage as he watched India get up from her resting place. "What have you to say for yourself, miss?" he demanded coldly.

India blushed to the roots of her dark hair. She opened her mouth to reply with a tart rejoinder, but could manage only an embarrassed squeak.

Lord Marlowe's face, in the meantime, had grown as white as his periwig as he observed the full extent of his fiancée's disarray—the bare feet and legs, mud-spattered breeches, and loose shirt whose deep vee neck revealed the alluring curves of her high breasts. Her hair had come loose from its chignon and tumbled down her back in a shining, tangled mass, decorated here and there with blades of grass. His eyes grew round with horror as, circling around the mortified girl, he observed twin grass stains gracing her well-formed behind. For possibly the first time in his life, Lord Marlowe was rendered speechless.

Sir William, it seemed, was the only one of the awkward company who had not lost his power of speech. He fixed his daughter with a gaze of contempt.

"I see you have nothing to say," he observed in a chilly voice. "That is just as well, miss, for I can think of no utterance you could make that would excuse you from such licentious and abominable behavior.''

India wished she could disappear, sink into the ground, die on the spot, anything other than stand there like a fool being slowly roasted over the fire of her father's anger.

''There is no point in carrying this unfortunate interview any further,'' Sir William continued acidly. ''Lord Marlowe has been enough distressed being forced to witness your wretched behavior. You will attend me in the library in two hours' time, dressed in proper and respectful attire. I trust by that time you will have recovered both your speech and your sanity!''

He looked significantly at Lord Marlowe, who by this time had reverted to a more natural color and was looking anything but distressed. He had, in fact, a remarkably healthy look as he continued to appreciate the visual impact of India's clothing. It was with some reluctance that he turned to mount his horse and follow Sir William into the trees.

India stood quiet and dry-eyed until they were well out of sight, then moaned softly and buried her face in the soft warmth of Brandywine's neck.

At the appointed time, India sat stiffly on the velvet settee that faced her father's desk in the Hillcrest library, trying to look composed and mature. She had dressed carefully for the interview, a light green afternoon gown with high neck and long, narrow sleeves creating a picture of modesty, but lace at neck and wrist and numerous ruffled petticoats preserving femininity. She knew she needed every ruse she could devise to survive this scrape.

Sir William sat behind his heavy carven oak desk with his wife standing by his side. Both their faces were identically forbidding. Both regarded India with eyes carved from ice.

''Daughter,'' Sir William began solemnly. ''I must regret the necessity of reminding you of your station in life, and the behavior required of a young woman in your position.''

Here we go again, India groaned silently—The Family Lecture.

Sir William continued stolidly, as if he had the words

memorized. "Our family is of undisputed honor and great distinction of character. I have always labored to preserve the dignity of the Carey name, holding honor to be above all things. You are my only child." His face tightened as he admitted his lack of a more suitable heir, and his eyes reflected a contempt for her that India couldn't quite understand. He composed himself to go on. "Through your scandalous behavior, India, you have brought disgrace down upon our heads, and shame to our honorable name. You have flagrantly ignored the precepts of decent behavior that have been taught you since your childhood, and by so doing, have laid our family open to the ridicule of our peers."

Sir William paused for breath, and India bowed her head in hopes that the appearance of humble contrition would stave off a longer diatribe. It was not to be, however, for in her husband's pause Lady Carey continued the lecture.

"Your father has given you every advantage in life," she said. "In addition, he went to great trouble to arrange a brilliant match for you with a very amiable, wealthy man, a match that will be advantageous to our entire family. I myself have endeavored to guide you in the arts of womanly grace, but in view of your adventure this morning, I fear I must admit defeat."

India eyed Lady Carey with dislike. She reflected bitterly that if she'd followed her stepmother's example of "womanly grace," she'd have been disowned as a trollop long ago.

Sir William regarded his daughter sternly.

"You've done us a very bad turn, India Catherine," he said. "Imagine my worry when Lord Marlowe called this morning and you were nowhere to be found! When the stablemaster told me you'd taken your mare out early and hadn't yet returned, I pictured all manner of dire things having befallen you. And poor Lord Marlowe was so beside himself with concern that I feared he was about to faint, poor man!"

India could not repress a smile at the picture of Lord Marlowe swooning in the parlor.

Sir William skewered his daughter with an icy glare. "Let me assure you, girl, there is no cause for levity in this discussion," he declared. "No cause at all!" After a few moments of silence, in which India looked properly chastened, he continued in a solemn voice.

"Unfortunate as this incident is, perhaps it is best that we have discovered this flaw in your character while there is still time to correct it."

India couldn't help but notice Lady Carey's smirk of triumph.

Sir William attempted a tight smile. "Now," he said, settling back in his seat. "I am a just man and a responsible father, and I hope you will regard my decision as being in your best interests, India Catherine."

India held her breath and waited for the ax to fall.

"You have a cousin who is presently residing in France, a gentlewoman of such virtue that she might mend the behavior of Satan if given a chance. She runs a school for young ladies of quality near Paris."

India's heart sank. Not cousin Prudence!

"Your stepmother and I have decided that you shall spend this winter with your cousin, and hope that you will profit by the example of her excellent demeanor. Arrangements have been made for you to depart in five days' time, so I suggest you spend your remaining time at Hillcrest packing whatever belongings you wish to take along."

India was stunned by her father's announcement. "Father," she begged, for once not having to act the role of humble penitent. "Don't send me away from Hillcrest! Please. . . . Surely my behavior has not been so bad as that! Just one little escapade!"

Sir William stood and leaned forward as anger began to erode his composure. "Silence!" he commanded in a tone befitting a former colonel in the Duke of Marlborough's forces. "Just be grateful that you have not ruined everything with your 'one little escapade'! Lord Marlowe has generously insisted that he still feels obligated to honor his contract to make you his wife. You will return to Hillcrest in March to prepare for an April wedding. I hope by then you have learned behavior that is appropriate to your station in life. But if you have not, at least you will be Marlowe's problem and not mine!''

With that statement, Sir William dismissed his daughter from his presence and, he sincerely hoped, from his responsibility. With a great relief he congratulated himself for suitably disposing of a child who was from the first an unwanted inconvenience and in recent times a nuisance beyond bearing. Months later he would think back on his self-congratulatory satisfaction with chagrin, and wish desperately that he'd never let the troublesome chit out of his sight.

CHAPTER TWO

Christopher Barnett stood by the rail of his ship, staring intently into the night. The rocky Cornwall coast, not more than a quarter mile from where the *Black Falcon* was anchored, sails furled and lanterns doused, was shrouded and invisible in heavy fog. The fog was all-enveloping. The railing dripped with it and the deck underfoot was slick. The night was all mist and darkness and silence. Even the sound of the wavelets slapping the sleek hull was muffled.

A bulky figure materialized out of the night to stand by his side at the rail. Christopher continued to frown into the night, then cursed softly, employing several epithets that would have done proud his most hardened seamen.

"They should have been back a full half-hour ago, Ian!"

Ian McCann leaned his three hundred pounds of heavily muscled, redheaded bulk on the rail and took his turn staring into the darkness, a frown creasing his freckled brow.

"Aye, Cap'n, they're taking their sweet time about it this

run. This be the last of the stuff to go, though." He hesitated before voicing the thought that had been plaguing him for the last quarter hour. "I could get the men up on deck and set the sails," he said tentatively. "They're nervous enough they'd not object to leaving those few lads behind. We know this cove well enough to get out even in this fog, and we could pick up the lads later at the rendezvous point."

Christopher left the rail to pace along the wet deck. He was an imposing figure even beside the bulk of his quartermaster. The sleek proportions of his broad shoulders, narrow hips, and long, well-muscled legs lent grace to his six-five frame. His strong face was framed by a thick but closely trimmed dark beard and short, dark brown hair. As he paced the slick deck, his stride was fluid and supple, but his coiled-spring movements betrayed his anxiety and impatience. His deceptively gentle brown eyes stared into the darkness as if trying to pierce the fog and discover what had detained his men.

"Give them another half-hour," he said. "I don't want to leave them here to be chased down by the revenue officers come daylight. Have the men stand ready, though," he ordered grimly. "We may want to leave in a hell of a hurry if something's gone awry. I'll be in my cabin. I want to be called the minute that boat is sighted."

"Aye, sir." Ian watched his captain cross the deck and fade into the fog. He was glad to sail with a man who would go to the limit to keep his crew safe, but he hoped this time Christopher didn't go beyond the limit. He had an evil feeling about this trip, and he didn't want his neck stretched before he'd enjoyed the fortune they'd made smuggling contraband from France and the New World these last five years. Even with the local revenuers thoroughly bribed, things could easily go wrong.

Things could go wrong, especially with that promotion-hungry naval lieutenant cruising up and down the Cornwall coast, hoping to assure himself a better post by securing the untimely demise of smugglers such as Christopher Barnett and his crew. And Christopher's delight in baiting the patrol officer only made things more dangerous. He would stand on his quarterdeck grinning with malice while the young officer and his crew searched his little brigantine from bow to stern without finding a trace of contraband. Last time that happened, two months ago, Ian had thought the hapless lieutenant's eyes were going to pop right out of his head with frustration. Aye, for all his success these years past, Christopher had better not stretch his luck too far. Ian had an uncomfortable feeling they'd best be away from here soon, before fickle Lady Luck turned her face away.

A faint voice called through the fog. "Ahoy the ship!" Ian recognized the voice of John Daughtery, who had led the last unloading crew to shore.

"Ahoy there!" he answered. "Is all well?"

"Well enough!" came the reply. "Light a lantern to guide us in, man. We're all muddled in this fog! We've been rowing in circles this last half-hour!"

Ian lit a lantern and hung it at the stern, then roused the ship's boy, a gangly lad of ten years, to fetch the captain. A few moments after returning to the rail to resume his anxious vigil, he was joined by a frowning Christopher. There followed several anxious minutes when Ian thought he'd been dreaming the voice. Finally, the muffled splash of oars reassured them that the lamp had been seen. In only a few more minutes a thump against the *Falcon*'s hull signaled the safe return of the tardy crewmen.

A ghost of a smile played at Christopher's lips. It appeared that luck was with him again.

"Get that boat secured and set the topsails," he instructed McCann. "We'll want to ease our way out with considerable caution, I think, but we can't wait here for the fog to lift."

He frowned into the darkness beyond the rail. "I think the fog's thinning a bit, anyway. Wait!" Christopher's features were set and grim as he stared into the night. "Look just off the bow there! Do you see it?"

Both men's eyes strained to pierce the shrouded darkness, and once again the light winked faintly through the slowly lifting mist.

"It's the shore watch," Ian groaned. "The revenue cutter must be coming down the coast. Though how the hell he spotted it in this fog I'd like to know!"

Christopher vented his frustration with a string of oaths that brought a smile of admiration to the quartermaster's freckled face. "What the hell is that son of a bitch Jeremiah doing off schedule?" he growled. "I'd hate to think the boy-lieutenant is beginning to use initiative in his crusade to rid the world of us villains!"

Ian could see ample cause for his captain's alarm. With the cutter close enough to be spotted by the shore watch, they had no time to set sail and maneuver out of the inlet before the revenuers would be upon them. On the other hand, if they were spotted in this cove, with no room to maneuver, every last one of them would end up on the gallows.

"Christopher," he ventured, "do you want to run for it?"

If luck was with them they just might gain open water in time to get a running start on the revenue cutter, or slip by the cutter in the fog without being seen. Only with a great amount of luck, though.

Christopher regarded the big Scot with cocked eyebrow and a devilish grin. "Don't you know suicide is mortal sin, Ian, my friend?"

Ian made a rude sound in answer.

"No," Christopher continued in a more serious vein. "This fog delayed up here to put us in trouble's way, and now let's hope it may save our necks. Douse the stern lantern. And pass the word to the crew—I want absolute silence until they're told otherwise. I don't want to hear a single whisper or the scuff of a boot on deck until that cutter is well away from us. With luck she'll never see us." He paused, thinking grimly of the odds. "And Ian?" He finally smiled.

"Aye, Christopher?"

"If you've ever bent that stiff Scots pride of yours to prayer, now'd be the time to do it!"

"Hmph!" he grunted, and disappeared into the night to relay his captain's commands.

Silence enshrouded the little brigantine. Only an occasional creak of the rigging or a muffled slap of the sea against the hull broke the stillness. Christopher stood alone on the quarterdeck, waiting in the dripping, clammy darkness for the lights of the revenue cutter to round the headland and either pass them by, ignorant of their presence in the blanketing mist, or head into the inlet and seal their doom. The fog was lighter than it had been, lighter than he would like it to be, but it still might hide them, he thought, with a fair amount of luck. It occurred to him, though, that this might be a trap sprung by an informer. If Mr. Jeremiah was varying his schedule because he knew of their plans for this night, no amount of luck could save them.

Luck! Christopher smiled bitterly. His crew thought he was the luckiest man to ever turn his hand to the smugglers' trade, and they were glad to sail with him. They believed his luck had made their fortune and kept them from the grasp of the law on the frequent smuggling trips and less frequent pirate operations of these past years, and probably they had faith that his luck would carry them through to safety this time, as well.

Christopher knew better, though. His success was due to meticulous planning and careful operations, not to mention substantial bribes placed in the right hands. He didn't trust to Lady Luck, that fickle patroness of all who lived, as he did, on the sharp edge of disaster. She had deserted him on a night in August, twelve years ago, and since that night he'd trusted only himself, surviving in a grim world by his considerable physical strength and sharp wits.

Christopher stood like a statue as his eyes strained through the night, seeking the outcome of this grim waiting. He saw only darkness, heard only silence. The memories that had haunted him through these years flooded his mind. The past twelve years disappeared as though they'd never been.

It had been a wet summer night in August 1704 when his life had shattered. Then Christopher Barnett had not existed. On that night he was still young, callow Christopher

Armstrong, second son to the Earl of Woodsford, just beginning to carve out a noteworthy career for himself as an officer in Queen Anne's army under the command of the Duke of Marlborough. On that night near the village of Blenheim on the northern bank of the Danube, grim tidings had reached him of the tragic deaths of both his father and brother in a carriage accident. No matter that he was on campaign and that battle with the French and Bavarians was imminent. As the new Earl of Woodsford and the only surviving member of his family, he was required to return to his estate, see to his family affairs, and ensure the orderly succession of the title.

And so he had done, or at least tried to do, pausing only long enough before the start of his journey to procure a good horse and a quick meal at the inn that served as temporary regimental headquarters. He had no sooner sat down to take his meal beside John Thomas, Colonel William Carey's valet, than the door had swung open, admitting gusts of wind and rain along with a cloaked figure whom Christopher immediately recognized as Phillipe Duquesne, a Parisian friend of some years past, whom he knew to be presently serving in the French cavalry. Since the Frenchman was wearing a British army uniform, there was little doubt in Christopher's mind as to Phillipe's current activities behind the British lines. What he was doing boldly walking into regimental headquarters Christopher intended to find out without delay.

As ill-luck would have it, just as Christopher was about to confront the Frenchman with his questions, Colonel Carey himself descended the stairs and entered the taproom, taking in the scene with a thoughtful frown. Not recognizing the newcomer who was still dripping rainwater on the taproom floor, he demanded Phillipe's identity. It was then Christopher made his damning error, a mistake of youth, ill-judgment, and a misguided sense of personal loyalty, all qualities he sincerely hoped he had left behind in the years since that dire evening. Instead of immediately condemning Phillipe for what he knew him to be, he maintained silence, hoping that somehow the situation could be resolved without his personally speaking out against a once-valued friend. His silence had been condemning, however, when that friend, caught in a hopeless situation and trying to protect his real contact, confessed and identified Christopher as his accomplice.

Three days later, Ensign Christopher Armstrong had been convicted of treason and condemned to a traitor's death on the testimony of Colonel William Carey and the already condemned Frenchman, Phillipe Duquesne. Colonel Carey, for his outstanding service to the crown, was awarded a knighthood and possession of the Earl of Woodsford's estates, which were forfeit to the crown. John Thomas, the man who could have testified to the innocence of Christopher's conversation with the Frenchman, mysteriously disappeared. Just as mysteriously, Phillipe Duquesne managed to escape before he met his fate. In the wave of patriotism that followed the French-Bavarian defeat at the Battle of Blenheim, no one cared to listen to Christopher's claims of innocence. They only wanted to spill the blood of one they believed had ignominiously betrayed his comrades on the eve of a crucial battle.

Even now, standing on the deck of a ship hundreds of miles and twelve years away from Blenheim, Christopher ached with frustration and anger at that betrayal. He had escaped his fate, thanks to jailers made less than vigilant by his substantial bribes. He had assumed his deceased mother's maiden name—Barnett—and signed on as a common seaman in Her Majesty's Royal Navy, laboring for nearly seven years before the mast, an experience that tempered both the strength of his body and the iron of his spirit. Year by year his thirst for revenge grew until it was the only thing that gave his miserable existence meaning. He meant to make sure that Sir William Carey someday sorely regretted making his fortune at Christopher Armstrong's expense!

He'd finally seen his chance in March 1711 when assigned to the prize crew of a captured French brigantine. He and several other less than worthy crewmembers had taken over from the young midshipman in charge, who in truth was not overly reluctant to join them, and had turned the little brigantine to smuggling and piracy, making good use of the talent for seamanship that Christopher had discovered in the navy. In the past daredevil years Christopher Barnett, his true identity known to only his closest officers, Ian McCann and Seamus Kennedy, acquired both considerable fortune and reputation. But only two goals really interested him. The first was to find John Thomas and, through his testimony, regain the good name and estates of Christopher Armstrong, Earl of Woodsford. The second was to make Colonel Carey, now Sir William Carey, pay for his overly hasty condemnation of a man who, proper investigation would have proven, was innocent.

Christopher was jerked back from his bitter memories by the appearance of a distant orange glow that could be none other than the light of the revenue cutter rounding the headland. He resisted the temptation to hold his breath as he followed its slow progress across the mouth of the inlet. Every eye on the ship followed the light as it inched along its course. Even the hardest and most seasoned of the smugglers waited with pounding hearts as they watched for the cutter to change direction.

Time dragged. At times the cutter seemed to stand still, so slow was her progress. Christopher finally began to breathe easier as the cutter reached the halfway point without altering course. The forty crewmen, standing silent and tense on the deck below, eased somewhat as the fortunate Mr. Jeremiah continued his unvarying course, ignorant of the fact that, not a mile away, his prey lay silent, dark, and vulnerable in the barely concealing mist.

As the cutter's lights finally faded into invisibility, Ian McCann moved out of the fog to stand beside his captain. "Orders, Christopher?" he asked quietly.

Christopher gestured him to silence, still staring in the direction the cutter had disappeared. When another few moments of silence had passed, he turned to his quartermaster and grinned. "If that young fool Jeremiah wants to catch smugglers, he'd best learn to sail a dark ship. If he'd not had his lanterns burning, we'd have sailed right into his guns in this fog."

"Aye," McCann agreed. " 'Twas a wee bit close."

"That it was, my friend!" Christopher replied, his deep voice jubilant with relief. "Just to ensure the good Mr. Jeremiah doesn't have second thoughts about this cove and come back to investigate, let's slip out of here as silently as possible—topsails only—and keep the lanterns doused. I'd rather risk the rocks than the gallows."

"Ay, Christopher," Ian acknowledge readily. "What destination?"

Christopher grinned. "We head for Falcon's Nest. The crew could use a rest, and I could use a few weeks to think up better ways to harass the worthy Mr. Jeremiah."

Ian smiled broadly, his face lighting up with a joy he took no pains to hide. Christopher glanced at the big quartermaster with amusement.

"Don't be so anxious to get back to that sweet young wife of yours that you run us onto the rocks, man." He shook his head in half-serious disgust. "There's nothing like a comely wench to turn a good sailor into a landlubber!"

"Aye, that may be." McCann grinned. "But there's not a man among us"—he paused and looked significantly at his friend—"who'd not profit by having a good lass like my Bess!"

Christopher smiled, but his smile didn't reach the flint of his eyes. "Stop trying to mellow me, my friend. My soul is hard and bloody and there's no room in it for a woman's affection. So stir yourself and sail us out of here, or we'll all hang on the gallows yet, and you'll leave your sweet Bess a widow!"

McCann turned with a tolerant grin and vanished into the mist, leaving Christopher alone to stare after the vanished lights of the cutter. He smiled at the recollection of Ian's many broad hints during this last trip. Once a man was snared by a woman, Christopher noted with amusement, he couldn't rest until every other available male was caught in the same trap. He pitied any woman who cast the net for him, though. She was likely to find the bait taken, enjoyed, and the trap still unsprung. In truth, Christopher thought, his heart must have turned to stone over these past hard years. And he would have it no other way. The world was a hard place, and the man who let himself become vulnerable to anyone was likely to reap a bitter harvest. Better to take his pleasure where he would and leave the tender ties of the heart to those who could afford them. Let Ian have his Bess, but any lass who sought to nourish herself on his own tender affections would starve on the barrenness she would find in his heart.

CHAPTER THREE

India shivered as she stood near the stern railing of the *Sea Gull* and clutched her cloak more tightly around her to ward off the knife-edged wind.

"I'm going to die, I swear I am, before we set foot on good English soil again!" wailed Helen, shivering beside her.

"Well, go below with Mollie, you silly goose!" India said. "You don't have to stay up on deck just because I'm here."

"Come with me!" Helen pleaded.

"No! But you go on." India had stayed up on deck in spite of the unpleasant weather during their Channel crossing, but she saw no reason why her companion should suffer just to keep her company. "That cabin makes me seasick. Besides, I feel like I'm in a coffin when I'm down there and the ship is tossing about like this."

"Oh, mercy!" Helen prayed. "Well, I won't leave you alone up here with those rough sailor types wandering wherever they will!"

India sighed in fond exasperation, but did not attempt to argue any further. She was truly glad of her companion's company and grateful for her willingness to brave the elements. She and Helen had grown quite close during the depressing months living with Prudence Wilson. In fact, India thought that if not for Helen's unfailing good humor and devotion, she would have gone crazy penned up in Prudence's cheerless house, trying to restrain her natural ebullience and mold herself into her cousin's idea of a well-behaved young lady.

India pulled her hood more tightly around her head, trying in vain to keep her long dark hair from whipping out in the wind. "I vow it's as cold out here as cousin Prue's parlor!" She smiled.

Helen giggled brightly in spite of the cold. "Oh, surely, nothing could be as cold as that dreary room! And to think of the hours she made you sit in there, reading the Bible and doing all that needlework!" Helen exclaimed. "Believe me, I was glad to be working in the kitchen! At least it was warm in there!"

India frowned to remember that her cousin had regarded Helen as little more than a kitchenmaid, using her as a servant in spite of the fact she'd been well paid for her keep, just as she was for India's.

"I would have joined you in the kitchen if I could," India replied with a smile. "Truly I would've preferred cutting vegetables to sewing those wretched samplers!"

Both girls laughed, glad to be going home again, glad that the "trial by Prudence," as they'd come to call the experience, was over at last. But India had learned at least one valuable lesson from her visit. Never again would she feel she could bemoan her lot in life. She was going to marry a rich nobleman. No matter that he was not to her taste. Unlike Prudence, she would never need to grub for enough money to maintain herself in genteel poverty by tutoring the daughters of the rich and kowtowing to their snobbish parents. And if her father had never shown her any affection, at least he had provided her with all the advantages of wealth. India knew that she should try to be more grateful for the good things in her life, and accept the not-so-good things with better humor. She was trying, but she still couldn't quite manage to accept dutifully the future her father had chosen for her, the future that awaited her on her return to her beloved Hillcrest.

Prudence's lifeless existence resulted from lack of both wealth and love. India wondered if the wealth in her own life could compensate for the lack of love. All her life she had longed for someone to love her. Her mother had died when she was only a year old. Her father only tolerated her, and all her childish attempts to win his love had met with cold indifference. As she grew older she realized her father would never regard her as anything but a nuisance. She took comfort in the affection of Helen and the household servants, lavishing them in turn with all the warmth of her young heart. But now she was about to be separated from those dear people and pushed into the cold embrace of Lord Marlowe. India knew she would never be anything more than a possession to her husband. Lord Marlowe was a man who enjoyed surrounding himself with showpieces of beauty and good taste. She would just be another piece in his collection. Could all his wealth compensate her for such a cold existence? Perhaps in time she could learn to substitute the companionship of friends and the affection of her children for that one special love she longed for.

Probably, after all, love was just a fantasy, an idea invented by poets and authors of romances. She was no doubt wasting her energy and making herself needlessly unhappy longing for something that existed only in her imagination. She thought back to Prue's drab existence and knew she should feel supremely grateful for all she had, but still she couldn't suppress the stab of rebellious discontent at the thought of her future. Would she never grow up and face the fact that the real world was a harsh place of practicalities, a place with no room for the romantic dreams of young girls?

The wind was getting stronger, whipping salt spray over the rail and dampening both the cloaks and the spirits of the two girls standing at the stern. A young officer approached them deferentially, occasionally clinging to the rail for balance as he made his way along the tossing deck.

"Your pardon, ladies," he began, touching his cap respectfully. "We're in for a bit of a blow, it seems, and the captain requests that you return to your cabin."

"Oh, mercy!" wailed Helen, instantly panicked. "Is there . . . are we . . ."

"Rest assured, miss"—he smiled reassuringly—"that the *Sea Gull* has made this crossing many times, and never have we failed to put our passengers safely on shore."

Helen was only slightly reassured, however, and regarded the lowering black clouds with doubt. India took her arm comfortingly and patted her hand.

"I'm sure there's nothing to worry about, Helen. These good men know what they're about."

India looked at the young officer regretfully. "Could we remain just a little while longer? It's really not so bad yet, and that small cabin is so . . . close." She dreaded the thought of three women—Helen, herself, and her maid, Mollie—crowded into one small cabin while the ship pitched and tossed in the storm. She wanted to avoid it for as long as possible.

The officer shook his head impatiently. "I sympathize, miss. I realize the unpleasantness. But, believe me, you will be much safer below. When it is safe to return above I will notify you ladies immediately."

India sighed in reluctant submission. She allowed the officer to take her arm as she and Helen moved haltingly along the slippery deck. Just the thought of that cabin in these heaving seas was beginning to make her queasy.

The unpleasantness of the storm far exceeded even India's expectations. It seemed as though an eternity had passed since they had first descended below and been shut in the tiny cabin. Surely, India moaned to herself as the seconds and minutes and hours dragged by, even hell could be no worse than being locked in the bowels of a ship being tossed to and fro by an angry sea.

All three women were sick, and the reek of the closed cabin was making them even sicker. The world had erupted into chaos as the ship lurched insanely, first rising, tilted precariously on its stern, then quickly dropping, leaning so far over on its side that it seemed doomed to capsize. The three women braced themselves against anything that looked secure, watching as loose items slid across the deck first one way, then the other. India's trunk, which a sailor had tied down at the beginning of the crossing, had broken loose and endangered lives and limbs with every movement of the ship.

Helen whimpered with each erratic roll. Gray-haired Mollie, usually so soft-spoken, had been cursing nonstop for at least two hours. India, who normally would have been fascinated by the virtuosity of Mollie's below-stairs language, huddled silently in her bunk.

The unfortunate *Sea Gull* creaked and groaned in protest with every lurch, and India wondered how long the ship could hold together. Life had never seemed so fragile. She tried to fight down a rising tide of panic by turning her mind to pleasant thoughts, but her mind refused to turn. Desperate imaginings crowded in instead, thoughts that the ship was dismasted and bound for certain doom, or that it would capsize on the next tilt and roll, turning their cabin into a watery coffin. Worse still, what if the crew were all dead, swept away by the waves, and the three women were the only ones left alive to ride out the storm in lonely terror until the ship was finally broken to pieces by the fury of the sea?

India's exhausted mind and body finally took refuge in fitful sleep, waking occasionally to nausea and terror and then uneasily dropping back into a restless, fitful doze. After what seemed hours of being tossed about, she was brought back to full consciousness by a lessening of the motion of the ship. She looked blearily at Helen, who looked back at her out of a pale green face.

"Perhaps it's over?" Helen pleaded quietly.

"Perhaps," India replied. How she wished they had a porthole to discover whether it was night or day, and what conditions were outside. They would have to wait for someone to come.

The deck still moved uncomfortably, but they were able to stand now and keep their feet beneath them. They resecured the trunk, picked up the loose debris that littered the cabin, and sat down to wait. The ship was ominously silent. Both Helen and Mollie wore faces blank from exhaustion, and India knew that she didn't look any better.

India fought the urge to go up on deck and see for herself what was happening. It was an almost irresistible temptation to escape the reeking cabin, breathe in the fresh, cleansing sea air, and reassure herself that up above all was indeed well, that the crew was simply too occupied to spare a reassuring word to three insignificant passengers. Someone will come, she reasoned, as soon as they can.

Two hours passed. India sat on her bunk, surveying her haggard companions, knowing she looked much the same as they and not caring. Occasionally one or the other of them ventured a word of encouragement or whimpered as the ship took a particularly erratic lurch. Other than that the silence was unbroken except by the creaks and groans of the *Sea Gull*'s overstressed hull and rigging. Eventually the motion of the ship became hypnotic, tempting India once again to give her tired body over to sleep. Yet uneasiness kept her awake, and she listened hopefully for the sound of someone coming down the companionway to tell them that all was well.

Finally her senses were jerked fully awake by the sound of feet running on deck, then voices raised above the steady sound of the wind.

"Listen!" she commanded. "Something's happening!"

"Is it good or bad?" Helen asked in a frightened voice.

"I don't know!" India replied. "At least we know someone is up there!"

More running feet. Then someone on deck screamed, a raw scream of naked fear.

"Oh, my God!" Helen wailed.

India had waited long enough. "I'm going up there!" she cried, her voice edged with rising panic.

Mollie grabbed her arm. "No! Miss India, calm down. You'll only be in the . . ."

A rending screech and violent jolt interrupted them, throwing all three women into a confused tangle of arms and legs at the front of the cabin. India screamed as she saw her trunk break loose and hurtle across the cabin straight toward Helen, who lay whimpering and immobilized by fear.

"Helen!" India screamed, and launched herself across the steeply tilted deck to pull her friend away. She succeeded only in placing herself in the path of danger, however. Fiery stars of pain exploded before her eyes as the heavy trunk hit her squarely on the shoulder, slamming both her and the helpless Helen into the bulkhead.

A chaos of sound erupted around them, a tortured symphony of tearing, twisting, splintering wood and the screams of terrified men. The ship bucked again and the trunk slid to the other side of the cabin. Water began to seep in under the door.

Helen was screaming every other breath. India tried valiantly to retain her consciousness in spite of the mind-numbing pain stabbing through her shoulder. Then Mollie's warm hand was on her good arm, helping her up.

"We've got to get out of this cabin, Miss India, or we're as good as dead, we are!"

India looked at her dizzily. Mollie seemed a sea of calm in a world gone mad. Blackness threatened to engulf her, darkening her vision and forcing her to clutch at Mollie for support. She couldn't tell if the roaring she heard was in her head or in the cabin.

"Helen?" she gasped.

"Right as rain," Mollie replied calmly. "Just a bit stunned, like yourself, Miss India. Come on, now. We'll just get up on deck and see what's about. Hold on to me, both of you. That's right."

Seawater swirled around their feet as they left the cabin and stumbled toward the companionway leading above. As they climbed the stairway, the frightened calls and angry curses of the sailors became louder still. The ship lurched again and almost sent the three of them sprawling from the top of the companionway, but Mollie's considerable strength managed to keep her charges upright.

The cold wind and driving rain that met them when they emerged on deck was immediately forgotten as they surveyed the scene before them. The groans of injured men mingled with the protests of the tortured wooden hull as the doomed *Sea Gull* was pounded on the rocks that impaled her and held her immobile. She was stripped of her rigging, all except for the mizzenmast, whose yards and spars creaked ominously above them. Men lay crushed and lifeless where tangles of lines and spars had crashed down on them. One sailor, still a youth by the look of him, lay practically at India's feet with a jagged splinter through his throat. His blood mixed with the rain and coursed down the deck in rivulets.

Helen stared blankly ahead, still too dazed for the bloody spectacle to have an impact. India retched. She cradled her injured arm closer to her body and fought down the tears of pain and fear. Sickness threatened to claim her again, but she fought it down. If she had to die, she'd try to go out with some dignity, at least! But she refused to give up. Surely there was a way to escape this deathtrap! There had to be a way!

India and Mollie hesitantly made their way along the canted deck, dragging the insensate Helen with them. Destruction and death were everywhere they looked, making India clench her jaw in an effort to keep nausea at bay. Mollie resumed her cursing.

"Heave away!"

The faint sound of a voice, barely noticeable above the sound of the wind, made India turn. She saw for the first time that several lifeboats had been swung out. One of them was about to be lowered into the churning water. Another was already trying to make its way through the treacherous rocks to the safety of the beach. Here was their escape, their chance for safety!

"Mollie!" India grabbed the older woman's arm to get her attention. "The lifeboats!" Her words were barely audible above the cacophony of wind, rain, and surf, but Mollie nodded to indicate she'd heard.

Between them India and Mollie guided the still-dazed Helen toward the rapidly filling lifeboat, where one pitifully young officer was trying to direct an orderly evacuation. His attempts were having no success with the panicky crowd of sailors jostling for a place on the boat. Finally one of the fortunate few who were already aboard unsheathed a wicked-looking blade and fended off the crowd still attempting to climb in. The already overloaded skiff was lowered over the side. It had no sooner hit the water than a wave smashed it against the *Sea Gull*'s hull. The cries of its passengers were carried away by the wind as they were dumped into the ice-cold sea. A few heads bobbed to the surface, only to be swept toward the jagged rocks and certain death.

India fought her rising panic as she watched the remnants of the second lifeboat pounded to splinters against the rocks. The first boat was still afloat and just barely visible through the rain. The passengers were rowing desperately toward what appeared to be a break in the deadly rocks. A wave hid them from view for a moment, and then they could no longer be seen. Capsized? Or just out of sight? India didn't know, but she was beginning to believe the sea was going to claim them all. It appeared that the problems of her future had just become irrelevant.

Helen was coming to herself, and with dismay was beginning to register the scene of destruction surrounding them.

"India," she whimpered fearfully. "India, what are we going to do?"

India attempted a reassuring smile. "We're going to get on the next boat. That's what we're going to do!" She gestured to the third and last lifeboat being readied. A slim chance was better than certain death, she thought grimly.

"But . . ." Helen started, her voice shrill with fear.

"Don't worry," India soothed, praying that these were not really the last few minutes of their lives, as she strongly suspected. "There's room for all of us. This boat won't be overloaded like the first two. We'll be fine."

Helen did not look reassured. Mollie was frankly disbelieving. But all the same, the three frightened women moved toward the boat as others began to climb aboard.

"Hurry up, there!" the young officer called in a worried voice. "We . . ."

Suddenly the *Sea Gull* shifted on the rocks, tilting the

deck at the opposite angle. The hull groaned and the timbers
of the one remaining mast creaked ominously.

A crewman yelled, "She's breaking up! Get the boat
down! Get it down, dammit!"

"No! Wait!" India screamed as she began to run across
the slippery deck. She frantically pushed Helen and Mollie
ahead of her toward the boat. They were almost there,
almost in reach of the crewman's hand outstretched to help
them board, when the agonized groan of twisting and
splintering timber riveted their attention aft. India did not
even have time to scream as a massive spar from the falling
mizzenmast buried her beneath its weight.

CHAPTER FOUR

Blue sea merged into blue sky as Christopher Barnett swept
the horizon with his glass. Not a cloud remained to recall
last night's storm.

"Looks like we lost him," he said, handing the glass to
his quartermaster.

"Aye," Ian commented. " 'Tis a shame that's not all we
lost!"

Christopher's eyes strayed to the splintered stump that
rose where the topgallant mast had been. "It could have
been worse," he said. "Much worse. We're not that far
from the rocks off St. Alban's Head."

Ian grinned unpleasantly. "Maybe that's where that damned
revenue cutter is—driven up on the rocks!"

Christopher leaned his tall frame against the railing. They
had just off-loaded a profitable cargo of contraband and then
survived a storm that could easily have sent them to the
bottom of the English Channel. On this beautiful morning,

with fortune seeming to run so well in his favor, he could not bring himself to wish harm even to that thorn-in-the-side Jeremiah. In fact, he had to admit, with a grudging admiration, that the young lieutenant was getting good. Christopher had regretfully scuttled two cargoes in the last three months to avoid being caught with contraband. Perhaps it was time to move on to different operations for a time and give the revenue patrol time to cool off.

Ian turned the glass toward the distant shoreline. "Ooh! There's one who wasna' so lucky!" He pointed to the listing dismasted hulk coming into view as the *Black Falcon* rounded the headland.

Christopher took the glass and examined the scene with interest. "It's not Jeremiah."

"Too bad!" Ian grimaced.

"She has the look of a merchantman about her, though it's damn hard to tell with all the masts down. Let's go in and have a closer look."

After an hour's careful tacking back and forth to avoid the treacherous shoals, they had a much better view of the wreck.

"It's a miracle she's held together this long," Christopher commented as he watched the precariously balanced hulk rock with the now gentle swells. The nearby beach was littered with the splintered remains of lifeboats. One body lay face down on the sand. No other evidence of the crew could be seen.

"I expect there's good salvage to be had here," Christopher remarked. "There don't appear to be any survivors to argue with us."

"Salvage?" Ian's brows shot up in surprise. "You're daft, laddie! 'Tis suicide to even think it! That wreck could break up any minute!" He shook his red-thatched head, declaring he'd have no part in such a useless scheme.

Christopher laughed at the quartermaster's discomfiture. "All that domesticity has made you soft as a grandmother, my friend! I've known you to bull your way into worse situations without a second thought for your skin!"

Ian grinned somewhat sheepishly. "Don't let my grand-

mother hear you say that. She's the grittiest old bitch in
Scotland!''

Christopher laughed appreciatively.

Ian turned his eyes back to the dismasted wreck and
continued in a more serious vein. "Use your head, man!
Why take such a risk when there may not be anything on the
tub worth claiming?''

"There may be, though, my cautious friend," Christopher
countered. "And we can't sail away without knowing, now,
can we?''

He turned to the boatswain. "Lower a boat, if you please,
Mr. Daughtery, and I'll need ten volunteers to strip that hulk
clean before she's carried off those rocks.''

Christopher spared one more moment to look at the
battered hulk. He was confident that there was something in
the wreck that was worth the risk of salvaging. It would
almost be worth the trouble just to see the look on Lieutenant Jeremiah's face when he sailed brazenly into Portsmouth
with legitimate cargo.

India swam up from unconsciousness with great difficulty,
surfacing to a blaze of pain and then sinking into comforting
blackness once again. Each time she awakened the pain
seemed more acute, and the enfolding blackness more
alluring. How nice it would be to sink into that soft oblivion
and not rise again!

But someone would not let her rest. Her name echoed
from a distance, again and again. The voice became louder,
clearer, until the blankets of darkness fell away and she
opened her eyes to bright light and a sea of faces. The faces
blurred as a searing pain in her chest and arm bore down on
her. Her head swam as she attempted to bring the world
back into focus.

Then she realized she was dead. The Devil was looking
down at her, his broad shoulders and dark-bearded face
blocking out the light behind him. The scene blurred again
as India's gasp of dismay started a new wave of agony
coursing across her body. Prudence had warned her that

Satan would claim her if she didn't mend her behavior. How unfair! She'd not even had time to reform!

"No!" India protested weakly. No, she didn't want to be dead. No, she didn't want to be in hell.

"Yes," the Devil said, and then he smiled. Who would have thought that the Devil could have a smile that would light up his eyes with gentle humor, a smile that would transform the hard planes of his face into a countenance of masculine beauty. No wonder that sin was so tempting, when the Devil wore such an alluring guise.

"Yes," he repeated. "I believe your lady is with us at last."

Mollie's gray face swam into view. "Oh, mistress! Mistress!" she sobbed. "You're alive! Bless you! Oh, thank the Lord!"

Beard-face moved and the sun glared down on her face. She tried to raise her arm to block out the light, but her arm wouldn't move. Helen's worried voice murmured somewhere out of her field of vision. This wasn't hell! Where was she?

"Where . . ." she croaked. Her voice would not cooperate. Something was pressing down on her, making every breath an agony.

Beard-face came back into view. If she wasn't dead, what was the Devil doing here, torturing her with this unspeakable pain? India's mind whirled and threatened to take refuge once again in oblivion, but the Devil's voice held her from the darkness.

"Now, mistress," he began. "You've got a sizable timber lying on you."

His voice was deep and went well with his face. Strange to be noticing such things at a time like this. Her mind was playing tricks, but her memory was slowly trickling back. Of course Beard-face wasn't the Devil. But who was he?

The deep voice continued. "We're going to lift it off you, my friend and I here. It may hurt when it moves, but you try to hold still."

Beard-face and the giant redhead behind him put their shoulders to the spar and pushed. India watched the muscles cord in the column of Beard-face's neck and the material of his coat strain across his powerful shoulders as the timber began to shift. He was right. It hurt.

"Lift! Now!" someone cried, and the terrible weight was gone. Mollie and Helen were both bending over her, and so was Beard-face. He ran his fingers gently from her collarbone down both sides of her chest. If she hadn't been in so much pain she would have thought him excessively rude to touch her so intimately. In spite of her acute discomfort, his gently probing touch sent unsettling currents coursing through her veins.

"Bruises," he commented matter-of-factly. "Maybe some cracks, but I don't believe anything's broken. Her shoulder's out of place, but we can fix that."

"Oh, no," India pleaded.

"Yes," Beard-face said. His smile was still alluring, but now she was afraid. She'd had enough pain. She couldn't cope with more right now.

"Easy," he said softly. "This will be over shortly."

His eyes, deeper and darker than the oblivion that had sought to claim her earlier, held her spellbound while the panic drained out of her. Something indefinable passed between them, some flame that leapt in his eyes as he held her momentarily entranced. India felt she had somehow been marked by that intense gaze, and then his eyes slid away from hers. He placed one big hand on her shoulder and grasped her arm with the other. Then he pulled. India screamed, finding her full voice at last. Finally merciful blackness washed over her and wiped out the pain.

She woke in a clean-scented bed, her injured arm bound to her side and her body draped in a fine linen shirt that was many times too big. Mollie sat by the bed.

"Where am I?" India sighed, heartily tired of awakening in strange places.

Mollie's face brightened, and a smile smoothed the worry lines around her mouth. "Oh, you're with us again!"

"Where am I with you?" India grimaced. She raised herself awkwardly on one arm and looked around. They were in a well-appointed cabin, much larger than their cabin on the *Sea Gull* but still of only moderate size. Bookshelves covered half of one bulkhead. The other half was occupied by the bed and a small writing desk littered with maps and charts. The rest of the space in the cabin was filled by a sea chest, a small wood-burning stove, and a single wing-backed chair. Hooks were fastened here and there and held various articles of masculine clothing. From one hook hung, ominously, a set of pistols and a sword. The wooden deck was partially covered by well-worn but colorful wool rugs.

India looked questioningly at Mollie.

"We're all fine, Miss India, so you just rest yourself, child."

"But where are we? And where is Helen?"

"She's up above with that fine young captain who rescued us, miss. This is his cabin, and he says we're to use it until he can put us ashore. Oh, Miss India!" she continued brightly. "He's such a fine, big man! He carried you off that wreck so gently, you'd think he was carrying a fragile child. And so much a gentleman!"

"The big man with the beard?" India shook her head, trying to bring her memories of their rescue into focus. "Is that who you're talking about? It all seems like such a nightmare!"

"Yes, miss," Mollie continued with enthusiasm. "A nightmare, indeed! And the Lord knows we'd have all been dead if this fellow hadn't come. But we're all lucky, you know, miss, because that lifeboat we were going to take got smashed just like the others. Helen and me, we wouldn't go without you, and you were lying under that awful mess. We were thinking you were most likely dead, but somehow we just had to stay, anyway. And we're mighty glad now, don't you know!"

"Yes, yes. Go on," India urged.

"Sure I thought we were dead, I did! Oh, the prayers I said! But the Lord was looking after us, because come morning we were still there, and still alive, though colder I've never been in my entire life! And then this ship sails out from behind the cliff, the prettiest sight in the world, if you ask me. Before we know it that big captain and his men climb right over the side, and here we are, all safe and sound!''

So, India mused, she had not been dreaming. He had been real. Imagine her thinking he was the Devil come to claim her soul for her misdeeds! But his eyes had seemed momentarily to mark her soul. She could almost imagine those deep brown eyes, boring into hers with that intense gaze, compelling her to . . . compelling her to what? What was she thinking? She must still be addled in the head! He was just a man who'd carried her off a doomed ship. She'd been dizzy and confused from the night's trauma when she saw him, and she'd imagined crazy things. He was undoubtedly just an ordinary, humdrum sort of man.

India sighed and leaned back against the pillows. For the first time she noticed a bandage wrapped tightly around her ribs, which ached considerably.

"Mollie?" she asked. "What's this for?" She indicated the bandage.

"Oh, the captain did that," Mollie said blithely. "He said your ribs are bruised, and that will make them feel better."

India gasped. "*He* did it?"

"Well," Mollie replied with some chagrin. "He seemed to know what he was doing. And I was right here with you all the time. He was a perfect gentleman, miss."

India blushed. She thought silently that if he'd truly been a gentleman, he would have turned his back and instructed Mollie how to do the task. In her opinion, this man had been entirely too intimate with her person!

What kind of ship was this? And what kind of man was her captain? They all owed him their lives, it seemed, but India could not suppress her uneasiness. There were scoundrels and blackguards aplenty in these waters, and this ship could as easily be some pirate or smuggler as a legitimate vessel.

And if Beard-face was some sort of criminal? Would he hold them for ransom? Or worse? After all, they were three helpless women, and completely in his power.

"Are you quite well, dear?" Mollie asked, bending over her in concern. "You do look white as a sheet."

"No. Yes, I mean...I..." India shifted uncomfortably. "Mollie, how does this fellow, the captain, strike you? I mean, what sort of man do you think he is?"

Mollie smiled reassuringly and helped India prop herself in a sitting position against the pillows. "Well, miss," she finally said, "he seems quite civil to me. Talks like a gentleman, he does, and handsome as a lord!"

"You don't think he's...he's somebody dangerous, do you?"

"Oh Lord, no, miss! The things that enter your head! Always looking for excitement and adventure, you are, letting your imagination run wild." She gave the pillow a final pat. "Miss Helen's up talking to him right now, and I'm sure she'll tell you..."

Helen danced through the door, her plump face beaming. "Oh, India! You're awake! We were so worried!"

"Not all that worried, I gather!" India commented, and immediately felt guilty. After all, Helen and Mollie had both braved almost certain death to stay with her. But Helen's cheerful mood seemed excessive in light of their situation.

Helen didn't notice India's frown, however. "We've fallen into a bed of roses, I vow!" she giggled. "I've just had the most civil conversation with our rescuer, and I do believe he's taken a fancy to me! Imagine! He certainly is the most well-set-up man I've ever seen!"

India looked at her friend in amazement. "What about George?" she asked.

"Who?"

"George! My stepmother's footman, you goose!"

"Oh, George! Oh, India, let me assure you, George doesn't hold a candle to this one!"

India was nonplussed.

"Christopher—that's his name, Christopher Barnett—has his own ship! Imagine! His own ship! He'd have to have money to have a ship, wouldn't he?" She perched herself on the side of the bed. "He's a bit tall for my taste, I'll admit, and rugged-looking—all that weather, you know—but then, nobody's perfect.''

"Indeed, Helen,'' India replied in mixed exasperation and amusement. "You sound like you're ready to run off with this fellow! You don't even know him!'' Some of India's fears were laid to rest, however, by Helen's attitude. If Helen was so taken with this fellow, perhaps her own imaginings were groundless after all.

"Oh, but I told you!'' Helen continued. "We just had the longest, most interesting conversation! You'll like him, India! Really you will! Why, I told him all about us, and he was really very sympathetic, and interested. He was very impressed when I told him who your father was!''

"You what?'' India exploded. "You told this complete stranger, whom we know nothing, absolutely nothing about, everything about us?''

"But of course!''

"What makes you think he's not some scoundrel who'll hold us for ransom?''

"La! You always did have such an imagination! Scoundrel, indeed! Small chance of that! I tell you he's every inch a gentleman.''

"That may be,'' replied India, still somewhat uneasy. "But I wish you'd been a bit more cautious.''

"You'll see! You'll like him,'' Helen declared happily. "Oh, I do hope he does like me! Imagine being married to a sea captain with his own ship. And so handsome! I vow I feel like swooning every time he looks at me. How romantic to be rescued by someone so . . . so dashing!''

Romantic, indeed! They were on a strange ship, at the mercy of an unknown man, and Helen thought it was romantic. India's spirits sank. She hurt all over, she felt dirty and disheveled from her ordeal, and here she was stuck in Beard-face's . . . no, Christopher Barnett's . . . bed and unable to leave it because she was wearing only Christopher Barnett's shirt. She had never longed so much for home, even with Lord Marlowe waiting for her there. Just to be in her own bed, surrounded by people who were familiar and safe, and sights and sounds she had known all her life.

India lay back on the pillows, feeling exhausted. How was it that she, who had always fancied herself strong and adventuresome, was so unnerved by this adventure when Mollie and Helen were taking everything in stride? The man who'd carried her off the *Sea Gull* was the source of her uneasiness, she was sure. She had never before had such a strong reaction to anyone. She'd only seen this Captain Barnett once, but that single encounter had made her feel strangely vulnerable, a new feeling for India and one she didn't much like. She was determined to persuade her rescuer to set them ashore as soon as possible. If it was out of his way, she would offer him a reward in compensation for his inconvenience. If her worst fears were true, and he was considering holding them for ransom, her offer of a reward might present him with a profitable alternative and assure their safety.

When she got home again, India told herself, she would recover, both physically and emotionally. Everything would return to normal. Yes, everything would be just the way it had been before.

CHAPTER FIVE

"Dammit, Ian! Don't give me any more of your nonsense! I will not tolerate interference in this! Even from you!" Christopher paced up and down the length of Ian's small cabin, his face grim. "I've never known you to be so squeamish before!"

"Aye," Ian replied calmly. "I'm no' squeamish, as you

well know. But neither do I wage war on women. I wouldna'
have thought you would, either, laddie.''

"I mean no harm to the girl. It's her father I aim at.''

"No harm is it, laddie? We're speaking of rape, here.''

"We're speaking of marriage, not rape. Why do you
think I want you to find me a parson in Portsmouth when we
dock?''

Ian continued stubbornly. "I think in this case there
would be little difference! She's a sweet-looking little lass,
and I'd not like to see her harmed.''

"Dammit, Ian!'' Christopher exploded. "Half the brides
in the British Empire are raped on their wedding night.
What I do with her once she's my wife is no man's concern
but mine—and her father's.''

Christopher grinned unpleasantly at the thought of William
Carey's reaction to his only daughter and heir being in the
hands of the man he'd condemned so carelessly to die.

"If you're that concerned about the girl, rest assured
she'll have gentler treatment at my hands than she would
from that lecher her father would have her marry. And when
I manage to clear my name, she'll be the Countess of
Woodsford. I've yet to meet a girl who wouldn't sell her
virtue ten times over for the sake of a title.''

Ian shook his head sadly. "You've become a cynic,
Christopher lad. You're obsessed by the thought of vengeance. You've got a good ship and a good crew who'd sail
with you into hell if you but gave the word. And we've all
made a fortune these last five years. Why can't you let the
past die?''

Christopher laughed bitterly. "You'd expect me to pass
up a golden opportunity that fate has dropped into my
lap—all for concern of a 'sweet-faced lass' who's about to
be served up to that wretch Marlowe to legally deflower. Not
a chance, my friend. I can think of no more appropriate
revenge than having Carey's estates, along with the estates
he stole from me, being inherited by the son I intend to sire
on his daughter, who happens to be his only living relative.''

Ian sighed. "You're determined to do this thing?''

"I am.''

"Then I suppose I'd better find you a parson while you're off-loading the salvage in Portsmouth. I wouldna' want the maid to suffer your attentions without benefit of the clergy's blessing!"

Christopher grinned, the grim lines of his face softening with humor. He gave the glowering Scotsman a clap on the shoulder that would have staggered a smaller man.

"Relax, my friend. She might even like me! Women have before, you know!"

He stooped to clear the transom on the way out of the cabin. Ian watched his friend in exasperation. Somehow he knew, this time, that Christopher had taken on more than he could handle.

Helen and Mollie had long since retired to the small cabin that had been vacated for their use, leaving India to sleep. And sleep she did, the exhaustion of her body finally overwhelming the uneasiness of her mind. She woke finally to a knock on the cabin door.

"Come in," she said sleepily.

The door opened and the source of all her uneasy speculation stepped into the cabin, bending slightly to clear the door. He was tall, with a broadness well-proportioned to his height. The face was as she remembered: dark-bearded, with dark eyes and hard planes that softened when he smiled. He was smiling now.

"Good morning, Mistress Carey. I hope you're feeling better today."

India studied him covertly. If he wore his character on his face, she guessed he was arrogant, ruthless, powerful, and . . . dangerous. She self-consciously slid farther under the bedcovers.

"I regret I haven't had the chance to introduce myself earlier," he continued. "I am Christopher Barnett, at your service, and this is my ship you are aboard, the *Black Falcon*."

India composed herself and found her voice. "I am very happy to make your acquaintance, sir." Her wide blue eyes belied the composure of her voice. "My friends and I owe you our lives," she went on quietly. "I hope someday to be able to repay you for all you've done."

Christopher looked amused. "I wouldn't trouble yourself on that account, mistress. The cargo we salvaged from the *Sea Gull* will more than compensate us for any trouble we took on your behalf." He was regarding her in an assessing manner that made India distinctly uneasy.

"Just the same," she insisted. "I am grateful."

She was acutely conscious that his dark eyes were resting on the spot where the loose vee neck of her shirt—his shirt, really—disappeared beneath the bedcovers. Awareness of the impropriety of carrying on a conversation with a man while in his bed, in his shirt, brought the beginnings of a blush to color her face.

"I feel quite well enough to get up, Captain, if you'll tell me what happened to my clothing."

His eyes traveled back to her face, and a smile quirked the corners of his mouth as he observed her heightened color.

"I'm afraid your clothing was beyond repair," he explained. "I believe our ship's boy is about your size, however, and could lend you some breeches and a sweater until you can get something more suitable."

India thought of the consequences of the last time she had worn breeches, and the thought of her forbidden riding costume made her heart twinge with homesickness.

"That would be very kind of him, I'm sure," she replied politely.

Then, as though a lamp had been suddenly doused, his pleasant manner was gone. His face settled into hard planes, and the light of humor fled from his dark eyes. He settled his big frame in the cabin's one chair, and, stretching his long legs out in front of him, leaned back and regarded her speculatively.

"We have a serious matter to discuss, Mistress Carey." His tone was casual, but his manner was somehow frightening.

"What would that be, Captain Barnett?"

India was puzzled by his changed manner. Had she been

right? Was he a scoundrel who was about to demand ransom for their safe return?

He sat up slowly. His face had become impassive. "You will better understand what I have to say to you if you realize who I really am." He watched her face intently as he continued. "I believe we met several times when you were a very young child and I was a lad on my father's estate in Hampshire."

India looked puzzled.

"Barnett is my mother's maiden name. My real name is Armstrong—Christopher Armstrong, rightful Earl of Woodsford."

For a moment India's face mirrored her consternation. She knew his name well, and she knew his story just as well. Her father had acquired the Earl of Woodsford's estates as a grant from Queen Anne, shortly after exposing the young earl as a traitor and spy. She'd been only six at the time, but had heard the story repeated many times by neighbors and friends who were horrified that a member of the nobility, and a Hampshireman at that, could turn out to be such a scoundrel. India's heart sank, but her chin came up in a show of defiance.

"My father said you were hanged as a traitor . . . for spying. How . . ."

"Obviously your father was wrong," he countered. "He condemned me to die—on one man's questionable testimony—and was very conveniently rewarded with his knighthood and my family estates, which just happened to border on his own land in Hampshire. As you can see, however, I escaped . . . escaped and survived to be a smuggler and a pirate with a price on my head."

India's heart pounded. All her fears were coming true, and worse. Not only was their rescuer a scoundrel, but a scoundrel who bore a grudge against the Carey family.

"You imply that my father condemned you wrongly, and that his judgment in your case was prejudiced by greed for your lands."

Christopher smiled, but the smile was not a pleasant one.

"You're wrong!" she went on. "My father would never

do such a thing. He values honor above all else. If you knew anything about him, you would know that his honor has never been questioned.''

''But you're mistaken,'' Christopher said softly. He regarded her with something akin to sympathy. ''I know much about your father. I know how highly he regards his family honor. It's a shame he has not always lived by the tenets he values so highly.'' His eyes held hers in an impassive gaze. ''I also know that you are William Carey's only child, his only living relative, in fact. And a kind fate has delivered you right into my waiting hands.''

India's heart seemed to stop. She longed to tear her gaze from his face, but his eyes were locked with hers, searing her soul with the intensity of his hatred. Hatred for her, or for her father? At this point, did it make any difference?

She was suddenly sure that he intended to kill her. He would strike at her father by eliminating the daughter. How would he accomplish his bloody designs? Her unbridled imagination paraded frightening scenes through her unwilling mind. Would he put those big hands around her throat, squeezing the life from her body, or hold her down and slip a knife between her ribs? Or maybe he would not be so kind and so clean. There were any number of messy things a man could do to a woman to make her beg for death. How would he take his revenge?

India could not still the quaver in her voice as she challenged him. ''If you think to hurt my father by killing me, you are quite wrong, sir. My father sets no great store by me. In fact, I'm sure he would just as soon I was out of his life.''

The grim set of Christopher's face softened. He hadn't intended to frighten her so badly, and behind the mask of her defiance he could see the panic rising. She looked helpless, appealing and incredibly beautiful sitting there in his bed, regarding him with her wide blue eyes.

''You mistake my purpose, mistress,'' he said softly. ''I've no intention of harming you.''

He quickly stifled an urge to take her in his arms and

comfort her as one might soothe a frightened child, but then he thought of William Carey and his heart turned to iron.

"What are your intentions, then, Sir Pirate and Smuggler?"

Christopher smiled engagingly. "Why, I intend to marry you."

India was dumbfounded, unable to answer. The man was insane! He had to be! Or perhaps this whole conversation was simply a nightmare, concocted by her uneasy mind, and soon she would wake. But the scene didn't fade, no matter how hard she tried to make it go away, and still he stood before her with that satisfied grin on his devilishly handsome face.

"An appropriate revenge, you must agree, Mistress Carey. Your father will know that the heirs to his carefully nurtured estates and his precious family honor will be sired by me, the so-called traitor he once condemned to die. When William Carey draws his last breath, he will know that all he has worked for will be in the control of a man he once sent to the gallows. I believe that knowledge will make his living as well as his dying very painful."

India stared at Christopher in disbelief. "You must be mad!" she declared, her voice trembling. "You must know that all my father needs do to counter your scheme is disinherit me. Believe me! He would do that in a minute rather than see his family brought so low!"

"I don't think so," Christopher replied. "He has no other kin to inherit in your place. He will lose either way. No, I think through you I will both regain my family estates and avenge myself on your father. I think you are going to make a very effective weapon, and"—he regarded her with a glint of desire in his hard eyes—"a very entertaining wife."

"You're wrong!" India vowed defiantly. "I will never be your wife. No parson will wed me to you if I am unwilling."

Christopher rose from his seat and moved toward the bed. His brown eyes were deceptively gentle as he looked down at her.

"You will be willing," he predicted. "You will either be my legal wife or bear my bastards. The choice is yours, and it makes little difference in the outcome. I can always have the heir legitimatized when the time comes.''

India looked up at him towering over her. She tried unsuccessfully to keep the fear from her voice. ''I will kill myself rather than let you touch me!'' she promised.

''You will have no opportunity to be so foolish,'' he answered calmly. ''Accept the fact that there is nothing you can do to keep yourself from me, one way or another. I mean you no harm, and if you behave like a proper wife should, you'll find that I can be a gentleman. If you insist on misbehaving, however, you'll find me a most unpleasant adversary.''

He reached for her hand and pressed his lips to her palm. A shiver of unwanted excitement shot through her body. His eyes lit with amusement as he noted her reaction. He cocked an eyebrow and smiled at her ominously.

''Be warned,'' he cautioned.

Before she could reply, he was gone.

A few minutes later a light tapping sounded on the cabin door. India was still seething. She'd vented her fury on everything breakable in the room, then collapsed on the bed and pounded on the unfortunate mattress until she hurt her injured shoulder. That made her madder still.

How right she'd been when she'd thought Christopher Barnett was the Devil. Only it wasn't her soul he intended to claim! How dare he propose to use her in such a way! She would escape somehow! She swore it to herself. She would jump into the sea, if necessary, before letting him cold-bloodedly possess her for his purpose of vengeance.

Unpleasant adversary, indeed! He expected her to meekly submit to him like a properly frightened maiden, or perhaps be overwhelmed by his animal masculinity. What arrogance! What insufferable egotism! She'd seen triumph register on his face at her unwilling reaction to his casual caress. She swore he would find her an unpleasant adversary also. If she couldn't manage somehow to escape, she'd make him regret the moment he thought of this disgraceful scheme!

The tapping sounded again. India covered herself quickly with the bedclothes.

"Who is it?" she demanded.

"India, it's me, Helen," came the anxious reply.

"Oh," she responded in a milder voice. "Come in, then."

Helen bustled through the door carrying a bundle of boys' clothing. She stopped short when she saw the condition of the cabin.

"Oh, India," she cried, looking around at the broken shards of mirror and porcelain that littered the floor. "What have you done?"

"I'd have thrown those at him if he'd been here!" India replied hotly. "But he wasn't, so I threw them at the wall instead."

"You mean Captain Barnett?" Helen asked, her eyes wide with horror.

"Yes, Captain Barnett! Do you know what that son of a bitch is planning to do to me?"

Helen's plump little hands fluttered with dismay.

"India! My heavens! Such words! Do please try to be calmer."

"Well?" India demanded. "You're so cozy with our brave rescuer! Did he fill you in on his scheme?"

"Well, yes, he did, just now. He said you were upset, that I should come keep you company."

"Upset!" India cried. "Of course I'm upset! He's going to . . . going to . . . Oh, Helen," she wailed, her anger giving way to misery. "What am I going to do?"

Helen stopped fluttering and sat down on the edge of the bed.

"You're not going to do anything but be the sweet girl you are and avoid making Captain Barnett angry." She looked significantly at the littered cabin. "I have a feeling that man can be dangerous when he's angry."

India looked at her companion in surprise. Where was the flighty Helen she'd known all her life? She should be all a-dither, not giving her calm advice to submit to that monster.

"You can't mean I should surrender to that renegade!"

she said incredulously. "He means to use me to break my father, to disgrace our family, to . . ."

"Why should you endanger yourself to help a father who's ignored you all your life? Besides, from what Christopher tells me, your father deserves anything he gets out of this."

India exploded. "Christopher, is it?" she cried angrily. "Helen, how could you believe him? He's a traitor, a spy, and considering the life he leads, probably a thief and murderer, as well! You wouldn't be so calm if it was you he was going to . . ." India's face turned crimson and she couldn't continue.

Helen arched her brows knowingly. "Oh, you're wrong. Believe me, India, I wouldn't mind at all finding myself under him some night!"

India's face grew even redder. "Helen!" she gasped. "You don't know what you're saying!"

Helen regarded her friend sympathetically. She took her slim hand in her plump one and patted it gently. "Poor India," she said. "So innocent! Do you think anyone can live as a servant under your father's roof and not quickly learn the ways of men, in a very intimate fashion?"

India didn't want to believe what she was hearing. "You were never a servant," she denied.

"You were the only one who did not regard me as such. My dear friend," she continued somewhat sadly, "you have been so sheltered. You don't realize how innocent you really are. You always played at being the scamp, running around the countryside like a boy, trying to win your father's attention, seeing everyone and everything through the eyes of your own inexperience."

"No," India denied hotly. "That's not true."

"Yes it is," Helen returned. "And if this all hadn't happened, you would have gone on obeying your father and married Lord Marlowe and been miserable the rest of your life. This Captain Barnett, or whatever his real name is, might make you happy if you would just cooperate with him."

"Never! He hates me."

"He hates your father. He doesn't hate you."

"No matter! I hate him. I'm afraid of him."

"And so you should be afraid of him. He's a powerful man. He'd make a terrible enemy. He'd also make a strong protector."

"Who'd protect me from him?" India wailed.

"You could make him love you, India. You're really a very lovable person, you know."

"No! No! No!" India punctuated her denials by beating on the covers, instantly regretting it as pain shot through her bruised ribs. "I don't believe we're having this conversation!"

Helen sighed and looked at her friend helplessly. She pushed the bundle of clothes onto the bed. "Here. Put these on. You'll feel better when you're out of bed." She paused, hesitating to add any more to her friend's dismay. "He said we'll be in Portsmouth in an hour or so. . . . You're to be married there."

India's face paled. "So soon?" she whispered.

"He's putting Mollie ashore to go back to Hillcrest. He says I can go, too, if I want, or I can stay, if you want me to."

India looked at the plump curate's daughter who'd been her companion from the age of eight. She'd always regarded herself as much stronger, more mature and sophisticated than her friend. Now suddenly, unexpectedly, their roles were reversed. India realized she'd never bothered to know Helen as she really was, just as she had wanted her to be. She knew she needed this new Helen's strength and support more than she'd ever needed anything in her life.

"I can't ask you to stay," she said regretfully. "It's too great a sacrifice."

"La! What sacrifice?" Helen chimed, her old cheeriness back in her face. "With all the rich, well-set-up men on this ship, I'll catch me a husband who can keep me in luxury the rest of my life."

India looked at her affectionately. Hot tears were threatening her eyes. "Oh, Helen!" She moved forward into her friend's embrace. "Thank you!"

Helen rocked the smaller girl comfortingly. "Never you fear, my lamb," she soothed. "We'll beat that big man at his own game, one way or another."

CHAPTER SIX

It was slightly past midday when the *Black Falcon* reached Portsmouth. Only a few minutes after the motion of the ship had stilled, a light tapping sounded on the door of India's cabin. She answered the knock with apprehension, fearful that her tormentor had returned. Much to her relief, the door opened and in sauntered a gangly collection of knees, elbows, spindly limbs, and the bluest eyes she'd ever seen, followed by a gray cat that was twice the size any self-respecting cat should be.

"I've brought you some food, mum," the youth said, offering her a tray of hard biscuits, moldy cheese, and an unidentified meat she didn't care to examine too closely. India regarded the food with thinly disguised distaste.

"Sorry it's a bit stale," the boy apologized. "The food'll get better soon, though, 'cause we'll be takin' on supplies here in Portsmouth."

He set the tray on the bed and looked around the cabin with some consternation.

"Ooh, mum, what happened in here?" His blue eyes grew wide as he took in the broken glass and ceramic that littered the floor. "Cap'n won't like this a bit, he won't!"

India raised her brows imperiously. "The captain can go to hell!"

The boy looked at her in awe, obviously impressed by her temerity. Then he gave her a freckle-faced grin.

"Had a fight, did ya?" he ventured. "You're probably safe, though. Cap'n's never hit a female. Far's I know, anyways."

India smiled. She couldn't help but be charmed by the lad. She was fond of children, and even in her present situation, found the boy's open friendliness appealing.

"Well," she said. "Thank you for the food, such as it is, Mr. . . ."

"I'm Theodore. Theodore Sykes, mum. Them's me breeches and sweater you're wearing."

"I'm happy to meet you, Theodore."

"Oh, you can call me Teddy. And I already know your name, mum. Miss Mollie's helpin' in the galley, and she told me."

"Well, Teddy. Thank you for the loan of your clothes. I hope it didn't inconvenience you too much."

"Oh, no, mum," he replied proudly. "I have three whole sets of clothes, I do. You can wear those for as long as you like."

Teddy folded his gangly frame into the cabin's one chair and made himself comfortable. Sitting and talking to the captain's lady was much more fun than attending to his other chores.

"Is that your cat over there on the bed eyeing my food?" India asked.

"That's Thomas," the boy replied. "He belongs to the whole ship, though Thomas thinks it's the other way around!"

Thomas continued to hunker on the bed and fixed her with an indignant cat glare. India guessed she might approach the food tray only at risk to life and limb.

"Oh, don't mind Thomas, mum," Teddy commented. "He don't like strangers. Come to think, he don't much like women, either. So it's nuthin' personal."

"Thomas doesn't like women?" India's curiosity was piqued.

"No, mum, he don't."

"Have there been many women in this cabin for him not to like?" she inquired with some asperity.

"Oh, a few. One or two, maybe three. None's what stayed long, though. Cap'n keeps most of his women at the island," he said candidly. He was, however, beginning to feel a little uncomfortable with this subject.

India didn't know why she was starting to feel more than a little irritated with this news of her captor's amorous habits.

"Island?" she asked. "What island?"

Teddy didn't like the way India's eyes were beginning to ignite with blue sparks.

"Little island off Scotland," he answered uneasily. "That's where we hole up when Cap'n doesn't feel like workin'. We haven't been there in, oh, three months or so."

"And the captain keeps . . . uh . . . mistresses there?"

She pictured a bevy of voluptuous ladies eagerly waiting the wretch's return.

"Well, generally he only keeps one at a time." Teddy wished he'd have kept his big mouth shut. He sidled casually toward the door.

"Guess I better go. Think I hear the boatswain callin'."

"Teddy, wait!" India called, suddenly forgetting the captain's women and remembering her own situation. "How long will we be here, in Portsmouth?"

" 'Spect we'll leave on the morning tide, mum," he answered. "Cap'n don't like to stay around these civilized ports too long."

"I can understand that!" India said caustically.

"I'll bring you somethin' more to eat come sundown, mum. Should have some better food by then." He looked at the cat, who was still hungrily regarding India's lunch. "Come on, Thomas," he called. The cat didn't budge. "Oh, well." Teddy shrugged.

"Stupid cat!" India mumbled as Teddy left. "Doesn't like women, indeed!" she murmured petulantly. "Sounds like your master doesn't share your tastes, Thomas!"

Thomas kept a green-gold eye on her while he reached out an experimental paw to a moldy piece of cheese.

"Oh, go ahead and eat it!" India offered. "I certainly don't want it!" The piece of cheese was gone in the twinkling of a cat's eye. Thomas regarded her somewhat more benevolently.

India sat down in the wing-back chair and stretched her shapely legs out in front of her. She sighed. Breeches were so comfortable. What a shame women couldn't wear them all the time instead of skirts. She wondered idly what Christopher Barnett-Armstrong thought of women wearing breeches. She pictured his mistresses clad in silks and jewels, purchased by his ill-gotten wealth, or clad in nothing at all, purring under the stroke of his caressing. . . . India blushed. The lecherous womanizer! Imagine parading all those women in and out of his island hideaway, and not even hiding his debauchery from an innocent boy like Teddy. To think that such a disgraceful libertine had sprung from a noble British family!

He must think he's quite the hot lover, India mused. She vowed he would get no pleasure from using her like one of his whores. A ray of hope had glimmered in her mind as Teddy left the cabin. If ever she was to escape, now was the time. They were docked in Portsmouth, which was in Hampshire not too many miles south of her beloved Hillcrest— maybe a day's hard journey by coach. If she was to take Teddy by surprise when he brought her dinner, chances were she could dash out the opened door and be off the ship before anyone could stop her. Once off the ship, she would be safe. Christopher wouldn't dare to pursue her into Portsmouth.

Her outrageous costume would be a hindrance, she knew. And even India was not so innocent as to believe that a woman abroad without protection in a port town, especially on the docks, was not taking a grave risk. The alternative was to stay here, though, and find herself wedded and bedded by that monster. Any risk was preferable to that fate. India was not certain what a man did to a woman once they were married, but whatever it was, she didn't want Christopher Armstrong doing it to her. The memory of her body's unwilling reaction to the feel of his lips pressed to her open palm, and of the satisfaction she'd seen in those dark eyes, made her shiver. No, any risk was worth escaping the plans he'd made for her. She regretted having to exclude Mollie and Helen from her flight, but she was sure that once she was safely out of his hands, Christopher would set them free. Without her in his grasp, he would have no reason to detain them.

There followed three long hours of waiting. India paced the room and agonized over the plans for her escape. There was nothing she could do to prepare. Time and again she looked longingly toward the place where earlier a sword and pistols had hung. If only Christopher hadn't thought to take them with him! She would have loved to greet him with the point of a sword on his return. What if Christopher returned before Teddy did? What if Teddy forgot her dinner and didn't come at all? What if? What if?

Weak rays of watery sunlight slanted through the small stern windows and made a pattern on the deck. India watched impatiently as the pattern inched its way across the cabin as the afternoon wore on. Thomas dozed contentedly on the bed, having finished the cheese and meat and declined the hard biscuits. Occasionally he woke and watched her restless pacing with mild curiosity.

Finally the sun dipped below the horizon, throwing the cabin into gloom. India found the flint and lit the two wall lanterns. She wished she could fire up the stove as well, for with the setting of the sun, the cabin was becoming uncomfortably chilly.

If Teddy didn't get here soon, it would be too late. Christopher would arrive with parson in tow, and she would be doomed. India set about to prepare herself for what she hoped was Teddy's imminent arrival. She searched through Christopher's sea chest, looking for a cap to hide her hair. No sense in advertising to the rowdies on the docks that she was a female. Instead she found a coarse woolen scarf, which she wrapped around her head, carefully tucking stray locks of her dark curling hair beneath the edges. She surveyed the results in the largest piece of broken mirror that she could find.

It would have to do, she thought. Even in breeches and a bulky sweater, with her hair bound and hidden from view, she would never pass for a boy to anyone who gave her a second glance. Her delicate oval face and thickly fringed blue eyes were anything but masculine, and the fit of Teddy's breeches revealed more than concealed the feminine curves of her hips and thighs. India turned from the mirror with a resigned sigh. Then her heart gave a lurch at a knock on the cabin door. This was it!

"It's me, Miss India. I've brought your dinner." Teddy's voice came from the other side of the door.

India gave a quick, silent prayer of gratitude while the boy fumbled with the lock. Then the door opened and in he stepped, holding the door with one hand and precariously balancing a tray with steaming food with the other.

India lunged. Tray, food, dishes, and boy hit the deck with a splat. Teddy howled with pain and surprise when his bony behind made sudden contact with the hard planking of the deck, but India didn't hear. She was through the door and running down the narrow corridor toward the companionway. She took the stairs two at a time, gasping not so much from exertion as from fear and excitement. Almost there! She was going to make it! She knew she was going to make it! She burst out onto an almost deserted deck and sprinted for the gangway. Freedom was just a few short steps away.

Suddenly she was brought up short, running headlong into a hard body that had seemed to appear from nowhere, directly into her path.

"Oof!" she grunted, and looked up into the laughing brown eyes of the man she least wanted to see.

"Going somewhere?" Christopher asked calmly.

Before she could move she was hoisted and held immobile by his strong arms. She was acutely aware of the feel of his muscular chest tensed against her body, even though they were separated by layers of sweater, breeches, and shirt. The few crewmen on deck were finding the scene hugely entertaining.

"Tch, tch," her captor mocked. "Could it be my lovely

bride was thinking of leaving me at the altar? How embarrassing that would have been!''

India's blue eyes grew smoky with anger. ''Put me down, you swine!'' she hissed.

''All in good time, my love.''

He made his way back to the cabin, moving as though her weight was no burden at all. An infinitesimally raised brow was his only reaction as he stepped through the cabin door and surveyed the chaos. Spilled food, broken crockery, and an irate Teddy rubbing his sore posterior was added to the mess she'd created earlier.

''You've been busy,'' he commented, and set her none too gently on her feet. Teddy glared at her. Somehow his look of hurt betrayal stung almost as much as the failure of her escape attempt.

''Teddy,'' Christopher said. ''Mr. McCann is needing you on deck.''

''Aye, sir.''

''Teddy, I'm sorry!'' India cried as the boy picked his way through the mess toward the door. He was still glaring, however, when he went out.

''He'll get over it,'' Christopher said, looking around the room. ''Looks like a typhoon blew up in this cabin.''

India looked speculatively toward the cat, who seemed a likely scapegoat.

''Oh, no.'' Christopher shook his head with amusement. ''Thomas Cat has much better manners than to make such a mess. Seems you need a few lessons in manners yourself, however.''

India glared at him in tight-lipped silence.

''Clean it up,'' he ordered.

She continued to glare.

''I will not tolerate tantrums.'' The light of humor fled his eyes and his face seemed suddenly threatening. ''The next time you display your childish temper, you will feel the weight of my hand on your little round bottom, and I guarantee you will not enjoy it. Now clean up that mess.''

India thought better of continued obstinacy and bent reluctantly to pick up the broken shards. He watched her for a few moments in silence. As his eyes traced the soft feminine contours outlined so well by Teddy's breeches, his face softened considerably.

"The parson will be here soon, little one, so I wouldn't dawdle—unless you want to stand in this garbage for your wedding."

India met his eyes with a defiant look. "I've already told you I will not wed you, sir."

Christopher smiled. "And I've told you that is your choice. The outcome will be the same in either case."

She stood and put one hand on her hip. "I also will not allow you to . . . to sleep with me."

He laughed. "And just how do you propose to keep me from sleeping with you, as you so delicately put it?"

"I'll kill myself, or better still, I'll kill you, before I let you lay a hand on me!"

"Oh, will you now?" He chuckled. "Seems we've covered this before." He looked at Thomas Cat, who still sat on the bed observing them with interest. "It's a stubborn wench," he told the cat. "A bit dense, too, about certain matters." The cat blinked in seeming agreement.

India was infuriated beyond reason by his casual dismissal of her threats. She lunged for the door. Before she had gone three steps, however, a steel-thewed arm caught her by the waist and lifted her off her feet.

"I wouldn't if I were you, little one," Christopher warned.

India howled in fury and struggled uselessly to free herself. Christopher only laughed, then grasped her uninjured shoulder in a firm grip, turned her toward him, and held her still.

"The next time you attempt to escape me, India, I will hurt much more than your feelings."

"Monster!" she spat. That was the second time he'd threatened to beat her. "You lie!" she accused. "Teddy said you've never hit a woman."

Christopher chuckled. "He did, did he? Well, in your case I may make an exception."

"Bastard!"

"Tch, tch!" He shook his head. "Such language from a gently bred lady! You should learn to mind your tongue, my love. Remember that the quality of your future life depends on my goodwill."

India's chin rose defiantly. "I will never allow myself to be bullied into submission."

Christopher regarded her speculatively. Even in breeches and sweater, with her hair tied ridiculously into that woolen scarf, she was beautiful, standing there with her chin held high and a gleam of rebelliousness lighting her blue eyes.

"No," he said quietly. "Perhaps you can't be bullied into submission."

He reached out and with one hand slid the scarf from her hair, allowing the lustrous dark curls to fall about her shoulders.

"I think perhaps with you there is a better way."

India's startled gaze rested on his face as the scarf fell from her hair. His dark eyes were regarding her in a manner that somehow set her blood to pounding. She moved to back away, but his hand on her shoulder held her still. He reached out his other hand and traced her lips, her cheek, then traveled down her neck to where Teddy's loose sweater stretched to allow him access to the soft upper curve of her breasts. Her breath shortened and a warm tingle began between her thighs.

"Quit!" she gasped.

"Why should I?" he asked softly. His face was becoming tense with desire.

India fought with herself as his hand dipped lower to lightly caress her erect nipple.

"Because you're being rude and obnoxious!"

Her breath was coming in short gasps.

"Rude and obnoxious, am I?" Christopher smiled. "Perhaps you'll like this better."

He moved his hand to the back of her head and brought his mouth down on hers, gently brushing her lips with his until her mouth with a will of its own opened to accept his kiss. He kissed her deeply, gently, and the warmth of his closely pressed hard body was lighting a fire that spread from her loins to quicken the beat of her pounding heart.

India was close to melting, her body throbbing with an unfamiliar passion. Surely this man was indeed the Devil, to have such an unholy power over her. Could she be brought into line so easily, with a touch of his hands, and a brush of his lips? Just like all his other women, India thought as his mouth seared a path down her throat, then back to her waiting lips. I'm no different from all the others.

All the others! The parade of Christopher's imagined mistresses marched through her mind like an army. She thought of them groaning with passion under his fondling hands, begging his lips to take theirs in unsanctified lust. The images drenched her newly awakened desire like a rain of ice water. She was not like all the others! Now was the time for action! She bit his lip, hard, and tasted his blood in her mouth as he jerked back.

"Son of a bitch!" he cursed, feeling his injured lip gingerly with a finger. He looked at her with newly born caution. Then he threw back his head and laughed.

"You are a nasty little vixen, aren't you!" he winced as he wiped the blood from his mouth. "I think taming you is going to be more interesting than I thought."

The parson arrived a half-hour later. India took an instant dislike to the man and gave up any hope of assistance from him. Her only contact with the clergy had been with Helen's father, the gentle and scholarly curate who had tutored her at Hillcrest, and Parson Wilson, who had looked to her father for a living for the past twenty years. Parson Ferris, as Ian had introduced him, was of a different ilk altogether. His cassock was badly stained and threadbare, and hung below his rumpled coat. His greasy locks stuck out from beneath his hat, and his reddish beaklike nose was in constant need of a handkerchief. He reeked of rum and other unpleasant odors India did not care to contemplate. The smell of him almost overpowered her when he breathed a greeting upon being introduced. For one horrible moment she thought he was going to reach forward with his grimy hand and chuck her under the chin, but he was promptly discouraged by a murderous glare from Christopher.

"Couldn't you at least have sobered him up!" Christopher frowned at Ian.

"Ah, now, laddie." Ian smirked. "This good parson is as well-suited to your purpose as any other, I think."

Christopher glared, but Ian remained unruffled. He'd known Christopher too long to be frightened by hot looks.

"Let's get on with it, then," he growled. He took India firmly by the arm and stood her beside him in front of the slightly swaying parson, who was fumbling through the grimy pages of his service book.

"Ah!" he finally said. "Here it is. Now, my children, are we ready to proceed?" He smiled a rotten-toothed smile that forced India to avert her eyes in disgust.

As the parson intoned the opening phrases of the wedding service, his thin features took on a caricature of solemnity that mocked the sanctity of the office he was performing. Christopher took India's arm and threaded it through his own. She felt his muscles tense, and the grip of his big hand on hers grew tighter.

I could end this, India thought. All I have to do is say no. Even this scrawny black crow would not dare to wed me against my will. Would he?

The parson droned on, taking full advantage of this rare opportunity to display his abilities. He paused only now and then to wipe a drip from his long nose.

Once it's done, India thought, there'll be no way out. I'll carry his name forever. India had heard of unfortunate heiresses being the victim of "Fleet Street marriages" in wicked London, but she never thought to be a victim herself. Divorce was near impossible, and any wedding performed by an ordained clergyman, even lacking banns and license, was legally binding. She had to act now or be forever in Christopher's power. He would use her to gain his revenge and to temporarily slake his animal appetites, but he would always despise her as her father's daughter. Being honest with herself, she knew she could easily fall under Christopher's spell, even knowing him for the rogue he was.

She could be beguiled by the way his handsome face softened when he smiled, by the crooked grin that pulled at his mouth when he was amused, and by the desire that sparked in his eyes when he looked at her. And if she gave in to his charm, he would break her heart like the fragile porcelain she'd earlier thrown against the wall. Other women would claim his attention, light his passions. He would keep her only as insurance of regaining his lands. She would be unloved, unnecessary except as a means to an end. Just as she'd been all her life.

The parson had stopped droning. He paused expectantly. Christopher was looking down at her, his face unreadable.

"Well?" the parson asked, his small, closely set eyes chastising her for her inattention. "Do you?"

"Do I what?" India inquired.

The parson sighed, and his breath almost caused India to choke. "Do you take this man, et cetera, et cetera?"

"Oh." India hesitated. He would take her anyway. He would carry out his threats and saddle her with his bastards. What would she gain by her defiance? No matter that the fault was not hers. She would be branded slut and whore and shunned by decent people the rest of her life. At least with his name she could preserve some trace of respectability.

India took a deep breath. "I do," she whispered.

She felt the hard muscles of Christopher's arm relax. She refused to look at his face and see the knowledge of his victory stamped across his features.

They were hastily pronounced man and wife and the parson was bustled ungently toward the door by Ian.

"Gently there, man," the parson whined. "This is a member of the clergy you're tussling! You got your money's worth, now, all tight and legal."

"You took long enough about it, you old crow," Ian complained. "Do you think we've nothing better to do?"

The parson's whines faded down the corridor, and Christopher cupped India's chin in his big hand and gently tilted her face up to his.

"Don't feel so low, little one," he commented softly.

"You'll be glad enough of my name when your belly grows big with child."

"Ooooooh!" she shrieked, infuriated by his crudity.

She aimed a kick at his shin, which he neatly sidestepped.

"There's the spirit!" He laughed and headed toward the door. He turned before he left, though, and regarded her with bantering eyes. "We sail on the morning tide, my love, and I've things to look to right now. Be assured I'll return, though, to fulfill my husbandly duties. I'd not want to disappoint you on your wedding night!"

India hoisted a thick book to throw, but Christopher just grinned and shut the door behind him. She heard the lock click firmly into place before his footsteps sounded down the hallway.

CHAPTER SEVEN

India lay huddled in her bed, still clad in Teddy's breeches and sweater. She was cold, her shoulder ached, her ribs hurt, and her stomach cramped with nervous apprehension. How many hours of the night had passed, she had no way of knowing. The minutes and hours dragged as she huddled under the blankets for warmth. She flinched at every sound, every creak of the ship, afraid that it was her tormentor's footsteps, afraid the door would open any minute and he would descend on her to claim what was now rightfully, legally his. She didn't know what frightened her most—the unknown mysteries of the nuptial chamber, or the hitherto undiscovered passions of her own traitorous body. Christopher Barnett could hurt her in many ways, if he wished, but India knew that only by her own actions could she suffer true dishonor. He had demonstrated already how easily he could ignite the appetites of her body. Would she betray her honor, her family, and herself by submitting willingly to the embraces of an unprincipled rogue who would use her for his own demeaning purposes? To be overwhelmed by her own passions would be the ultimate dishonor.

Shortly after the wedding Mollie had come by, bringing a light meal and, much to India's delight, hot water for washing. She'd tried to reassure her young mistress, patting her on the shoulder and mumbling that all girls have to become women sometime in their lives. In spite of the awkward situation, she'd gone on hopefully, Captain Barnett didn't seem like such a bad sort of man, and, well, at least she was married. Yes, Mollie had nodded sagely, India should be grateful she was wed, considering the circumstances. Things could be a lot worse, and maybe everything would turn out for the best.

India thought she would cry through Mollie's hesitating, uncertain efforts to console her. She had cried when they finally embraced good-bye, unwanted tears spilling from her eyes and wetting Mollie's shawl. Would she ever see the faithful old servant again? Mollie had been with her as long as she could remember, and her leaving opened an empty place in her heart that even dear Helen couldn't fill. It seemed as if her final tie with a secure childhood had been severed with the old woman's departure. She felt very frightened and alone.

India had almost slipped into an uneasy sleep when the banging of the door brought her eyes wide open. Christopher was standing by the sea chest, stripping off his coat and loosening the buttons of his linen shirt.

"Good Lord, woman! Why didn't you light the stove? It's freezing in here!"

She looked at him with heart pounding and breath laboring in her chest. How could he talk of such mundane things at a time like this? Panic was rising in her throat, threatening to cut off her breath.

He discovered the lack of wood. "Hell!" he cursed. "What a night!" Sticking his head out the door, he bellowed, "Reed! Bring a load of wood down here before I freeze my . . .'' He remembered India's presence. ''Just get it down here right away!''

Five minutes later a fire was crackling in the stove, and the chill of the room began to dissipate. India's heart pounded even louder as she watched Christopher stand by the stove and undress. Flickering shadows cast by the dim wall lamps outlined the powerful muscles in his chest and arms as he stripped off his shirt and cravat, laying them neatly across the back of the chair. She averted her eyes when he unlaced his breeches, thinking that the male anatomy could remain a mystery a few moments longer. He chuckled when he saw her head buried in a pillow.

A few moments later, the bed creaked with his weight and she felt the warmth of his body as he stretched out beside her, laying his hand on her thigh in a gentle caress.

He chuckled again, low and throaty. ''Do you always go to bed fully clothed?''

She looked up from the pillow indignantly. Thank heaven he'd doused the lanterns! ''I have nothing else to wear, sir!''

''You don't need to wear anything at all in my bed, little one.'' He took hold of Teddy's sweater and pulled it over her head in one swift, efficient motion.

She shrieked. ''Ow! Ooh, my arm! That hurts!''

He covered her mouth with his hand. ''Do you want the whole ship to think I'm beating you?''

''What do you care what the ship thinks?'' she demanded when he released her.

He smiled, thinking of his still-indignant quartermaster. ''Believe it or not, you do have some guardians who are determined to see to your continued welfare.''

''Then I shall scream to high heaven if you touch me!''

''Tch, tch.'' He grinned devilishly. ''Then I will just have to gag you. You wouldn't like that, I think.''

He next attacked her breeches. She gasped and attempted to slap his hands away.

''Stop struggling, my sweet, or you will hurt your shoulder again.''

The brush of his fingers against her bare skin sent unfamiliar and unwanted sensations racing through her nerves.

"If you had anything of a gentleman in you, you'd at least wait until I recover to force yourself on my person!" She gasped as he slid the breeches down over her hips and legs. They disappeared somewhere beneath the bedclothes.

"Remember my shoulder!" she demanded. "I'm injured! Let me be!"

He laughed. "It's not your shoulder I'm interested in!"

He moved forward to kiss her, but she scrambled to the far side of the bed, trying to cover her exposed breasts with the bedsheets. In her hasty flight, she unknowingly delivered a glancing blow with her foot to an unprotected and highly sensitive area of Christopher's body. He grunted in pain and surprise, then tightened his lips and glared.

"Damn little hellcat!"

He reached for her angrily and pulled her struggling body under him, bringing his weight down on her and pinning her hands on either side of her head with his own. She felt his coarse body hair scratch her tender skin and moaned in misery and embarrassment at the feel of his hard body against hers.

"Now, little virgin." He looked down at her, his face unreadable in the darkness. "Are you going to make this difficult for yourself? Or are you going to be a good girl and let me take you like a gentleman?"

She glared at him. "What makes you think I'm a virgin?" she asked breathlessly, hoping to prick his ego.

"It's only too obvious, little India."

He lowered his mouth to hers, gently parted her trembling lips, and, teasing with his tongue, tasted the freshness of her sweet breath and probed the soft contours of her mouth. His kiss, begun so gently, rapidly grew hungrier and more demanding until she thought he would devour her entirely. Then he released her mouth and held her wide blue eyes with his dark, brooding ones as he moved his body against her own. He smiled knowingly as he wedged his knee between her thighs, rubbing gently against that tender, secret place that no man had ever touched. India groaned, but she couldn't move. Unfamiliar sensations ran riot through her body, and she felt helplessly confused and out of control. Things were moving too fast! Entirely too fast!

"Don't!" she begged. He ignored her, though his eyes never left hers.

Again his warm mouth came down on hers, not gentle, as before, but plundering, demanding, seeming to suck the very soul from her body. Her breath came in ragged gasps as his lips moved to trace a fiery path down her throat. His mouth moved from the valley between her breasts, brushed lightly over her tingling skin, and, fastening on an erect nipple, teased it gently with his tongue. India felt a surge of warm moisture between her legs as her traitorous body responded to his urgent demand. Panic warred with passion as she felt herself being overwhelmed by a flood of unfamiliar desire.

Then he moved off her. Even in the dark she could see him smiling, a smile of conquest, of triumph. She fought to rise, but his strong arm pinned her securely to the bed. His eyes slowly and deliberately traveled the length of her slender body, lingering on those places she most wanted to hide, noting with appreciation the inviting contours of her long legs, gracefully curved hips, slender waist, and small but beautifully formed breasts. Then his appreciative gaze moved to the piquant, exotic face with the slanting blue eyes and wealth of raven hair. He grinned. Even in the dark he could see her blush scarlet under his scrutiny.

"Beast!" she accused. "Crude, obnoxious beast! You have no right to use me in this demeaning fashion!"

He smiled urbanely, refusing to rise to the bait of her anger. "I've every right, little one, if you remember!"

He lowered himself to her side and gathered her close in his arms, gently fastening his mouth once more on the rosy nipple of one firm round breast. While he suckled her like a babe, easily subduing her indignant struggles, one hand slipped between her legs to lightly caress the hidden moist recesses of that most feminine part of her. India gasped and abruptly stopped her futile struggling, shocked into immobility by the fire that ignited at the intimate touch of his fingers. She fought an urgent impulse to run her hands through the softly curling brown hair that rested against her breast and to arch her hips against the hardness of his caressing hand between her legs.

"No, please." She didn't know whether she was talking to him or to herself. She squeezed her eyes shut and tried desperately to regain control of her clamoring senses.

Then his mouth moved, traveling slowly, tantalizingly over the firm contours of her breast, down over her flat belly, to replace his hand between her thighs. She cried out as his hot tongue flicked here and there, teasing and inflaming with its soft touch. She couldn't move, immobilized by shame, breathless with wanting, not knowing quite what she wanted. He moved back to her mouth, kicking the confining bedcovers to the foot of the mattress.

With desperate effort she pulled away from him. Her eyes had adjusted to the darkness, and she could clearly see the satisfied, knowing, infuriating smile on his satanic-seeming face.

"Monster!" she spat, trying to still the pounding of her own heart. "Stay away from me!"

"Is it so horrible?" Christopher laughed softly. "By God, I don't think you find it so!"

He reached out for her. "India, my little virgin child," he whispered hoarsely. "Do you know how very beautiful you are? I'm going to love you like you deserve to be loved."

"No!" she denied desperately. "This isn't my idea of love! Stay away from me!"

She could see clearly now the swollen shaft of his manhood, and the sight terrified her and excited her at the same time. She lunged for the opposite side of the bed in an effort to escape both his passion and her own, but his arm caught her around the waist and he pushed her gently down on her back. Her shoulder and ribs throbbed with pain from her struggles to escape. Suddenly he was on top of her, holding her so she couldn't move.

"It would not be wise to fight me, India," he said softly. His whole body was tense with passion as he crouched over her. He kissed her lips with surprising gentleness, then, firmly parting her thighs, rubbed his swollen manhood gently against her until her whole body throbbed. She wished now that she had watched the stableboy and kitchenmaid more closely on that long ago evening so she might know what was about to happen.

"What are you doing?" she squeaked in a frightened voice.

"Making you my own," he whispered, his lips warm against her ear. "My very own."

He spread her legs wider still and pushed himself very gently into her moist body. She gasped at the pain as he filled her, breaking the fragile barrier that separated him from her inner recesses. He groaned softly, kissing her mouth, her throat, her breasts, then, slowly moving, gently at first, then more urgently, plunging ever deeper, massaging her firm buttocks with his hands, lifting her hips to meet his thrusts.

India was lost. She thought she would die, first from the pain, then from the tension that surged in her body in time to his urgent thrusting. She arched her back and wrapped her legs around him, wanting to be closer, wanting somehow to weld their two straining bodies into one. Then he gave a deep moan of satisfaction. She could feel him emptying his seed with powerful pulses inside her. Her body contracted in a spasm of ecstasy that sent her soaring into a world she never knew existed. She closed her eyes as she reached the pinnacle and spiraled slowly, slowly back to earth, listening to her heart pounding, thinking curiously she could hear his heart beating in unison with hers.

When she opened her eyes some moments later, Christopher was propped on one elbow, smiling down at her. His smile was enigmatic, part tender, part cynical, and part amused.

"Well, India." He cocked one brow sardonically. "Now you are truly and legally mine."

India felt as though she'd been slapped. For a few moments during his lovemaking she had actually felt cared for, wanted, warmed by his tenderness. The primitive female in her had been secretly pleased at his urgent arousal. His cynicism brought her back to earth with a painful thud. She was, after all, merely a tool to be used for his vengeance, insurance that he would regain what he regarded as rightfully his. She had no importance to him as a person, a woman, or a lover.

"Swine!" she accused, and rolled away from his warm body to the opposite edge of the bed. The sheets were cold there. She shivered with the chill.

Suddenly his arm encircled her waist and pulled her back into the warm curve of his naked body. She could feel his breath in her tousled hair.

"Slimy bastard! Let me go!" She struggled against his hold, but only succeeded in entangling their limbs in a disturbingly intimate manner. "Haven't you done enough already?"

He chuckled low in his throat. "Such maidenly protests! A few moments ago you were pleased enough to accept my caresses." He pressed his thigh between her legs and felt her quiver in response. He was laughing at her!

Tears of humiliation and shame spilled from India's eyes. How easily he'd drawn her into the currents of his passion. How easily he'd conquered her defiance, pride, and hatred, all burned to cinders in the heat of his animal masculinity. She hated him more for lighting her passions than for taking her body. If he'd simply raped her and been done with it, she'd have been left with an abused body but an intact spirit. She could have spit in the face of his gently mocking laughter. Now all she could do was weep out her shame. At that moment she hated him more than she'd ever hated anyone in her life.

Twice more that night she woke to the feel of his hands and lips caressing her body, and the mounting throb of desire pulsing in her loins. Both times she fought both herself and him. Both times she lost, clinging to him in the end as he sent her soaring above the world on a flight of ecstasy. He didn't mock her again. Instead, he treated her with a warmth and tenderness that might have bespoken affection had he been some other man, and she some other woman. As she fell into sleep, cradled in his arms against the warmth of his hard body, she vowed that never again would she leave herself open to that mocking laughter, never again would she let him hurt her with his cutting cynicism and his uncaring, ironclad heart.

When India finally woke from exhausted slumber, the morning sun was slanting through the stern windows and painting a cheerful pattern of sunlight by the side of the bed. The pattern slid back and forth, back and forth, with the rhythmic motion of the ship. Rippling reflections of the ship's wake danced on the deck above her head. India lay for a few moments, wrapped in the warm, secure cocoon of semi-sleep. Then her eyes opened to the rumpled, empty bed beside her, and the memory of the night came flooding back. She groaned and turned her face into the pillow. She had absolutely no desire to arise and face the world, a world that was a place far different from what it had been yesterday morning.

The door creaked open, and a soft footfall sounded on the deck.

"India," Helen sang cheerfully. "India, dear, wake up!"

She dumped a large bundle of cloth on the bed. Thomas Cat followed hard on her heels, gingerly sniffed the bundle, and, deciding it contained no food, settled down stolidly on India's legs.

India mumbled and waved them both away with one bare arm.

"No, no," Helen chided. "Get up now, India. See, I've even brought warm water to wash in."

She put the bucket down and moved to the bed, observing India's tousled form and the small splotches of crimson that stained the sheets.

"Tch, tch. We'll have to see about changing these." She shook India's shoulder gently.

"Ow!" India complained. "That's my bad shoulder. Stop it!"

"Well, then, get up, lazy goose!"

How could Helen be so damned cheerful when her life was in tatters, India moped to herself. Some friend!

"I don't want to get up. I want to die. Go away!"

"No, no," Helen scolded. "Don't pout. You're not a child anymore."

Not a child, indeed! India felt at least a hundred years

old, used, soiled, and discarded. She was sore and chafed. Her pride was in shreds. How could she ever face the light of day after last night!

"Come on, now," Helen prodded. "You'll feel better once you're up and washed. We've a lot to do, you know. That ugly boatswain Mr. Daughtery brought us some fabrics from Portsmouth, and we'd best be making you some decent dresses before you cause a riot in those breeches! And I could use two or three myself."

India gave her friend a sour look, but managed to stumble from the bed with the sheet wrapped around her naked body. Thomas glared at her indignantly as she jostled him off her legs. She winced at the raw soreness between her thighs as she padded toward the washbasin. After splashing the sleep from her face, she wet a towel and carefully sponged her entire body, wishing fervently she could lie for hours in a hot bath and soak away every trace of Christopher from her aching body.

Helen observed with relief that her friend bore no bruises or other overt signs of mistreatment. She herself had spent the night being lustily entertained by Seamus Kennedy, a handsome young Irishman with black hair and vivid green eyes. When she'd emerged abovedeck in the early-morning hours, the crew had been abustle preparing the *Black Falcon* to set sail. Christopher was overseeing the preparation with the quartermaster, Mr. McCann, whistling a low tune and looking mightily pleased with himself. When he'd spotted her he motioned her to where he was standing. He'd told her about the fabric Mr. Daughtery had brought on board, and then added with a smile that she should let India sleep another several hours. As he turned back to his work, humming snatches of a disreputable sailor's ditty under his breath, she wondered what had happened to the grim, embittered sea renegade of the day before. This morning he looked like a cat who'd just devoured an exceptionally fat canary. She'd been afraid that India might have been that unfortunate morsel, and was relieved, therefore, to discover that her friend seemed not much the worse for wear after a night spent with her new husband.

India pulled on Teddy's breeches and sweater, then set about braiding her long hair and winding it about her head in a coronet. Helen observed with relief that some of her friend's spirit seemed to be returning.

"Well, now," she said, pulling the soiled linen from the bed and shooing an irritated Thomas from his nest. "It looks like you've survived, after all. It wasn't so terrible, was it?"

She personally thought Christopher had the look of an extremely sensuous lover, and she was even a bit envious when she thought on what must have happened in that rumpled bed.

India shot her a look of pure misery. "It was awful!" she cried. "It was . . . just horrible! Cruel! Oh, cruel! Helen, he . . . I swear he is the Devil himself. He humiliated me . . . laughed at me! He did terrible things . . . forced me to want him. Then he laughed at me!" India buried her face in Helen's plump shoulder.

Helen patted her back soothingly. "So that's it!" She smiled. "Don't be embarrassed, my lamb. You're supposed to feel something when an attractive male is making love to you. It's nothing to be ashamed of."

"Not when you're trying to hate him!" India wept.

"Ah, yes." Helen sighed. "Even then."

"He was using me, the despicable swine! He was just showing me how much power he has over me! He's horrible, and I'll never be able to face him again! I hate him! I hate him!"

"Perhaps you feel that way now. But you must remember, India, that you have the same power over him."

"Bah! I don't even have any power over myself when he . . . when he . . . I don't have any power over him."

Helen laughed as India turned scarlet. "Yes, you do, sweeting. You just don't know it yet."

She remembered the captain's softened mood in the early-morning hours and smiled knowingly.

"Our brave captain may think he has an impervious heart, but I think before this adventure is over, he's going to find himself ensnared in his own trap!"

CHAPTER EIGHT

As the *Black Falcon* sailed westward out of the English Channel and into the open sea, India's days took on an almost pleasant routine. Her only experience on board a ship had been in the Channel, and she found the great rolling ocean to be of different character altogether. She was fascinated by the ever-moving, ever-changing expanse that stretched away from her to what seemed the edge of the world. No land in sight. Just water, forever and ever, on and on. She could understand why just a few hundred years ago seamen had believed they would fall off the edge of the world if they sailed far enough west. She could also understand why men became enamored of the sea, taking her as a mistress in place of the comforts of home and family on dry land. Standing at the rail hour after hour, day after day, India began to understand the sea's personality, to feel her awesome power, and to comprehend the seductive nature of her always beautiful face. The sea's immensity made her own problems seem insignificant. She enjoyed losing herself in the grandeur that stretched all around her.

They were sailing to the Caribbean, Christopher told her on their first day out. Daughtery the boatswain had a seafaring cousin in Portsmouth who reported seeing John Thomas on New Providence Island, a notorious pirate stronghold in the Bahamas. Christopher's features grew grim as he told her he would turn the pirate island inside out, if need be, to find her father's former manservant and persuade him to tell the truth about that long-ago night in Blenheim. India frowned in anger, asserting that if he thought to clear his name in this manner, then he didn't need her to regain his properties. Christopher regarded her with a knowing gaze that brought a hot flush to her face. Perhaps that was true, he admitted, but she did appear to have other qualities that would make her useful on a long voyage. Then he smiled sardonically, saying that in any case he didn't trust King George to return what Queen Anne had taken away, even if he did clear his name. And there was still the matter of her father to be considered. She turned on heel and stalked angrily away. The man had an uncanny knack for breaking her composure, for bringing out the hot-tempered child that India thought she'd conquered during her stay in France. She had pointedly avoided him the rest of the day.

All in all, however, her days on board the *Black Falcon* were pleasant. She and Helen were allowed the run of the ship now that they were at sea. While India was still dressed in Teddy's breeches, she was too self-conscious to spend much time abovedeck. The seamen were unfailingly polite, undoubtedly out of fear of Christopher's watchful eye, but she could imagine the sniggers and winks exchanged behind her back. She and Helen spent most of the first week at sea industriously laboring over the cloth Mr. Daughtery had purchased in Portsmouth, turning out three dresses for each of them, plus chemises, drawers, and petticoats. India blessed her redoubtable tutor Miss Adams for insisting that she acquire sewing skills herself instead of having all her clothes made by professional seamstresses, as was the usual case with young ladies of fashion and wealth.

She made one dress of wool with a light muslin under-dress, and the other two she fashioned of light-colored muslin and linen. The dresses were designed to be modest and practical, and were far from being fashionable. Still, somehow India had never felt so feminine than when she climbed out of Teddy's breeches and oversized sweater and donned her new blue wool dress, with closely fitted bodice and long narrow sleeves. The full skirts swished around her feet, and she wondered why, back at Hillcrest, she had so enjoyed playing the hoyden in boys' clothing.

As days passed, India found herself enjoying shipboard life almost to the degree that she began to feel guilty. The weather held fair and mild, and every day the white billowing sails glared against a blue sky. The breeze was strong and steady, and the little brigantine pushed steadily southwestward, rising and plunging with the white-tipped waves as though she had life of her own. India would spend several hours every day at her favorite place by the rail, as far toward the bow as she could get, and revel in the rhythmic rise and fall of the ship, the creaks and groans of the rigging, and the occasional thunderous crack of the sails when the helmsman steered too close to the wind. As they approached warmer climes, she delighted in watching swarms of tiny flying fish break from the waves and skim over the surface, or occasional schools of dolphin cavort in the ship's bow wave.

Sometimes Helen would keep her company, and they would reminisce about the people and places of their former life together, or comment about the new experiences they were sharing. Most often, though, Helen would be keeping company with one or another of the seamen, and India was left alone with her own thoughts. During those long idle days at sea she came to a better understanding of herself, of her relationship with her father, and of her life at Hillcrest. Those days saw the ending of her girlhood and the beginning of her womanhood. She came to terms with herself and realized that she had the strength, if need be, to stand on her own. Much as she might long for the warmth and security of love, if life never gave her her heart's desire, she had the character to find contentment, if not true happiness, within herself. With all the philosophical musings that passed through her mind as she stared out to sea, though, she still could not think of a solution to the problem presented by her future life, or an understanding of the enigmatic man who controlled it.

While India was enjoying the ship and the sea, Helen was enjoying the seamen. She cut a wide swath through the eligible men on board the *Black Falcon,* much to Christopher's amusement and India's consternation. India found it impossible to condemn her friend's flirtatious and at times promiscuous behavior, however. She understood now that in spite of being together most of their young lives, Helen had actually lived in a different world and operated by different rules from those that governed her.

The crew understandably warmed to Helen right off. They treated her variously as a sister, friend, or a lover. None of the men seemed to mind that she distributed her favors so freely among the crew, casting flirtatious gazes to one, teasing and giggling with another, and granting a kiss, or possibly much more than a kiss, to still a third. She was someone who would listen to their woes, to their stories of home. She would be properly awed by their tales of adventure, liberally laced, of course, with their own heroism. With Helen they felt manly, attractive, gallant, even, at times, chivalrous. Christopher swore that he'd never before seen such a crowd of fancified, prissed-up dandies as the young bucks of the crew took to shaving, hair-combing, and even an occasional washing under the hose of the seawater pump to impress Helen and win her favors.

One man in particular pursued Helen with unusual intensity. Seamus Kennedy was a handsome, black-haired, green-eyed Irishman who served the *Black Falcon* as sailing master. He had "entertained" Helen the night the ship had anchored at Portsmouth, and was apparently overwhelmed by her charms. Since that night he had wooed her with single-minded devotion. Unfortunately, however, after a single night in his company, Helen did not share his feelings.

"An Irishman! Of all things!" she complained to India one day as they stood by the railing, watching the topmen scramble up the rigging to lay on more sail.

India commented that she couldn't see why, if Helen didn't mind his being a smuggler and pirate, she objected to his being an Irishman. Helen sniffed with disdain and replied that one must maintain some standards, at least.

India herself found Seamus Kennedy charming. His intelligence and easy humor made him an entertaining conversationalist, and she spent on more than one occasion several happy hours conversing with him about politics, the theater, literature, and philosophy. His sophistication and experience made her feel like an ignorant country girl at times, and made her realize what she had missed by spending her entire

young life at Hillcrest. But somehow Seamus always made
her feel that she had something to say, that her opinion was
worthwhile. He never condescended, never talked down.
His cultured speech, with just the hint of an Irish brogue,
his education, and his fine manners all bespoke breeding
and wealth. India wondered how he had ended up serving
on this outlaw ship but knew better than to question him
about such personal matters.

As India became acquainted with many of the crewmen,
she was amazed to find herself liking most of them. She had
expected villains and cutthroats, but found instead rough,
hardworking men who were staunch supporters of their
captain and loyal friends to their comrades. They were not
ashamed of their way of life. Indeed, they considered
themselves the most fortunate of men. They could be
slaving under the discipline and abysmal pay of His Majesty's Royal Navy, or working their hands to the bone for
some autocratic English landlord. Instead, they'd made
themselves a fortune the easy way, by taking a few risks
with a swift ship and a daring captain who always seemed to
have luck on his side.

The crew came from all parts and all levels of British life,
and after discovering they were not the villains she had
imagined, India welcomed the friendship they readily offered.
As the evenings grew warmer, the off-duty seamen and
officers generally gathered in a knot in the ship's waist,
smoking their pipes and spinning yarns, sometimes telling
stories of themselves or of their friends and acquaintances.
Helen usually sat with them, and after a few evenings'
observation from a distance, India joined them, also. She
listened to their stories with fascination, learning of a whole
side of life in the British Isles that she'd never before
realized existed. Her heart stirred when young Peter Reed,
the sailmaker's apprentice, told of being disowned by his
father after marrying far below his station, then being
deserted by his new wife when he'd lost his inheritance.
And grizzled old Tom Smith the sailmaker, who had deserted from the HMS *Plymouth* after fifteen years of service,
told of conditions in the Royal Navy that made her stomach

turn with disgust. And then there was poor Thomas Crowley, with only one leg and one eye, who'd suffered the tortures of imprisonment in Newgate for stealing a loaf of bread, and who'd seen his older brother hanged for the crime of copping a gentleman's fat purse in hopes of feeding his starving family.

Tales of derring-do were numerous, and many of the *Black Falcon*'s self-styled professional adventurers were not loath to embellish the excitement of their lives at sea. Garrulous Timothy Hawkins, with hardly a tooth in his mouth or a hair on his head, loved to spin tales of his great-grandfather's adventures with the original *boucaniers* of Hispaniola. Most horribly enthralling of all were the boatswain John Daughtery's yarns of his two years pirating in the Caribbean with one-armed Henry Johnson.

India thought the boatswain was possibly the ugliest man in the entire world. He'd been the victim of fire, and the features of his face appeared to have melted and run together to form a countenance that was barely human. All his visible skin was mottled, red, and hairless. One ear had been burned completely away and was covered by a bright red scarf he tied around his head. His mouth was a lipless gash. Daughtery's unfortunate deformities added even more horror to the stories he told of the brutalities and monstrous cruelties practiced by the rovers of the Spanish Main. His tales sent chills deep into India's soul. She knew Christopher had spiced his smuggling activities with a bit of piracy, but she couldn't imagine his committing such acts of barbarism as Daughtery described. But then, and she shivered at the thought, how well did she really know the man whose bed she warmed every night? Not well at all.

The one thing that marred India's enjoyment of those long, idle days at sea was her relationship with Christopher. Where he was concerned she was puzzled and confused. Her feelings for him defied understanding. In all her young life, no one else had been so successful in getting under her skin. He could provoke her temper with a single word or a sardonic look. He brought out the worst in her—temper, rebelliousness, stubbornness—and seemed to delight in doing so. After their first few days at sea, however, his manner toward her was courteous, cool, and distant. At times she would catch him gazing at her with an enigmatic, almost questioning expression; but upon noticing her glance, his face would become impassive, unreadable.

All of Christopher's humor and warmth seemed reserved for their times alone, in his bed. He would come to their cabin usually long after she had already retired. She would wake to the feel of his big hands caressing her silken skin and his mouth moving gently against hers. She learned quickly not to fight, for that seemed only to inflame him all the more. So she would lie still, trying to ignore the tingling that began between her thighs and the delicious languor that stole over her body, urging her to relax and invite him into her body with open arms and open legs. Her silent battle with herself was always lost nearly before it began. He seemed to know just what it took to bring her to the point of relenting to her own passions, and his skillful hands and mouth would quickly achieve their purpose. He took delight in driving her to higher and higher peaks of ecstasy, gently and skillfully teaching her the secret needs of her own body. Under his passionate tutoring she became familiar with every square inch of his hard, muscular body, just as he explored her every soft curve and recess that was hidden to all but him. The mystery was fading, but the passion stayed and grew.

Try as she would, India could not hate him, though at times she hated herself for her helplessly wanton behavior in his arms. His mind and thoughts were ever a puzzle to her. How could he treat her like a stranger during the day and possess her in such gentle and passionate lovemaking each night? Could pure lust evoke the tender expression she saw in his eyes when he brought them both to fulfillment? Or was there truly some affection for her lurking deeply hidden in his soul? Moreover, did she really want this man to love her, this renegade who had forced her into his bed for his own dark design of revenge? Questions, questions, questions! They seemed to run riot in her head every waking hour. She knew she was becoming inexorably caught in his spell, that in spite of her resolutions he had achieved a hold on her heart that might be impossible to remove. Whether his hold stemmed from love or from some darker fascination she didn't know, but she swore he would never know her feelings. She felt terribly vulnerable to this man who held her in his power. Where before he could only hurt her body, had he wished, now he could strike clear through to her spirit. He must never be allowed to realize the extent of his hold on her.

As India was trying to puzzle out her feelings for her captor, Christopher was fighting a battle of his own. He had married India for two purposes only—to secure revenge against her father and to ensure redemption of his lands. Everything was neatly planned. He had his revenge on her father. He would find John Thomas, clear his name, resume his rightful place among his peers, and, either through recompense from the king or inheritance through India, he would regain his family's beloved seat in Hampshire. Very neatly planned. But things were not working out quite as he expected.

There had been many women in his life, and he expected that there would be many more. He'd always taken women with a practiced skill and passion that had nothing to do with emotion. Though one or two in the past had engaged his affections briefly, the feeling had been short-lived and halfhearted at best. The life of a smuggler and pirate did not encourage long-lasting relationships. But now there was India, with her defiance, her rebelliousness, and her reluctant but deeply ingrained sensuality. He watched her watching the sea, moved by her fascination and deep appreciation of the elements he most loved. He watched her make friends with his rowdy crew, amazed that these rough men, who usually regarded women as mere vessels for their lust, could treat this one woman as a comrade and a friend. And where he knew her best of all—in his bed—she continued to intrigue him night after night. Her allure had not waned after several encounters, as he expected it would. Instead of fading, his passions continued to grow. He was captivated by the depths of her sensuality, seduced by a sweetness of face and body that he sensed reflected a sweetness of spirit he'd not before encountered. She was blossoming from a girl-child to a woman before his eyes; and while he had been amused and captivated by the girl, his heart was in mortal danger from the woman.

Christopher did not want to fall in love with India. Love had been the furthest thing from his mind when he married her, but from the night he'd first bedded her, he realized that this was no woman he could use and discard at will, not unless he kept a very firm rein on his feelings. Poetic justice, he mused, that such an unconscionable breaker of hearts should finally set his own heart on a woman who hated him, and hated him with good reason. Would it amuse her to know how desperately he was attempting to evade the silken net of her sweet charm? Would it comfort her, when she reluctantly yielded under his caress, to know that her slender woman's body drove him out of control with desire, that as the days wore on he could not tear his thoughts away from the curve of her smile, the timbre of her voice, and the sweet silken feel of her skin under his hands? Christopher fought, finding in himself the very unpleasant adversary he'd warned India about. He knew it was a losing battle, as long as he had India readily under his eyes and nightly under his hands to unwittingly bewitch his heart with her sorcery. But she would not know of his feelings, he vowed. No telling what form her revenge would take if she realized his heart was not, after all, made of iron.

Ian McCann watched Christopher's restless pacing with amusement. He was sorely tempted to say I told you so. Any fool could have seen, he thought, that putting those two together under any circumstances was like applying spark to dry wood, and now the captain was getting burned. Ian couldn't sympathize, though. It wasn't as if the lad hadn't been warned. Tampering with innocent maids usually led to trouble, in Ian's experience. Besides, though he loved Christopher like a brother, he recognized that his friend needed someone like India, someone who could curb his hot temper and soften his growing cynicism. He could sense the tension between the two of them, but he guessed once they both resolved their differences they could do each other a world of good. If only the situation would continue calm. If only they didn't kill each other first.

Unfortunately, the peaceful days of easy, idle sailing were about to end.

CHAPTER NINE

As the *Black Falcon* approached the southern latitudes, the fair weather and easy sailing came to an end. The sun was merciless. By noon of every day the deck planking was hot enough to be uncomfortable even through the soles of India's shoes, though the horny-footed seamen didn't seem to notice as they went about their tasks barefooted as always. The men worked without their shirts and grew almost black from the sun. The least amount of exertion would cause sweat to run in rivulets down their chests and backs. India wished fervently she could discard as much of her clothing as the seamen did.

Daily tropical cloudbursts were the only relief. Every afternoon brought violent but short-lived squalls that battered the ship with driving rain and turbulent winds. India could stand at the rail and watch them approach, amazed at how sharp a line divided blue sky and calm seas on one side from boiling clouds and gray rain-ravaged waves on the other. Sailing into one of these squalls was like sailing through a curtain separating fair weather from chaos.

India retreated to her cabin during these short bouts with the weather. The memory of that horrible night aboard the *Sea Gull* was still too fresh for her to pretend any bravery while the little brigantine was tossed about and the wind and rain battered her shortened sails. Fortunately for her peace of mind, most of the squalls were over before they had fairly begun, but occasionally the ship would sail into a line of storms that lasted all afternoon. Then she would sit on the bed with knees drawn up to her chin, heart pounding loudly at every pitch and roll, until the cooler air of evening brought calmer seas and gentler winds.

The tropical squalls were a boon to the *Falcon*'s fresh water supply, as every available container was set on deck during the storms to catch the precious rains. For the first time since the beginning of the voyage, India had fresh water to wash her hair and clothes. She indulged herself in luxury by washing her hair every day, letting the soft warm breezes dry it to a shining curling mass that fell around her shoulders and down her back. Since the beginning of the voyage she had worn her hair in thick braids atop her head; she had almost forgotten the delightful feeling of having it free to move in the breeze.

It was particularly hot on the afternoon that the uneasy truce between India and Christopher was broken. The afternoon rains had passed without cooling the air much. The decks steamed from their recent soaking. The sails fluttered occasionally in the fitful breeze, but mostly hung limp from the yards. Tempers were on edge from the heat and from the idleness forced by lack of wind. Most of the crew were gathered in the waist of the ship dozing, daydreaming, or swapping tales with their comrades. India stood at her favorite place in the bow, trying to take advantage of what little breeze there was. Beside her, the young sailmaker's apprentice Peter Reed leaned on the railing and looked out upon the vast expanse of calm sea.

India had formed a close friendship with Peter over the last few weeks. He inspired her motherly instincts, India told herself. Although Peter was actually a few years older than she, he looked like a mere boy. He was tall and thin, with near-white blond hair and light gray eyes. An adolescentlike awkwardness made him look younger than his years, and his features had a childish quality—with thickly lashed eyes, slightly pug nose, and a sensitive mouth—that he would probably never outgrow. Peter had a quick and intelligent mind, and over the last few weeks India had enjoyed their frequent conversations. As Peter sought her out more and more, she was aware that he was becoming infatuated with her. He was obviously so lonely, though, and she saw no harm in giving him a bit of the feminine sympathy that he seemed to crave.

Peter had taken great pains to explain to India that he was not a criminal by choice, but that unfortunate circumstances had forced him into his current lawless life. He was the eldest of three sons, she learned, whose father was a well-to-do squire and local magistrate in Suffolk. His father had ruled both his family and his tenants with a hand of iron, and, as eldest son, Peter was groomed to carry on the tradition. A brilliant match was made for him with the daughter of a wealthy London merchant, a girl who would bring both additional wealth and influence into the squire's family. Unfortunately, Peter and his intended bride had loathed each other on sight. But, of course, their feelings had little influence on the planned nuptials. Persons of quality were expected to accommodate themselves to such situations.

Peter was a quiet and biddable boy by nature, but in this one instance he could not see sacrificing his own happiness for family position. The thought of spending his life with a woman he regarded as a sharp-tongued shrew with ice water in her veins was insupportable, so on impulse he defied convention and eloped with the pretty daughter of one of his father's tenants, a girl whom he'd found very accommodating several times in the past. His father promptly disowned him. That wasn't much of a surprise. What did surprise him was that his pretty young wife, who, when she found out she had not indeed married up to a life of wealth and luxury, flew in a dither back to her father, spinning a tale of abduction and rape. Peter, unfortunately, had no home to return to, his father being an unforgiving sort. And now he had earned a reputation as kidnapper and rapist of innocent maidens into the bargain. His wife and her father were very vocal about their accusations. There was nothing left for him but to live outside the law, circumstances being what they were.

Peter had recited his tale of woe so often that India knew it by heart. She felt sorry for him. He was an immature boy who had handled a bad situation in a very foolish manner, she thought, and been paid in very hard coin. He needed a sympathetic ear. She knew she shouldn't allow him to seek her out quite so often, and that she shouldn't so readily fall into conversation with him when he did. But the puppy adoration in his eyes was balm to her senses.

India's relationship with Christopher had ravaged her feminine pride. Peter's worshipful regard could make her temporarily forget that Christopher degraded her nightly to satisfy his animal lust, while all the time holding her womanhood and individuality in contempt. Peter treated her as though she were an untouched maiden, full of virtue and free from any taint of unpure and unholy passions. He made her feel clean again. The thought that young Peter might some day step out of line had never occurred to her.

Peter was particularly moody today as he leaned on the rail and stared out at the calm, almost greasy-looking sea. India was lost in her own thoughts and paid little heed to Peter's attitude. Everyone was out of sorts today. It was the heat, and the stillness. Soon the trades would blow again and they'd be on their way. Everyone's mood would lighten when that happened. Peter continued to stare moodily out on the glassy blue surface.

"We'll be making land soon," he said.

Another long period of silence.

"You'll like the Bahamas," he finally went on.

India pretended interest. The only land she really wanted to see was her beloved England.

"Have you been there?" she asked courteously.

"Oh, no. But I've heard stories. Palm trees, warm sand beaches, exotic flowers and birds."

"Well," India returned, "I don't think I will like it where we're headed. New Providence is a pirate stronghold, and I hear no one but scoundrels and rogues go there. Mr. Daughtery says even the British governor of the Bahamas encourages piracy and takes a cut of the loot! Can you imagine a British official being so corrupt?''

Another long silence.

''A lady like you shouldn't have to put up with such foul places,'' Peter commented.

''Well, I don't plan to go ashore.''

''No.'' He frowned. ''Not just New Providence. I mean you should be somewhere in some rich drawing room, surrounded by servants. It's a crime that you have to live on a scummy ship, surrounded by lowborn dogs like . . .''

''Now Peter,'' India interrupted. ''Most of the crew are really very nice, you know, and treat me with respect. You shouldn't get upset over my . . .''

''Not him!'' Peter asserted with clenched jaw.

''Him?'' India questioned uneasily. She was made a little uncomfortable by Peter's intensity.

''Barnett!'' Peter looked at her with bitterness in his gray eyes. ''Our gallant commander!'' he spat. ''I can't bear the thought of him touching you. He treats you like a . . . like a . . .''

''Don't say it!'' India's face grew stony. ''I am his wife, and he can treat me any way he wants.''

''No!'' Peter's knuckles turned white where he gripped the railing. ''You shouldn't talk that way! You shouldn't think that way!''

India was glad they were out of sight of the crewmen in the waist.

''You don't have to put up with it,'' Peter asserted, looking up.

India laughed bitterly. ''What would you suggest I do?''

Peter had the opening he longed for. ''Come away with me! We could get off at New Providence with no trouble. No one asks any questions there!'' He was begging. He wanted to fall on his knees, clasp her little hands in his, and convince her of his devotion.

Dread flooded India's heart and momentarily paralyzed her thoughts. She'd had no idea Peter's feelings ran so deep.

''Peter.'' She shook her head, backing away slightly from

the ardor he had unmasked in his eyes. "You don't know what you're saying!"

"Yes, I do! India," he begged. "I love you! I'd treat you right—as you should be treated. We'll go to one of the other islands, buy a place—a rich place with servants and slaves. I've got money. Really! All I need to do is send back to England for it. Please! Trust me! You'll never have to see this ship or . . . or Christopher Barnett again!"

"Peter, please!" India shook her head again. "It's out of the question. Please stop talking like this. Let's just forget this whole subject came up."

"India," he pleaded, his face looking very much like a petulant child's, "I'm offering you freedom . . . and love. . . ."

"No, Peter. Even if I wanted to go with you, Christopher would never let me go. It's impossible."

"He'll never know you're gone," Peter promised desperately. "He'll be busy on shore the whole time in New Providence, looking for that man. We could do it, India. Really. It would be so easy."

She fixed him with what she hoped was a stern, level gaze.

"Peter," she began softly, "you must understand. I like you very much. You're my good friend. But I don't love you. For that reason, if for no other, I couldn't go with you."

She moved to leave, but he grabbed her arm.

"You don't love him, either. Everybody knows he forced you to marry him. He has no right to hold you."

India gave up trying to reason with him. The best thing to do now, she decided, was leave. Maybe later he would calm down and see his plan held no hope for either of them. She was desperately glad that no one could overhear their conversation. She lifted her chin with the shreds of pride that were left to her.

"I don't want to discuss this anymore, Peter, and I mean it. So I will bid you good afternoon. And I think we should both just forget this conversation ever took place."

She shuddered to think of Christopher's reaction should he ever learn of Peter's ambitions.

"No! India! You can't go yet! You've got to listen!" He moved to block her path.

India was becoming seriously annoyed.

"Peter! Stop it! You're acting like a child! Now get out of my way!"

She was beginning to sympathize with his father for disowning him.

Peter grabbed her by both arms and backed her against the rail. His grip was amazingly strong.

"A child, am I?"

Suddenly he no longer looked like a boy. He looked like a man—an angry man. Fear was beginning to blossom in India's chest. How could she have underestimated him so?

"I'll show you what kind of child I am!"

He covered her mouth with his, holding her head in a harsh grip so she couldn't move. She pounded against him with her fists, to no avail. His mouth was wet and unpleasant and ground against hers painfully.

Suddenly and unexpectedly she was free, and Peter was flying ungracefully through the air to land with a thud on the deck ten feet away. India wiped her hand across her bruised, wet mouth and looked up into the stony face of her husband.

Oh, my God! she thought as her heart sank into the pit of her stomach. He looked calm—too calm. The hard planes of his face seemed cast in immovable bronze. Only his eyes betrayed him. They were black with anger. If eyes could reach out and strangle, surely she'd be dead at this very instant. India wished she could sink through the deck, or evaporate into thin air, but she managed to draw herself up to her full height, lift her chin, and meet those fearsome eyes with a defiant gaze. After all, she had done nothing wrong. Well, not much, at least.

"Go to the cabin," he ordered in a low voice edged with steel.

India turned and left without a word. She looked back only once to see Christopher lift Peter bodily from the deck and slam him against the deckhouse. Peter yelped with pain, and India didn't stay to learn his fate. She turned and ran the rest of the way as if the Devil were nipping at her heels.

An hour passed, then two. India paced the length of the cabin. Up and down, back and forth, with swishing skirts and angrily clenched fists. She watched the light fade slowly from the windows. Up and down, back and forth, again and again. Thomas Cat watched her curiously.

"Can't you find someplace besides my bed to sleep!" India snapped, and she threw a pillow at him. Thomas sidestepped adroitly, shook himself indignantly, then settled down again and fixed her with an irate cat glare.

"Hell!" India cursed, and she kicked Christopher's sea chest, grimacing as pain lanced from her toe up her leg to her hip.

"Hell and damnation!"

She grabbed the injured toe and sat down hard on the wing-back chair.

"I hate you, Christopher Barnett-Armstrong!" she declared to the cat, who looked at her with the beginnings of alarm. "You arrogant, traitorous, lecherous, son-of-a-bitch pirate, you! Ooooooh!"

He was deliberately letting her stew, she thought, letting her wonder what was in store for her.

"Dirty slimy bastard renegade!" she muttered to the cat. Thomas decided he'd taken enough abuse. He flattened his ears and hissed.

"Oh, shut up! You mangy alley cat! Why don't you find someone else to follow around. I thought you didn't like women."

Surely Christopher would listen to reason if she explained. After all, she was the victim, not the offender! What could he do, anyway? Beat her? Christopher didn't beat women. Teddy had told her so. Besides, he just wasn't that kind of man. Or at least she didn't think so. Keelhaul her? Strap her to the mast for thirty lashes? That was a laugh. It would defeat his whole purpose if she died before she delivered him up a child.

One little kiss! It wasn't that great an offense, after all. He couldn't know anything about Peter's plans to carry her away. He'd be cooled down by the time he came to the cabin. Of course he would. It wasn't as though he'd be jealous. Just a little tweak to his pride—seeing another man fool with something that belonged to him—and something he didn't much care about anyway.

India had almost convinced herself by the time Christopher walked through the door. But one glance at his face told her he was still angry, very angry. Furious, India thought, would be a better word. He looked more fearful to her than he ever had, even on their wedding night. His coarse-weave muslin shirt seemed to emphasize the broadness of his shoulders, and the close-fitting breeches outlined the thick muscles of his thighs. His face was as dark as a tropical storm. Every movement seemed to spell menace as he walked slowly toward her.

She sprang from the chair and backed toward the bulkhead, raising her hand in front of her to fend him off.

"Now, Christopher, let me explain. I can explain. Really!"

Christopher perched on the arm of the chair, folded his massive arms across his chest, and regarded her grimly.

"So explain."

India took a deep breath. Yes, so explain. Explain without getting Peter into deeper trouble than he was now. Think, India, think!

"I . . . that is, he . . . well, it wasn't my fault, really . . . you see. . . ."

"If you can't explain better than that, I may as well beat you and get it over with."

"Beat me?" India cried. "Beat me? You wouldn't beat me! You don't hit females!"

"In your case I'll make an exception."

India forgot the need for caution. "You wouldn't dare, you bastard!"

Christopher's eyes narrowed. "Wouldn't I?"

"It wasn't my fault! I didn't do anything wrong! I didn't ask him to kiss me!"

Christopher just looked at her with those dark, terrible eyes. How would eyes usually so warm turn suddenly so cold, so hard?

"I tried to get away! But he just . . . just . . . I didn't even know he felt that way," India lied.

"Didn't you?" Christopher asked quietly.

There was a long silence as they held each other's eyes. Then India tilted her chin and glared at him angrily.

"All right. I did know. But I didn't think he would step out of line. I didn't encourage him."

"You did encourage him," Christopher accused. "I've seen you flirting with the boy, smiling at him, fluttering your eyelashes."

"I did not flutter my eyelashes!" India denied indignantly. "I was friendly to him. There's nothing wrong with that! He was nice to me. He makes me feel like a lady!"

"And I don't?" Christopher raised a sardonic brow.

"You!" she cried. "You make me feel like a . . . like a whore!"

"Seems appropriate," he mused calmly, "since that's the part you've been playing."

"What!" she exploded. "How dare you accuse me of . . . of . . . something like that when it's you who lie in my bed every night! You damn lecherous dog! You treat me like a whore . . . doing things to me . . . and making me feel like no decent woman should feel. . . . Then you laugh at me, you bastard! How dare you accuse me of . . ."

"Enough!" He rose from his seat and advanced toward her menacingly. "I've a good mind to turn you over my knee and let you feel the weight of my hand, you little hellcat! But I won't, this time. But listen to me well, India! The next time I catch you waggling your tail at any one of my crew, you'll get the beating of your life. And you'll be restricted to this cabin the rest of your time on my ship!"

India saw red. Her mouth dropped open incredulously.

"Waggling my tail, is it! How dare you, you filthy-minded swine!"

She drew back and slapped him full across the face with all the strength of her slender arm. When she saw the look on his face she was immediately sorry. She gasped and backed into the bulkhead, but he grabbed both wrists and dragged her toward him.

"You should learn, madam, that if you initiate violence, it is likely to be returned."

She clenched her teeth, but the expected blow never fell. Instead, he pushed her back on the bed, raking her with hot, narrowed eyes.

"So, you think I treat you like a whore, do you? I doubt very much, India, that you know what a man does with a cheap whore." He grinned unpleasantly. "Perhaps you need a lesson, so next time you'll know the difference!"

India regarded him with amazement. Her heart twisted with both fear and a hint of perverse excitement. It occurred to her that she'd never seen him truly angry before, and his anger was both fearsome and magnificent. With an aura of barely restrained violence, he seemed coiled tight and ready to spring at her.

"Take off your clothes, whore," he growled. "I want to see what I've bought."

"You can go to hell!" India tried hard to control the quaver in her voice.

A hard smile twisted his lips. "Playing hard to get? Pity I'm not in the mood."

He took one quick step toward her, grasped the neck of her dress, and in one quick yank ripped it halfway down to the hem.

"Nooooo!" India wailed, seeing her painstaking work destroyed in his big hands. "Get away from me!"

"Step out of that dress, then," he ordered, "unless you want more damage done."

She did as he ordered, looking at him with eyes smoky-gray and burning with fury.

"You damned lowborn grunting animal." She could not prevent the husky note of desire in her voice as she watched him hurriedly unbutton his shirt and begin to unlace his breeches, which were already strained with the swelling evidence of his desire. "I hate you for this!"

"You already hate me," he commented coldly. "Take off your drawers and lie down, India. If you're going to be a whore you've got to remember that the only thing about you that matters is what's between your legs."

India's face blanched with fury. She lunged at him with nails poised to make a bloody shambles of his face, but he caught her easily and forced her down on the bed, bending her back over the edge until she was helpless to move. Then, holding her easily with one hand, with the other he ripped away the last shreds of material that separated the soft skin of her belly from the throbbing shaft of his manhood.

"You'd make a lousy whore, India," he whispered hoarsely. "You don't know when to stop fighting."

He poised himself at her hot, moist portal and looked down at her pale face with eyes gone black with anger and desire. There was no warmth in those black eyes. At that point even his lust was icy-cold and remorseless.

"Remember this next time you think you're being treated like a whore."

He rammed himself into her, ignoring her cry of pain and fury as he felt the full length of his hot flesh enveloped by her moist warmth.

She writhed under him, heaving up, trying to escape his merciless, punishing invasion. Then, as he thrust again and again, she was carried helplessly into the storm winds of his passion. Of its own volition her traitorous body surrendered to his. Her hips moved in rhythm with his, trying to take him harder, deeper, faster. She alternately cried out her passion and cursed him in words she'd only recently acquired from his own crew.

He finished quickly, holding her down as he pumped his seed deep into her body. She lay limp, ashamed, and exhausted as he rose from between her legs and relaced the front of his breeches. Hot tears coursed down her cheeks to soak the bedcovers. Somehow the fact that he hadn't even bothered to undress made the experience that much more humiliating. She snatched at her torn dress to cover herself, then curled into a tight ball and buried her face in the bedclothes.

"Lesson over," he said finally. "Now that you've discovered you don't like being a whore you can go back to being a lady—and leave my men alone."

She looked at him, blue eyes dark with venom. "I'll never forgive you for this."

Halfway out the door, he turned and regarded her sardonically, one eyebrow slightly arched. "I don't recall having
asked your forgiveness."

He shut the door quietly behind him.

CHAPTER TEN

The whole ship suffered the aftermath of Christopher's
temper. He left the routine sailing of the ship to the
quartermaster and spent the next few days pacing the quarterdeck with a black scowl on his face. Even Ian approached
him only at the risk of being glared at by hooded dark eyes
and having his character and ancestry evaluated in highly
unpleasant terms. But in spite of having to walk softly
around his ill-humored captain, the quartermaster was secretly
delighted by this display of raw emotion from his friend,
whose composure could seldom be pricked by even the
direst circumstances. Here he was, pacing and scowling and
fit to be tied over a lass who he claimed meant nothing to
him. Ian's faith in human nature was restored. He'd expected
this from the first. Christopher's using the little maid for his
own purposes, trying all the while to stay uninvolved, was
like setting a match to gunpowder and expecting no explosion.
It was gratifying to have his estimation of the situation
prove correct. Ian's knowing, grinning face, however, only
drove Christopher into a fouler mood, if that were possible.

Shortly after leaving India weeping in the cabin, Christopher's anger had cooled somewhat, allowing room for
more rational thought and a healthy dose of remorse. When
he was in a calmer frame of mind, his actions of the last
hour made Christopher despise himself for a fool, and a

brutal fool at that. If it were physically possible to kick his own tail around the quarterdeck, he would have done so.

Christopher had never before mistreated a woman. And though he had not physically injured India, he knew he had shamed and humiliated her in ways more painful than a simple beating would have accomplished. He was furious with himself for allowing her to goad him into losing control. His women before India had always been easily dealt with. He had enjoyed them in bed and mostly ignored them out of bed. None had mattered enough for him to care one way or another what they did. So why had a bright red haze clouded his vision when he'd seen Peter Reed pressed against India at the railing, hungrily devouring her lips with his? The damned little minx had gotten under his skin to the point he was acting like a jealous husband.

Christopher was confused by his feelings about his unwilling bride. She was the daughter of a man he hated, a spoiled brat and a hellcat into the bargain. But he had to admit that there was something there, something that had never entered into his relationships with other women. Her hold on his heart was growing stronger every day, and yet he was driving her farther away from him. He could keep her prisoner forever, possess her unwilling body every night, sire a dozen children on her, and virtually make her his slave; but he knew none of those things would truly make her his. And suddenly he knew he wanted her to belong to him. More than her body, he wanted her soul and spirit also. He wanted to talk with her, laugh with her, enjoy her companionship. He wanted to see those deep blue eyes light with love when he was near; he wanted to touch her without feeling her flinch; and he wanted her to crave his body as he did hers, to long for his company as he was beginning to yearn for hers. But how could he hope to win her affection after all he'd done? He might have won her after forcing the marriage. He had a way with women, and he knew it. Had he been smart he might have mastered her heart as easily as he had mastered her passions. But now, after brutally violating her pride and spirit as well as her body, he'd made himself a monster in her eyes. She would never forgive him.

Several days of mental tail-kicking were followed by nights of heavy drinking. Christopher would fall into bed with a bottle sitting nearly empty on the desk, to be chased in his dreams by the same goblins that haunted his daytime thoughts. India had moved into Helen's cabin to sleep, silently daring him to prevent her. He hadn't, having temporarily lost the will to do battle.

On the morning of the third day he woke with the evil taste of stale liquor in his mouth and an uneasy feeling of nausea in the pit of his stomach. He swung his legs over the side of the bed and groaned as a throbbing pain shot from behind his eyes to reverberate around the inside of his skull. He gingerly pressed his hands to his temples as the pain settled into a dull, throbbing ache.

"A pox on all women!" he mumbled.

He rose slowly and grimaced at the sledgehammer in his head increased in tempo. He regarded his face in the small mirror hanging above the desk.

"Damnation!" He scowled at his bleary-eyed reflection. "You damned stupid ass!" he commented.

He left the cabin and stumbled to the seawater pump on deck, letting a stream of tepid tropical seawater free him of the grime of liquor and sweat as he stripped off his soiled clothes. The heavy muscles in his back, arms, buttocks, and legs bunched and released as the stream of cool water drove the tension out of his body. Finally, his dark hair plastered to his head and his big body glistening with a dew of clean seawater, he strode back to his cabin, never giving his nakedness a second thought.

If he'd been a fool before, he thought as he pulled on clean breeches and shirt, he'd been doubly a fool in the last few days. When had he ever admitted defeat or failed to pick up the gauntlet thrown at his feet? Never! He wanted India to love him in every sense of the word. Therefore, he would win her, no matter how long it took. He'd never yet met a woman who could stand long against the relentless pursuit of a man who was really determined to have her.

And he was determined to have India. He was determined to fan the ember of passion he felt in her until it burst into flame and consumed her entire being. He wouldn't give up until he held her heart in his hands, just as she unknowingly held his.

India and Helen were standing at the bow railing when Christopher emerged on deck. India's dark blue eyes clouded with displeasure as she noticed how cool, clean, and refreshed he looked on such a sweltering, breathless morning. She had enjoyed seeing him squirm over the last few days. She didn't really believe he could be suffering the pangs of conscience. The beast probably didn't know what a conscience was. He was probably brooding over a case of hurt pride, amazed that a woman could find pleasure in arms other than his own. She had conveniently forgotten that Peter Reed's impulsive embrace had given her no pleasure at all.

Poor Peter! Helen had told her he'd been given ten lashes and might be put off the ship at the next port. India felt partly responsible for his plight, though she told herself that most of it was due to his own foolishness. Still, she had to admit that she had not discouraged him, and in fact might well have encouraged him, for the pleasure of seeing the adoration in his eyes. When she'd sought him out to apologize for her part in the disaster, as she felt she must, he had avoided her as though she carried the plague. Helen had scolded her soundly for seeking him out at all, accusing her of trying to get both Peter and herself in even more serious trouble by her foolishness.

In fact, Helen had not been a very sympathetic listener to India's tales of woe. When she had bawled out the story of her mistreatment at Christopher's hands, Helen just shook her head and said she hoped India had learned her lesson. You don't deliberately provoke a man like the captain and expect to get nothing in return, Helen told her. She was lucky to get away as lightly as she had. Most men would have had her black and blue and then put her on her back.

Helen's lack of sympathy didn't stop India from maintaining a stony, grim-faced silence during the day and crying herself to sleep every night. At this point she wasn't sure whether she was crying over Christopher's cruelty or the belief that she'd forever lost the chance to win his regard. Had she ever really wanted his affection? And if she had, did she still, in light of his soul-destroying brutality the other night? Did his lack of objection to her move into Helen's cabin mean he didn't want her anymore? Perhaps he hated her so much he couldn't force himself to be with her, even for his grand purpose of producing a legitimate heir to her father's estate. And if this was so, why wasn't she grateful? Why wasn't she sighing with relief at the thought she would no longer have to endure the feel of his big hands moving over her, or need to look into his eyes and read the triumph there when her body responded instinctively to his hard-thrusting invasion.

Questions, questions, and more questions! Her confusion produced countless wakeful hours in the narrow bunk she shared with Helen, tossing and turning, questioning and weeping. Helen bore it all in stoic silence, hoping her friend would come to her senses and go back to Christopher, where she belonged, or that Christopher would stop sulking and drag India back to his bed, where Helen was convinced she really wanted to be, for all her weeping and wailing.

Both girls were silent as they stood by the railing and looked out upon the tropical sea, each wrapped in her own private thoughts. A quiet footstep behind them made India jump, and she turned to find her husband regarding her with a smile quirking the corner of his mouth. The ice was gone from his eyes and the warm humor was back to soften his hard-planed face. She struggled to wipe the confusion from her features and to bring the old chin-up defiance into her stance. From the amused expression on his face, she knew she was not being totally successful.

"I want you back in our cabin tonight," he informed her.

She was barely able to meet his level gaze. "And if I won't come?" she asked.

He folded his big arms across his chest and sighed. Must he put up with this kind of cheek forever?

"You'll come back to our cabin either on your own two feet or thrown across my shoulder like a sack of flour. I suggest it would be more pleasant for you to come on your own.''

With that he turned and left, his supple, long-legged stride taking him out of reach of her tongue before she could think of a suitable retort. Helen looked at her and shrugged meaningfully. India grimaced. She supposed that, after all, there was nothing more to say.

The day slogged by slowly. The air was heavy and sultry with the heat, and not a breath of air stirred the limp sails as they hung lifeless on the yards. The sea and the sky were as one, lost in the bluish-white haze of the long tropical afternoon.

By midafternoon India would have given five years of her life to feel a breeze, even a small puff of a breeze, sift through her damp hair and lift the wet, clinging material of her bodice off her skin. A feeling of uneasiness nagged at her as she paced up and down in the scant shade of the mainsail. Helen was deep in conversation with several seamen lounging idly at the rail. Teddy was perched atop the deckhouse, cheerfully whistling as he whittled away on a chunk of wood. Old Tom Smith sat in the waist with a younger seaman—the new sailmaker's apprentice—repairing the damage to a sail that had split in the last little rainsquall they'd encountered, two days ago. All was quiet and orderly. The tension of the last few days, with everyone going about on tiptoe trying hard to stay far out of the captain's way, had dissipated along with Christopher's black mood. So why, India wondered, was she so persistently uneasy? Perhaps because of the hazy stillness of the air. Perhaps because every time she glanced toward the quarterdeck, Christopher and Ian McCann were scowling out at the horizon, as if they could see something she couldn't. Whatever they saw, India mused restlessly, they didn't appear to be pleased. What could be wrong on such a quiet day as this?

The hours dragged on. As India continued to move about uneasily, following the sail's shadow as it swung back and forth across the deck with the ship's wallowing movements, she finally felt a breath of air against her damp face.

Erratically at first, then with slowly increasing force, a cool
breeze combed through the damp tendrils of her hair and
lifted the clinging muslin from her body, drying and cooling
the skin underneath. The sails flapped loudly once or twice
and then filled. The little brigantine woke to life as timbers
creaked and sails began to strain at the rigging. The helmsman swung round to take full advantage of the breeze, and
soon the white foam of the bow wave testified to their
progress through the gentle swells of the now choppy sea.
India sighed with pure pleasure as the cool air ruffled her
hair and molded the lightweight material of her skirts to her
legs and hips.

"All hands! Prepare to shorten sail!"

The order was trumpeted from the quarterdeck, where Ian
stood, tree-trunk legs spread far apart to maintain balance
on the now rolling deck. He raised his hands to either side
of his mouth and shouted again.

"To the rigging, you lazy sons of bitches! Look sharp
now!"

Then he noticed India standing in the waist and cleared
his throat in embarrassment.

"Uh . . . sorry, Miss India," he apologized.

At his words, Christopher turned and noticed her, apparently for the first time since their encounter that morning. In
three long, fluid strides he was off the quarterdeck and
coming toward her. She turned to look in the direction he
had been looking, with the wind blowing, hard now, straight
in her face. Her heart leapt and stuck in her throat. There on
the horizon—no, much closer than the horizon—was what
Christopher and Ian had been watching for. Black, roiling
clouds, shot through with occasional flashes of lightning,
were massed in a continuous bank to the north and rapidly,
inevitably bearing down on them. This was no transient
rainsquall! She could imagine with grim certainty the
murderously high foam-topped seas and driving wind and
rain that would accompany those boiling clouds. A chill of
fear prickled her skin as she remembered the nightmare on
the *Sea Gull*.

India jumped at the touch of Christopher's hand on her

arm. His hard-planed face was serious. His eyes were dark with concern.

"Get below, India," he ordered brusquely. "And take Helen with you. Stay in the cabin until I tell you differently."

He was looking at the approaching storm and didn't see the panic rise in her wide blue eyes.

"Christopher," she pleaded, "is it . . ."

"Not now!" He frowned. "I don't have time for argument, so for once just do as I say!"

He took her by the shoulders and gave her a gentle push toward the companionway. Helen was scurrying to join them from the railing. India turned at the entrance to belowdecks and watched Christopher vault to the quarterdeck, taking the steps in two long strides. The wind was blowing gale force now, and whipped her hair stingingly around her face as she watched Christopher pull up to stand beside Ian. They both raised their faces to watch the men precariously straddling the yards, working to shorten sail before the wind could tear the sheets. The wind plastered Christopher's linen shirt to his skin, and she watched the play of thick muscles in his arms and chest as he braced himself against the rail. She had to admit he made a magnificent picture. Would she ever see him this way again? She remembered the deck of the *Sea Gull* after the Channel storm. In a few hours, Christopher might be a bloody corpse crushed beneath a tangle of timber and rigging. Or they might all be corpses floating toward the bottom of the sea, with staring eyes and water-filled lungs.

India felt hot tears of terror well up in her eyes to be whipped away by the wind. Her knees were turning to water. How she longed to run to Christopher to hide her face against his massive chest and feel his big arms surround her. If he told her they would survive she would believe him. But he had no time now for mewling women, she knew. He had his hands and mind full with the storm, and she must behave like a grown woman and face whatever came with courage. India, however, did not feel courageous as she turned and descended the companionway into the bowels of the ship.

*   *   *

Hours had passed, or so it seemed to India. She sat alone in the cabin, curled tightly in the wing-back chair, watching the hypnotic sway and shift of the dim lantern that hung from the deck above. Helen had elected to brave the storm in her own cabin, where she could be sick in private. So India sat alone, wide-eyed and white-faced. Her heart beat in terrified tempo with the pitch and buck of the ship. At every precarious roll, her breath stuck in her throat until the little brigantine had once again righted itself.

Nightmarish visions of the *Sea Gull* flashed through her mind—the tossing, airless, reeking cabin where three terrified women stared at the death written in each other's eyes; the tortured, rending shriek of the ship as she was impaled on the rocks; the trunk hurtling at Helen with crushing force, then silence, and the ominous, quiet flow of seawater under the door. The memory of the devastation on the *Sea Gull*'s deck and the bloody ruins of seamen caught up in the destruction haunted her mind. Could the same thing be happening up above as she sat unknowing and frightened in her cabin? Christopher might even now be gone from her, swept overboard to his death, or crushed beneath falling timbers. And all the rest, all of the crew she had come to think of as friends—Seamus Kennedy, Tom Smith, hideous John Daughtery, and even Peter Reed—what was happening to them now? And Teddy! Surely Christopher wouldn't make the lad work on deck in such circumstances! That mischievous lad had wormed his way into her heart like the little brother she never had. Losing him would be like losing family. And Thomas Cat. Where was that damned cat when she needed somebody, anybody, to share her terror and her misery? Had he managed to scamper below before the sea began to wash across the decks? She would miss even him, that overgrown, woman-hating, food-stealing puss. But then, she probably wouldn't miss anyone for very long. She would soon be dead with the rest of them.

She was sure of it now. They were going down. Of course they were going down. What hope had this little ship against the fury of the sea? No more hope than the unfortunate *Sea Gull*. Even Christopher was not indestructible. He was not the Devil, as she'd first imagined on that long-ago morning. He could not stretch his strong arms out to the tossing waves and summon the demons of the sea to his aid. He would die with the rest of them. He would never know the hold he had on her heart. Would it have pleased him to know he had captured more than her body, or would he have cared?

A crash above India's head brought her out of the chair with a start. Ominous splinterings and thumps were followed by the faint sound of a voice cursing in loud, angry tones. Then silence, punctuated by the creak of the strained wooden hull and the squeak of the swinging lantern. If the deck had not been pitching so violently, India would have paced to and fro in her agitation. As it was, she folded herself back into the chair, hugging her legs tightly against her chest, and hid her white, strained face against her knees. She sat there maybe five minutes before the cabin door banged open.

India looked up to see Christopher step into the cabin, balancing easily on the pitching deck. Blood poured down the left side of his face from a gash in his forehead.

India started from the chair. "My God! You're hurt!"

Christopher winced as he looked in the mirror above the desk. "Looks worse than it is," he commented briefly. "Fetch me a towel, will you?"

How could he be so calm when they were sinking? They were all about to die, and he was standing there admiring his damned bloody face in a mirror!

"What happened?" she demanded. "Are we sinking? Are we . . . are we . . ."

"No, of course we're not sinking! Now, will you fetch me that towel?"

Very well, she thought. She could be as stoic as any damned lowbred pirate! She stumbled across the pitching deck to where she'd braced the ceramic water pitcher in a corner, hoping all the water had not slopped out. Then she wet a towel and stumbled back to where Christopher balanced himself gracefully against the roll of the deck. A particularly erratic roll sent her lurching into him, but he steadied her in a strong grip before she could send them both sprawling. Then he held her at arm's length, noticing for the first time her strained face, wide blue eyes, and white knuckles as she wordlessly handed him the dampened towel. He took the towel but ignored his injury for the moment.

"You're terrified, aren't you?" he said gently. "Of course you're terrified, after what happened to the *Sea Gull*. It just never occurred to me that such a little blow would send you into the rafters."

Little blow! How could he call this a little blow? He was taunting her for lack of courage in the face of death. Still, his presence took the edge off her panic. She looked at him wordlessly. His grip still held her steady against the heavings of the deck. Then came another great roll. The deck tilted, steeper, and still steeper, and held for a terrifying breathless moment. Then the ship swung back and righted itself. India's breath expelled in a shaky sigh of relief. Christopher grinned.

"India," he said, "look at me."

She dragged her blue eyes up to be caught by his—those dark brown eyes that could be so deceptively gentle when he wanted them to.

"India, we're not going to sink. We're running very well under a storm sail, and everything is very orderly and under control. I know it seems terrible to you down here, but really, this is not a bad storm. Not nearly as bad as I thought it was going to be. We're in no danger."

She looked at him, wanting to believe.

"Trust me, India," he went on gently. "If we were in any danger at all, do you think I would be down in this cabin talking to you, instead of up on deck minding my ship?"

She lowered her head and pulled away from his steadying hand. Her heart still jumped with every lurch of the deck.

"What happened to your head?" she asked quietly, schooling her voice to calmness. She didn't want him to see how scared she still was, after he had told her there was no reason.

He suddenly remembered the towel in his hand and started dabbing at the crimson on his face.

"Stern chaser broke loose," he explained. "Knocked me off my feet, and I plowed up the deck with my face."

"Oh," she replied simply, and turned back toward her chair. "Was anybody else hurt?"

She tried to sound casual. The deck under her feet fell unexpectedly, throwing her against the arm of the chair, where she held on for dear life. An animal whimper escaped her throat as the ship then lurched in the opposite direction.

"India."

His voice was soft and deep, and his hand on her shoulder was firm. She turned into his arms, the last shreds of her reserve worn through by her terror. She felt secure with his big arms encircling her and her cheek pressed against the hardness of his chest. His heartbeat was slow and steady in contrast to the rapid tattoo beating in her chest.

"Christopher, stay," she whispered, almost against her will. "Don't leave me alone down here."

A persistent voice niggled at her mind. This was the man who had raped her, humiliated her, degraded her numerous times for his own pleasure. How could she sink so low as to turn to him for comfort. But the mind-numbing fear and the sweet feel of his strong arms tightening around her blotted out the voice of reason. The ship rolled again, and she clutched him tighter, burying her face in the wet, cold linen of his shirt, inhaling the clean salt smell of his skin.

"Don't go."

Anything to take her mind off visions of splintering timbers and bloody corpses and tons of seawater pounding in on them, filling their mouths, their throats, their lungs.

Christopher lowered his head and breathed in the sweet scent of India's hair, enjoying the feel of her slender body against his. He'd never seen her so frightened before, even when he'd been at his worst with her. Strange that after all his efforts to break her defiant spirit, all it took was a simple storm to bring her to her knees. Stranger still that right now he wanted nothing more than to see that old spirit leap back into her eyes.

"I'll stay, then," he said softly, "if that will make you feel better. But trust me, India. The ship is in no danger."

It was true. Ian and Seamus had things well under control and would call him the minute he was needed. There was no reason he couldn't stay and play the gallant cavalier.

But in the next few minutes, as India helped him shed his drenched clothing, he knew that gallantry was going to be out of the question. She had just finished struggling with his boots and reached for the lacings of his cold wet breeches as he held a towel to his bloody forehead. As her fingers brushed against him he felt a hot throbbing begin in his loins. Damn! He couldn't be near this woman without wanting to get on top of her! He dropped the towel and caught her wrists in his big hands.

"India," he warned in a strained voice. "Unless you want much more than just comfort from me tonight, I would advise going no further. You hold the towel, and I'll undress myself!"

Tonight she had extended a tenuous trust. He didn't want to betray that trust by taking advantage of her when she was so vulnerable.

India looked at him in surprise, noticing the tense set of his darkly bearded face and the animal heat that glowed in his eyes. She jerked her hands away from his as if they'd been burned. She'd had her mind full of the ship and the storm and death. He, apparently, had his mind full of her. He was warning her, and she got the message.

Then, suddenly, she knew exactly what she wanted, what she needed, to drive away the nightmarish terror that was still pounding through her veins. If she ended up cursing herself for a trollop in the morning, it would be worth it to survive this terrible night.

"Love me, Christopher," she said hesitantly. "Please."

Her hands went tentatively back to the laces, and she blushed to the roots of her dark hair as she felt him swell with desire beneath her hands. Christopher looked at her with searching eyes but said nothing. He finally leaned back in the chair and closed his eyes as he enjoyed the feel of her fingers lightly brushing that most sensitive part of his body.

When she was through with her task he took her hand and pressed it against him, holding her eyes with his own. India turned a deeper shade of scarlet as she felt his hard shaft throbbing against her fingers.

"Is this truly what you want, India?" His eyes seemed to be sending heat waves into her body. "I won't force you, not tonight. But God help me, girl, tell me now. Don't try to back off later."

India bit her lower lip nervously. Her heart was beating faster, but not out of fear of the storm. Why did he have to choose tonight to play the gentleman—the one night when she would gladly have him swarming over her, forcing out all thought by the powerful maleness of his body?

"Truly, Christopher," she breathed, shamed even as she said it. "I need you tonight."

He did not mock, as she half expected him to, but his coiled-spring stillness ended. She turned away as he rose from the chair and stripped off his breeches in one fluid motion. She reached up to douse the lantern, but his hand caught hers and gently pulled it away.

"Don't you want the lantern out?" she asked nervously.

"No."

His hands were deftly unfastening the hooks of her dress. It slipped off her shoulders to lie in a pile around her feet. Her chemise dropped a few seconds later.

"It . . . it's still light." India quavered. He'd barely touched her, but flames of desire were leaping at her, turning her knees to water and spreading a delicious languor throughout her body.

"I know," he whispered hoarsely. "I want to look at you."

He pulled her gently against him, her back against his hard chest, and braced her against the erratic roll of the deck. She felt the pleasant scratchiness of his beard as his lips traced a tingling line from her ear to her shoulder. His hands cupped her breasts and held her firmly against him, then moved down across her waist to her flat belly, pressing her gently back against his hot, swollen manhood. A small moan of pleasure escaped her lips at the feel of his naked, hotly aroused body against hers.

Then he took her by the shoulders and turned her toward him. His eyes devoured her, the exotic face framed in tumbling dark curls, the slender, graceful arms, high rounded breasts, tiny waist, flat belly, and long graceful legs. India had a sudden urge to curl onto herself, suddenly finding that being naked with a man in the glare of lantern light was much more revealing than being naked with him in a dark bed. Her face flamed with embarrassment, though the heat of his gaze and the look on his face showed he found her pleasing.

She tried to look away, but her eyes were drawn irresistibly to his magnificent body. He was huge. Thickly muscled shoulders and chest tapered to a narrow waist and flat, sinew-corded belly. His legs were strong, straight, and well-shaped. What stood at attention between them made her finally look away in embarrassment.

"Damnation, you're beautiful!" he whispered intensely. "Have I ever told you how beautiful you are?"

He stepped forward and lowered his mouth to hers. His kiss was deep, gentle, exploring. Her arms encircled his broad chest with a will of their own, and pressed him tighter against her. She allowed herself to float on the waves of his passion, to surrender languorously as his searching mouth drew her into the maelstrom of his desire.

Without taking his mouth from hers, he picked her up and laid her gently on the bed. She opened her legs willingly to his caressing hand. His fingers lightly teased at her moist entrance while his mouth playfully nipped and sucked at her breasts. She was impatient. She wanted to be one with him, linked to him through his hard flesh and driving desire. She arched against his lightly caressing hand, guiding him to the deeper recesses of her womanhood.

He rose to one elbow and looked down at her with amusement.

"Easy, infant," he smiled. "We have all night, remember."

She was past the point of inhibition.

"Take me, Christopher. Please. Now."

He ran his fingers lightly from the valley of her breasts to gently cup the mound of her womanhood. She closed her eyes and sighed with pleasure at the feel of his warm, hard hand between her legs.

"Patience, little one. Patience makes the rewards all the greater."

He took her hand and placed it on his hard body, gently guiding it in exploration until it moved of its own volition. India was amazed at her own wantonness as she caressed the hard-muscled ridges of his arms and chest, her fingers drawing teasing circles around his erect nipples and then running lightly down through the coarse hair that formed a line from navel to groin. Then, inevitably, her soft fingers encircled the hard, swollen shaft of his manhood, and its hot pulsing set up an urgent throbbing in her own body, as if the two of them lying there were attuned to the same primitive beat of desire. She blushed scarlet at her own boldness, but she was far past the point of reining in her own desires for the sake of maidenly modesty. She longed to be impaled by him, to enfold him in her warm flesh and abandon herself to his hard-thrusting conquest of her body. She massaged him with the untutored skill of innate sensuousness, and felt him grow to even greater proportions in her encircling fingers. Christopher groaned and finally thrust his hips up to meet her hand. He deftly shifted and poised himself over her waiting, eager body. His eyes as he looked down at her were dark and seemed to glow with the power of his naked hunger.

"Impatient wench," he growled, but there was tenderness in his face. "Is this what you want?"

He grinned wickedly and pressed himself into her, slowly, slowly, making her feel every ridge of his flesh as it penetrated the most intimate recesses of her womanhood. She heaved up beneath him, longing to take him entirely into her being, but he held her hips firmly with his hands, refusing to yield his control over their union. When he had sheathed himself within her entirely, he lowered his mouth to hers and kissed her tenderly, gently, then lightly ran his callused hands over her breasts and down to her buttocks. Still he held her unmoving beneath his body's weight.

"Christopher, please," India whispered in a ragged voice.

She was drowning with him in a sea of passion. Her whole being centered around the hard male flesh that filled her, torturing her with the urgency to make their union complete. She longed to heave up under him, writhing like conquered prey impaled by the shaft of a primitive spear. But he held her down while his hands and mouth drove her mad with wanting him.

Finally he moved within her, slowly, sensuously probing her depths. Then harder, deeper, faster, until she teetered on the brink of ecstasy. He would let the tension ebb, and then begin again, driving into her body until a wave of passion carried them both up to the heights, but never allowing that wave to crest and submerge them in the violence of release that they both ached for. Then finally his passion rose and took control of them both. India closed her eyes and abandoned herself to the violence of his hard-thrusting invasion of her inner being. He sent her crashing through the barriers of sight and sound to a new dimension of feeling, and then joined her there in sweet release. They were fused into one being, one pounding heartbeat, one flesh, one mind, as they spiraled slowly, gently back to earth.

Christopher looked tenderly down at the woman-child beneath him. Her eyes were closed, and her peaceful face still showed the traces of ecstatic fulfillment. She slept, with her arms still around him and his flesh still deep in her body. In the throes of their union she had said she loved him. He believed her.

Such a woman as India would never limit her love to moments of sexual abandon. Now he knew that he had fastened onto her heart just as she had unknowingly fastened onto his. She might not admit it, even to herself, with the coming of daylight. But the hold was there, for both of them.

Christopher pulled her closer and buried his face in the fragrance of her hair. So many barriers of misunderstanding and mistrust stood between them and the happiness they could share. Ian had been right. This time he'd taken on more than he could handle. But what a sweet battle it was going to be.

CHAPTER ELEVEN

India was awakened by a loud knocking at the cabin door. She burrowed more deeply under the covers, not yet ready to come back to reality.

"India," Helen chimed as she stepped across the threshold. "Why is it when I come into this cabin you're always abed?"

India opened one eye and regarded her sleepily.

"Lazy twit," Helen went on. "The sun's been up over three hours!"

"Mmnlmph!" India scrunched deeper into the bed.

"So you didn't get much sleep last night! So neither did I. I'm sorry I deserted you last night, dear. Really I am. I know you were terrified out of your mind, but I was too sick to be scared. And when I'm turning myself inside out every five minutes, I don't want an audience."

India reluctantly peeled the covers back from her face and regarded her friend with concern.

"Are you better, Helen? You look better."

"Oh yes, I'm fine, dear. My illness went out with the storm."

India settled cozily back into the pillows and smiled. She still felt warm and languorous from a surfeit of fulfillment. She looked at Helen with a twinkle in her blue eyes.

"Well, I'm awfully glad you're better. That shade of green you were wearing on your face was most unbecoming."

"Hmmph!" Helen replied jauntily. "You should talk! Your face was as white as a dead fishbelly. I thought you were going to expire from fright right in front of my eyes."

Another loud knock on the door.

"It's Teddy, Miss India," a voice piped. "I've got tea and biscuits."

"Oh, my!" India dove under the bedcovers to hide her nakedness. Helen opened the door.

"Oh, hullo, Miss Helen." Teddy peered around her plump form. "Where's Miss India? Cap'n tol' me to bring her down this tray."

Thomas Cat slipped between his feet and jumped onto the bed. Helen indicated the mound under the sheets.

"Oh," Teddy commented. "Ought to get out of bed, Miss India. It's a rare fine day, it is! Shouldn't miss it!"

India's muffled voice came from beneath the bedcovers.

"Get out of the cabin, Teddy, so I can get dressed. And take the cat with you!" She nudged at the oversized ball of gray fur on the bed. "I know you're there, Thomas!"

"He won't come with me, Miss India. He likes you." Teddy grinned impishly as he set the tray beside the bed. "Do you want some tea and biscuits, Miss Helen? Cook made 'em up fresh this morning, believe it or not."

"Oh, yes, Teddy. I could eat a whole pan of biscuits, I vow!" Helen's face brightened at the thought of food. "Just set it outside the door when you come back."

"Aye, aye," Teddy answered, moving toward the door. "Come on, Thomas!"

The cat curled himself into a tighter ball on the bed. Teddy shrugged.

"Told ya so."

India's head popped from beneath the covers. "Is he gone?" She nudged the cat with her foot. "Damn cat!"

"He likes you," Helen said.

"Bah! He likes food! He's got his eyes on my biscuits. Where was he last night when I needed company!"

India could not suppress a smile at the thought of the company she eventually got.

"Well, you'd best get up and eat, then, before he gets

them. As for me, I'm going to intercept Teddy with my breakfast and go up on deck, now that I see you've survived. Actually, for a girl who spent the night in mortal fear for her life, you look remarkably well this morning,'' Helen said with a twinkle of suspicion in her eyes.

"Who, me?'' India replied with wide-eyed innocence.

Once she had dressed and tied her hair back neatly with a ribbon, India regarded herself critically in the small mirror above the desk. Same face, she thought. Slanted dark blue eyes, pert nose, curving full lips, and softly rounded chin stared back at her from the mirror—the same face that had left Hillcrest so many months ago, and yet somehow changed. There was a new dimension in the face that stared out of the mirror. She didn't look like the child who had left England to visit her cousin in France. India tilted her head thoughtfully. Neither did she look like a trollop, or a slut, in spite of her wanton behavior of the night before.

India sighed and turned away from the mirror, hastily rescuing a biscuit from an encroaching cat paw. No decent woman would throw herself at a man, any man, even her husband, as she'd thrown herself at Christopher last night. A decent woman dutifully tolerated her husband's carnal needs, although it might offend her sensibilities. She didn't delight in seeing her touch arouse a man to animal passion, and she certainly didn't abandon herself to uncontrolled ecstasy whenever a man got between her legs. India had always thought herself a decent, modest girl. So what was wrong with her? If she was driven out of her mind with fear last night, why hadn't she swooned or died of fright? Why had she permitted, no begged, Christopher to take her? She had thrown herself at him like a street harlot, knowing that when he possessed her, nothing would matter but the urgency of her own passion.

She regarded herself in the mirror for a long moment. She knew the answer. She was not a harlot. She was not a woman who could willingly give her body without giving her heart also.

God help her! She loved the scoundrel! She loved a traitor and an outlaw, a man who meant her nothing but harm, a

man who would use her, then discard her when his purpose
was accomplished. However had she let herself come to
this?

India had no illusions about Christopher. She had learned
enough about men, during this voyage, to know that a man
did not require love to enjoy a woman in bed. And Christopher
did enjoy making love to her. He was gentle, considerate,
and even loving in his passion—usually. But he couldn't be
in love with her. He probably didn't even know what love
was. He was a cynical, ruthless pirate who was embittered
toward England and hated her family. She shouldn't love
him, but she did. How many times had Helen told her that
the heart didn't listen to reason?

So what could she do, if she couldn't help loving the
man? Give up? Show a proud face to the world and then
weep and wail when he broke her heart? Not a chance, India
thought grimly. She was no frightened mouse to resign
herself meekly to such a fate. He taught her the passions of
the body; she would teach him the passions of the heart. A
difficult task for an untutored girl, to teach him love where
so many sophisticated women had failed, at least according
to the voluble Teddy. But she would not give up without a
fight. The gleam of battle was in India's eyes as she
prepared to join Helen on deck.

It was indeed a "rare fine day," as Teddy had said. The
sails billowed with a gentle but steady breeze. The deep
blue of the sea stretched away from the ship to join with the
lighter blue of the tropical sky. The only remains of last
night's storm were a few wispy white clouds low on the
horizon.

Christopher was deep in conversation with Helen at the
rail. India joined them hesitantly, somewhat fearful of seeing
the old triumphant mocking in Christopher's eyes. But the
look that met her was the enigmatic, questioning regard he
generally turned on her when he thought she wasn't looking.
Then he favored her with a slow, knowing smile that almost
took her breath away, made her feel like she was back in bed
with him on top of her. She looked away quickly, feeling her

face grow hot with embarrassment. He obviously knew his power over her and was intending to remind her at every opportunity. But she told herself not to care. If she ever got a grip on that iron heart of his, she promised herself, she'd squeeze until he cried for mercy. He'd find himself trapped in the same spell he'd so skillfully cast over her, writhing in torment as she was writhing now. She brightened at the thought of Christopher in torment over her. How sweet it would be to see him squirm from the same doubts and passions that had invaded her own heart. She allowed her eyes to be caught by his, and turned on him a smile so sweetly, innocently sensuous that his heart skipped a beat. The battle was on.

Helen watched them both with a twinkle in her eye.

"Well," she said finally with an ill-concealed smirk, "I'll leave you two alone. Thanks for showing me the sights, Christopher."

They stood alone at the rail. Christopher smiled, apparently perfectly at ease. India suffered through an awkward silence as she tried to ignore the effect of his nearness.

"What sights?" she finally asked.

"We're passing a small island." He pointed to a smudge of green on the horizon, crowned by a few puffy clouds. "That island's only about thirty miles off the coast of Hispaniola. Right now we're about two hundred miles due east of Tortuga."

India's imagination soared. Tortuga! Headquarters of the old buccaneers who had attacked Spanish shipping and Spanish strongholds in the last century. Shades of Sir Henry Morgan and Bartholomew Sharp. Pirate country, indeed! India felt a shiver of apprehension travel up her spine as she remembered John Daughtery's bloody tales of pirating in the Caribbean. Once again she wondered if the man standing beside her was as ruthless a killer as the men the boatswain had described. How little she really knew about this man she thought she loved! Would her stubborn heart still take his side if he proved to be a callous mankiller?

"Are we going to stop here? On this island, I mean?" she asked.

"No. We've been blown a bit off course, but we should land in New Providence in just a few days from now, given fair winds."

Another awkward silence. India squirmed inwardly. How could they stand here and talk of trivialities with all that lay between them? She took a deep breath and plunged into deeper waters.

"Do you really think you'll find my father's old manservant there, just on the secondhand word from Daughtery's cousin?" she asked skeptically.

A slight frown darkened Christopher's face. "It's a chance," he admitted. "I questioned the man myself, and he described John Thomas right enough. He'd be a hard man to mistake."

"Why is that?"

"He's got a long scar running from his temple to his chin on the left side of his face. Pulls his whole face over to one side. I'd have thought you'd remember that."

"The last time I saw John Thomas was a long time ago. I was very young when my father left to serve with Marlborough. He had a new manservant when he came back."

"Ah, yes," Christopher replied with a grin. "You have ways of making a man forget how very young you are. A mere child."

India shot him a slant-eyed look of irritation. "Well, at least I'm old enough not to believe every story I hear. I think you're on a wild-goose chase." She tilted her chin in her old stubborn defiance. "Not that I believe for a minute that John Thomas can really clear your name. If he'd seen something that proved you innocent, he would've told my father."

Christopher smiled tolerantly. "Yes, he would've, wouldn't he."

India scowled at the implication of her father's duplicity, but Christopher decided against starting an argument on such a beautiful morning.

"No matter," he said. "I needed to get out of English waters for a while, in any case. A certain ambitious naval lieutenant was hanging uncomfortably close to my stern.

Maybe we'll get lucky and pick up a few good prizes while we're down here.'' He grinned wolfishly.

Visions of murder and mayhem flashed through India's mind at his casual words. She studied him with fearful eyes.

"You mean to play the pirate while you're in these waters? Why? You're rich as a lord already. Ian told me so.''

"I am a lord. An earl, in fact. Or had you forgotten?'' He laughed.

India opened her mouth to deliver a tart rejoinder, to remind him of just how unlordly his behavior had been, when visions of her own behavior of the previous night assaulted her memory. She closed her mouth abruptly. Christopher regarded her with amusement, as though he were able to read her mind.

"Besides, my love,'' he continued, "one can never be too rich. I'm certainly not going to just sit here if some rich Spaniard comes within range of my guns.''

As if on cue, a hail sounded from the crow's nest.

"Ship off the port bow. No . . . ships! There's two of them, I think, sir!''

Christopher vaulted up the stairs to the quarterdeck and took the glass from Ian. India was hard on his heels, apprehensive that at last she might be forced to see her outlaw husband in action.

"There's two of them, all right,'' Christopher commented. He held the glass steady for some moments. "Looks like it may be a *guarda-costa* and a prize,'' he finally said. "One of them's dismasted, so they're not going anywhere very fast.''

India strained her eyes in the direction Christopher was pointing the glass, but she could see nothing through the haze.

"What's a *guarda-costa*?'' she finally asked, hoping that it was something Christopher wouldn't dare attack, dismasted or not.

Christopher handed the glass back to Ian.

"*Guarda-costas*,'' he explained, "are Spanish ships that protect Spain's prohibitive trade laws with her colonies.

They stop and search English ships for contraband. The Spanish only allow one English ship per year to trade in the Spanish colonies, but of course English ships smuggle in as much in the way of trade goods as they can. The colonies are a rich market they're not willing to pass up, so the *guarda-costas* do a rich business. It's an easy way to make a fortune.''

''What do you mean, an easy way to make a fortune?''

Christopher's face was grim. ''Those *guarda-costas* are manned with the worst scum Spain could dredge up. Their crews work without pay and take a cut of anything they capture. Naturally they're not too particular about what they attack, and the crews of the ships they impound end up dead or rotting in some Spanish prison. They're worse than most of the pirates in these waters.''

''But why doesn't England stop them,'' India asked, ''if they're attacking ships that aren't actually smuggling?''

Christopher's mouth quirked in a cynical smile. ''Maybe they will, someday. But England would have to go to war with Spain to stop them, I suspect, and we just made peace with Spain, remember? Right now a few English lives aren't worth the trouble to the important men in London.'' His grin was cynical. ''But that doesn't keep me from giving them a taste of their own medicine.''

India eyed him apprehensively. ''What are you going to do?''

''Capture her, of course. If we're lucky she may be loaded with a fortune in confiscated cargo.''

India raised an eyebrow. ''I thought perhaps you wanted to avenge all those poor Englishmen.''

Christopher laughed unpleasantly. ''Don't mistake my motives, little one. I don't give a damn what the Spanish do to the English. There's no soft spot in my heart for England or Englishmen. However,'' he said, and a familiar gleam came into his eyes as he looked at her, ''there is a concern for one particular Englishwoman. I want you and Helen belowdeck before we get in range of that fellow's guns, and I'll hear no argument.''

She placed her small hand on his hard-muscled arm.

"Christopher, please, how can you shed men's blood over a little money when you've got so much already? Such needless violence. Can't you just pass them by?"

He regarded her with darkened eyes. "Violence is a way of life, India, and it's addictive in its way. In my world only the ruthless survive, and I'm one of the best survivors I know. You will do well to remember that there's no room in this world for weakness or mercy." His voice was soft but edged with steel.

India withdrew her hand as if she'd been stung. "Are you always so merciless, then?" she whispered.

"Mercy is irrelevant." The softening of his gaze belied his words as his eyes sought out her own. "What I set out to have, I always get. No matter what the cost."

India's throat tightened at the warning in his words. She knew he meant far more than just the unfortunate Spaniard on the horizon. Her brave plan to gentle his violent heart with a woman's love might be ill-conceived indeed, like trying to turn a lobo wolf into a pet dog. She might very well be mauled in the process.

Christopher turned to Ian. "Alter course to intercept those two, then clear the deck for action and run out the guns. I don't want that Spaniard to think he's got a chance in hell if he chooses to fight."

"Aye, Captain," Ian acknowledged.

Christopher went back to examining his prey through the glass. India stood tensely at his side, wondering how everyone could be so casual about seizing other men's lives and property. Crewmen were calmly spreading the deck with sand, carrying powder to the gun stations, checking their guns and pistols. A few had appeared in their battle dress, jerkins and trousers made of sailcloth and coated with pitch to withstand the thrusts of daggers and swords. The *Black Falcon* swung around to head for the crippled ships, the sails flapping thunderously as the ship crossed through the wind. It was like a nightmare, India thought, inexorably progressing to its bloody conclusion. Violence had never been a part of her life until that disastrous night aboard the *Sea Gull*. Since then she'd had her fill of blood, pain, and death. The thought that she was about to see the man she loved turn into a beast of prey sickened her.

India stood helplessly, watching the ship prepare for battle.

"What's the sand on deck for?" she asked Christopher.

He was still examining the two ships, trying to determine their armament and fitness to defend themselves.

"Soak up blood," he answered tersely. "Keeps the deck from getting too slippery."

India grabbed the rail for support and closed her eyes. She thought she was going to retch. Then she felt a warm, hard hand cover hers and looked up into Christopher's dark eyes. She read a trace of sympathy there, and understanding. How could that be? How could those gentle eyes regard her with compassion when he was about to plunge into a bloodbath of his own making? Could a man be gentle one moment and a killer the next?

"I'm sorry, India," he apologized. "I keep forgetting what a tender heart you have. There's no need to be upset, little one. I doubt we'll see any fighting today. The Spaniard's badly crippled, and he'll probably surrender without firing a single shot." His face turned grim. "At least he will if he's not a complete fool."

India's delicate brows puckered in an exasperated frown.

"Christopher," she said, "one of these days you're going to meet someone who is fool enough to take you on. And he's going to blow you and your ship straight to hell. Doesn't that mean anything to you? Doesn't that give you pause at all?"

"Hell, is it?" Christopher threw back his head in delighted laughter. "No doubt where I belong! But I don't think this fellow's the one to send me there." He continued to chuckle, then turned amused eyes on India. "You wouldn't be concerned about my safety, would you now, little wife?"

India lifted her chin in scorn, but a revealing flush spread over her cheeks. "Of course not! You can get blown out of the water, for all I care, as long as you don't take me and Helen with you!"

He regarded her thoughtfully, a sensual smile slowly

spreading across his face. "I don't think I'm ready to give up the pleasures of life yet."

India blushed. She opened her mouth for a sharp retort, but his finger pressed to her lips forestalled her answer.

"You go below now, until this is all over. I don't want to have to worry about you up on deck."

The look that momentarily flashed across her face told him she was truly concerned about him. The thought made him uneasy. He didn't want someone fretting over his safety. He stepped forward and lowered his mouth to hers in a gentle kiss that got much harder and more demanding before it ended. Then he released her and grinned wickedly.

"Never fear, my love. I'll be back for more after this chore is taken care of."

He noted with satisfaction the angry set of her face as she turned on heel and left. At this moment her anger was more easily dealt with than her concern.

When India and Helen had disappeared below, Christopher turned back to examine his intended victims. They were almost within range now, and he could see the crew of the *guarda-costa* standing at their guns and swarming in the rigging with swords and pistols at the ready. The other ship appeared deserted. The Spaniard must know that the fight was hopeless. He was dismasted and lay dead in the water, while the *Black Falcon* could maneuver away from the Spanish guns and rake the enemy ship at will with her own fourteen-pounders! If he chose, Christopher could cut the ship to splinters with very little risk to his own ship and crew, but he would prefer to take the Spaniard intact if he could. Senseless slaughter had never appealed to him. Besides, the Spaniard was bound to have cargo aboard, since he had apparently just taken a prize before he was damaged by the storm. It would be a waste to send valuable goods to the bottom of the ocean.

They were well within range now, and he saw no preparation by the Spanish gun crews to open fire. The *Black Falcon* was angling across her bow, which did not give the Spaniard an easy target.

"Mr. Hawkins!" Christopher hailed the chief gunner.

"Aye, sir!" he answered with a gap-toothed grin.

"I want a shot across her bow. And have the other crews stand ready. I want that bastard to know we mean business!"

"Aye, sir!" Hawkins acknowledged with a bloodthirsty grin. He would just as soon have given them a broadside and seen a few dons go up in smoke, but orders were orders. He carefully gauged his distance and angle as the ship came within firing range.

"Number-one crew! Fire!" he bellowed.

A flash of fire and a cloud of acrid smoke belched from the number-one gun position. A fountain of water erupted on the other side of the *guarda-costa*'s bow, bearing witness to Hawkins's skill. The Spaniards stood tense at their stations, awaiting their captain's commands.

Christopher took a speaking trumpet and hailed the Spanish ship, picking out her name from the lettering on her side.

"*Navarre!*" he cried. "Surrender and keep your lives!" He smiled to remember India's prediction of his own fate. "Or fight and get blown straight to hell!"

In the face of the *Black Falcon*'s bristling armament and his own storm damage, the Spanish captain had little choice. Before a minute had passed, the Spanish flag was struck and the boarding nets were lowered.

"Bring us alongside," Christopher instructed the helmsman. "Grappling irons! Ready the grappling irons and prepare to board."

Crewmen stood at the rail and prepared to throw the heavy iron hooks as soon as the two ships closed. The gun crews stood alert at their stations, prepared for any trick on the Spaniard's part.

"Heave!"

The grappling irons were set; the ships were linked, and crewmen from the *Black Falcon*, Christopher at their front, swarmed over to the *Navarre*'s deck, swords at the ready. They were met by a lean dagger of a man in a soiled, ill-fitting uniform. Thin strands of graying hair spilled from beneath his hat and fell to his narrow shoulders.

"Lieutenant Ortega, at your service, sir," he addressed

Christopher in halting English. With a perfunctory bow he offered his sword hilt first. Christopher accepted it.

"Are you the commander of this vessel?" he demanded.

The lieutenant shifted uneasily. "I have the honor of serving under Captain Juan Alfonso Garcia y Velaques, who is commander of this ship."

Christopher was not in the mood for niceties. "Where the hell is he?"

The Spanish officer did not answer, but shifted his eyes uneasily to the hatch.

Christopher sighed. "Ian," he growled. "Find the son of a bitch and bring him to me aboard the *Falcon*. Kennedy" —he turned toward the sailing master—"check the other ship for cargo as well. And find Daughtery. Tell him to get together with the carpenter and jury rig a mast on this thing."

The unfortunate Spaniards were being herded together in the waist, prodded by the swords and pistols of their captors, as Christopher vaulted across to his own ship.

India had just emerged on deck, being towed by an excited Teddy. The ship's boy had burst into her cabin and gleefully recounted to her the entire encounter, embellishing a few points here and there to make the incident seem more exciting than it really was. He was as excited as if he'd taken the Spaniard single-handedly, and begged her to come up on deck and look at the prize. Piracy was a good bit more exciting than smuggling, he assured her knowledgeably. Maybe when the cap'n sails back to England, he'd stay here and become a full-time pirate himself.

In Teddy's enthusiasm to drag India to just the right vantage point to see his prizes, he ran headlong into his captain.

"There you are!" Christopher said, after hauling the youngster up off the deck. "I've got work for you, boy. Go help Mr. Kennedy check the cargo on the captured ships. And be careful crossing over the side. I don't want to break in a new ship's boy after spending so much time on you!"

Teddy composed his elfin face to the solemnity appropriate to his assigned responsibility.

"Aye sir, Cap'n," he acknowledged. Then he looked at India in a fair imitation of gentlemanly regret. "Sorry, Miss India. I've important work to do!"

Christopher smiled. "You can leave Miss India in my care. I think she'll be safe enough with me."

India wasn't too sure about that, having an idea she was in trouble again.

"Aye, Cap'n!" The boy grinned, then shot off toward his assigned task.

Christopher took India's arm in a none too gentle grip and steered her toward the quarterdeck.

"Why aren't you in the cabin where you belong? Won't you ever learn to obey orders!"

She looked up at his face and couldn't decide whether he was amused or angry.

"Teddy told me the fighting was over. He . . . well . . . it is over. Isn't it?"

Christopher sighed in exasperation. "There was no fighting, my disobedient little wife." He gestured to the still cleanly sanded deck. "As you can see, my lady, no blood."

"He surrendered, then?"

"He did."

"And nobody was hurt?"

"Not yet, at least."

Christopher looked suspiciously over at the *Navarre*, where Ian still had not appeared with the Spanish captain. His attention was diverted by India's hand on his arm.

"What are you going to do to those poor men?"

She was frowning with concern over the despondent-looking group of Spanish seamen huddled in the waist of the captured ship. Upon noticing her, one of the Spaniards made a lewd gesture in the direction of the quarterdeck, and promptly received a heavy blow from the grip of Tom Smith's pistol. India looked away in embarrassment, and Christopher raised his brows meaningfully.

"That was one of the reasons you should have stayed in the cabin," he said.

"You've never before been concerned with my sensibilities, that I remember."

"I reserve to myself the privilege of outraging your sense of righteous morals." He grinned.

India pressed her lips together in a tight line of irritation. "You still haven't told me what fate you intend for those unfortunate prisoners."

"For a person who detests violence, you've chosen some inappropriate characters to champion." He looked across to the Spaniard with contempt. "Those poor men, as you label them, are probably the bloodiest cutthroats in the Caribbean. Given a few moments in their care, India, and I assure you, you would be only too glad to return to my tender attentions."

"You attack their ship and then call *them* cutthroats?"

Christopher smiled grimly. "I've never been reluctant to knock a few heads together, or to use a blade when it comes to that, but I've never killed a man just to see his blood run, or raped a woman for the satisfaction of feeling her rip to pieces inside." He looked down at her stubbornly set face. "It might interest you to know that those poor men murdered the entire crew of that English ship over there, the *Lady Mary*. That's the sort of character we're dealing with here, India, so don't waste your sympathy."

India grew pale as she looked up at his harsh face.

"So what are you going to do with them?"

He regarded the band of Spaniards thoughtfully. "I suppose I could line them up at the rail and shoot them. It would certainly raise the average quality of the human race." He cocked an eyebrow at India to see her reaction.

"You must be joking!" India gasped.

"That's right. You're offended by the sight of blood, aren't you? Well, in that case we'll just throw them overboard and let them drown. Saves the mess."

"You wouldn't . . . you couldn't . . . just kill men in cold blood!"

"Couldn't I?" Christopher's suddenly impassive face told her nothing. "Aren't you convinced I'm cutthroat and scoundrel enough to kill without thought to mercy?"

"I never said that," India said softly, though she admitted to herself she'd wondered about it several times. "You were the one who said that mercy is irrelevant," she accused. "I guess I don't know you very well, but I can't believe that... that you could just wipe out all those lives... cold-bloodedly."

"You're right," Christopher admitted. "You don't know me very well. Perhaps you should learn to know me better before assigning me the role of bloodthirsty villain."

India felt a fool. He'd been goading her into making an ass of herself, and she'd fallen for his little act.

"You needn't worry yourself about those fellows," he continued. "They'll be put in a boat with food, water, and a sextant. There are any number of places they can go before their supplies run out. Not that they don't deserve to be shot, my tenderhearted lady, but because I promised them their lives if they surrendered."

India was indignant. "Why did you lead me to believe the worst? You knew all along they were to be set free!"

Christopher laughed softly. "Because I like to see you irritated. And you're so ready to believe the worst. I hated to disappoint you."

India made a sound of annoyance and moved to go. Christopher held her arm, though.

"Wait," he ordered. "I don't want you wandering around alone on deck right now. Stay here with me."

His eyes were on Ian and a resplendently garbed Spaniard crossing over from the captured ship. As they mounted to the quarterdeck he motioned her back.

Ian pushed his prisoner forward until he was standing directly before the captain.

"Here's your commander, Captain," Ian growled. "This scum was trying to sneak off to his prize ship. Figured he'd take it right from under our noses, he did. Had three men with him."

"Did he now?" Christopher drawled. "Leaving his men behind to our tender mercies once he's made his escape?"

The Spaniard replied in an angry rapid-fire Spanish that India couldn't follow. She quietly moved toward John Daughtery, who was standing a few paces away.

"Do you know what he's saying?" she asked.

John's hideous face split into a parody of a grin. "Well, ma'am, cleaned up a bit, he's saying we had no right to take his ship, and the mighty power of Spain is going to wipe pirates like us from these waters." He laughed softly. "He also appears to have a pretty definite opinion of the captain's lineage."

Christopher gave his prisoner a calm answer in fluent Spanish. India looked to Daughtery for translation.

"The captain's saying he's lucky to get off with his life. If he'd known the crew of the English prize had been slaughtered, he wouldn't have accepted their surrender. He'd have blown 'em out of the water."

India looked at Daughtery in consternation. "They really murdered the English crew of that other ship?"

"Yes, ma'am," Daughtery replied. "One survivor—some rich lord they had tied in the forechains—and he'd been beat pretty bad."

"Oh, my God! That's unbelievable!"

"Well, you can believe it, ma'am. That scum would just as soon kill a man as look at him. I'm surprised the captain hasn't strung him up by his . . . uh . . . by his neck, promises or no promises!"

The Spaniard was growing more vociferous by the minute, while Christopher stood and watched him with icy calm.

"What's he saying now?" India asked the boatswain.

Daughtery cleared his throat uneasily. "I don't think you want to know, Miss India."

Suddenly Christopher cut the diatribe short with an order.

"Take this piece of filth and put him in the boat with his crew. Cut them loose, before I decide to hang the lot of them."

The Spaniard uttered a guttural curse and sprang. A knife suddenly appeared in his hand, aimed at Christopher's throat. Christopher cursed and grabbed the Spaniard's wrist. There was a brief test of strength as their eyes locked venomously. The muscles in their necks, shoulders, and arms stood out in stark relief as they each struggled for supremacy. No one spoke; no one moved to interfere in the contest between the two leaders.

It was over as suddenly as it had started. With a low grunt of exertion, Christopher twisted his opponent's arm viciously. A sickening sound of snapping bone was accompanied by the Spaniard's ragged scream. The knife clattered to the deck, followed by the thud of the Spanish captain landing on his back. Christopher's sword was at his throat before he could move an inch.

The onlookers were silent, waiting expectantly for the final thrust. The Spaniard looked up and saw the bloodlust in Christopher's grim face. He hadn't expected the devil Englishman to be strong enough to best him. Now he waited to pay the ultimate price for his misjudgment. He spat an insult in his conqueror's face, hoping to anger him and win a quick death.

Christopher's tight-lipped mouth twisted in disgust. "Scum!" he sneered. He leaned forward slightly. A trickle of crimson appeared where the blade pricked the Spaniard's throat. "I should gut you slowly for the entertainment of my crew, but I don't want to dirty my blade with your foul slime." He removed the sword and wiped it on the downed man's jacket. "Get this bastard out of here before I change my mind and mess up the deck with his bowels."

His eyes were as black and grim as a pit of hell as the cursing Spaniard was roughly towed away. Then he turned an impassive face to India, who was staring at the scene with eyes gone dark with revulsion. He gestured to Daughtery.

"Take her below. Put a guard on her door until we get these sons of bitches on their way."

A quarter hour later the Spanish crewmen had been lowered in one of their own lifeboats with enough food and water to keep them for at least three days. They cut loose from the *Black Falcon* and hauled up a small sail, flinging curses and threats back at the ship as they slowly widened the distance between them. The *Black Falcon*'s crew laughed and jeered as they watched at the rail. Christopher stood with Ian in the stern. His face was set and cold as he watched the boat depart.

"I'm turning soft, Ian my friend," he commented. "I should have cut that bastard's throat, then hanged every one of his crew for good measure."

"Aye, laddie," Ian agreed in a neutral voice.

"Not too long ago that's what I would have done."

"Aye," Ian agreed again.

Christopher shook his head, half amused, half despairing.

"There's nothing like a comely wench to ruin a man for a bit of action."

Ian grinned broadly. "Aye, Christopher, so you've told me, time and time again."

Ian thought warmly of his own Bess, then chuckled as Christopher made a rude sound and headed toward the hatch.

CHAPTER TWELVE

The following morning the *Black Falcon* and her two prizes, the *Navarre* and the *Lady Mary*, approached the island they had sailed past only the day before. The captured *guarda-costa* was too heavily damaged to sail to New Providence, so Christopher had decided to stop for repairs. While they were there the *Navarre* would be repaired and all three ships would be careened and scraped.

India thought Pig Island, as the chief gunner Timothy Hawkins had dubbed it, was the closest thing to paradise that she had ever seen. It sat like a verdant oasis in the warm azure sea. One black, bare spire of rock rose from the island to point like a huge steeple to the blue tropical sky. Skirts of lush green vegetation spread from the beaches over gently rolling hillocks to halfway up the imposing monolith. The windward side of the island was outlined by ever-changing arcs of white as the Caribbean waves rolled up on the beaches and broke to foam on the shallow sands.

Pig Island, India complained to the chief gunner, was really not an appropriate name for such a lovely place. Hawkins, a crafty-looking old man of indeterminate age and seemingly infinite knowledge, assured her that it was a good name, right enough. He favored her with his gap-toothed grin as he boasted of his great-grandfather, who'd roamed Hispaniola and its bordering isles with the original bucca-neers, or *boucaniers*, as they'd originally been called. He told her how those desperate men had lived at first by hunting the wild cattle and pigs that roamed loose on the islands, preparing the long strips of smoked meat, or *boucans*, that had given them their name. Eventually they'd turned to raiding Spanish shipping in their *piraguas*—long, swift canoes hollowed out from tree trunks—and evolved into the powerful buccaneer brotherhood who terrorized the Spanish Main from their headquarters in Tortuga. Wild pigs and cattle still roamed these islands, Hawkins assured India. Perhaps while they were here a hunt could be organized and the crew could have some fresh meat for a change.

India listened to Hawkins with half an ear as the *Black Falcon* slipped smoothly into a long, narrow cove on the lee side of the island. The beauty of the scene almost left her breathless. On one side of the cove, tangled vegetation rose from the very edge of the water to flow over a low bluff that hid the cove from the open sea. On the other side the jungle was bordered by a beach of such pure white that it seemed to glow in the reflected sunlight. Palms and the huge fronds of banana trees shaded the upper beach and joined together in an impenetrable-looking wall of green that rose and blocked off from view all but the very peak of the black spire in the distance. The water of the cove was an amazing cerulean color, and much to India's delight, she could look straight down through the crystal water and see the white sand ripples slip beneath the ship's hull as they drifted slowly to their anchorage.

The rest of the day was busily occupied with ferrying supplies to the beach and constructing a camp of temporary lean-tos. India occupied her time in packing up any breakable items in the cabin and tying down everything that wasn't packed, in preparation for the ship's being careened the next day. Then she set to work helping Teddy and the cook organize and pack the food and cooking utensils they would need on shore, loading them onto the boats, and then unpacking them on the beach. By the time she had helped the cook prepare a dinner of salted meat and freshly caught fish for the hungry crew and then helped clean up, she was too exhausted to move a step away from the cook fire. She slumped wearily on a makeshift driftwood bench and wished she'd not drunk so much wine as she sat eating and listening to Hawkins's garrulous accounts of the early buccaneers. Her arms and legs felt weighted with lead, and her head was becoming much too heavy to hold up. If she just knew where she was supposed to sleep, she'd try to work up enough energy to crawl off to bed.

India had almost dozed off by the fire when a pair of hands lit gently on her shoulders, then started to massage her tired muscles. She jumped at first, then sighed and leaned back against the hard-muscled legs of that body she had learned to know with such shameful familiarity. She could recognize the touch of the big hands almost as if they were her own.

Christopher moved from her shoulders to the tight muscles in her neck. She sighed with weary pleasure.

"It appears we've worked you too hard," he commented.

"Hmmmm," she answered drowsily.

"Or perhaps you've wined and dined too well?"

"Mmmmmm," she agreed.

He laughed and pulled her to her feet, turning her to face him.

"Well, why don't you go to bed, little one? Everyone else has."

"Becauth...because...I don't know where I'm to sleep."

"With me, of course."

"Um...of course."

Her head was definitely too heavy for her neck, so she allowed it to fall back and gazed sleepily up into his face.

The flames of the little cook fire cast flickering shadows across his darkly bearded features, and his eyes mirrored the red of glowing coals. She smiled, warmed by the wine and the feel of his hands at her waist, thinking of her old fantasy.

"Did thoo . . . did you . . . know, when I first saw you on the *Sea Gull*, I thought I was dead, and you were the Devil come to carry me away."

Her eyes threatened to close. He said nothing, but a slow smile spread across his flame-shadowed, red-bronze features.

She smiled crookedly. "You're not, are you?"

His brow arched mischievously. "What do you think?"

"You did carry me away."

She frowned in tipsy confusion. Her mind suddenly jumped back to the day before, when Christopher had defeated that horrible Spaniard. Bloodthirsty, murderous intent had been written across his face, the face of death personified, but at the last minute he'd let the man go. Why? She leaned against him wearily, suddenly very tired of the games they played between them. She was lulled by the feel of his strong arms around her.

"I think maybe you are." She sighed. "I think maybe you're not a man at all. You're the Devil in disguise, and you aren't required to act like a normal human being. That's why I can't understand you."

"Why should you want to understand me," he asked, an edge of malice to his voice, "if I'm such a monster?"

India leaned back in his arms and regarded him foggily, the wine clouding her vision now as well as her reason. His eyes seemed to glow even more red in his bronzed face.

"You're not such a monster, maybe," she admitted softly. "But you've invaded my soul, do you know that? Do you do that to everyone before you carry them off to hell?" She giggled, but it was a mad, despairing sound. "Do you make every woman crave your touch before sending her off to burn for eternity? Maybe that's how your victims burn. Not with fire but with . . ."

"I think you're staggering drunk," Christopher interrupted.

An amused smile played around his lips as he picked her up in his arms and caught her eyes with his.

"Do you know what you've made me?" she asked, her voice husky and slurred.

"What?" He smiled.

"You've made me a . . . a . . ."

"A woman, I think," he finished for her. "And a very tired and tipsy woman at that."

Her head fell heavily against his shoulder and her eyes gave up the battle.

Christopher shook his head and grinned. "I surely do hope you're drunk enough to not remember this conversation in the morning!"

When he set her on the pallet in their lean-to and gently undressed her, she opened only one weary eye. She was too tired to resist or even respond when he covered her body with his and gently opened her legs to receive him.

"I want to go to sleep," she murmured drowsily, but she made no effort to escape his caresses. Her body seemed heavy and immovable, but still tingled deliciously when he pressed himself against her.

"Go right ahead," he invited with a smile, and gently sheathed himself in her warm, enfolding flesh. She arched involuntarily to take him.

"I'm too drunk for this." She sighed. "Why do you do this to me?"

He smiled wickedly and arched one brow. "I thought you craved my touch."

His movements against her, inside her, sent an aching warmth spreading through her body that turned into fire as his thrusting became deeper and harder. She groaned as the familiar, unbearable tension tightened her body, centering all her senses on the joining of their flesh.

"You've no morals at all," she moaned hoarsely. "Do you know that?"

His powerful body tensed as he drove her to her release and simultaneously found his own. As they settled back to earth together, he whispered teasingly against her ear.

"Just trying to live up to your ideals, lady mine."

But India didn't hear; she lay sprawled beneath him, peacefully and deeply asleep.

India woke the next morning not knowing where she was. Her head throbbed painfully and insistently, and waves of nausea threatened her when she attempted to sit up. She was lying naked on a pallet in a shelter constructed of palm fronds and the wide leaves of banana trees. Her body missed the constant motion of the ship, and her head tried to compensate by making the ground tilt back and forth in a manner much more distressing than the familiar motion of the *Falcon*'s deck. She looked around in a confused apathy until her eyes fell on Christopher's shirt lying in a crumpled mass.

India groaned as she rose to one elbow and was assaulted by the urge to turn herself inside out. Of course. They were on the beach, and this must be her hut—hers and Christopher's. She remembered the toil of the day before, loading and unloading, packing and unpacking, she and Helen helping to cook and wash up for fifty crewmen. In her last clear memory she was sitting down to eat herself, and her cup always seemed full of the good wine they'd broken out to celebrate their safe landfall. After that the evening became blurred, but she faintly remembered saying some silly things to Christopher and then ending up with him on top of her, as usual, with her enjoying everything he did to her, as usual. Lord! What a slut she'd become! She wondered if she was really in love with the man or if he had cast some wicked spell over her that made her blood race whenever he touched her or even looked at her. She hoped she hadn't made a fool of herself in her wine-inspired stupor. It wouldn't do to let her defenses down in front of a man who would only use her weaknesses against her.

India managed to dress and stumble out of the lean-to into the glare of the tropical sun. She winced as the bright sunlight stabbed through her eyes and bounced painfully off the oversensitive nerves in her head. Never again, she swore, would she overindulge from the bottle.

"Oh, there you are, sleepyhead!" Helen's voice chimed. "You've missed breakfast."

At the thought of breakfast India's stomach rebelled. She moaned and pressed her hand to her mouth. Helen came closer and peered into her friend's face.

"Oh my, you do look terrible!" She could not suppress the grin that spread over her plump, pretty features.

India glared at her resentfully. "How can you be so cheerful this morning?" she croaked. "You drank more than I did!"

Helen smiled mischievously. They had both consumed a good deal of wine last night, sitting with Timothy Hawkins, listening to the old chief gunner's tales of his buccaneering great-grandfather. But Helen had considerably more tolerance for alcohol than her more inexperienced friend, and the only penalty she was paying was a slight headache.

"I know what you need," Helen said cheerfully. "Seamus told me there's a fresh-water hot spring around the headland only half a mile or so. I wanted to go take a bath, but I didn't want to go alone. So now we can go together."

India groaned and put her hand to her throbbing head.

"A half mile!" she complained. "Oh no, I can't."

"Of course you can!" Helen assured her. "Just think how good a warm soak will feel!"

She disappeared into the lean-to and came out with soap and towels. Then she prodded India's unwilling body up the beach toward the headland.

The hot spring was indeed everything Helen had promised, and as India lay soaking in the steaming, sulfurous-smelling water she felt the aches and sickness flow from her body. It was almost worth the miserable walk, even though she had been forced to stop several times while her empty stomach had tried to force itself up her throat. She could happily laze here all day, she thought, lying against the smooth-worn volcanic rocks, letting the hot water soothe her aching body, and resting her eyes on the wall of cool green vegetation that surrounded the steaming pools. Paradise, indeed! If only she didn't have to go back to the beach and face the grim realities of her life.

"Want the soap?"

Helen giggled as the bar slipped out of her hands and

landed with a splash that covered India's face and hair with warm water.

"You looked about asleep."

India sputtered, thoroughly awake now. She shot Helen a look of bleary-eyed irritation, but took the offered soap and lathered her face and hair, dunking herself until she was sure every trace was rinsed from the luxurious black mane that fell to the middle of her back. Then she set to work soaping every inch of her body until her skin was rosy and tingling from her energetic scrubbing. Feeling somewhat alive again, she combed her fingers through her wet hair and lay down on a sun-warmed rock to let herself dry.

"You're going to get sunburned," Helen warned.

"Uh-huh," India agreed. "I won't stay here long."

Helen sighed quietly as she watched her friend stretch out languorously in the warm sun. She wondered how it would feel to be as slim and graceful as India, with her long legs, slim hips, and small, high breasts. Not that she was dissatisfied with herself, of course. She had soft, plump, voluptuous curves that were made to pillow a man's harder body, and there had never been any lack of men anxious to take advantage of her soft embraces. She enjoyed men, enjoyed their caresses, and wouldn't willingly trade places with India, who sought only to fight the natural sensuousness that nature endowed upon her. God! The girl didn't know how lucky she was, to be taught the arts of love by someone like Christopher Barnett.

Helen smiled sensuously, just thinking of him. Now, there was one man she would dearly love to feel on top of her. Oh well, there were certainly plenty of other attractive men to be had, and there was a certain satisfaction in watching that arrogant, powerful male animal turn to putty in the slender hands of the girl he'd meant to enslave for his own purposes. He hid it well, Helen admitted, but her knowing woman's eyes detected the signs, even if India herself couldn't see. She couldn't help but chuckle when she thought of how, those many weeks ago, she'd told India she could beat the man at his own game. And here the little chit, without even knowing it, was accomplishing that very thing.

"You'd better turn over," Helen warned, "and roast the other side, too."

India obeyed. She rested her chin on her hands and lazily watched Helen twirl the steamy water with her toes.

"This place is marvelous. I could stay here all day."

"Mmmmm," Helen agreed. "We'd better start back soon, though, or someone might come looking for us." Helen rose reluctantly from the pool, looking like a lush wood nymph. "They'd get quite an eyeful if they barged in right now," she commented.

The walk back was far more pleasant than the walk there. India was glad to have dry land under her feet after being weeks on board a ship. The earth still seemed to sway now and then, however, and she wondered how long it would take to regain her "land legs."

"Did you say Seamus Kennedy told you about that spring?" she asked Helen as they emerged from the jungle out onto the white beach.

"Yes," Helen replied. "He and that Englishman we rescued off the Spanish ship . . . they went exploring yesterday and found it."

India's eye twinkled with mischief. "I thought you were avoiding Seamus. Is he finally breaking through your resolve not to like him?"

Helen puckered her face in irritation. "La! I like him well enough, I suppose, even though he is an Irishman. But . . . well . . . Seamus is quality. You can tell by just listening to him talk. He'd not give a poor curate's daughter a second glance under normal circumstances. One of these days he's going to tire of all this adventuring and go back where he belongs, and you can be sure he'd not be taking me with him!"

"Would you want to go with him, do you think?"

"That's the trouble, I guess," Helen admitted with a sigh. "I think I might, if I allowed myself to get involved with him. It's never wise for a girl to get ideas above her station. So I'd rather just stay away. And I wish he'd stay away from me."

Helen thought with a mixture of longing and regret of the

single night she'd spent with Seamus, before she'd realized
what a danger to her heart the Irishman could be.

"I think you're underrating your own worth," India
commented. "Seamus is too much of a gentleman to pursue
you just for . . . for . . . well, sleeping with you."

Helen sighed. "Still have your illusions, don't you? Who
else would he pursue if he feels like some sport in bed?
You? Certainly not, my dear! Not after what happened with
Peter Reed!"

They had rounded the headland now and could see the
camp. The *Black Falcon* had been towed to the beach and
turned on its side by means of several block-and-tackle
arrangements fastened to sturdy palms. Most of the crewmen
were hard at work scraping barnacles and other encrusting
sea life off the hull. When that work was completed, India
knew, the hull would be coated with a mixture of tallow and
sulfur to protect the wood from worms and weed. She didn't
look forward to being in camp when that odoriferous process was taking place.

India noticed a tall man she didn't recognize talking with
Christopher in the shade of the upper beach.

"Is that the English prisoner from the *Navarre*?" she
asked Helen curiously.

"Yes," Helen replied. "You haven't met him? He's a real
gentleman. A viscount I think, though I don't remember the
title exactly. Cold fish, though. Can't say I like him much,
though we spent some time together yesterday and he was
quite nice to me."

"He and Christopher seem to be getting on well."

Helen laughed. "Well, they should both be happy.
Christopher saved him from being tortured and killed by the
Spaniards, and he's offered Christopher a huge sum to set
him safely on shore."

"You'd think Christopher would take him to safety without the benefit of a bribe," India said disdainfully. "After
all, he is a fellow Englishman."

Helen looked at her friend with a trace of sadness, noting
the bitterness in India's voice.

"I thought after all these weeks you two might get to

understand one another. Do you still think Christopher is the traitor and criminal your father says he is?''

India shook her head in sad confusion. "I don't know what to think anymore. I'm not sure it makes a difference. Whatever he was then, he's certainly a renegade now.''

Helen frowned in exasperation. "Sometimes I just don't believe how dense you can be. You don't appreciate what you've got.''

"What I've got?'' India cried. "I'm a prisoner of a man who hates me, who enjoys hurting me . . .''

"Oh, twaddle!'' Helen interrupted impatiently. "When has Christopher ever really hurt you? I think you hurt yourself! Or maybe you hurt each other. I've never known such a pair of stubborn fools!''

"That's not true,'' India insisted. "You don't know what he's done to me.''

Helen grinned wickedly. "I can imagine!'' she smirked.

"Oh, Helen,'' India cried. "For the love of God! How do you want me to feel? I'll admit I enjoy his . . . his lovemaking, when he's not being hurtful and cruel. Sometimes I think that if he loved me, really loved me, I wouldn't care about anything else. I wouldn't care what he was or who he was. And then I'm so ashamed, because I should be thinking about my poor father and what a dishonorable rogue Christopher is. But he doesn't love me, in any case. He's just using me, and I guess he enjoys it. But he'll finish with me and go to some other woman.''

"India,'' Helen broke in softly, "I think you're wrong. I think Christopher loves you.''

India stopped as they approached the camp and faced out to sea pensively.

"I don't even know if I want him to love me. Sometimes he scares me so. There's something very . . . savage . . . about him sometimes.''

Helen sighed dreamily. "Yes, isn't there, though.''

"I guess I'm being a fool,'' India said finally, smiling.

Helen's eyes twinkled. "Well, I suppose I'll let you be a fool if you want. But when Christopher gets what he's after, and you're a rich countess back in England, you'd better

just take me with you. Otherwise,'' she groaned, ''I'll be
back at Hillcrest with nothing but George the footman!''

CHAPTER THIRTEEN

The first days on Pig Island seemed to pass as if in a
pleasant dream. India allowed herself to live for the present
only, forgetting the past and ignoring the future. The warm
days and balmy, perfumed nights lulled her into a state of
peaceful acceptance, though a demon voice deep in her
heart told her this idyllic respite could not last forever, and
that her problems would return full force when she left the
magic aura of the island.

Her daytime hours were mostly her own. She volunteered
to help Cook with the meals, but those chores took very
little time. She spent long hours with Helen, lazing at the
hot springs or just talking companionably on the beach.
More often she was alone, though, left to her own devices
for entertainment. She would watch with interest as the
seamen worked on the ships, or when that became boring,
hike up her skirts and wade in the shallow waters along the
beach, letting her mind go pleasantly blank. On one occasion she walked entirely around the island, though it took
her three-quarters of the day and resulted in muscles sore
and stiff from slogging through the loose sand. It was worth
it, though, to be completely alone, with only the sea gulls
and the foaming breakers for company. To be able to tie her
skirts up to midthigh and explore the shallow beach reefs
without fear of drawing silent, teasing leers from the seamen,
or just sit and marvel at the panorama of sea and sky, with
no raucous voices in the background to disturb her inner
peace.

If her days were idle, though, at least her nights were well occupied. Christopher was never too tired from his day's work to make love to her at the end of the day, and she had stopped resisting him when he pulled her down on the pallet beside him and put his big hands on her. She knew that to resist him now would be pure hypocrisy, for they both knew how easily he could inflame her desire. Her mind still rebelled at the dishonorable use he was making of her, but her body willfully enjoyed the touch of his hands and mouth and the primitive union of their flesh. Lying beside him at night with the naked length of his muscular body pressed close to her, she felt secure, loved, needed, even though her mind knew this was far from the truth.

As India's enjoyment of their nights together grew, she became bolder in her role and experimented, learning which caresses would bring him to the highest peak of passion. One part of her cringed at the thought of such wanton behavior, while another part of her enjoyed the power of being able to inflame him with a single touch. Once, with the fever of desire burning in her own blood, she had tentatively taken him in her mouth. His response had been instant and gratifying. He had let her tease him a few moments, every muscle in his body tense while her hair brushed softly against his thighs and her tongue prodded him to new heights of throbbing agony. Then he had lifted her, turned her, and taken her with a savagery that had momentarily awakened her dormant fear of his powerfully thrusting body. When his breathing and heart had finally slowed, he looked down at her and sighed.

"Where did you learn that?" he asked in a hoarse voice.

India looked at him in pert innocence. "From you." She smiled. "You do that to me all the time. I just wondered what it was like."

He groaned softly and buried his face in the soft hollow of her throat, shaking his head slightly as if in disbelief.

"I've created a monster," he murmured. "No one would ever believe you were a frightened virgin not too many weeks ago."

India smiled as she felt his heart beat heavily against her.

At that moment she began to wonder who, of the two of them, was truly the slave.

A week passed, and the novelty of the unrestricted freedom of the island began to wear off. The long, idle daylight hours began to drag. India paced up and down the white beach, watching the laboring seamen in bored frustration. She pestered Cook for extra chores until he threatened to chase her out of the camp area with an iron skillet. Helen for the most part found her time occupied in dodging the attentions of both Seamus Kennedy and the English prisoner, Phillip White, so India was deprived even of her companionship. Christopher she saw only at night. From early morning to long after she would fall asleep on their pallet, he was totally occupied by the work on the three ships. It seemed to India that the only time he knew she was alive was when he would collapse on the pallet beside her and pull her sleep-warmed body gently against his.

They had been on Pig Island eight days when Peter Reed approached India as she brooded in the shade of a banana tree on the upper beach. He moved stiffly; the stripes on his back were still only half healed. His eyes no longer held the puppy-dog adoration that had catapulted them both into trouble two short weeks ago, but glinted with something darker that India did not care to define. She was astounded that he would dare approach her after what had happened, but she greeted him with a friendly smile, remembering that, after all, she had been largely responsible for his misfortune.

Peter squatted down beside her. In two short weeks his face had changed from boyish to bitter. His voice was sullen, even in the carefully neutral pleasantries they exchanged in greeting.

"Have you met the English fellow we took off the *Navarre*?" he finally asked.

"Yes, I've met him," India said.

She agreed with Helen that Phillip White was cold and hard to like. Somehow his aristocratic snobbery seemed out of place in the easygoing atmosphere of the island encampment. His gentlemanly mannerisms, which India might have admired back at Hillcrest, seemed artificial and out of tune with the ice that lay behind his eyes.

"He's going to buy a ship in New Providence—and a crew—to sail back to England," Peter went on.

"Isn't that dangerous?" India asked. "Considering the type of men on New Providence?"

"He'll pay them enough to keep them out of mischief," Peter said confidently.

India glanced uneasily to where Christopher was helping hoist the *Navarre*'s new mainmast with a series of ropes and pulleys. He looked in their direction, an irritated frown puckering his brow, but looked away again as India met his eyes. He didn't look very disturbed, she mused, to see her in conversation with the man who earlier had taken such liberties with her. She wondered if he thought he could trust her, or if he just didn't care anymore.

"Are you listening, India?" Peter scowled petulantly.

"Hmm?" India's attention turned back to the man beside her. "Oh, yes, Peter. Go on."

"Well"—Peter frowned in Christopher's direction—"I'm going with White. It seems our great leader doesn't want me around anymore. I'm sailing back to England to try to make a new life for myself." He smiled confidently. "I've got plenty of money now, and I don't have to worry about my father or anyone else."

"That's good, Peter. It's probably for the best, you know." India listened to Peter with half an ear. Would Christopher care if Peter tried to kiss her again? Would he be as violently angry as before? Had he been jealous, that other time, or had he simply been upset that his rights had been usurped? It wasn't worth the risk to find out, of course, either to her or to Peter, but she couldn't help but wonder, just the same.

"India?" Peter interrupted her thoughts.

"Hmm?"

He frowned at her obvious distraction.

"I said the offer still stands. You can come with me. No one in England would ever have to know you're not my wife."

India looked at him in surprise.

"Come with me, India," he urged. "I'll make you happy, I promise!"

He looked at her pleadingly, and a hint of the puppy-dog adoration slipped back into his eyes.

"Peter, no," she said firmly. "Nothing has changed, except that we both know now what a risk it is for you to be here talking to me like this." She looked significantly in Christopher's direction.

Peter's adoring gaze became a sullen glare. How like a spoiled child he is, India thought.

"Every woman I've ever met was a whore at heart." He sneered. "I thought you were different. I thought you were unspoiled and pure, in spite of what he's done to you. But you're just like the rest, aren't you?"

He rose to his feet and looked at her with contempt.

"Whore!" he spat. "Do you enjoy spreading your legs for him, or is it just that you hope he'll make you rich someday!"

India flinched as though he had hit her.

"Filthy, disgusting whore!"

He turned on his heel and left, but the look of contempt in his eyes stayed with her.

India felt the muscles in her chest tighten convulsively. She wanted to cry aloud, to release the sudden pressure of shock and mortification in great wracking sobs, but Christopher was regarding her closely from farther down the beach, and she refused to create a scene. So, instead, she lowered her head to her bent knees and cried inside.

She wasn't a whore! She wasn't! Peter was a sullen, spoiled child who hadn't gotten his way, and he had simply called her that dreadful name in revenge. How dare he presume to judge her! She was not a whore! She had no choice but to stay with Christopher. Peter had not been offering a way out, simply a change of masters. He would have expected the same privileges as Christopher, only without even the sham of marriage that she had now. She had been right to refuse. Of course she had been right!

Slowly the emotional agony subsided and reason returned.

What she had discovered that bright morning after the storm was still true. She loved Christopher in spite of the dictates of reason.

It was only natural that this man who mastered her passions should master her heart, also. But it made no difference. She deplored his reasons for kidnapping her, and she would escape if she ever got a chance. She was still ruled by her head, not her heart, India reassured herself. Escape—the only way to deliver herself and her family from Christopher's revenge—was still uppermost in her mind. Wasn't it? India examined her heart and mind and tried to be painfully honest. She should be thinking of her father's pain and disgrace, but all she could think of lately was the sound of Christopher's voice and the way his eyes lit up when he smiled. Would she leave if the opportunity presented itself? Had she been so enslaved by this man that she could no longer do the honorable thing? She didn't really know anymore.

India sat for a long time, thinking of her predicament. She finally raised her head to the sound of voices laughing not far from where she sat. The sun was resting on the horizon, a huge red ball that streaked the sea and sky alike with bands of fire. Several seamen who had finished their day's work were holding a mock fencing contest on the wet beach. They had been joined by Phillip White. Time to help Cook prepare the evening meal. The men were entertaining themselves now, but they'd soon be demanding their dinner. She rose and brushed the sand from her skirts.

As India cleaned and scaled the day's catch of fish, her thoughts wandered back to her husband. She had to admit that her brave plan to capture his heart as well as his passion seemed to be failing dismally. In fact, even his passions had cooled lately. The last few nights he had come to their shelter exhausted. Without giving her as much as a greeting, he had dropped down beside her and taken her, quickly and efficiently, like he would tend to any other physical need. He'd been asleep as soon as he rolled off her. India suspected he wouldn't even bother with her if he weren't so determined to produce an heir.

So what was she to do? She'd allowed herself to accept
her role as his wife, accepting and, yes, enjoying his
lovemaking with hopes of eventually winning his love.
Now, not only was he not surrendering his heart, he was
growing bored with her body, as well. She was beginning to
feel more and more like a discarded mistress. Perhaps she
should try to escape with Peter after all and try to keep him
at arm's length until they got to England. Then she thought
of Peter's sullen face and bitter words. There had to be a
better way.

India's eyes strayed from her task to the mock battle on
the beach. Phillip White was demonstrating one of his more
complex fencing moves to old Tom Smith. He was really
very good, India thought as she watched him disarm Smith
with a graceful turn of his wrist. Smith made a rude gesture,
grabbed a cutlass from a watching friend, then turned to
White with a fierce grin on his face. White laughed and
waved him away, admitting defeat. His slender foil, even
wielded with consummate skill, was no match for the
heavier, clumsier cutlass.

To be able to hack and cut at an opponent with a cutlass
was all very well, India thought, but she wondered how
many of these brigands could boast of skill with the more
refined épée that White handled so well. She remembered
when, as a hoyden of thirteen, she had persuaded a young
neighbor, James Leighton, to coach her in the gentlemanly
art of fencing. She'd blackmailed the poor boy, she remembered, by threatening to inform his mother of a particularly
embarrassing amorous escapade. He'd worked with her for a
full year, finally admitting that she had talent, a grace,
style, and quickness that made up for her lack of brute
strength. She smiled a secret smile and wondered how many
of these rough men she could outduel.

Suddenly, the seed of a wild idea began to germinate in
her mind. The secret smile spread until it was a wide grin. It
just might work! She remembered Ian's words as if it were
yesterday, instead of weeks ago, that they had sat with the
crew in the waist of the *Black Falcon*, the steady, warm
breeze filling the sails and the brilliant stars whirling over-

head. Ian had been imbibing liberally from the bottle and boasting of his exploits in a thick Scots brogue. He'd mentioned, in an offhand way, that Christopher was an adequate swordsman, but just adequate. Had he meant it? Or had he been simply building himself up at his captain's expense? If Ian had been accurate in his estimation of Christopher's skill, perhaps she could actually defeat Christopher in a duel with foils, where grace and nimbleness counted more than brawn. With Phillip White's coaching, she might have a chance. She could goad him into accepting a challenge, and the stakes would be her freedom. Once and for all, she would prove to everyone, herself most of all, that her will had not buckled under Christopher's assault, that she was still a woman of independent mind and spirit.

The longer India thought about her idea for a duel, the higher her spirits soared. She would restore her own self-respect while winning her freedom. Perhaps she could get in a few strokes of revenge, as well. It wouldn't hurt to prick him a couple of times before sending his foil flying in final defeat. Her eyes glowed with satisfaction as she imagined the look of humiliation on his face, and the look of hurt surprise. He thought he had her down; he thought she was so securely trapped in the spell of his damned masculinity that she couldn't make a move to defend herself. Well she would teach him better, the arrogant, cocksure fool! Indeed, she would!

In the vivid scenes of her imagination, India grew more and more confident of victory. She brushed the idea of defeat from her mind. Her reluctant childhood coach had admitted her talent. With Phillip White's tutoring she could become really good, she was sure. And Christopher was only adequate. Adequate! What a wonderfully descriptive term for mediocrity, India thought. Ian wouldn't have said that about such a good friend unless he'd meant it. Now what she had to do was persuade White to coach her, then, when she thought she was good enough, persuade Christopher to fight her.

She approached the rescued English nobleman as the evening meal was ending. The tropical sun had set an hour before, and the cook fires cast a wavering ruddy glow across the beach. He sat alone on the upper beach, watching the activities of the campsite with a slightly supercilious air. One slightly raised brow was his only acknowledgment of her approach.

India had thought carefully about what she should say. Their conversations to this point had been few. India had formed a mild distaste for the man from the very first, and whenever he had approached her she had been polite but cool. As a result, he had turned for female companionship to Helen, who was just as cool but lacked the advantage of having a powerful protector on the island. Asking Phillip White for a favor was going to be awkward.

They talked casually for a few minutes, with several strained silences. He was being as cool to her as she had been to him. The tables had turned, India thought ruefully. She had to put this request in a way that he could see advantages to himself—a way to occupy his time and display the skill he was obviously so proud of. She took a deep breath and told him the reason why she had sought him out. He laughed condescendingly.

"Why on earth, my sweet lady"—he put an unpleasant emphasis on *lady*—"would you want to indulge in such an unwomanly activity?"

India was vexed at his tone, but she carefully schooled her voice to pleasantness.

"Exercise," she said. "It would be something different to do. Surely you've noticed there's nothing to do on this island unless you're working with the crew."

"Indeed," he drawled.

"Besides, I've had some instruction, about five years ago, and my instructor said I was good. I saw you on the beach today, and it's obvious you're a master." She hoped she could appeal to his vanity. "I thought it might be a way we could both occupy our time."

She tried to sound casual, and hoped he wouldn't get the wrong idea. It wouldn't do at all for him to think she was flirting. That might provoke the kind of attention from Christopher that she really didn't want.

He thought it over silently for a few moments.

"I don't see any harm in me giving you a few pointers, I suppose. Lord knows I don't have anything else to do. But knowing your husband, I think we better get his permission first. He's a man I'd just as soon not cross, not now at least."

India clenched her teeth to hold in an oath of frustration. So close, and yet so far! Christopher would never consent! She'd counted on his being too busy to notice her activities. She forcibly pulled her face into a casual smile.

"Of course," she agreed sweetly.

Christopher laughed when she asked him that night in their lean-to.

"Of course," he agreed cheerfully. "Do whatever you want. We still have about two more weeks of work to do here. Maybe this will keep you out of trouble." He grinned.

India slanted him a look of irritation. He didn't suspect her plans, because he was so sure of her docility. His offhand dismissal was almost as infuriating as a refusal. Never in her life had she met a man who could with so little effort provoke feelings of such intensity in her. This swinging from passion to anger must surely drive her mad if she remained with him much longer! She attempted an impassive face.

"Then you won't mind if I borrow a foil?"

"Just make sure the tip is blunted," he cautioned. "I wouldn't want any scars on that pretty skin of yours."

She was tempted to reply that she was not going to be the one to come away with scars, but she simply nodded her consent instead.

"I just wanted to make sure you knew there was nothing going on between me and Phillip," India ventured. "He said he wouldn't work with me unless you gave permission."

The look of irritation on India's transparent face brought a gleam of amusement to Christopher's eyes.

"Considerate of him." He smiled. "But don't worry. I know nothing's going on."

"You do?" India's brows rose. Vexed by his confidence,

her voice took on an acid tone. "Just how do you know nothing is going on?"

He looked at her with deceptive mildness. "Because every man on this island knows what I'd do to anyone who laid a hand on you."

India felt a chill go up her spine. "And what would you do?" she asked, trying to sound casual.

"I'd make him sorry he ever experienced puberty," he stated in a matter-of-fact tone. "Very sorry."

India shot him a look of disgust. "Do you solve everything with violence?"

"It's worked so far." He grinned. "For someone who claims to hate violence, you seem mighty anxious to learn about it."

"Fencing is an art." India's chin lifted defensively.

"A deadly art," he corrected. "But go ahead, learn all you want about swordplay. Just don't get overconfident."

India looked at him apprehensively. Was that last statement a warning? Perhaps he understood her better than she thought. But his expression held no hint of suspicion.

He took a step toward her. His fingers gently pushed a tendril of hair from her face, then traced the line of her cheek and chin. Her pulse quickened at his touch, and her irritation washed away in a flood of heat.

"You can play at fencing all you want, for all I care," he said quietly. His voice had grown husky. "But right now I have a different sport in mind."

All thoughts of leaving him fled to the back of India's mind as he bent, slipped his powerful arm beneath her knees, and carried her to their pallet.

The gray light of early dawn reflected off the mirror-smooth wet sand as India sat yawning, waiting for Phillip White. These early-morning hours were all very well when one was stimulated by the strenuous exercise of lunging and parrying, but right now India wanted nothing more than to go back to sleep. Damn Phillip for being this late! It had been he, after all, who had insisted on these early-morning lessons, saying he wanted no gapers to watch him teach a mere woman how to fence. She supposed he'd been up late, drinking and pestering poor Helen, who, when India had passed them on her way to bed, had been politely trying to escape from his unwanted attentions. India wondered if she should mention to Christopher that Helen needed more protection from the fellow. She'd have to do it quietly, though, because if Phillip ever found out, that would be the end of her fencing lessons.

For four days now they had spent the predawn hour on the smooth, glassy beach, quitting when the sunrise brought the camp to life. India practiced lunging until her legs burned. She breezed through the basics and concentrated on learning strategies of attack and gaining facility and confidence in fending off an opponent's thrusts. In the afternoons she would take a foil and slip around the headland, where she couldn't be seen by the men working around the ships. There she set herself up to duel a convenient palm tree, lunging and thrusting until she imagined her unfortunate opponent crawling in the sand and begging for mercy.

From her very first lesson she felt her natural instincts guide her hand and arm. After four days of hard work she felt as confident as she had felt after a year's instruction from the reluctant James Leighton. Phillip White might have been a jackass, but he was a skilled swordsman and a good instructor. He worked her until she wanted to drop. He drilled her until she parried his blows from instinct rather than thought, and until her footwork was as natural and graceful as if she'd been doing this all her life. She knew it was to satisfy his own vanity that he showed her complex movements he thought she would never duplicate, but in her afternoon practice sessions she drilled herself on every movement until even Phillip could find very little fault with her technique.

As her strength grew, so did her confidence that she could win her planned duel. Christopher had said they would be on the island through the following week. She would give herself five more days, then put forth her challenge. Then, when they left, he could honor his bargain by putting her ashore on the first civilized island they sighted. Assuming that she won. But, of course, she would win. She couldn't let her confidence wane at this point.

India jumped at a sound behind her and turned to see Phillip, red-eyed and bleary-looking, coming toward her without the usual swagger in his walk.

"Whose stupid idea were these damned early-morning lessons," he croaked.

"Yours." India sniffed. "Though it's not so early now. The sun's almost up."

Phillip grimaced and put a tentative hand to his head. "Well, the lessons were your stupid idea. Don't know why I ever let you talk me into it. Damn me, I don't!"

India wrinkled her nose in disgust as she caught a whiff of the stale smell of liquor that still clung to his clothing.

"Don't take it out on me if you drink all night," she said indignantly. "Maybe we'd better skip this morning's lesson. The camp is almost ready to get up anyway, you're so late."

"The night's drinking was the fault of your sweet friend's charms." His crooked smile came close to a leer. "She certainly does know how to play coy. You'd think after having to put up with this riffraff, she'd be glad of a gentleman's attentions."

India frowned at him, wanting on the one hand to warn him off Helen and on the other hand to remain in his good graces for the sake of her lessons. She compromised.

"Helen is a lady," she asserted. "You should treat her with more respect."

Phillips's puffy face twisted in a sneer. "Lady, my . . . Oh, well," he gave in. "You're right about one thing. I'm in no condition to teach you anything this morning. Tomorrow, maybe . . ."

He groaned and turned to walk toward the cook fire, where Cook had water boiling for tea.

India felt like throwing something in frustration, but there was nothing handy. The morning was wasted. She would just have to practice extra hard this afternoon. Damn men and their lecherous, carousing ways!

Three days later India had additional reason to curse men and their ways. She was half dozing on their sleeping pallet, snuggled tightly against Christopher to ward off the predawn coolness. Phillip had appeared for only one lesson in the last few days, and she had finally given up on him, admitting that, now his enthusiasm had waned, she was better off simply practicing what she had been taught. It was nice, for a change, not to rise long before the sun, nice to be able to lie against Christopher's warmth, feel his breath in her tousled hair and his naked arm pressing her close to him even in his sleep. Soon, if her plans went as they should, she would be sleeping cold and alone again. If only they had met in different circumstances, before his heart had turned to iron and her will had settled into unshakable stubbornness. India burrowed even closer to him, enjoying the feeling of letting down her guard in these few moments when he was sleeping and harmless. She was drifting back into warm sleep when a scream ripped the air.

CHAPTER FOURTEEN

India's heart jumped into her throat as the shrill scream jerked her to befuddled wakefulness. Christopher had pulled on his breeches and was pushing through the doorflap, sword in hand, before she had scrambled out of the blankets. She grabbed her dress and pulled it hastily over her head, cursing as her arm caught in the sleeve.

Helen! India knew the screams could only have come from Helen, the only other woman on the island. She ran across the cool sand to where the commotion was broiling, stumbling once or twice as her bare feet collided with stones and driftwood. In the darkness of predawn she couldn't see what was happening, but she heard angry masculine voices clashing above a background of feminine sobbing. Lord! If one of these swine had hurt Helen, she'd kill him with her bare hands; she'd see the wretch strung up by his damned . . . Her unladylike conjectures were cut short as she pushed through a circle of crewmen to observe the drama that was being enacted at the entrance to Helen's lean-to. Christopher held Phillip White in an iron grip, one arm around White's throat and the other pinning his arms behind his back. Another crewman restrained Seamus Kennedy. Helen sat on the sand in the shreds of her dress, her face tearstained, puffy, and bruised. Her sobs and distressed hiccups accompanied the shouting match developing between the men. India quickly circled the ring of observers and dropped down beside her friend. At her touch, Helen's sobs grew louder and she buried her face on India's shoulder.

"You slimy son of a bitch!" Seamus shouted at the nobleman. He struggled in his captor's arms. "Let me go, dammit! Let me kill him, like the bastard deserves!"

"Shut up, Seamus!" Christopher ordered. "Calm down, and maybe we can find out what's happening here!"

Seamus's face was flushed with anger. "I already know what happened here. That piece of English filth raped Helen, and I'm going to kill him for it!"

Helen's wails grew louder. Seamus's eyes blazed.

"I caught him in the act, the pig. Grunting and heaving like a boar while he'd already beaten her half senseless and gagged her into the bargain." He looked at Helen sobbing loudly on India's shoulder. "I'm going to make you wish you'd never learned to use that cock you're so proud of, you English son of a bitch. You just see if I don't!"

Phillip's face was white with fury as he struggled for some shred of aristocratic dignity while still pinned by Christopher's arm.

"I'd hardly call getting a little rough with a whore rape," he sneered. "That little tart's probably been with every man in this camp. What's one more going to matter to anyone?"

Seamus lunged, but was held back by the brawny arms of the crewman.

"She's been playing coy and hard to get ever since we got to this godforsaken strip of sand," Phillip continued. "Thought she could hold out for money, I'll wager, her being the only available piece on the island. I just gave her a lesson in how to treat her betters, that's all."

Helen's sobbing had quieted to forlorn sniffs punctuated by an occasional miserable hiccup. India looked at Phillip White's arrogant face and felt her stomach turn in revulsion.

"He's lying," India proclaimed. "None of that's true!"

"Be quiet, India," Christopher ordered quietly. "Let me handle this."

He released his prisoner suddenly, with a jerk that threw him into the middle of the circle of curious observers.

"You admit you forced yourself on this girl and beat her to make her submit to your advances?" he asked, his face a grim mask.

"As I said . . ." Phillip began.

"Just a simple yes or no will do," Christopher cut him short.

Phillip's face grew whiter still as he looked at the faces of the men surrounding him. He nodded tensely in agreement. He couldn't deny the obvious facts.

"What is your business with this, Seamus?" Christopher turned to the Irishman.

Seamus shrugged off the restraining hands of a crewman and straightened proudly. "I intend to marry Helen," he declared.

India shoved Helen's head to her own shoulder to muffle her friend's denial. Her screech of indignation was taken by all to be simply another wail of distress.

Seamus continued. "By defiling my intended wife, this man has delivered me a deadly insult, Christopher. You can't deny me the right to fight him."

"Oh, Lord!" Phillip exploded. "How can one defile a bitch who's already been mounted by a pack of dogs! You're insane, Kennedy!"

Seamus reached for his knife, but his wrist was caught in Christopher's grip of steel.

"Shut up, White!" Christopher commanded. "You'll

either fight Seamus now or you can start swimming for the nearest island. We don't hold with a man who backs down from a challenge. Cowards and woman-beaters don't last long in this company.''

Phillip recovered his aplomb and once more looked every inch the haughty aristocrat.

''I'm no coward.'' He sneered. ''I'll fight this fool and anyone else who cares to die by my sword this morning. I've no need to fear such a pack of lowborn ruffians.''

''One fight will suffice,'' Christopher said tersely, taking two foils from the surrounding crew and handing them to the combatants.

Seamus grinned a death's-head grin. ''To the death, with no quarter asked or given.''

Phillip was amused. ''Of course.'' He shrugged.

The circle of men expanded to give the duelists space. Excitement of anticipated bloodshed lit every face as the first gray light of dawn outlined the deadly contestants and hovering spectators. The shadowy, macabre scene seemed to India to be part of a bizarre nightmare. She dragged Helen from the circle and left her wide-eyed just inside her hut, then ran to Christopher's side.

''You can't let this happen!'' she begged.

He didn't answer.

''Phillip will kill him!'' she cried urgently. ''Please . . . Stop them! This is murder!''

Christopher looked at her calmly. ''Seamus has a right to fight his own battles,'' he told her evenly. ''I don't have a right to stop him, and neither do you. Don't be so sure that he doesn't know what he's doing.''

India groaned. Her fists clenched in rage and anxiety. All eyes riveted on White and Kennedy as the first metallic clash of their foils broke the tense silence. India couldn't bear to watch. Neither could she look away. The sight of two men furiously intent on doing murder held her fascinated and at the same time sickened her. How could these men just stand here and permit this to happen . . . and yes, even enjoy the spectacle of two men determined to spill each other's lifeblood? In the horror of the scene she forgot her own recent lethal intentions toward her friend's assailant.

Kennedy and White circled each other warily. The Englishman's point flicked and wove an intricate pattern as he attempted to draw Kennedy into an ill-timed and hasty attack, but Kennedy was too astute to succumb to any swordsman's tricks. When he did attack it was with a grace and deadly skill that left India breathless with admiration and White hard-pressed to defend himself. The English nobleman had expected his opponent to be an easy kill; he hadn't prepared himself for a contest of equals.

The rage had left Kennedy's face. In its place was a mask of passionless concentration. The gentle and philosophical Irishman whom India had so admired had become an efficient killing machine. Phillip White was the most skilled swordsman India had ever seen, but Kennedy parried his attacks with ease. The effort of defending himself against the Irishman's intricate swordplay was bringing a sheen of sweat to White's face. After five minutes, few had any doubt about the outcome of the match. Kennedy could have killed his opponent several times, but he chose instead to prolong the agony and give the Englishman more time to contemplate his coming defeat. A pallor of fear was spreading across White's face, and his attacks were growing clumsier and more desperate.

Finally Kennedy grew tired of the game. His face still showed no emotion as he opened a shallow but bloody gash from White's collarbone to crotch. The Englishman gasped in agony and stumbled, but he recovered his feet and raised his foil to parry the next thrust. A fierce grin split the mask of Kennedy's face.

"Did you think I would give you a quick, easy death after what you've done to the woman I love?"

He attacked again, easily penetrating White's faltering defense and whipping his point across the Englishman's face. Blood flowed from the gash across White's forehead into his eyes, blinding him. He raised his hand to clear his vision, but Kennedy's point had cut again, this time between his legs.

"You won't be needing this any longer," Kennedy said grimly, and White screeched in agony, dropped his foil, and clutched at his bloody groin.

"Oh, God!" India pressed her face to Christopher's arm and felt her stomach heave. "God! God!"

Christopher's arm tightened around her and pressed her face firmly into his shoulder.

"Enough, Seamus!" he said. "Kill him and be done."

"Aye, aye, my captain," he acknowledged grimly.

India pressed her face tighter against the hard comfort of Christopher's shoulder as the Englishman's screams ended in a sharp gasp, followed by silence. Deadly quiet prevailed as Phillip White slumped gracelessly to the ground, Seamus's blade buried in his chest. For a few heartbeats the crowd stood as if stunned, staring at White's lifeless body. Then the tense silence broke as the spectators voiced raucous approval.

The crowd of blood-sated spectators had drifted off to the cook fires by the time India gathered the courage to leave the circle of Christopher's arm. She glanced at the bloody corpse, then looked determinedly away. Her stomach was still crowding her throat, and the earth seemed unsteady under her feet. How could a good man like Seamus Kennedy, a man she had trusted and gladly called friend, how could such a man have done this gruesome deed?

She moved uncertainly to where Helen sat, stunned, inside the entrance of her lean-to. Muddy tearstains marred her usually pert face, and her gray eyes were red and puffy.

"Did you see it?" India sank down beside her friend and touched her gently. Helen's face threatened to crumple. She nodded.

"Are you all right?" India asked gently, then thought immediately, of course she's not all right! How could she possibly be all right with all that had happened in this early dawn?

Helen sniffed ominously, then nodded.

Two crewmen were dragging the corpse away as Christopher and Seamus talked in muffled tones some distance away. India's gaze was drawn in horrible fascination to the blood-soaked sand that just a few short minutes ago had been the battleground for two mankillers. She was more determined than ever to escape this world of violence and passion, and to escape the man who ruled it. She had thought to win him, maybe even reform him by her love. She saw now that her goal was hopeless. She hadn't realized the magnitude of what she had thought to do. Perhaps all along it had merely been an excuse to stop fighting him, and herself, an excuse to surrender to the passion and the fascination he inspired. She had to be strong enough to ignore the tug of her heart when he touched her, and the warmth that flooded through her veins at his smile.

The leader of the pack is always the most ferocious, she thought, or he wouldn't be the leader. She had believed she could tame a killer wolf with a mere pat on the head. What she had witnessed this morning was the reality of this world—blood, cruelty, death, degradation. What she saw in Christopher's eyes in the intimacies of their warm tropical nights was mere fantasy. She had to remember the reality. She had to have the courage, determination, and luck to complete her plans and win her duel.

India looked up as Helen pressed against her in distress. Christopher and Seamus were standing in the entrance to the shelter. Christopher looked amused. Seamus just looked determined. It was Seamus who spoke.

"Helen," he began, "I have something to discuss with you, and I'd appreciate it if you'd listen to what I have to say."

Helen looked at him wide-eyed and gripped India tighter.

"Now, I just killed a man here because of you," he said grimly. "It was none of your fault what happened, and I'm not implying that it was. But it's true you're a woman who likes a man's attention, and in this company that means trouble. These are good lads, most of them, but they think of females as only two kinds—the untouchable ladies and the trollops. They aren't accustomed to anything in between."

India bit her lip in anxiety, and Helen whimpered. What was he getting at?

Seamus shifted somewhat uncomfortably, then continued.

"Now, I'm wondering how many more men I'm going to have to pull off you in the middle of the night. I didn't mind killing that son of a bitch White, because he needed killing. But I'd hate to have to go after any of our own lads who mistake your flirtatious ways for a come-hither. Now, I've declared myself for you tonight, so I'm bound by my honor to run through any of these studs who try to insult you. And I intend to do that. But the whole problem can be easily avoided by your marrying me right now."

Helen looked at him in amazement. "You can't mean it!" she squeaked.

"I do mean it," he replied firmly. "My feelings have been clear to you for some time now. And though you've been avoiding me, for some reason, I think you feel the same for me as I do for you."

"I didn't . . . I mean . . . you really do want to . . . to . . ."

Seamus smiled for the first time. "My bride is obviously overwhelmed, Captain. Perhaps it would be best to get the ceremony accomplished before any more confusion breaks out."

Christopher seemed only too happy to accommodate. "Whatever you say, my friend." He grinned.

"Wait!" Helen stuttered. "You can't . . . it's not . . . it wouldn't be legal . . . would it?"

Seamus took Helen's arm and lifted her gently to her feet. He guided her into the lean-to.

"Legal enough, my love," he assured her. "And we can be married again when we get to Ireland, if you wish."

"Ireland?"

Christopher chuckled at the confusion in Helen's voice as he lifted India to her feet.

"Perhaps you should put on some shoes for the wedding, little one." He smiled at her with warm eyes.

India looked at Christopher doubtfully, ignoring his amused look at her sandy, bare feet.

"What gives you the right to force Helen to marry Seamus?" She frowned.

"We're not forcing anyone," he replied. "She loves him.

It's in her eyes every time she looks at him. And he loves her.''

"You know so much about women, then, and love, that you can tell how Helen feels better than she can herself?'' she asked sarcastically.

He just smiled gently at her barb. "I know enough.''

"She's been running away from him for weeks.''

"She wanted him to catch her, though. You know it as well as I do.''

India shook her head in confusion. Too much had happened, and the day had not yet really begun.

"Helen deserves someone gentle and good. Not . . .''

"I thought you liked Seamus,'' Christopher said.

"I did . . . I do. But . . .'' She waved vaguely to the blood-soaked sand.

"But you're upset because he got a bit angry with our friend Mr. White.''

India grimaced distastefully. How could he be so casual about the carnage that had taken place here? But then, to him such violence was an unremarkable, perhaps even essential, part of his life.

"Don't worry about Helen,'' Christopher reassured her. "Seamus will take her back to Ireland when we get back to Britain. He has plenty of money, land, and even a title, if that's what she wants.''

"Seamus has a title?''

"Yes.''

India looked at him expectantly.

"You'll have to ask him about it if you want to know anything more,'' Christopher said with a gleam of amusement in his eyes.

India tried hard not to pout, but her curiosity had been thoroughly piqued.

"As long as Helen's safe and happy. That's all I'm concerned about,'' she declared.

He grinned at her attempt to hide her dissatisfaction.

"Then you better go clean up. You don't want to look like a disheveled beach rat at your best friend's wedding.''

Seamus and Helen were pronounced man and wife by

Captain Barnett just as the orb of the sun rose entirely above the horizon. Symbolic, India thought. At least she hoped this would be a grand new beginning for Helen, whose life had been so different than what India had believed all these years they had been together.

India stood watching the ceremony with mixed emotions. Helen was beaming, looking young and happily innocent in her light muslin dress, with face freshly scrubbed and free of the traces of her earlier agony. Seamus looked stalwart and respectable, if that were possible after the morning's display of the more dangerous side of his nature. The ceremony was brief, but much more meaningful, it seemed to India, than the sham she had been put through so many weeks before. Helen repeated her vows with the sound of conviction in her voice, and when she looked at Seamus the light of adoration in her eyes was plain to see. Now the fear of his eventual rejection was gone, she was free to release the feelings she had in her heart.

India watched the scene and tried not to feel envy for the difference in their situations. She was happy Helen had a strong man who loved her, who would give her children and grow old with her. No matter what violent instincts were hidden behind Seamus's gentle exterior, he would never turn on Helen, hurt her, or discard her. It was obvious from the look on his face as he stood beside his bride that he loved her very much. India wished she could be as optimistic about her relationship with Christopher.

A holiday was declared in celebration of the happy event. The gruesome happenings of the dark predawn hours were all but forgotten as the seamen drank, cavorted on the beach, and drank some more. India sat in the shade of a palm, watching. She felt too morose even to slip away and practice her fencing. Christopher had been right. Fencing might be an art form in some ways, but how easily it was transformed into a deadly method of butchery!

She should challenge Christopher today and get it over with, India knew. She could set the date of their fight several days forward, but if she broached the subject to Christopher today, there would be no backing off. And if she brooded on the morning's events much longer, she would no longer have the courage to fight. Not that their duel would be anything like that gruesome scene in front of Helen's lean-to. There would be no real anger, no fight to the death, or even to first blood. Just two people laboring to show who was the better artist with the foil. And then she would be free. Maybe. She hoped. She had to believe she could win, or she could never go through with it. Both her conscience and her good sense demanded that she make her bid for freedom, that she defy her ever-deepening attachment for the iron-hearted, warm-eyed man who held her prisoner and win through to an honorable, decent life with honorable, decent people. Even if she would be lonely, and miserable, and bored, with only honorable, decent, boring people to keep her company. India shook her head. This line of thought was leading to disaster. She obviously had to make her move before her will had decayed entirely.

The right opportunity did not present itself until after dinner. The meal had been leisurely, and somewhat sparsely attended, with many of the crewmen too drunk to eat. Christopher sat by her side and talked in inconsequential trivia. The flickering light of the cook fire outlined the cleanly chiseled planes of his face and shadowed the darkness of his eyes. His voice was deep, resonant, and expressive. She would miss that voice, that face, the feel of his short, coarse beard on her skin. India closed her eyes and clenched her jaw. She mustn't allow herself to think of those things. He was a beast who would trap her in the snare of his masculine charm to turn her into a weapon of his own dark revenge. He had no regard for honor, or mercy, or love. He didn't care for her, she told herself. Oh, he probably liked her well enough, but he would never love her in the way she longed for love. His charm, humor, tenderness, all these qualities were a sham, a disguise that hid the inpenetrable, embittered, bloody-souled thing that was his inner core. She had to escape before she was completely lost to all pretensions of decency and honor, before this devil disguised as a man had her shamelessly begging for his love.

She looked up into his questioning eyes. She hadn't heard a word he'd said for the past five minutes. They sat for a few moments in awkward silence. His expression seemed to invite her to speak what was on her mind.

"Christopher?" she began in a slightly quavering voice.

"Yes?"

His dark eyes seemed to see through her, to witness the struggle that tormented her soul.

"I'm going to challenge you to a duel."

Silence. Then he smiled, and the smile turned into a grin, and the grin ended in an uninhibited shout of laughter.

"You what?"

India frowned in irritation. He wasn't taking this as seriously as she intended.

"I'm going to challenge you to a duel," she repeated more firmly. "I want to fight you, with swords . . . with the foil, to be more exact, since I can't handle a cutlass."

Christopher was having a hard time speaking through the laughter that bubbled in his throat.

"Why, may I ask, do you want to fight me? Have I offended you so mightily that you wish to carve me in the manner Seamus demonstrated this morning?"

India's face reddened with both anger and embarrassment.

"I would appreciate it if you would stop laughing," she said sharply. "I'm serious about this!"

Christopher managed with difficulty to present a more sober mien.

"Of course you're serious," he conceded. "But I'm intensely curious as to what you think you're going to accomplish by this lunatic suggestion."

"It is not a lunatic suggestion." India's chin rose in its old defiant tilt. "I'm good with a foil. I think I have a good chance of beating you."

His face was settling into hard-planed impassivity. "Do you hate me so much you wish to see me dead by your own hand?" he asked quietly.

India was startled by his assumption. "Of course not!" she denied. Then, more quietly, "I never said I hated you. At least I haven't said it lately. And I don't."

His face softened almost imperceptibly. "Then what is the purpose of all this, India?" he asked gently.

"I had in mind a contest of skill, with the aim being disarming rather than maiming."

"Indeed." His voice took on a sardonic tone. "And what would be the stakes in this contest of skill, as you call it?"

India took a deep breath and plunged ahead.

"My freedom," she explained. "If I win, you must promise to set me free at the nearest civilized port, with enough money to take me home."

"Ah." His brows raised in understanding. "And if I win?"

"If you win?"

"Yes." He smiled, somewhat threateningly, India thought. "If I win, what do I get?"

India drew a blank. She hadn't really thought of the possibility of his winning. "I . . . I don't know. What do you want?"

He thought for a moment.

"You," he finally said. "If I win, I get you."

"That's ridiculous! You already have me!"

"No," he replied. "I want all of you, willing, a wife in every sense of the word. No escape attempts. No fighting to get out of my bed."

India lowered her head. This was a twist she hadn't considered.

"I haven't fought to get out of your bed in many days," she murmured.

He raised a mocking brow. "I want that a permanent situation. If I win, you give yourself to me. No reservations."

India was silent. He was asking for the final surrender of her pride, the final defeat of the last shreds of her honor.

Christopher smiled. "Not willing to risk it, are you? I thought not." He rose to add another stick to the fire. "Don't feel too bad," he counseled. "I wouldn't have fought you anyway."

India lifted her eyes to his. They were slate-gray with anger.

"And just why won't you fight me, you damned arrogant pirate? Are you afraid you'll lose?"

He returned her gaze mildly. "I won't fight you because you might get hurt. You can't always control what happens when you draw a blade on an opponent."

India sneered. "That's right. Maybe you can't control what happens. Maybe you'll lose. You're afraid you'll lose, and then where would your grand plan of revenge be?"

Christopher's face tensed in the beginnings of anger. "You're out of your mind."

"No, I'm not. I agree to your stakes. I'm willing to take the risk. Why aren't you?"

Christopher looked at her thoughtfully for a few moments. "All right," he finally said. "If that's what you want, I'll agree to fight you."

India was suspicious of the gleam of satisfaction she saw in his eyes. Had she been manipulated while she thought she was doing the manipulating?

"Done, then," India agreed somewhat shakily. "Friday. Three days from now. Early morning."

"As you say."

All traces of anger had left his face, and there was a hint of a smile in his eyes. India had a sinking feeling she'd put herself right where he wanted her.

"Until then, I want to use Helen's lean-to. She won't be using it."

He smiled knowingly. "Don't you trust me, my love?"

"No," she answered tersely. "I want you to stay away from me until this is settled."

"All right," he said. "If that's the way you want it."

He didn't seem very upset. Somehow the whole thing had been too easy. India sat a few moments in silence, thinking. Then she rose and started toward their shelter, intending to remove her belongings to Helen's former bed.

"India." Christopher's voice reached her as she started to leave.

"Yes?" she asked.

"Just don't forget your part of the bargain."

CHAPTER FIFTEEN

Friday came much too soon. India spent all the daylight hours in endless practice. She and Christopher had agreed on a site out of view of the encampment, both admitting that there was no need for witnesses at this contest. Every dawn found her at the chosen site, drilling herself until her whole body ached. She didn't leave until the sun was far down on the horizon. Just drilling wasn't enough, though, and she wished desperately for a practice partner, someone who could really test her skill and help her polish her technique. The thought of asking Seamus to coach her had risen several times, but the memory of the last time she'd seen him with sword in hand was too fresh. Besides, India reasoned, Seamus was much too busy to bother with her problems.

She spent her evenings and nights alone, retiring early and tossing for hours on her pallet. The darkness had never seemed so lonely, and her body ached rebelliously for Christopher's touch. She frequently found herself waking from restless slumber, reaching for a hard, masculine body that wasn't there. Her sleep was plagued by nightmares of the duel between Kennedy and White; only the combatants were now Christopher and herself, battling on blood-soaked sand, surrounded by a ring of leering crewmen. The dreams had two endings, both equally frightening. In one dream Christopher was the victor. His foil would impale her body, filling her not with pain, but with naked, burning desire, radiating from her doomed soul for all to see. Then, as she would sink to the sand, he would laugh. From somewhere the flickering red glow from a fire would outline the planes of his face and transform him into a figure half demon, half human. The last thing she would see as darkness overwhelmed her was the hard and callous rejection in his eyes.

In another dream she was the victor. She would battle in righteous fury, knowing she had to win at any cost, overcome with a euphoric surge of her own prowess and strength. Without knowing quite how, she would score horribly, cutting Christopher from shoulder to groin. He would take a long time to die, standing there with his blood pouring out onto the sand, gazing at her with his face an impassive, unreadable mask. Then she would suddenly realize what she had done. The intoxication of battle gone, she wouldn't understand why she'd done this terrible thing. Great tearing sobs would wrench from her throat as she realized her loss, and when they dragged him away she would scream for them to stop, scream endlessly that she hadn't meant it, begging them to let things be as they were before. The nightmares repeated over and over again, leaving her to wake with a heavily pounding heart and a strangely aching throat.

India woke early on Friday morning. She'd gotten little rest during the night, and a throbbing headache was already beginning behind her eyes. Her body and mind alike felt weighted down with lead as she pulled on Teddy's shirt and breeches. She wanted no skirt to tangle her legs in the upcoming fight. She pushed aside the doorflap and breathed in the cool, salt-scented morning air. The stars were just beginning to fade in the dark gray of the morning sky. She could just barely make out the white splash of the breakers rolling onto the lower beach. The tide would be all the way out in another hour or so. They would have a wide area of firm, wet sand for easy footing.

India walked across the beach with foil in one hand and boots in the other. Her stomach was roiling with nervousness and her bowels threatened to turn to water. She wondered if she should have stopped by the camp kitchen for a piece of bread and cold tea. But that might have made matters worse, she thought. The only remedy for this particular ailment was to put this duel behind her—as the victor, she hoped. She enjoyed the feel of the cool sand squeezing between her toes, and only donned her boots when she reached the rocky headland that hid their private cove from the rest of the island. The climb across the rocks was not a difficult one, and the route was one she'd followed every day for the past two weeks, but this morning her shakiness made her falter and slip several times. Not a good beginning for the morning, she thought ruefully as she finally climbed down onto the beach and gratefully removed her boots to wiggle her toes in the fine sand. By the time she'd reached their designated site, a red glow on the horizon was signaling the imminent appearance of the sun.

She didn't have long to wait. After a few minutes of warmup, taking a few practice swipes at an unresisting palm tree, her concentration was suddenly broken by a deep voice.

"I hope I put up more of a fight than that poor tree!"

India's heart lurched. Christopher stood behind her, stance relaxed, arms folded casually across his broad chest. He was dressed in snugly tailored breeches and a loose linen shirt that was open most of the way down the front. His foil hung from a woven sash that crossed from right shoulder to left hip. All in all, he presented a picture of piratical arrogance that threatened to take India's breath away. She attempted to ignore the nervous pounding of her heart as she fixed him with an irritated frown.

"You needn't sneak up on a person that way, you know!"

He smiled with easy nonchalance. "Just checking out my adversary."

"And?" India inquired archly.

"And I think you could defeat the whole palm population of this island with no problem at all," he observed calmly.

India's eyes narrowed slightly. His mocking tone grated on her raw nerves, and his apparent unconcern over the coming duel annoyed her.

"Perhaps you won't be so cocksure after this fight is over," she shot with an angry glare.

His mouth twitched in amusement. "I have no doubt that one of us will be wiser at the end of this duel."

He drew his foil from its scabbard and tossed the sash

aside. His big hand closed over the hilt in easy familiarity. The mocking light in his eyes left no doubt as to who he believed would learn an unpleasant lesson on this morning.

He gestured with the long, slender sword. "I suggest we move down to the firmer sand, unless, of course, you prefer to flounder here among the driftwood and shells."

India tilted her chin proudly and started for the lower beach.

"Of course," she acknowledged coldly.

Her breath seemed to come faster with every step she took. Her hand was moist and slippery on the hilt of her foil. At last she turned. Christopher stood about six feet away, facing her. The mocking amusement was gone. He stood and looked at her for a moment, noting the rapid pulse evident in the hollow of her throat, the tiny beads of perspiration forming along her upper lip and brow. He smiled slightly, his face unreadable.

"Are you ready to give up this insanity?" he inquired.

India stiffened in proud determination. "Are you afraid to fight me?"

Christopher shook his head in resignation. "You're a fool, my love," he told her softly.

His sword came up in traditional salute. India raised hers in answer. They held for a long moment as their eyes locked. Then the clash of metal on metal signaled the beginning of the contest.

India felt her confidence return as the beginning moves of the duel took on the familiar pattern of her drills with Phillip White. Her first tentative thrusts met with an adequate but somewhat lackluster defense. She easily deflected his first attack with an instinctual grace and quickness that brought a smile of reluctant admiration to Christopher's face.

The first indecisive encounter was over, and they circled each other warily. India's confidence was tempered with caution. She knew she had to end the duel quickly, before his superior strength and stamina could become a deciding factor. She had to use her quicksilver nimbleness to penetrate his defense during the next five minutes or so. The goal of disarming her opponent was considerably more difficult than just drawing blood, India acknowledged to herself, but considering his marginal defense of the first encounter, she should be able to meet the challenge without too much trouble. After all, this was a contest of skill; she had no desire to add injury to insult. A momentary vision of her nightmares flickered distressingly through her mind as she shifted her weight for the next attack.

The momentary break in India's concentration did not escape Christopher's watchful eyes. Just as she positioned herself to attack, his perfectly timed thrust caught her completely off guard. She felt the cold point of steel brush past the skin of her throat without leaving a scratch, then move down to cut the top two button loops of her shirt, leaving it gaping to well below her breasts. She drew back in surprised consternation; then a hot flush of anger and embarrassment spread over her face as she observed his mocking smile. She did not condescend to satisfy him further by attempting to close the front of her blouse. Instead she attacked with fury, catching him somewhat off balance as he admired the view revealed by her unfastened shirt. He recovered quickly, though, and parried her attack with an effortlessness that increased her fury. She broke off, and they circled each other once again, she panting and angry, he with the cool grace of a stalking tiger.

"You sneaky bastard!" she gasped.

He smiled winningly. "Didn't your instructors bother to tell you never to become angry during a duel, India? Destroys your concentration."

She fought for control, for calm, but her blood was pounding in her ears and her breath came in desperate gasps. Icy fingers of fear began to claw at her heart. She had to end this fast. He was much, much more skilled than she had anticipated, and he had deliberately led her on during the first round, feeding her overconfidence until it was too late.

She feinted, hoping to draw him into an ill-timed attack that would leave him open to her next thrust. He didn't rise to the bait. She shifted her attack, trying to get under his defense and disarm him with an upward cut of her foil. He parried easily, and metal rang on metal. With the fury of desperation she allowed her point to dip and her foil to slide off his in an apparently aimless fashion. Then she thrust forward. Surprisingly, her point slipped past his defense. A crimson stain spread over his shirt from shoulder to opposite breast.

India gasped and drew back. What had she done! Visions of her nightmare pounded at her consciousness. But Christopher only raised an eyebrow in acknowledgment.

"You're better than I thought," he said calmly.

"I...I..." India groped for the words to explain that she hadn't intended for this to happen.

"You shouldn't have broken off, you know," he continued in an undisturbed voice. "Once you have an enemy off balance you should always press your advantage."

Before she could reply he attacked, driving her back until she was close to where foamy seawater advanced across the sand. His attack had the fluid grace of a master swordsman, and with sinking heart India realized that up until this point he had simply been playing a game. He wasn't playing around anymore, however, and India fought down the panic that threatened to engulf her. She tried to let her instinct take over her defense, as Phillip had taught her, but her arm was growing tired, and the lightweight foil felt like a lead weight in her hand. Her heart pounded heavily in her breast. She began to actually fear for her life. Had she made him angry enough to kill her?

She retreated steadily toward the water. Then they locked hilt to hilt, and his foot somehow moved to the exact spot to trip her. She hit the sand hard, but managed to hold on to her sword. He made no attempt to press his advantage, as he'd advised her to do earlier. Instead, he laughed at the undignified picture she made sprawled on the sand.

India sputtered in anger. "You cheating son of a bitch!"

"Never fight fair, my love." He chuckled. "Rules don't matter here. The only thing that matters is who wins."

"Unprincipled swine!" India muttered as she rose shakily to her feet. "Let's see how you like a taste of your own medicine!"

She flung a handful of sand full into his face, or at least where his face should have been. He neatly sidestepped.

"Glad to see you're getting into the spirit of things." He smiled.

She attacked with fury, determined to create an opening that would allow her to knock the foil from his hand. His shirt was soaked in the blood from her earlier score, but he seemed not to notice as he easily deflected her attack and pressed home an attack of his own. It was all India could do to keep from going to her knees at the relentlessness of his thrusts. She knew she was leaving him numerous openings. He could have killed or disarmed her several times over, but he continued to beat her back toward the sea. She didn't know how much longer she could stay on her feet.

The shock of cool water swirling around her feet brought India renewed energy. She attempted to change the direction of her retreat, to get back on dry land, but he pressed her even harder. The water was around her ankles now. She felt the sand being sucked from beneath her feet as the water receded. She stumbled, then recovered to meet his next thrust. The water hit her again, foaming to her knees. She lost her balance. A quick twist of Christopher's wrist sent her foil flying from her hand as she stumbled backward, landing hard on her rump in the salty foam. She rose soggily to her knees, her breeches gritty with sand. Then, as she gathered herself to rise to her feet, she felt the cold tip of Christopher's sword at her throat. Her very heartbeat seemed suspended in a cold well of fear as she felt the steel trace a line from her neck down to between her breasts, then back to the soft hollow of her throat.

She raised her eyes to his face and regarded him stonily, determined not to give him the pleasure of seeing her terror. The tip of his foil didn't move for what seemed an eternity of strained silence. Then he spoke in a level, calm voice.

"If you ever again take up a weapon against me, India, you'd best be prepared to kill me with it, or suffer the full consequences of defeat, the same as any man. These weapons are not playthings. They're instruments of murder, and you'd best remember that."

He lowered the sword, then tossed it on the upper beach beside her own. She released her breath at the break in tension and sat back on the sand, heedless of the sandy seawater that foamed around her as the next wave crashed on the beach. The shrill cries of the seabirds, the muted roar of the surf, the sparkle and glare of the early-morning sun on the tropical sea were all very vivid in her mind. Suddenly it was very good to be alive. She looked up. Christopher was standing directly in front of her. The wound she had opened on his chest still oozed droplets of blood. She rose shakily to her feet, grimacing as her sand-filled breeches chafed against her tender skin.

"You ought to do something about that," she said tentatively, gently touching a finger to his chest. She felt uncertain what to do or say. Their relationship had changed somehow. It seemed to her she was facing an imposing stranger, and she was unsure how to act. She had underestimated him this once. Had she underestimated him in other things as well?

"Forget it," he said.

"But you're bleeding."

"It's not serious."

His voice was deep, quiet, somewhat husky. He was obviously not interested in the fact that the front of his shirt was soaked in his own blood.

He took a step closer and, cupping her chin in his hand, lowered his mouth to hers in a gentle kiss. When she stiffened and tried to push him away, he caught her hands and drew them behind his neck. His mouth released hers, and he smiled.

"We had a bargain, remember," he whispered against her ear.

India's heart thudded heavily in her chest. She was confused enough right now without his touch to muddle her mind even further. She struggled halfheartedly to free her hands.

"It's broad daylight, you animal," she protested. "Someone might come."

She was unprepared for this sudden swing from violence to lust.

He nuzzled her ear and neck. "If anyone comes I'll put out their eyes so they can't watch, and maybe cut off their ears, as well."

"You're revolting." She gasped as his lips found a particularly sensitive place at the base of her throat, the spot where the cold steel of his sword had lain only moments earlier. "This is ridiculous. Let me go!"

He smiled and released her wrists. "All right," he said softly.

Somehow her hands stayed locked around the back of his neck. His hands moved to the small of her back and pressed her tightly against him. She could feel the hard swell of his manhood against her belly, and her body responded instinctively to his obvious arousal.

He looked down into her face with mocking eyes. "You're not supposed to resist, you know. Loving wives don't protest their husbands' demands. Or had you forgotten that part of the bargain?"

His mocking tone stung. She longed to draw back her arm and slap him, but knew the consequences of that would be unpleasant in the extreme. And what he said was true, damn him! She'd gambled and lost, and now he expected her to live up to her part of the bargain. She looked up into his dark eyes and saw the fire in their depths. She felt him swell against her stomach as his eyes searched her face. So be it, she thought. It remained to be seen whether he could handle what he had won without being trapped himself. She had underestimated him. Perhaps he had underestimated her, also. This would be a new beginning to their battle.

His big hands brushed past the gaping front of her shirt and gently cupped her breasts, lightly teasing the rosy nipples until they were taut and erect. She relaxed and let her body arch against him, letting the fire that had kindled in her loins wash over her entire body. His mouth came down on hers, insistent, demanding, possessing, while his hands and fingers gently traced the contours of each breast. Her eyes closed, and she allowed herself to be sucked into the maelstrom of his passion. The only focus of her consciousness was his mouth and hands, and the urgent ache that pulsed between her legs. He pushed the shirt from her shoulders and tossed it carelessly away. His mouth trailed a line of fire down her throat and across her breasts. A small whimper of satisfaction escaped her throat as his mouth grasped her taut nipple and sucked. She twined her fingers in his hair and pressed his face closer to her, lost in the sensual pleasure of his caress.

In one deft movement he lowered her gently to the sand. He lay beside her for several aching moments, propped on one elbow, watching the seawater swirl and foam around her white skin. Then his hand moved to unfasten her breeches. She lifted herself to assist him in pulling the soggy, sand-encrusted material over her hips and down her long legs. The breeches were discarded in the same manner as her shirt. Still he made no move to possess her. He simply lay there and let his eyes travel over her body, as though he were truly seeing her for the first time. The seawater ebbed and flowed over her legs, the slight curve of her belly, and the twin mounds of her breasts. The cool, caressing water seemed almost to be an agent of his will, seeking out and touching every secret recess of her body. She lay perfectly still, open to his gaze. His eyes swept over her and seemed to brand her in their passing. His forever, his alone, to use as he chose.

Then it was her turn to watch. He rose and quickly divested himself of shirt and breeches, flinching slightly as his blood-stiffened shirt brushed against the shallow cut on his chest. He stood above her like some bronzed statue, his golden tanned skin burnished by the morning sun, the lean and corded sinews of his powerful body tense with desire. The engorged shaft of his manhood stood as witness to the intensity of his passion.

When he knelt beside her and gently, almost reverently placed a hand between her parted thighs, she arched against him, longing with her entire being to be filled with his throbbing flesh. He smiled as his light caresses brought a frenzy of desire to her eyes.

"Impatient little witch, aren't you?" he teased.

Though his breathing was ragged and his face was taut with passion, he controlled the wild flow of his own desire in order to enjoy the urgent response of her body for a few moments more.

She gasped as he lowered his head and allowed his tongue to seek out the intimate passages where seawater had gone before. She tasted of sea salt and sand . . . and passion. He lifted her buttocks with his hands and probed deeper. A wave washed over them, flowing around them and between them, seeming somehow to weld them into one unit. The salt water stung the open gash in his chest and set it to bleeding again. He ignored it. The urgency of his desire could be denied no longer.

India gave a low cry of satisfaction as he lowered himself between her open thighs and thrust his hot, swollen flesh into her body. She arched herself to take his entire length, then moved her hips in counterpoint to his in a slow, sensuous rhythm as old as life itself. The focus of her entire being was the throbbing shaft that stretched her, filled her, an extension of the man who demanded possession of her spirit as well as her body. The seawater ebbed and flowed around their straining bodies, but seemed only a part of that wave of force that pulsed with the rhythm of his thrusting.

Christopher lifted her head above the wash of the encroaching sea, then suddenly shifted and, without breaking the union of their bodies, brought her over on top of him with her legs astraddle his hips. He held her firmly with his hands as he arched against her, groaning with satisfaction as his flesh drove even more deeply into hers. As the water swirled around them again, he half sat up, twining her legs around his hips and gathering her close to him with powerful arms. She pressed her face tightly against his chest, feeling as if her flesh had truly melded with his. The thunder of the incoming tide became one with the thunder of her own pulse, and he continued to move within her, lifting her higher and higher on a wave of ecstasy that finally crested and broke as he brought his own explosive release with a final powerful thrust. They were one with the sea and with each other, melting into perfect harmony of elemental male and female. Life given and taken, then given back again.

It was a few minutes before their slow descent to earth gave them back their separate identities. They lay on their sides in the sand, heedless of the warm tropical seawater washing over their bodies, leaving gobbets of foam and seaweed on their skin. India was still cradled in Christopher's arms, her face pressed tightly against his chest, her legs intertwined with his. She could hear the steady beat of his heart and the even rhythm of his breathing. Lying motionless in his arms, she savored these few moments of intimacy before the real world could again intrude on their fragile peace. She thought of her promise not to leave, or even try to leave—part of her bargain in the duel. So now her honor bade her leave him and her good faith required her to stay. And in these past few moments she had come to realize that even if she escaped him she could never escape his hold on her heart. She was bound to him by far more than just her marriage vows. Never could she belong to another man. She shut her eyes and pressed tighter against the length of his body, shutting out her confusing and uncertain vision of the future. But the peace was broken. He stirred, and she found herself on her back, looking up into his boyishly grinning face. He looked extremely pleased with himself, India noted. She smiled back, unable to resist his contagious pleasure.

"You're going to sunburn some very tender places if you don't get dressed," he teased.

"Oh, I don't know about that," she countered saucily. "I'm not the one with my bare backside pointed toward the sun!"

"Point well taken!" he agreed, and rolled on his back, bringing her over on top of him. "Now who has her backside to the sun?"

She screeched in protest and scrambled off him just in time to avoid a playful swat on the behind, then danced lightly away from him when he attempted to tackle her at knee level.

"Your backside isn't the only thing that's going to get

burned if you insist on going around like that!'' she pointed out cheerfully.

Neatly sidestepping another attempt to grab her, she started toward deeper water to wash off the accumulated sand and the streaks of his blood on her skin. She turned to look back at him, appreciating the imposing figure he made, standing there with legs apart and arms folded across his chest, naked as the day he was born and not at all self-conscious. He really looked more like a bronzed god than a devil, India noted, wondering that she hadn't noticed it before. A lithe, powerful, black-haired, dark-eyed Neptune risen from the depths. Only the crimson streak across his chest marred the picture. A mischievous gleam lit her eyes as she splashed water over her shoulders and between her legs. It would be nice to prolong this interlude, to gather a few pleasant memories, however wicked, to carry into her uncertain future. She glanced over her shoulder and smiled impishly at the tall figure on the beach, then stretched sensuously in mute invitation as the next wave foamed about her thighs, arching her back and letting the sun and warm breeze play tantalizingly over her skin. Then she ran at the next breaker and dove cleanly into its smooth green swell, swimming with strong strokes to the calmer water beyond the surf.

Momentarily a hand closed about her ankle and pulled her down. She struggled briefly, then surfaced, sputtering, to find herself pinioned against Christopher's strong body. He pushed her back to arm's length and held her there, taking in every detail of her face as though he would memorize it. The impish smile still played around her lips as she watched him watching her.

"Sea witch!" he accused with a smile.

He moved his hands to her waist and pulled her forward to meet his kiss. Her heart pounded with familiar urgency as she willingly opened her mouth to his invading tongue and wrapped her legs sensuously around his hips. His hands moved from her waist to her firm buttocks, lightly brushing the soft down between her legs, pressing her against him with a renewed urgency that matched her own.

India allowed herself to melt against him for a moment, enjoying the feel of his hard, lean body pressing into hers. Then with an agile wiggle and twist, she escaped the circle of his arms and laughingly pushed away, deluging him with a spray of seawater in the process. A sputtering string of oaths followed her as she swam toward shore, putting a safe distance between them before she rolled playfully onto her back and waved mischievously. But Christopher was no longer where she'd left him.

"Yeek!" India squeaked in surprise as strong fingers closed around her ankle and pulled her down into the green water. She bobbed to the surface, only to be caught and held in the viselike grip of his legs as he dragged her under again. It was the first time she'd ever been kissed under water. It was a strange but oddly sensual feeling, floating with him in the eerie green, enveloped by the undulating veil of her hair, his powerful thighs clamped securely around her legs and his mouth plundering hers. In the magic of the moment she hardly gave a thought to the need for air. But that need finally drove them to the surface, gasping for breath as they bobbed in the gentle swells.

Christopher shook the water from his hair and eyes and gave her a lecherous grin. Droplets of water clung to his eyelashes and beard. The planes of his face were softened with humor, and the hard gleam of desire in his eyes was tempered by a twinkle of merriment. India hardly recognized her grim opponent of an hour past.

"Through playing mermaid?" he asked.

She smiled sweetly and kicked away. This time he was too fast for her, though, and she found herself locked against him in a hungry embrace. The rock-hard swelling pressed against her thigh left no doubt as to his intentions, and she willingly, achingly opened her legs to receive him. She relaxed against his hard body, letting him support her in the water as he prepared to take her. It was then that she looked over his shoulder.

"Oh, damn! Oh, noooooo!"

A mountain of green towered above them, then crested and crashed down, hitting them with a wall of foam and water that bowled them over like two flimsy pieces of straw. Over and over they rolled, a tangle of arms and legs, painfully scraping the sand, gasping for every available breath. After what seemed an eternity of painful buffeting, the water receded, leaving them on the sand like two pieces of limp seaweed.

Christopher was the first to move, rising to his hands and knees and shaking the water from his eyes. India lay on her back gasping for breath. Then she laughed. She continued to laugh until Christopher loomed above her, pinning her shoulders to the sand with his hands.

"Damn you, woman!" he groaned. "You are a witch! You summon the very sea to frustrate me!"

She laughed again, clear peals of merriment that lifted on the morning air to join the crash of surf and raucous cries of seabirds. She couldn't stop.

Christopher shook his head, half amused and half resigned. Her laughter finally faded away to a mischievous smile.

"You have to admit it was funny," she prodded.

He glared. "Not to me it wasn't!"

"Oh, come now!" she chided lightly. "You didn't lose anything but a little pride. And maybe a little skin here and there," she conceded.

He cursed under his breath.

Her smile became the least bit tantalizing. "It isn't as if you can't take up where you left off."

He looked at her in amazement. "Your expectations are limitless, little one. You demand the impossible."

She teasingly trailed a finger along the inside of his naked thigh, eliciting a response that showed her expectations were really not all that impossible.

A smile twitched the corners of his mouth. He tried very hard to maintain a grim face.

"You little hellion," he accused. "Do you think I have all day to lie around here, servicing your insatiable needs?"

India blushed slightly, but that was indeed a very good idea. She noted with satisfaction the growing evidence of his desire.

"All day?" She raised one brow mockingly. "Do you think you're up to it?"

He groaned at her blatant pun. "Shameless hussy!" He lowered himself onto her body and grinned knowingly at her response. Then he rose to his knees. "Then again," he mused aloud, "you were the one who pointed out the disadvantages of having my bare backside to the sun."

India found it difficult not to squirm in frustration. He was being very difficult, the cad! He was determined to make her play the hand to the finish.

"Well, there is the shade, you know," she said impatiently.

He laughed, an uninhibited bark of delight. "You are an absolute jewel."

He stooped and picked her up with no effort at all. So much for his being tired, India thought, and nuzzled her face into his neck as he carried her toward the trees and laid her down on the cool grass.

"All day, hmm?" His eyes traveled the length of her waiting body. She smiled.

"All day it is, then," he concluded.

CHAPTER SIXTEEN

The three ships of Christopher Barnett's "squadron," as the men were beginning to call it, lay at anchor, fully rigged, hulls scraped and sealed, brass polished, and decks scoured to pristine whiteness with holystone. All was ready for departure. In a few days' time, they would sail into New Providence. There they would sell the *Navarre* and the *Lady Mary*, reprovision the *Black Falcon*, and, most important, search for the elusive John Thomas. When that business was concluded they would be off again for British waters.

India watched the ships float at anchor and glumly thought of the gray and misty chill of England in the winter, as it would be when they returned. The tropical fantasy was coming to an end. Soon they would leave these warm, clear waters for the cold, slatey seas around the British Isles, where Christopher would once again have his Scottish hideaway castle with its parade of mistresses, and she would have to face the real world once again.

Not today, though. Today was a celebration. Christopher had bowed to the wishes of the crew and agreed that a day of sport was well deserved. The ships' boats were being readied for the short trip to a neighboring isle, somewhat larger than the one they were on, which old Tom Smith swore was inhabited by a sizable herd of wild pigs. He'd seen them three years ago on a trip to this same area on a British man-of-war. If the *Black Falcon*'s hunting parties returned with a pig or two, Timothy Hawkins had promised to show them how to smoke the meat as his great-grandfather and fellow *boucaniers* had done. India had her doubts about Hawkins's talents as a cook, but she was excited by the idea of the hunt.

At first Christopher had been reluctant to let her participate.

"I thought you didn't like violence," he protested.

"This isn't the same thing," she told him confidently.

"Tell that to the pigs."

"I can shoot," she insisted. "I'm a good shot. I've known how to handle a gun since I was thirteen."

He wasn't impressed. "If you shoot as well as you fence, the pig population will be in very little danger." He laughed.

Her chin came up in indignation. "I can fence as well as any man here!" she protested with a slight blush. "Except you . . . and Seamus."

He grinned at her irritation. "Fortunate for me that you're no better than you are," he conceded, gingerly stretching the stiffened muscles of his chest where she'd cut him three days before. "All right, you can go. But you have to stay close to me, and follow orders. I'll have none of your stubbornness. You do what I say when I tell you to."

"I'm not stubborn," she denied mildly.

"Neither is a mule!"

She made a face at him, then smiled brightly. "May I have a pistol?"

Christopher laughed. "How would I guard my back, with you carrying a loaded pistol?"

India opened her mouth to protest, but he cut her short.

"No pistol," he repeated.

"You don't really think I'd shoot you!" India said.

"Wouldn't you?" he replied with a mocking look.

India wasn't sure if he were joking or serious.

"Of course I wouldn't!" she protested finally. "Besides, I promised I wouldn't try to escape. Remember?"

He grinned lustily. "How could I forget?"

"Well, then?" she said expectantly.

"No pistol," he repeated.

India glared. "You don't trust me!"

"Damn right I don't!" he admitted. "I haven't survived this long by trusting sneaky slant-eyed females who have very good reasons for wanting me dead!" He softened his words with a smile.

India sputtered indignantly, "Who are you calling sneaky, you . . ."

Christopher promptly cut her off with a kiss. In a few moments her protest faded and her arms wound around his neck. Presently he smiled down at her.

"Be good about this, now," he warned as the light of battle came back into her eyes, "or I'll leave you here with Seamus and Helen. And I assure you, with what those two individuals have on their minds, they won't be very good company!"

"You should talk!" she commented with a mischievously cocked brow.

"Yes, well . . ." He released her with reluctance. "If we don't get going, I'm going to have you down on that pallet, and the hunt will leave without us."

"Wait!" she said as he shoved two pistols in his belt and started toward the boats. "I have to change clothes! Where are those damn breeches?" she muttered, searching with impatient exasperation through his sea chest.

He turned and regarded her with an affection that he would not have allowed to show had she been looking at him.

"Wear the dress," he said finally.

"What?" She looked up in surprise. "I can't wear a dress where we're going!"

"Yes, you can. Besides, I don't want the men looking at your backside instead of looking for pigs. You have no idea what effect those breeches produce."

He smiled and pulled her out of the shelter and toward the boats. She looked up at him in irritation.

"You're impossible, do you know that, Christopher Barnett-Armstrong!"

"Try to put up with me," he advised.

"Do I have a choice?"

He grinned. "As a matter of fact, you don't."

The trip to the larger island took over an hour. By the time the hunt was organized and on its way, the morning was well advanced. Another couple of hours creeping through the hot and often prickly tangle of island vegetation finally resulted in Tom Smith's locating a trail—a pig trail, he swore—where the dense jungle had been trampled by the repeated passage of animals. The little party of hunters carefully concealed themselves downwind in a nearby thicket with hopeful expectations of the imminent arrival of their intended prey.

"Are you sure this is the accepted method of hunting wild pigs?" India asked Christopher skeptically as she swatted a bloated mosquito from her arm.

It had been several hours since she began to regret coming on this ludicrous adventure. To think she could have been lounging in the hot springs, or sunning on the beach, instead of sitting in a hot jungle infested with an army of creepy crawlies, waiting for some unfortunate pig to come along and offer himself for slaughter. She grimaced with disgust and boredom.

Christopher gave her a crooked grin. "How should I know? I've never hunted pigs before." He shrugged broad shoulders. "Old Tom claims he knows what he's doing."

"Old Tom has eaten one too many green bananas, as far as I'm concerned!" India said irritably.

She could feel sweat trickling down her scalp and between her breasts. Her bodice stuck to her skin in soggy discomfort. She fanned her skirt, surreptitiously lifting it to admit more air, when she noted with horror the many-legged green insect that was crawling over her bare foot.

"Yeek!" She squealed in disgust as she gingerly brushed the thing from her skin.

Young Teddy Sykes, the only other of their party who was in plain view, fixed her with an impatient glare.

"Be quiet, Miss India!" he admonished in a loud whisper. "You're going to scare them pigs!"

"What pigs?" she snorted in disbelief, and made a face at Teddy. "I'm beginning to think there's nothing on this island but bugs!"

Lounging easily against a vine-tangled tree stump, Christopher fixed them both with what he hoped was a reproachful scowl. He tried hard to conceal the smile that lurked at the corners of his mouth.

"Have a little patience, India," he advised. "You're the one who wanted to come on this hunt."

Teddy snickered.

"And you show a little more respect, youngster, or I'll have you hanging from the bowsprit and painting the *Falcon*'s figurehead for the next week!"

The snickering stopped abruptly. "Aye, aye, Cap'n," he acknowledged reluctantly, and turned his attention back to watching the trail.

India slumped down in resigned boredom. Every now and then her eyes strayed to her husband relaxing against the stump, idly whittling on a soft piece of wood to pass the time. His gleaming white shirt was open to the waist, revealing the hard, lean muscle and dark curling hair of his chest. Two loaded pistols were stuck in his wide belt. He looked every bit the dashing pirate of popular romance, India thought, with his darkly handsome, chiseled features and the slightly sinister look about his eyes and mouth. No, maybe not sinister, she decided on continued examination, just hard, and maybe cynical. And sometimes, rarely, that face was open, and boyish, and relaxed, and the hard, cynical mask disappeared.

The thick, close-trimmed beard didn't help much, India thought. It was attractive enough, and it fit his face rather well, she admitted, but it did manage to give him a more piratical look. How would he look if he were clean-shaven? she wondered. He had a strong, well-defined chin that would do well without the beard. He probably would appear considerably more civilized, more gentlemanly, without it. He certainly wouldn't look like the Devil anymore. India smiled secretly to herself, imagining him with horns, tail, and pitchfork. Christopher looked up and caught her eye.

"Amusing yourself?" he asked, smiling as he noticed her startled blush.

She sniffed indignantly and looked away. It was infuriating the way he always seemed to know what she was thinking!

He turned his eyes toward Teddy. "No signs yet, lad?" he inquired.

"No, sir."

Even the boy's voice held a hint of impatience now.

India sighed and glanced toward Christopher. "How can you look so cool and unperturbed when I feel like a wet rag?" she asked in irritation.

He grinned. "You do look rather like a bedraggled kitten," he observed.

India fixed him with a disgusted glare. "You needn't look so jolly about it."

He got up and brushed the wet leaves and dirt from his breeches.

"Why don't we go look for a nice cool swimming hole in that little stream we passed on our way here," he suggested, offering India a hand up. "I could stand to cool off some myself."

India noted a suspiciously warm glow in his eyes as he pulled her to her feet. She suspected he was looking to cool the heat in his loins rather than the heat in his body. At the moment she felt anything but sensuous, with her wilted dress clinging damply to her body and her skin prickling from the heat and what seemed to be at least a hundred insect bites. But she had to admit that a cool swim in a shady pool, with his hard, lean torso sliding through the water next to her, just might change her mind. In any case, it was certainly more appealing than staying here and being eaten alive by mosquitoes.

"Aw, Cap'n," Teddy complained. "Aren't you going to stay and shoot pigs?"

"I'll let you shoot the pigs, Teddy," Christopher granted generously. "Tell the others we've gone for a walk and we'll meet them at the boats."

India could imagine the smirks on the crew's faces when they heard that!

They walked in amiable silence beside the stream for a while, his hand occasionally taking hers to help her over a difficult spot. In one place the bank had caved in and made their way impassable, so they waded through the shallow water until a clear path appeared once more. The cool water felt heavenly as it flowed around her feet and ankles, and India was sorely tempted to simply sit down, clothes and all, and let the stream wash away all the itchiness and grime and sweat from her skin.

India finally broke the silence. "Didn't you say there was a village somewhere on this island?"

"Mmm," Christopher replied absently, his eyes fixed with interest on the length of shapely leg revealed by her hiked-up skirt.

"Won't they have some objection to our barging in here and shooting their pigs?" she persisted.

"The pigs aren't theirs," he replied finally. "They're wild. The villagers will probably be grateful if we rid the island of a few. They make a damn nuisance of themselves rooting around the women's gardens. Besides, these people are fishermen. They don't care much for hunting, and a wild pig can be a mean son of a bitch when he's cornered, or even when he's not. I'm sure the villagers would just as soon see the entire herd cleaned out."

"You seem to know quite a bit about this village," India commented.

"I paid it a visit about two weeks ago," Christopher admitted. Then he smiled teasingly. "You didn't even know I was gone. I think I'm insulted."

India arched her brows haughtily. "You expect me to follow your every movement like a lovesick schoolgirl?"

His smile was enigmatic. "Might be nice at that," he observed.

"The needs of your vanity are boundless," she scolded with a grimace. "But seriously, why did you visit the village?"

"Just doing a bit of bartering, really," he explained. "It's actually a pretty civilized place. There are a few whites who live there, and a Spanish missionary who's determined to rescue all the natives from the pit of hell."

He shot her a disturbingly devilish smile that set her vivid imagination to spinning again. Damn him anyway!

"Well," she finally said. "As long as they don't come after us with spears for shooting—or maybe I should say trying to shoot—their pigs."

It did not occur to India until much later that all during the traumatic hours that followed, not once did she think of the village as a route of escape from her captivity.

They finally found a pool that was deep enough for swimming. It was perfect, set in a shady, secluded nook of the jungle with a merrily splashing waterfall at one end and a natural dam of rocks at the other. In several places trees overhung the pool so closely that their verdant branches almost dipped into the still green water. The air was scented with exotic perfume from a riot of large red blossoms that hung in clusters on one bank. All in all, it was the perfect picture of paradise.

"It seems we're not the only ones who find this spot attractive," Christopher noted.

"What do you mean?"

He indicated a set of tracks at his feet.

"Oh, my!" India exclaimed. "What made those?"

"I can't tell for sure." Christopher knelt to examine the

tracks in more detail. ''They're a bit muddled, but there are quite a few different sorts of prints around. I would guess that this is a pretty popular watering hole for the local animal population.''

India looked into the surrounding wall of vegetation somewhat hesitantly. ''Perhaps we shouldn't stay,'' she suggested.

Christopher didn't look concerned, however.

''I doubt anything is going to venture near while we're around.''

The gleam in his eye showed he definitely had something else on his mind. He gently brushed a damp tendril of hair from her cheek, then allowed his hand to trail down her throat and lightly brush the tip of her breast.

''Didn't I hear you say something about taking a swim?'' he asked.

''Lecher!'' she laughed. ''What if some hairy creature is out there watching us right now?''

He smiled tolerantly and allowed his hand to drift inside the loose neck of her bodice.

''Hairy creatures don't exist in paradise, little one.''

Unfortunately, Christopher was wrong.

India pulled away from him, but smiled invitingly. ''A swim would feel good, wouldn't it?''

She turned her back and began to unfasten the buttons of her bodice. His touch had quickened her pulse to a rapid tattoo, as it always did, but there was no sense in feeding his already overconfident masculine vanity. Behind her she heard his belt and pistols fall to the ground, followed momentarily by the splash of his long body cutting the calm surface of the pool. She smiled in anticipation.

Then the nightmare began. A slight rustling drew India's eyes to the dense underbrush next to the waterfall. An ugly snout pushed its way through the vegetation, followed closely by two small, evilly glittering eyes that regarded her with a businesslike air of menace.

For the first few short moments, India wasn't really concerned. How ironic that a wild pig should show up here while the hunting party waited so patiently back at the trail, she thought. Then she took in the pig's size, the razor-edged teeth, the yellowish tusks curving around the moist, ugly snout. Suddenly she was very frightened, so frightened she merely stood there in wide-eyed paralysis as the pig lowered its massive head and started to squeal in fury.

"Christopher!" she screamed.

The pig squealed again and angrily ripped the ground in front of it.

Christopher was lazing on the far side of the pool when India's scream brought him to full alertness. He took in the situation immediately, cursing under his breath as he realized that both the pig and India were between him and his pistols, and that the pig was about to charge. There was no time to swim across to his weapons before India would be downed by the huge boar. She was standing like a terrified statue, unable to move, barely able to breathe as she looked at the apparition of horror that was preparing to sweep her away.

Christopher lunged out of the pool, waving his arms to attract the pig's attention.

"Move, India!" he commanded. "My pistols, dammit! Move, girl!"

India ran for the weapons, jerked out of her trance by the sound of his voice. The boar was confused, now presented with two targets that were moving in opposite directions. The man was dancing around in a purposeful attempt to infuriate him, though, and the pig's attention finally riveted on him. He charged.

India clawed at the pistols, which were wrapped in Christopher's belt on a branch above her head. He'd put them out of her reach, damn him! Damn him to hell! She screeched in frustration and jumped at the belt, missing by a wide margin.

Without weapons, Christopher stood helpless before the boar's assault. His face was stony calm, however, as the hideous animal thundered toward him, and when the pig reached the object of its fury, he was no longer there. Sharp tusks tore at the air where Christopher had stood.

Christopher timed his jump perfectly, and the moment the

boar was past him, he ran for India and the pistols. The infuriated pig turned, squealed in fury, and without hesitation charged again. Christopher turned to look back on the onrushing horror. His foot struck a protruding root. He stumbled and went down, landing hard on his back. The boar was on him before he could move to defend himself. He slashed and tore with teeth, tusks, and sharp hooves at the creature who had dared to provoke his rage. Christopher grunted in agony as he tried to push the boar away, but the animal was too powerful. In only seconds, his victim was silent and unresisting.

"No!" India screamed, and screamed again.

It seemed to her that her screams reverberated around the jungle clearing, sounding as though they came from far away, issued from some throat other than her own. She waved her arms frantically, trying to lure the pig's attention to her, away from Christopher, who lay in a pool of crimson, too silent, too still.

"God! Oh, God! Dammit. Damn! Damn! Damn!"

She looked at the scene with senses clamoring in near-hysteria. Finally the pig turned its attention to her, its tusks and snout covered with gore. India sobbed. Her knees were turning to water. She backed a step, then two. The boar followed her movements with glittering eyes. Then she stumbled backward, gasping as she connected painfully with a rotten branch hidden under the mulch of dead leaves and loose soil.

"Stupid, useless little bitch!" she denounced herself. "Why didn't you see this before it was too late!"

She grabbed the branch and rose slowly, watching the boar warily. The pig grunted, then began to paw at the ground with his sharp hooves. India turned quickly, hit at Christopher's belt with the branch, and grabbed the first pistol that clattered to the ground.

"Please, God," she sobbed, "let it be loaded and primed."

It was. The boar charged, squealing. India pulled back the hammer, aimed, and fired. Acrid smoke stung her eyes, and the explosion deafened her ears. The boar hesitated, stumbled, then screamed in fury and started toward her again. India picked up the second pistol. She prayed as she pulled back the hammer, prayed as she never had before in her young life. Another explosion. More smoke. The boar shrieked, stumbled, then crashed to the ground and lay twitching. India whimpered, still holding the now useless pistol pointed at the pig's head. Tears streamed down her face, and her white-knuckled hand tightened convulsively on the grip of the gun.

She gave the still-twitching boar a wide berth as she ran to Christopher and knelt beside the silent body. Ground and body alike were stained with bright crimson, and his left side from upper ribs to hip was such a mess she couldn't even guess at the extent of his injuries.

"Christopher!" she sobbed. "Oh, God, Christopher, wake up!"

She gently brushed the dirt and blood from his face, hardly daring to look at the mess below his shoulders. He stirred slightly at her touch. His eyelids flickered open, closed, then opened again as his eyes focused on her face.

"Christopher!" she breathed. "Oh, my God, you're alive. No! Don't move! Please don't try to move!"

His face twisted in agony as he attempted to raise a hand to touch her face. The effort left him panting. Finally, a tense grimace that might have been a smile crossed his face.

"I guess I should have given you a pistol, after all," he whispered hoarsely.

India tried to control an overpowering urge to blubber hysterically, to give way to the panic that was flooding through her mind. What could she do? How could she get help? My God, what was she going to do?

"Christopher, listen to me!" she cried. "You can't die, do you hear me? No! Don't go back to sleep! You listen to me. Don't you dare die and leave me alone! I'm not through with you yet, do you hear!" She sobbed and brushed her finger gently along the line of his cheek. "Besides, you damned, arrogant, stupid pirate. I love you."

His eyes were fastened steadily on her face, but she didn't know if he could hear her.

"But you know that, don't you," she accused softly.

"You overbearing, cocksure, overconfident animal. You've known it from the very first."

A genuine smile was on his face as he slipped back into unconsciousness. India found his pulse, weak, barely discernible. His breathing was shallow and uneven.

"Damn you, you bastard!" she cried. "You can't do this to me! Don't leave me!" Her cry seemed to echo around the clearing, or maybe it just reverberated through her soul. "Don't leave me!"

CHAPTER SEVENTEEN

The search party from the *Black Falcon*, consisting of Ian McCann, John Daughtery, Tom Smith, and Timothy Hawkins, did not find Christopher and India until the golden orb of the sun was well down toward the horizon. The pig hunt had been successful, finally, and two pigs had been shot on the trail where the hunters waited. India and Christopher hadn't been missed until after the unfortunate pigs had been bled, cleaned, and loaded in the boat for the trip back to camp. Then their absence began to draw notice. A search party was hastily formed, but was at a loss where to start looking. Teddy didn't remember where the pair had gone, just that they were supposed to meet the rest of the hunters at the boats. Only by luck did the searchers blunder within the sound of India's hoarse cries for help.

"Oh, thank God!" India sobbed as the four men burst into the clearing.

India's eyes widened in alarm at the scene before him. Christopher lay as still as death, his chest tightly wrapped in multiple layers of bandages that were soaked through with blood. Even his breeches, which India had managed to pull on him to ward off the ravening insects, were beginning to show a crimson stain where the bandages could not soak up the seeping blood. His face was white, his breathing shallow. All in all, Ian thought, Christopher looked like a man who was spending his last hour this side of the gates of hell.

"Ian? . . ."

The question choked up in India's throat. She looked as pale as Christopher, her face tearstained, hollow-eyed, and blood-smeared. The tatters of her skirt and petticoat bore evidence to the source of Christopher's bandages, but she seemed totally unaware of the immodest state of her attire as she knelt beside the captain and looked at Ian, half pleading, half afraid. Ian wished he could tell her what she obviously wanted to hear, but he couldn't.

"I don't know, lass," the burly Scotsman said gently after kneeling by the captain and quickly assessing the damage to flesh and bone. He looked at Christopher again, noting that at least most of the bleeding seemed to have been stopped by the tightly wrapped bandages. "Tell me what happened."

India gave him a brief account of the boar's attack. Ian went over to look at the pig, then looked at India with new respect.

"That's not a bad job you did there, lass," he told her solemnly. "He's a monster. That was good shooting to bring him down in two shots."

India blinked away the tears that were welling up in her already red eyes. She didn't want to think of what would have happened had the pig not died on her second shot. She didn't want to think at all, in fact. She just wanted Ian to tell her that Christopher would be all right. Then she wanted to go to sleep and not awaken until everything and everyone was back to normal.

"Let's get a stretcher made, lads," Ian said.

Then he turned to face the miserable questioning of India's eyes. He draped what he hoped was a fatherly arm across her slender shoulders. The little lass had pulled at his heartstrings since the day she came on board, Ian had to admit, and now he felt a surge of protectiveness overcome his usually crusty soul. He might well have lost his closest friend today, but he knew that this diminutive maid whom Christopher had alternately frightened, manhandled, ignored, and, whether or not the captain would admit it, loved, would feel the loss even deeper than he would.

"You never can tell, India lass," Ian lied gently. "He just might make it. Christopher's a tough one, tough as they come. Why, he's too contrary to die until he's damn good and ready."

The men politely averted their eyes from India's display of leg as they loaded their captain onto the hastily constructed stretcher of vines strung between two straight branches. Several warning glances from the quartermaster ensured their continued discretion. As they exited the clearing, Tom Smith and Timothy Hawkins slung the pig, legs tied together, over a pole and hefted the pole onto their shoulders.

"No sense in wasting good pig meat!" Timothy replied to India's questioning look.

The sail back to the encampment seemed to India to take an eternity. Christopher lay unmoving, his head pillowed on her lap, covered by an old canvas to protect him from the sea's spray. India made no attempt to hide her concern. At this point, she didn't care what the crewmen knew about her feelings for Christopher, or her lack of virtue, character, pride, or any other trait that she must have abandoned when she gave her heart and soul to her enemy.

She could have escaped while Christopher lay unconscious in the jungle clearing. She could have left him and made her way to the island village, but she had stayed. Finally, she'd made the choice between Christopher and her conscience. No longer could she consider herself a victim with no opportunity to foil her captor's plans. But somehow that didn't matter anymore. Nothing mattered anymore except Christopher's continued stay in the land of the living.

The next few days passed for India in a haze of exhaustion and anxiety. Christopher was carried aboard the *Black Falcon* as soon as they reached the encampment. While the crewmen on shore carried on with the feast and celebration, butchering the three wild pigs that had been shot, roasting one on a spit and smoking the rest for use in the weeks to come, India and Ian gently unwrapped Christopher from the encasing strips of India's skirts. They cleaned and dressed his torn flesh, then rewrapped him in clean bandages provided by Cook, who generally doubled as ship's surgeon. Only once did India leave his side, to rush abovedeck to the railing as her empty stomach tried to convulse its way out of her exhausted body. The sight of Christopher's torn side and the smell of warm blood had been finally too much. For hours she had sat in that clearing, steeling herself against the heat, the fear, the scents of blood and death. Now, safe at last, she allowed herself the luxury of succumbing to her nausea.

She was at the *Falcon*'s rail when Helen came on board.

"India!" Helen said gently. "Oh, my Lord, India, I just now heard."

India composed her face as she looked at her friend, trying with difficulty to hold back the sobs that were clawing at her throat. But Helen quickly moved forward and took her in comforting, plump arms. The dam burst then, and India's tears gushed forth on Helen's shoulder. She allowed her grief to pour out for several minutes in the comforting circle of Helen's soft embrace. Then with an effort to pull herself together, she backed away.

"Bah! Enough of this!" she said. "I have to get back."

It was then that she noticed Seamus standing somewhat awkwardly in the background. She felt a brief stab of embarrassment at having so completely abandoned her composure in front of him, then admitted to herself it didn't really matter anymore.

"My Lord, India, look at you!" gasped Helen as she took in her friend's wild hair, hollow eyes, torn skirt, and hands, arms, and legs smeared with blood. "You are an absolute fright!" Helen continued. "Why, when Christopher wakes up and sees you, he'll pass out from horror!"

"Oh, what does it matter what I look like!" India frowned impatiently. "I've got to go below. I've been gone too long as it is. Christopher might . . . might . . ."

Seamus stepped forward and laid a brotherly hand on her shoulder.

"Ian won't let anything happen without calling you, India," he said with gruff sympathy. "You listen to Helen, girl, and go down to our cabin to clean up. We cleaned out your lean-to and brought your sea chest on board with us, so you won't have to leave to go on shore if you don't want to. You'll do Christopher a lot more good if you wash up and get some food in your stomach. You get sick, and we'll have to take care of you as well as him."

India reluctantly let Helen pull her down to the cabin she shared with Seamus, now that they were married. The sick feeling returned as India sponged the dark red smears from her skin, but she took deep breaths and willed it to pass. No more weakness, she told herself. No more tears, no more squeamishness. There'll be plenty of time for crying if he dies, but until then she had to be strong. She resolutely donned a clean dress, brushed and tied back her hair, and choked down the cold meat and biscuits that Helen had brought her from camp. The food renewed her strength and steeled her determination. Christopher wouldn't die. She wouldn't let him. If he thought he could steal her heart and then leave her alone to face the world without him, well, he had better think again. She'd hound him clear to the gates of hell, if necessary, and pull him back with her. There was no way she was going to let him leave her alone, she resolved angrily.

When she stepped back into their cabin, Ian greeted her changed appearance with a smile.

"Ah, lassie," he commented. "I'm glad to see you looking more yourself. For a wee minute there I was afraid I'd be stuck with two patients. That I was!"

India pulled the wing-back chair to the bed and sat down. Christopher was so pale, so still, that her heart caught painfully in her throat. His skin seemed almost translucent as it stretched tautly over the strong bone structure of his face. She shot Ian a frightened look.

"Don't you be looking like that, now," the big Scotsman said, moving to her side. "I've seen him survive worse, indeed I have. It's cleaner than I thought at first. Deep, but cleaner than you'd expect, considering the beastie that did it to him. Knowing Christopher, he's likely to come out of this with nothing worse than a few more scars to show what a tough son of a bitch he is, begging your pardon, lass.''

"Really, Ian?" India asked in a small voice.

He attempted a hearty reply. "Really." But one way or the other, we should know for certain in the next few days.'' He looked at the dark circles that ringed India's blue eyes. "Why don't you get some sleep, lass," he suggested. "Go on to Helen's cabin. I'll call you if there's any change.''

India's tired face hardened with determination.

"No," she answered. "I'm not going to leave him, Ian.''

Ian read the unshakable resolve in her features and didn't attempt to argue.

"Well, then," he decided, "maybe I'll go scrounge something from the galley that we can force down the lad's throat.''

In the next few days the shore camp was dismantled and the ships were readied to sail. The *Black Falcon* came alive with the sound of renewed activity, but India didn't notice the shouts, clanks, thuds, and rattles that accompanied the unloading and stowing of the myriad items that had been transferred to the beach and now were being secured back on board. She never left the cabin and rarely left her perch in the chair beside the bed. Ian came in frequently to help change bandages and clean the wounds. Helen brought her food and made sure she ate, brought her water to wash, and occasionally kept her company in her lonely vigil. Cook came in his capacity of ship's surgeon to look at the torn flesh and cluck disconsolately. But in the final analysis, none of them could do much of anything but watch as Christopher battled for his life.

The first morning, India roused from a restless doze in her chair to be met by Christopher's too-bright eyes staring blankly at her face. His skin was flushed and hot to her touch. He muttered several unintelligible phrases as she bent over him, sponging the fine sheen of sweat from his face.

For the rest of the day he tossed restlessly in the bed,

sometimes requiring India's entire strength to prevent him from trying to get to his feet. He stared at her unseeingly, groaning out words and sentences that had no meaning and twisting his face in horror as he battled the fever-bred apparitions that were assaulting him. As his delirium grew worse, he lashed out wildly when she attempted to soothe him and wipe the sweat from his face and shoulders. Once, grasping her by the throat with surprising strength, he shouted obscenities and tightened his fingers until she nearly blacked out. Then he lost interest and began muttering inanities in a childishly petulant voice. Finally India sent for Ian to help hold him, fearing the struggles would break open his wounds and renew the bleeding.

"Maybe we should tie him down," she suggested doubt-fully when Christopher finally drifted into a calmer state.

Ian considered for a moment. With Christopher's frantic strength, even ropes might not hold him unless they were tightened to the point where they might do more harm than good. It would be far better if he and the lass could hold him down and keep him from hurting himself, if possible.

"No," he finally told India. "This shouldn't last much longer. That fever of his will either burn itself out or burn him out."

Ian was too tired to be tactful, and the past two days had increased drastically his respect for India's strength. Small the lass might be, but she had more spirit than most men Ian had met.

"Next time he starts thrashing around like that, you call for me before he gives you another black eye," Ian instruct-ed with mock severity. He regarded the swelling around India's left eye with chagrin. "He can't be too bad if he's still got enough strength to give both of us a battle like that," he finally assured her.

The next day Christopher was easier to handle, but India was approaching the limit of her strength. Anxiety and lack of sleep were taking their toll, in spite of her determination. Helen's efforts to get her to rest in her cabin while she and Ian kept watch were to no avail. She could sleep just as well right here in her chair, India claimed. Besides, she had a gnawing, illogical fear that the minute she left the cabin Christopher would be gone. It seemed almost as if her presence by his side could prevent his spirit from slipping its bonds.

On the third day Christopher's thrashings ceased, for the most part. But his delirium didn't. Most of his ravings were meaningless to India, but some gave her a glimpse into his soul that afforded her some small measure of understanding of this enigmatic man she loved. He wasn't made completely of iron, after all, India decided as he relived the pain of loss at his father's and brother's deaths, and then the disillusionment, fear, and anger of his trial at Blenheim. He cursed her father in terms that made India's face turn scarlet even in the privacy of the cabin. The look in his unseeing eyes made India understand the depth of his hatred for the man he thought had falsely condemned him and then stolen his family lands.

Christopher was innocent, then, she thought with a lift of her heart. He was innocent of spying on that day long ago, but surely he was wrong about her father. It had to have been an innocent mistake on her father's part, India was sure—a mistake that was disastrous for Christopher Armstrong, Earl of Woodsford, but not a deliberate plot. That would be murder, and India knew her father would never stoop to such a heinous crime, no matter what the motivation. Sir William Carey was a hard man, but nevertheless a man who valued honor above all else.

Late the third day India was jerked from an exhausted trance in her chair by the sound of her name. She sat up groggily and heard it again.

"India," Christopher whispered hoarsely.

"Christopher!" India cried happily, her eyes flying open when she realized he'd called her name. "I'm here, right here!" she assured him, leaning over the bed.

But his eyes looked through her, still unseeing. He didn't respond at all to the gentle touch of her hand on his arm.

"India!" he said again in a clearer voice.

"Christopher," she whispered, although she realized now that he was not awake, as she'd thought at first, but still caught in some hallucination. She longed to shake him and bring some look of recognition into his eyes. She wasn't at all sure she wanted to hear any delirium-induced truths concerning his feelings for her.

"Witch!" he whispered, and his eyes clouded with pain. Then they grew softer. "Little witch, you've won. Damn you for making me love you."

He was silent for a moment, and India sat back in the chair hardly able to breathe. He loved her! He said he loved her! All this time she'd been wallowing in self-pity, fiercely guarding her vulnerable heart from his view, and he'd been fighting and losing a similar battle of his own. It seemed too incredible to be true, that this iron man of violence and cynicism could have softened enough to love the daughter of the man who'd robbed him of his inheritance, condemned him to death, and forced him into a lawless life of uncertainty. Just as incredible, she thought then, that she should come to love the man who'd kidnapped and raped her, the man who with one hand stripped her of all honor and pride and with the other hand taught her about a kind of love she'd never known existed.

"India," Christopher's voice whispered again.

India tried to see some sign of lucidity in those dark eyes, but they seemed to look through her at another India entirely. What was he seeing that made his face so dark with regret? India wondered.

"My life," he muttered on. "My love, forgive. Too late . . . I can't forget . . . forgive . . . India . . ."

His voice drifted into a faint mumbling, then stopped. His eyes closed and his breathing slowed to a peaceful, even rate. Some of the flushed tightness of the past several days had left his face.

India laid a hand gently on his cheek. His skin was cool and dry. The fever, as Ian had predicted, had burned itself out. He was resting for the first time since the attack in a natural, healing sleep.

India was too exhausted to feel anything but a dull glow of relief. The tightness in her chest that had constricted her heart since that terrible day of the hunt began to release, and the tense energy that had sustained her began to dissipate. She was too tired, even, to wonder overmuch about those last incoherent mutterings that Christopher had addressed to the India of his fevered visions. She allowed her head to sink, for just a very few seconds she told herself, to rest comfortably on the uninjured side of Christopher's broad chest. She closed her eyes and listened to his even, deep breathing and the strong beat of his heart. Before those few seconds had passed, India had joined him in the peaceful haven of deep, dreamless slumber.

When she woke some hours later she was stretched out full length on the bed beside Christopher, who was still resting in deep sleep. She quietly swung her legs over the side of the bed, careful not to wake him, then brushed the wrinkles out of her skirts, ran a brush through her tangled hair, and stepped out into the darkness of the corridor. For the first time she noticed the motion of the deck beneath her feet and the slight heel of the ship. In the agony of the last three days she hadn't even noticed the ship getting under way.

At the top of the companionway the fresh night breeze ruffled through her loose hair and seemed to clear some of the cobwebs from her brain. She stood there a moment and took in the familiar beauty of the scene: the swaying masts, the occasional green glow of a foaming swell of the black expanse of sea, and the billowing sails, invisible except as a black curtain blotting out the bright stars of the tropical sky.

For a short moment India thought she was alone on deck, but then she spied the tall, lean shape of Seamus Kennedy standing watch on the quarterdeck. He waved when she saw him, and she realized he'd been watching her from the moment she'd stepped out of the hatch.

"Ho, there!" he greeted her. "I see you've decided to rejoin the world of the living."

India smiled tentatively. She still felt a trifle uncertain around this man who had cut down Phillip White with such ruthlessness. But his smile was friendly, and his eyes held only a faint sparkle of brotherly affection.

"Christopher is sleeping, so I thought I'd come up for some fresh air," she explained.

"Aye," he replied with a grin. "Ian told me our good captain appears to be over the worst. Said you were both getting some well-earned rest."

India glanced up at the sky. From the position of the stars she could see that the night was well advanced.

"I slept for a long time," she finally commented. "I'd no idea it was so late." She paused as a tempting idea entered her head.

"Are you the only one on deck?" she asked curiously.

"Me and the helmsman over there," he replied. "Most of the other lads are below. Not much to do on a calm night like this."

"Is there anyone aloft?"

"Not until morning," he answered.

India cleared her throat in slight embarrassment.

"I would dearly love a bath right now, Seamus. I haven't had any chance to really wash since we brought Christopher back. And if I invade the galley at this time of night for wash water, Cook will have my hide."

Seamus laughed. "Aye, that he would!"

"If I went to the stern and used the seawater pump, do you suppose you could . . . uh . . . well . . . make sure no one wanders down that way?" Her eyes pleaded. A good scrub would be like heaven!

Seamus chuckled. "Aye, I suppose I could do that for you, little India. Just don't take too long. The dawn will be peeking over the horizon in not too long a time. If you don't want to be caught by the morning watch in your . . . uh . . . natural state, you'd better jump to it."

"Oh, thank you, Seamus!" She flashed him a grateful smile and fled.

The pleasantly cool seawater was like a balm to India's senses. Blanketed by the dark, warm, tropical night, she stripped off her musty clothes and scrubbed until her skin tingled. Then she directed the hose over her head, lathering her hair and hoping that she could scrounge at least enough fresh water from the galley to rinse the salt water from the long, thick tresses. She set to work again on her skin, enjoying the feel of the pleasantly cool seawater as it washed away some of the tension of the last few days. She let her mind drift where it would, feeling refreshed, safe, and at last willing to explore some of the startling revelations of the last few days.

Christopher loved her. She reveled in the knowledge, letting it wash through her, exhilarating her mind and filling her heart. True, he'd not been in his right mind when he said it, but it must be true nonetheless. It explained so much—his inconsistent behavior, his moods of alternating passion and disdain, the strange tenderness that she could feel in his action even when his words were harsh and hurtful. How he must have fought it, falling for the daughter of a sworn enemy. He must still be fighting it, she mused, and perhaps he would never admit to any tender feelings he harbored for her. But it was a comfort, just the same, to know for sure that his heart was not after all truly made of iron, that he really did regard her with something more than just physical passion.

India sighed and wrapped herself in a towel. She wondered if she could scamper down the hatch and get below without showing an indecent amount of skin to either Seamus or the helmsman.

Back in their cabin after a successful dash across the starlit deck, India pulled on the modest nightdress she'd made herself and climbed under the blankets beside the still-sleeping Christopher. She felt as though she could sleep around the clock and still be exhausted when she woke up. In the darkness she could barely make out Christopher's face, but she could discern enough to appreciate how much younger he appeared with the lines and tightness gone from his features. He doesn't look nearly so fierce, India thought fondly, when his face isn't masking that all too human heart of his. She indulged herself and brushed her hand gently along his lean cheek. He stirred restlessly; his big hand rose from his side and fumbled for hers. Having found and captured it, he settled back into restful slumber with her hand trapped in his like a delicate bird in a steel cage. She smiled and snuggled down beside him. She could really see no happy ending to this strange adventure. At the moment the barriers between them seemed insurmountable, in spite of their hidden affection for each other. But India fully intended to enjoy being with him while she could. A dark premonition told her that upon their return to Britain she would pay dearly for the happiness she was stealing now, but that couldn't be helped. If there were dark times ahead, she might as well store up happy memories against future loneliness.

CHAPTER EIGHTEEN

Christopher was on his feet by the time the *Black Falcon* reached New Providence three days later. Much against the advice of Ian, Seamus, and Cook, who'd taken much more interest in his captain's injury since it became apparent he would survive, he stood on the quarterdeck, once more in command of the squadron of ships as they approached the notorious pirate island. His bandage-swathed chest was hidden by a clean white shirt, and he compensated for the occasional unsteadiness of his stance by a tight grip on the quarterdeck railing.

India stood with Ian at the rail and looked curiously at the low green smear on the horizon that boasted such an unsavory reputation. They were sailing toward the harbor at Nassau, Ian told her, which was the headquarters of the pirate colony.

"It's no place for a lady such as yourself, lassie," Ian admonished. "Christopher would likely skin you alive if he knew you were entertaining notions of going ashore."

"Oh, but Ian," India pleaded. "After all the stories I've heard about this place, I'd really like to see it for myself!"

She knew Christopher would squash her ambitions, so she had attempted to cajole the big Scotsman instead.

Ian shook his great head. "Even if I took you with me, Christopher would just send you back. Then he'd stretch my hide along a yard to use like a topsail. He may not be up to his full strength yet, but where you're concerned he's got eyes like a hawk."

India made a face, but Ian continued.

"And you should be glad he's looking out for you, little lassie," he scolded in as near to a fatherly tone as Ian could manage. "You wouldna' like what you see ashore, and that I'm sure of. There's some females in that town, but they're only there to get on their backs for the men. Begging your pardon for some blunt speech, lass, but that's God's own truth. And those pirates dinna know the difference between a class lady and a trollop. You'd find yourself in trouble before you went ten steps up the beach."

"Bah!" India thought Ian was exaggerating, but she didn't feel like arguing any further. It was obvious Ian could not be swayed.

The green smear on the horizon had resolved itself into two separate islands. The larger rose from the sea in low, jungle-covered bluffs behind a white-and-pink coral beach. A much smaller, lower island lay off the main one. It was this combination, Ian explained, that made New Providence such an ideal pirate lair. The low island formed an ideal harbor that had two ways in and out, while the bluffs of the larger island gave the pirates a sweeping view of the horizon. A well-armed fortress on the outer island commanded the only channel deep enough for a warship, thus protecting the harbor from attack by the agents of law and order.

India sniffed at the breeze with some distaste as they drew nearer.

"What is that ghastly smell?" She turned to Ian and wrinkled her pert nose in disgust.

Ian laughed. "Aye, well, as I said, these are rough sorts

that live here, and they dinna pay much mind to cleanliness. You'll get used to it after a while.''

India couldn't imagine getting used to anything so vile. As a stronger breeze wafted out from the still-hidden harbor, India thought she would gag. She couldn't imagine any human habitation producing an odor quite so foul.

But when they rounded the point past the frowning pirate fortress and sailed slowly into the harbor, the sight that met her eyes made her begin to doubt that Ian had been exaggerating the bestiality of the island's population. Well over a hundred ships of all types were anchored in a harbor of generous proportions, and a good part of the crewmen of those ships seemed to be sprawled on the filthy beach, heedless of the early-morning sun, in varying states of sleep, drunkenness, and several different stages of copulation with the female population. The noisome odor emanated from a polluted stream emptying into the harbor. The outgoing tide swept all manner of garbage, sewage, and a few bloated bodies, at least one of which was recognizably human, into the sea. India choked with horror, fighting back a sudden urge to retch.

She jumped slightly as a pair of firm hands came down on her shoulders, then slipped down to rest lightly on her small waist.

''Oh, Lord, Christopher, it's you!'' India gasped as she turned in his arms. ''You gave me such a start! Must you always sneak up on a person like that? I swear sometimes I think you're worse than that sneak-thief cat of Teddy's!''

Christopher raised a brow. ''And who else do you think would be coming up behind to grab you like that?'' he teased.

''You're the only one I know who has such wretched manners!''

She tried to make a face, but smiled in spite of herself, made slightly giddy by the nearness of his lean, muscular body and reveling in the look of warm affection in his eyes. She finally extricated herself from his grip, embarrassed at the amused looks they were receiving from the crew.

''I don't believe people can actually live like this,'' she

finally commented, gesturing to the tent town crowded between bluffs and beach, flapping in the trade winds like so much dirty linen. The sounds of the day were beginning as a combination of raucous screaming and laughter erupted from what India assumed to be a tavern, one of the few permanent structures in the settlement. The sound of a dog fight drifted out over the harbor, followed by the angry screech of a woman and a frightened yipping as one of the dogs departed the scene. India leaned against the rail with a depressed little sigh, then glanced down at the water sliding slowly past the ship. With a loud thump, something bloated and unidentifiable bumped the hull.

"Uck!" India screwed up her face and looked quickly away.

Christopher couldn't hold back a chuckle. "Why don't you go below," he suggested, slipping an arm around her and urging her toward the hatch. "We'll only be here a day or so, and you needn't come up at all if you don't want to. Helen can keep you company while we're gone."

India turned in surprise. "Gone? Christopher, you're not going ashore, are you? Can't you let someone else tend to your business here? You should still be in bed, you know!"

Christopher smiled, but his face was determined. "Much as I hate to turn down an invitation into your bed"—he grinned at the exasperation that crossed her face—"this is business I must see to myself."

India was tempted to stamp her foot at his foolishness.

"You're not nearly strong enough to go traipsing off into such a den of scoundrels!" she insisted vehemently. "If you must go, at least wait a few more days until you have your strength back," she pleaded.

Christopher was not accustomed to having a woman fuss over him, and he was showing signs of impatience.

"Don't be ridiculous," he tried to reassure her. "I'm as strong as an ox!"

"Oh, you great bloody fool!" she returned. "You've got the brains of an ox! What if someone should jump you?"

"Why should anyone jump me?" he demanded.

"If the stories Ian and John Daughtery have told me about this hellhole are true, someone might jump you just for a lark! Why, the tales I've heard about these men, they make you look virtuous!"

Christopher laughed and placed a light kiss on top of her raven-haired head.

"I never thought to hear you admit I'm not the vilest, bloodthirstiest villain you've ever met!"

India gave into temptation and stamped her little foot in a fit of temper.

"Idiot!" she cried. "You've not listened to a thing I've said!"

Christopher smiled tolerantly. "Yes I have, little one," he told her. "And I appreciate your concern. But I can take care of myself, so just stop trying to mother me."

"I'm not trying to mother you!" she replied hotly. "I'm just trying to . . . oh, forget it! There's nothing in this world stupider than some big, bloody man who thinks he's tough!"

With that parting shot she turned and huffed down the companionway.

Christopher grinned as he followed India's stiff-backed descent belowdeck. Ian lolled nearby and watched the scene with a twinkle of amusement in his eyes.

Christopher cocked an eyebrow at his friend. "She loves me," he grinned with a shrug of his broad shoulders.

"It would appear so," Ian agreed. "I'd not try to convince her of that right now, though." Ian paused thoughtfully. "The lassie does have a point, you know. You're not up to snuff, and this is a mite dangerous port. It might be best if you just let Seamus and me take care of what needs taking care of here."

The relaxed humor left Christopher's face as his mouth tightened into a grim line. "No, Ian. Seamus can take care of disposing of the *Navarre* and the *Lady Mary*, and Daughtery can see to the reprovisioning, but you and I are going hunting for John Thomas, and when we find him I want to be there to wring some answers from his miserable throat. That's a job I won't leave to someone else. Not even you, my friend."

"Well," Ian said mildly, "you might be able to wring more effectively if you waited a while to get your strength back, at least a few days. We're in no hurry to get back to merry old England, are we? We can stay here for as long as you need."

"I've waited years for this." Christopher frowned. "Another few days shouldn't make any difference, but it does."

"Aye, aye, Captain." Ian waved a half-mocking, half-respectful salute. "I'll tell Daughtery to have the boat ready as soon as we drop anchor. I can see you're not wanting to waste any time."

A short time later India sat on her bed and listened to the rattle of the hawser as the anchor was dropped. She was furious that Christopher would place himself in such a precarious position so soon after rising from what very well could have been his deathbed. She was also a bit piqued that, while he felt free to take ridiculous risks with his own person, she must stay pampered and hidden away from anything that hinted of danger or excitement. He treated her like some fragile female who would get the vapors at the first sign of unpleasantness. He should know by now, India thought peevishly, that she was no languishing, delicate creature who must be cosseted and protected like an innocent child. She could damn well take care of herself—well, in most situations she could, at least.

After an hour had passed, the noise level on the ship reduced to lonely silence. Most of the crew had gone hunting for pleasure and excitement on shore, and only a skeleton crew was left to guard the ship. They lolled at their posts, waiting impatiently to be relieved so that they, too, could take their turn exploiting the vices of this notorious community.

India sat in sulky boredom. Shortly after the anchor was dropped Helen stopped in to keep her company. India was in no mood for idle girlish chitchat, however, and when Helen failed to sympathize with her indignation at being left behind, India's mood only grew darker.

"Sometimes I think you're still a child, India," Helen scoffed. "When are you going to grow up and realize that there are just some things in this world that a decent woman doesn't do?''

''It's not fair!'' India insisted.

''I don't understand why you would want to see such a wretched place anyway. You're just asking for trouble.''

''So it's a wretched place. I still would like to see for myself rather than just hear everyone else's stories. Are you going to be content all your life to sit around listening to other people's tales of adventure and excitement and never experience any of your own?''

''I've had enough adventure in the last few months to last me a lifetime,'' Helen insisted. ''Besides, I don't regard an island full of cutthroats and filthy whores as an adventure—rather as a hellhole to be avoided at all costs.'' Helen looked at her friend thoughtfully. ''Sometimes I think you fight against all these conventions just to prove you're independent and don't need anybody or anything. You did that back at Hillcrest, too. I think maybe you should start facing the realities of life, India Catherine.''

Helen's voice had taken on the slightly patronizing tone she had used at Hillcrest when arguing with India on the necessity of ladylike behavior. Suddenly India found she'd lost the desire for any more of this conversation.

''You don't know what you're talking about.'' India frowned ominously. ''I can stand on my own two feet. I don't need to prove that to anyone, much less myself!''

Helen wisely took her leave before India's temper got any hotter than it already was. But India was not left alone for long with her brooding thoughts. A few minutes after Helen's departure, Teddy's tousled head peeped around the door with a mischievous grin plastered on his face.

''Ho, Miss India,'' he greeted her cheerfully. ''Were you stranded here, too?''

India made a disgruntled reply, but, ignoring her frown, Teddy sauntered through the door and plunked his gangly frame down on the wing-back chair.

''Quiet around here with most everybody gone,'' he observed.

India sighed and resigned herself to the cabin boy's company.

"Where's that cat of yours?" she asked with a bit of annoyance in her voice. "Don't tell me he's gone ashore, too!"

"Naw," Teddy replied good-naturedly. "He's asleep. He don't like to move around much anymore. His stomach drags the deck."

India chuckled in spite of herself. "If you didn't feed him so many biscuits, maybe he wouldn't have that problem!"

"If I didn't feed him biscuits," Teddy commented, "he wouldn't follow me around no more. Then who'd keep me company?"

Not very many minutes passed before India felt her spirits lifting as she listened to Teddy's ebullient chatter. It was impossible to maintain a long face, India realized, in this barrage of the boy's contagious good humor.

"Kinda lonely around here," he finally concluded. "If you wasn't a girl we could hop a boat and mess around on shore a bit. Too bad," Teddy mused thoughtfully. "But if any of those fellows caught sight of you, well, there's no telling what sort of trouble we'd be in for."

A wayward idea formed in India's head.

"I could wear your breeches!" she suggested.

Teddy crowed. "Begging your pardon, Miss India, but that won't do us no good. A fellow surely can tell you're a female when you're wearing those breeches!"

India frowned and thought some more. She was reluctant to give up on a chance to explore the notorious pirate colony, but she admitted the danger of walking around the tent town as a woman.

"We'll just have to find me some loose clothes that make me look like a boy," India declared. "What about Timothy Hawkins?" she asked. "He's big enough to wear a tent!"

Teddy laughed. "Ol' Hawkins don't have anything clean enough to scrub the deck with, much less wear." He thought a minute, then his puckish face lit up with glee. "What about the cap'n?" he chortled.

"Christopher?" India's eyes grew wide at the audacity of the idea. "Wear Christopher's clothes?"

"Sure." Teddy shrugged casually. "Why not? He and Mr. McCann won't be back 'til late tonight. He'll never know you took 'em. The cap'n's big enough to make two of you, Miss India. No one'll ever know you're a female in his clothes!"

India smiled. Why not, indeed! The idea was beginning to appeal to her.

"Do you think we could get a boat?" India asked, her voice tinged with excitement.

"Well . . ." Teddy hesitated thoughtfully. "We'd have to get past Mr. Daughtery. He's on watch now. He wouldn't give one to me, that's for sure. But he might give one to you, if you told him the cap'n knows and says it's all right. He wouldn't expect a lady to lie."

India was taken aback for a moment with that problem. She was a rotten fibber, but it was worth a try. The worst that could happen would be Daughtery's keeping them on the ship, then reporting their attempt to Christopher when he returned. That might be awkward, but she supposed it was worth the risk.

She turned to Teddy with a mischievous grin. "You go round up a couple of knives while I change clothes. And a pistol, if you can manage it. We don't want to go over there unarmed."

Teddy gave an uninhibited whoop of joy. "That's the spirit, Miss India! We'll have us a time, we will!"

When Teddy had made his usual ungraceful exit, India opened Christopher's sea chest and started to assemble an outfit that would hide every trace of her femininity and still be inconspicuous enough not to attract undue attention. Instead of breeches, she chose the lightweight sailcloth trousers and shirt that many sailors favored for these tropical climes. Sturdy sandals and a scarf from her own meager wardrobe completed the essentials, and another scarf belted loosely around the waist kept the voluminous shirt, which was made to be comfortably loose even on Christopher's broad chest, from looking completely outrageous.

India surveyed herself critically in the small mirror and decided that the disguise would be adequate. A bit of dirt smeared here and there would help the overall effect. Teddy confirmed her opinion when he returned with the two knives he'd scrounged from one of the arms lockers.

"Oooooh." He giggled. "You look like an undergrowed runt, just like me!"

India wasn't positive her vanity appreciated his frank assessment.

"Well, it'll have to do," she said, tucking the last stray wisp of dark, curling hair beneath the scarf.

Teddy handed her the knives, one of which was little more than a whittling knife. The other was a long, wicked-looking dagger with a carved and ornamented hilt.

"That's all I could find," Teddy explained apologetically. "Those fellows cleaned out all the good stuff to take ashore."

India smiled reassuringly. "We'll just avoid any trouble that comes our way," she reasoned. "I don't know how to use one of these things anyway. So here, you take the big one."

Teddy beamed as India handed him the dagger. "I'm good in a fight, Miss India," he bragged. "You don't need to worry as long as I'm with you!"

India didn't comment, but made a mental note to keep Teddy from trying to prove his prowess while they were in the pirate colony.

The next obstacle was hurdled with more ease than India expected. John Daughtery the boatswain hardly blinked an eye when India told him she wanted a boat to go ashore. For a moment she thought she detected a gleam of cunning in his eye as he asked how long she would be gone, but who could tell what thoughts were going on behind that hideously scarred face. Poor man, she thought with a shudder. No one could be as evil as he looked.

They finally decided that she and Teddy would be rowed ashore by one of the crew on duty, then return when the same crewman came to pick up the next duty shift from the beach some three hours hence. Teddy was about to voice a loud objection to any limit on their time, but India silenced him with a glare. Now that she was getting a closer look at the squalid tent town, she was beginning to have second thoughts about the wisdom of this escapade. Maybe Helen was right and she was simply behaving like a stupid, rebellious child.

The short trip across the harbor to the beach landing was an assault on both the ears and the nose. The noxious fumes that rose from the sewage-laden water came and went with the breeze, but the noise from the crowded colony was constant. India wondered how even hardened pirates and whores could get used to such cacophony.

As she and Teddy stepped out onto the beach she began to regret ever having left the safe haven of the ship. This place wasn't as dangerous, India decided, as it was just plain offensive. Not ten feet away from where they landed, a man eyed them with mild curiosity while he squatted on the beach answering nature's call. A little farther along a haggish bawd moaned and heaved while an obscenely fat man, his breeches down around his knees, pumped furiously between her legs. India's stomach churned as she turned quickly away.

"Come on, Miss India!" Teddy's eyes grew wide as he realized he shouldn't be calling her name. "Oops! Sorry!" He grimaced. "Come on, let's see what's in the town! Isn't this terrific!"

"Terrific." India grimaced with notable lack of enthusiasm.

They proceeded into the town, if town it could be called. Most of the tents were simply spars driven into the sandy ground and covered with sailcloth that flapped constantly in the trade winds. They followed a confusing network of dirt pathways that wound among the tents, gingerly avoiding the filth that was strewn everywhere. It seemed only the most fastidious of the town's residents even bothered with taking their garbage down to the water's edge. Most of the ragged dwellings were surrounded by heaps of refuse rotting in the tropical heat. Young children and dogs played and fought among the odorous piles. Gangs of older brats, too old for toddling and too young to ship out as cabin boys, raced between the canvas hovels wreaking as much havoc and mischief as they could manage. Hawkers and whores were everywhere, assiduously plying their wares, shouting over the unending noise and confusion of crying babies, screeching women, and runny-nosed filthy brats yelling and laughing at the top of their voices. Somehow, India thought with disgust as she stepped aside to avoid a drunk staggering from the door of a tavern, this was not what she had pictured as a notorious pirate lair.

Long before their allotted time was up, India was wondering how to persuade Teddy to return to the ship. She had decided she'd seen enough of this vermin's den when all hell seemed to break loose on the beach. The level of noise coming from the waterfront doubled as India strained her eyes in the direction of the commotion. Finally she saw that two boats laden with the crew of a newly arrived ship had rowed ashore. The men were garbed outrageously in silks, satins, and plumes. With whoops, hollers, and pistol shots into the air, they headed raucously for the nearest tavern, pulling a couple of bored-looking whores along with them.

When the din and confusion of the new arrivals had finally calmed somewhat, India touched Teddy on the arm.

"I think maybe we better get back to the ship, Teddy," she suggested. "This place is getting a bit wild for us, I think."

"Oh, come on!" Teddy whined. "There's lots more to see yet. Look at that fellow over there with the parrot! I bet he talks."

"Who"—India sniffed—"the parrot or the pirate?"

"Come on, India," Teddy pouted. "Don't give out yet. Besides, the boat won't pick us up for another hour or so. We have to stay longer!"

India stepped around a prostrate, loudly snoring figure whose reek of alcohol could be detected ten feet away.

Teddy stopped suddenly and strained to see through the crowd around him.

"Isn't that Mr. Daughtery?" He pointed to three men deep in conversation by the door of a tavern a short distance from where they were standing.

India looked in the direction Teddy was pointing.

"Yes, it is," she agreed. It was impossible to mistake those twisted features even at this distance. "I wonder what he's doing here. I thought he was on watch until this evening."

Teddy shrugged and made to move on, but India continued to watch the little group. For some unexplainable reason, an uneasy knot was growing in the pit of her stomach. She thought she saw Daughtery gesture in their direction several times, and those were certainly a couple of unsavory-looking characters the boatswain was talking to. But then, there weren't very many gentlemanly types on this island!

Suddenly Daughtery nodded, and he definitely pointed right at her. The little knot of men broke up, and the two unsavory types were headed in their direction!

"Teddy!" India grabbed her young companion by the arm. "Teddy, I don't feel good about this!"

"What?"

Teddy was engrossed in the nearby scene of a lad about his age bargaining for the services of an even younger whore.

"Those men that were talking to Daughtery are coming straight for us!"

Teddy seemed unconcerned. "Maybe he wants to let us know the boat's leaving early."

"I don't think so!" India quavered.

She tightened her grip on his arm and pulled him down the pathway, remembering the gleam of cunning she'd imagined in Daughtery's eye when they asked to go ashore. Perhaps it hadn't been just her imagination! But what possible motive could the boatswain have for wishing harm to either herself or Teddy?

She darted between tents and in and out of the crowd

trying to lose their pursuers. Time seemed to slow to a crawl, and her feet felt weighted, as though she were fleeing through a nightmare. Teddy ran breathlessly beside her.

"You really think they're chasing us?" he gasped between breaths.

"I really think they are!" she panted.

"Why?"

"I don't know. I'm not going to stop and ask them, though!"

She pulled Teddy abruptly into a narrow alleyway between two taverns and flattened with him against the rough plank wall. Several minutes passed without a sign of either pursuer. The bedlam continued as before. After long moments, their breathing slowed to normal. Teddy looked at her with wide eyes.

"Do you think we lost 'em?" he whispered.

"Don't know for sure," she answered quietly. "Maybe."

They stepped cautiously out into the glaring sunlight. The men were nowhere in sight. Teddy shifted uneasily, his former confidence gone from his stance.

"Maybe we should try to find the cap'n or Mr. Kennedy," he suggested.

"Maybe," India agreed hesitantly.

She didn't know which would be worse, running into their unknown pursuers again or having to face Christopher's wrath when he saw them in the tent town.

"Let's make our way back to the beach," she decided. "It's almost time for the boat anyway."

They turned down the crowded path that led most directly to the waterfront. Everything was back to normal. Maybe the whole pursuit had been a figment of her overactive imagination, India began to think. Then a gasp from Teddy made her heart jump. He was no longer beside her. She turned to see a meaty fist on its way to her face. Then the world exploded into pain and blackness.

CHAPTER NINETEEN

Christopher was tired and frustrated when he returned with Ian to the ship in the small hours of the morning. They had searched through half the squalid taverns and tents of New Providence without finding their quarry, or even finding anyone who had seen a man answering to John Thomas's description. Christopher was beginning to fear he was following a false lead. If Thomas was shipping in and out of Nassau on a pirate vessel, as their informant in Portsmouth had said, surely someone in the colony would recognize his description. He would give the search one more day, Christopher decided, and then have a little talk with Daughtery about that cousin of his who had so willingly supplied them with information.

His thoughts were cut off by a hail from Seamus Kennedy, standing on the quarterdeck with Timothy Hawkins.

"What is it, Seamus?" Christopher replied, and climbed wearily to the quarterdeck to stand beside his two officers. He may have overestimated his strength a bit, Christopher admitted reluctantly. His only wish right now was to go below, climb into bed beside India, and sleep as long as he could possibly get away with.

"India's gone," Seamus said tersely.

All thoughts of sleep fled Christopher's mind.

"What do you mean, gone?" he snapped. "I left specific orders for her not to be allowed ashore! How could she possibly be gone?"

Seamus's face was grim. "Helen went to her cabin to eat supper, and she wasn't there. She looked all over the ship and couldn't find her. Said India had been talking earlier about wanting to go ashore."

"Did anyone see her go ashore?" Christopher asked tersely.

Ian stumped up to the group with a worried frown on his face.

"Jack Smythe just told me he rowed both India and Teddy over to the town on Mr. Daughtery's orders, sometime in the early afternoon. They were supposed to return in the boat with the second shift, he says, but they weren't there when he went to pick them up."

Christopher took on a hard-eyed, grim-faced look that Seamus knew only too well. Several somebodies were going to be mighty sorry, he guessed, before this was over.

"Where is Mr. Daughtery?" Christopher asked in a measured tone.

"Smythe claims he rowed ashore about an hour after India and the boy went over," Ian told him. "He hasna' come back yet. Do you want Smythe up here so you can question him?"

Ian thought of young Smythe's timorous reluctance to face his captain with the bad news. With good reason, he admitted, noting the icy blackness of Christopher's eyes. He wasn't so happy about facing him either.

"No." Christopher frowned. "Let him be for now."

A tense silence reigned as Christopher glared across the harbor to the dark colony. Then he startled all present by bringing his fist down sharply and loudly against the rail.

"Damn! Of all the stupid, idiotic . . . Hawkins! Ready a boat to go ashore." He swept the men beside him with a fierce glance. "Ian, Seamus. . . . Are you with me?"

"Aye," both men answered at once.

Ice-cold anger was gripping Christopher's soul as he loaded his pistol and secured knife and cutlass at his hip. The pieces of this puzzle didn't fit. He'd guessed that the little minx would try to go ashore, so he left specific orders with the officer of the watch, Mr. Daughtery, that she wasn't even to be allowed abovedeck. He hadn't wanted any of those horny ruffians on neighboring ships to see her and decide she was worth going after. There was no reason for Mr. Daughtery to disobey his orders, but he had, and evidently with some purpose in mind, as he'd followed closely behind India. But whatever the intent of Daughtery's actions, India and Teddy had not shown up for their ride back to the ship. That was ominous, indeed. Even India would have more sense than to stay in Nassau after dark.

Christopher felt like a lead weight had been placed on his heart. He fought down the desperate visions that clamored at his brain—India laughing, India defiant, India loving and passionate, India lying like a broken doll on a New Providence refuse heap. The pain of losing her now, before he'd won her, before he'd shown her how much he loved her, would be more than he could bear.

He welcomed the rush of deadly anger that wiped away his panic. India and Teddy might well be beyond help; it had been at least seven hours since they had failed to appear at the appointed spot on the beach. But they had to be found, and if harm had come to them they had to be avenged. Then he could think of his loss, but not yet. The hours ahead would require a cool head and a strong arm. There was bloody work to be done before he could allow himself the luxury of succumbing to his anger and fear—and his grief. There was no hint of the former weariness in Christopher's movements as he climbed down into the boat and gave the order to push off.

India clawed her way to consciousness through a sea of pain and confusion. Her head throbbed mightily, and every muscle in her body ached. Unfamiliar voices and snatches of rough laughter filtered in and out of her awareness. Memory returned, then faded again, confusing her with visions of running, hiding, then running again. Where was she, anyway? And what was she doing here?

The pieces of memory gradually fell into place—the two men, the pursuit, the dark alley where she and Teddy thought they'd shaken off their followers. They'd been caught, obviously. Those men must have known all the time they were hiding in the alley. She remembered seeing Teddy snatched, then being hit with what felt like an anvil. The question was . . . why? What would anyone want with her and Teddy? Especially John Daughtery the boatswain, if he indeed was the one behind this craziness.

One of the voices came closer, a young voice, nasal and whining.

"She's still out," it said.

India schooled herself to limp relaxation as a boot prodded ungently at her ribs.

"Maybe you hit her too hard, Jake," the whining voice said again.

"Nah," came Jake's deep, gruff reply. "She'll wake up. Just keep your breeches on, laddie."

"Maybe we just ought to go ahead and kill her now," an older, nervous voice suggested. "Ol' John'll be mighty displeased if we don't do the job right. Going to be dawn in another couple of hours."

"We can't kill her afore we all has some fun, Cory," the young voice asserted. "Dead meat's hardly worth the effort."

"Shouldn't let you on her anyway," the voice named Jake growled. "You let that kid get away. Could've got us all into bad trouble, that!"

"The little bugger pulled a knife on me!" the first voice complained. "Besides, he just ran like a dog with its tail afire. He's not going to make no trouble!"

India's spirits lifted with a spark of hope. Teddy had escaped, bless him. Maybe rescue was on the way! Then again, how would Teddy know where to find her, if he had escaped and run before they reached wherever they were now? Her spirits sank again. It looked like she had to depend on herself to get out of this one. She had only her own foolishness to blame for her situation, after all. But how on earth was she going to avoid the grisly fate these cutthroats were planning for her? How long could she fake unconsciousness? How long would they wait to do their job, even if she could continue to fool them? A sick feeling of despair was threatening to block her ability to think, just when she needed that ability the most.

"I still think we ought to kill her now," Cory's voice

piped up again. "Let's get it over with and get out of here. That runt running away makes me nervous. What if he turned around and trailed you? You should've hung on to that kid, Dundee."

"Aye, Cory, you're just mad 'cause you like boys better than women," Dundee sneered. "I been hard since we brought that little piece of tail in here, and I'm not letting you snuff her out afore I has me some fun!"

"Well, she better wake up pretty soon," Cory complained. "This whole business is making me a mite nervous. You know who that piece belongs to, don't you! I tell you that Barnett has a reputation as a mean son of a bitch when he's riled. If he ever finds out it was us that done for his woman, here, likely we'll be grateful when he lets us die. I don't like the thought much of killing a female in cold blood anyway."

The voice named Jake chuckled obscenely. "Cory, old boy, you don't know what pure pleasure is. A female can give a man a right good ride, with him stuck between her legs and choking her at the same time. They sort of thrash and heave and buck, trying to get air. Makes me hard just thinking about it."

India felt a cold flood of terror wash through her mind at Jake's words. The full import of her situation finally hit her. Death was one thing, but the kind of perversions those three were talking about gave a whole new meaning to the word fear. Somehow she had to think of a way out.

They weren't going to leave her alone much longer, she knew. Ever so carefully she tested her bonds. Her hands were tied securely above her head and fastened to something behind her. Her feet were unbound, but that wasn't much help. She dare not open her eyes to find out where she was, though from the smells of the place she would guess a tavern somewhere, or maybe the back of a tavern. Even in this notorious place they couldn't very well haul an obvious kidnap victim into a public gathering place.

If she screamed suddenly, someone out in the tavern, if that's what this was, might well hear her. But probably no one would give a woman's scream a second thought, considering the activities that were commonplace on this island. They would just figure some bawd was getting more than she'd bargained for and leave well enough alone. She might offer to bribe these cutthroats, but the only thing she had to offer they planned to take anyway. And since they seemed to be afraid of Christopher, a promise of money from him on her return probably wouldn't work. And well they should be afraid, India thought grimly. It was some comfort, however small, to think of Christopher catching up with this perverted crew and sending them all to hell. She wasn't even very ashamed of the thought. India noted with some chagrin that she was getting as bloody-minded as her renegade husband.

She nearly flinched when Dundee prodded her again with the toe of his foot.

"It's getting late, Jake," he said.

There was the scrape of a chair on the plank floor and the clomp of heavy boots as Jake came over to peer into her face.

"All right, laddie," he said. "If you're so damned impatient, go get a bucket from the well and wet her down. That ought to bring her around, right enough."

India's mind convulsed with fear as she heard Dundee leave the room, muttering under his breath. This was it. There had to be a way out! She didn't want to die, and she particularly didn't want to die in the manner these men planned. But what was she going to do?

As Christopher stepped onto the beach in front of the tent town, anger warred with despair in his rigidly controlled mind. He had little hope of getting to India and Teddy in time to do them any good. There were so many hiding places in the maze of flapping tents and shoddy taverns, and he had no idea even where to start. This wouldn't be the first time someone had disappeared without trace in this den of thieves and murderers. He was angry at India for being foolish enough to disobey his orders, but he was angrier by far with the men who had taken her from him, whatever their reasons. If he could find them, he vowed, he would see to it they died very unpleasantly.

The night was almost peaceful as Christopher, Ian, and Seamus walked up the beach. The revelers were for the most part lying drunk in their tents, or passed out on the waterfront. Candles and lanterns gave a soft glow to tavern windows and tentflaps, and the milky sweep of stars across the tropical sky lit the beach and bluffs with a cool radiance. The only sound that disturbed the night was the snore of a pirate lolling in drunken stupor on the beach, and faint off-key singing issuing from a tavern the revelers had not yet quit. Christopher decided the tavern was as good a place as any to begin. At least someone was awake there.

As they passed the first disorderly row of tents, a shadow detached itself from a canvas wall and moved toward them. Christopher froze, pistol in hand. Then the shadow resolved itself into a frightened boy.

"Cap'n!" Teddy whispered urgently as he came to a swaying halt. "It's me, Teddy! I been waiting for you all night, Cap'n. Something horrible's happened!"

Christopher grasped the distraught lad by this thin shoulders and knelt to bring his face on a level with the boy's.

"Teddy! Where's India?"

He felt like shaking him, but controlled the urge.

"Calm down, Teddy. Where's Miss India?"

Teddy shivered in his captain's grasp, but took a deep breath and haltingly related the events of the afternoon. The story tumbled out in an unintelligible mixture of sobs and broken sentences, but Christopher was able to comprehend the gist of it.

"They've still got her, Cap'n," Teddy concluded. "The fellows that jumped us, they've got her in this tavern up in town."

"Do you know where?" Christopher asked urgently.

"Sure. I escaped and ran, but then I doubled back and followed the blokes. I been waiting here all night for you to come."

"Lead on, then, and make it fast, boy. Why didn't you send a message to the ship for help, dammit?"

"I . . . I didn't know which of the crew I could trust, sir," Teddy stammered. "It was Mr. Daughtery that set them fellows on us. We saw him talking to them just before they came for us. I didn't know who else was maybe working for him."

"When did all this happen, laddie?" Ian interjected as they ran quietly up the twisted path through the main port of the town.

"Must have been about suppertime," Teddy estimated. "We was about to go down to the beach to meet the boat."

"That long ago! My God!" Christopher's voice was hoarse with despair.

"Steady on, now, Christopher," Seamus advised. "If they'd meant to kill her they would've done it in the street and left her there, not dragged her off to some tavern and take a chance of getting caught."

"Not necessarily!" Christopher said grimly, knowing the predilections of the men who frequented this port.

"Quiet, now," Teddy whispered. "We're getting close."

They approached a shantylike plank building whose windows gleamed with the soft glow of lantern light. The somewhat muted sound of voices coming from within indicated that at least some revelers in this part of town had lasted out the night.

"They got her in a back store room," Teddy whispered. "There's another door around behind."

Christopher clapped the boy on the shoulder. "Good work, lad. Now move away. We've got work to do."

"Aw, Cap'n. I want to stay and watch," Teddy pleaded with bloodthirsty curiosity, his fear gone now that Christopher had arrived.

"No you don't," Christopher assured him. "Get back to the beach and wait by the boat. That's an order, Mr. Sykes."

"Aye, sir," he groaned.

Knife in one hand, cutlass in the other, Christopher moved silently around to the back of the tavern with Ian and Seamus by his side. His face was set and grim. Never before in his life had he felt such a feeling of sick dread in the pit of his stomach. He was afraid of what they would find in that room. It had been so many hours since she'd been brought here. How could she possibly be still alive, or unhurt? He knew only too well how most of these lawless men would treat a woman like India if she were completely at their mercy. If she were dead, he suspected, she would not have died pleasantly. And if she were dead, the light would go out of his life. There would be a few more souls in hell before this night's work was done, he vowed, if those scum had touched so much as one hair on her head.

The back of the tavern was dark as the Pit, but faint slivers of light outlined a door on the far end. Wet footprints led from the door to a well a short distance away and then back again. Faint starlight reflected in water that had been slopped into the footprints. The puddles had not had time to even begin to dry. At least, Christopher thought, we know someone is here, or has been very recently. He flattened himself beside the door and listened.

India sputtered and jerked against her bonds. A cold bucket of water had effectively ended her masquerade of unconsciousness, and now the time for stalling had run out. Her three captors stood and looked at her with anticipation in their eyes.

"Ain't she nice!" A man whose voice identified him as Dundee leered down at her. "Look at those little tits bounce under that wet shirt! Man, I'm going to enjoy this!"

Dundee was young and thin, with wet lips and hot eyes. He looked ready to pounce.

Jake's voice came from a heavyset man with ruddy complexion and small eyes set deep into a beefy face. He regarded her with a businesslike manner of menace that was somehow even more frightening than Dundee's open lust.

"You ain't going to enjoy nothing, boy, unless you like watching it done by a real man. We've got to get this done fast. The dawn's going to be here any minute, and if ol'

John catches us with her alive there'll be hell to pay. So you just back off and let me do the job.''

"Dammit, Jake! You promised!" Dundee whined. "I been hard since we drug her in here! It'll only take a minute!"

"Minute, my ass!" Jake sneered. "Last time you was on a woman you took a half-hour to come, boy, and don't say it ain't true, 'cause I was there watching. I thought we was going to have lots of time, but we don't. If you're that bad off, go hump yourself a whore. I mean to do for this one right now.''

India watched the argument in macabre fascination. She knew she was going to die horribly in just a very few minutes unless she came up with a miracle real fast. But her brain seemed frozen with fear, and even simple thought seemed beyond her grasp right now. A miracle wasn't going to happen. As Dundee continued to whine she desperately worked at the bonds that held her hands, but her attempts to loosen the cord only seemed to tighten it more painfully around her wrists. She was still struggling futilely when an abrupt silence fell in the room.

"Well, now that that's settled, let's get to it!" Jake said.

He turned to regard India with a hungry look that made her stomach turn over in revulsion. Dundee gave him a stare of pure venom and stamped off to sit at the table with Cory, who seemed at the moment uninterested in anything except finishing the job.

Jake chuckled obscenely as Dundee continued to glare.

"Maybe you can learn something, boy, while you watch me pleasure this little lady, here.''

India felt a wave of dizziness engulf her as Jake knelt beside her and ripped open her shirt. Before she could gather her wits to scream, he'd stuffed a dirty handkerchief into her mouth and secured it tightly with another.

"Not that I generally mind humping a yowling she-bitch," he grunted. "But we wouldn't want any unwelcome visitors in here, would we?''

India gagged on the dirty cloth in her mouth and thought

she would choke. She kicked futilely at her tormentor, to no avail. He just laughed at her struggles.

"You're going to make this real interesting, aren't you, darlin'!" He leered. "That's just fine with me!"

He grabbed her breasts with both beefy hands and squeezed painfully. She jerked and fought, but her thrashing only brought a gleam of satisfaction to his eyes.

"Don't like that, honey?" He grinned unpleasantly. "Let's see if you like this"

Suddenly he took her trousers by the belt and jerked the fastenings loose. He quickly hauled them down around her hips. His two partners had joined him now, and pulled the trousers the rest of the way off her legs. She lay there completely naked from the waist down, exposed to the open air and to the three men's avid eyes.

Jake's breathing became noticeably more rapid as he knelt there looking at her. His lips were wet and his eyes looked as though he was in a trance. He moved one hand to his own crotch and began to massage himself urgently.

"Ain't she sweet!" he breathed.

His two partners just stood there looking, Dundee with a sick longing on his face and Cory with a marked nervous twitch.

India closed her eyes and attempted to blot out the scene. She squeezed her legs tightly together, only to feel them pulled apart again by one of Jake's cronies. The humiliation was more than she could bear. She wished she could die this very minute instead of waiting on Jake's evil pleasure.

"Open your eyes, sweet thing, and look at what ol' Jake has for you."

She kept her eyes firmly shut. Without warning, a fist exploded on her cheek.

"Open your eyes, you little slut!" Jake sneered.

She obediently opened her eyes. Jake had moved to kneel between her open legs. His trousers were down around his knees, and he held a huge erection in his hand. He chuckled as her eyes grew wide and terrified at the sight of him.

"Nice, huh?" His thick-lipped mouth twisted into an

ugly grin. "I'll bet your man never humped you with anything like this!"

She struggled to get away, sick with fear and loathing, but Jake nodded to his two partners to hold her legs spread apart.

"We can get bigger," he mumbled. "Yes, we can."

He moved forward and fumbled at her crotch, finally pushing two thick fingers up inside her while his thumb dug painfully into the tender flesh between her legs.

India gasped and screamed at the pain, but no sound escaped the crude gag binding her mouth. Her writhing, jerking attempts at escape only inflamed Jake further as he grunted and grasped himself, urging his engorged member to even larger dimensions as his fingers moved painfully in and out of her cringing flesh. India thought she would go mad from pain and humiliation. She felt her stomach heave and bile rise burning into her throat. Then he withdrew his hand and sat back on his haunches and licked his lips like a ravenous animal.

"Too bad I have to make this fast, sweet thing." He grinned. "Just be grateful you have a real man to pleasure you afore your lights go out."

India longed to spit in his face. The only thing left to her now was defiance. Her earlier fear was being submerged by hatred that burned her soul with white-hot intensity. She wanted to scream her contempt into their faces and let them know what low, cowardly vermin they really were, but all she could do was mumble into her gag and watch with wide, terrified eyes as Jake positioned himself to thrust his engorged flesh into her unwilling body.

Suddenly he jerked upright and clutched his throat. Dundee and Cory watched dumbly as Jake gurgled once, then fell forward onto India's body as blood welled out of his gaping mouth. The reddened tip of Christopher's knife was protruding from the front of his neck. Dundee found his fate seconds later as he turned to face the cold green eyes of Seamus Kennedy. The tip of Kennedy's light foil wove back and forth before his staring eyes.

"What shall I do with this one, Captain?" Seamus asked casually.

"Kill him," Christopher ordered coldly. Seamus had Cory pinned against a wall with his cutlass while Ian dashed into the barroom of the tavern to see if by chance Daughtery might be there.

Christopher regarded his victim coldly.

"Tell me who put you toads up to this, and I'll let you die clean," he offered.

Cory's eyes grew wide with fear. He searched Christopher's face, but could find no trace of mercy there.

"I didn't hurt your lady, Cap'n Barnett. Honest I didn't! I'm just here 'cause this is my tavern. They wanted the back room, but, God as my witness, I didn't know what they was going to use it for. You got no call to..."

The man's protestations were cut short by the sharp edge of Christopher's cutlass pressing gently against his throat.

"I'm not interested in your babbling," Christopher warned. "Tell me who's behind this, or I'll make a very messy job of sending you off to hell. Ten seconds and I start cutting. Starting here."

Christopher lowered the cutlass to rest at the frightened man's crotch.

Cory's mouth moved up and down soundlessly a time or two as he felt Christopher's blade press more firmly into his genitals.

"I'll talk!" he finally cried. "It was John Daughtery what paid us. They was to snatch the girl, and I was to provide a place to kill her quiet-like. I swear I didn't know Jake planned anything dirty. Honest! I thought it was going to be just a nice, clean killing. Daughtery, he's the one you want. I'm just a..."

The babbling was cut off by a swift slice of Christopher's cutlass across his throat.

"Well, old man," Christopher commented as he wiped his blade on the shirt of the man crumpled at his feet. "That's about as clean and quick as it comes."

Ian came back in the room and shook his head. Seamus stood cleaning his foil with Dundee's handkerchief. Christopher moved to haul Jake's limp body off India, who lay in a shocked stupor beneath him. He gestured both his friends from the room, indicating they should guard the door.

"Right!" Seamus turned his face away from where India lay below Jake's bleeding hulk. "We don't want any surprises, do we? Take your time, Captain," he added in afterthought.

India saw Christopher's face swimming above her in the blackness that kept sweeping across her vision. Confusion reigned for a moment, then reality snapped back into focus. She groaned, then, rolling over into a fetal position, covered her face with her arms and gave way to uncontrollable sobs. Christopher called her name softly, reassuringly, but the sobs that tore from her throat refused to stop.

She felt unredeemably soiled, contaminated by Jake's unspeakable touch. If Christopher had ever loved her, India thought desperately, he couldn't possibly love her now that that creature had put his hands on her, in her, and used her as the object of his perverted animal rutting. She couldn't even stand to be near herself. She wished she could shuck this body like a piece of soiled clothing and exchange it for something clean and fresh. India knew she'd never feel clean again.

The worst part of all was that it was her own stupid fault. She had almost gotten Teddy and herself killed, and had forced Christopher, Seamus, and Ian to risk their lives to rescue her. And all because she'd wanted her own way, and wanted to prove that she didn't have to listen to anybody. She didn't want to live with herself anymore. Maybe she could die of terminal humiliation and shame. She certainly felt at this moment that something inside her was dying.

India felt herself being gathered gently into her husband's strong arms. She struggled briefly, wanting only to be left alone to die, but his gentle embrace was nevertheless like steel bands surrounding her. She continued to sob against his bandaged chest and felt his big hands running soothingly through her tangled hair.

"Hush now, India," his voice crooned. "Be quiet now. It's all over and done with."

She shook her head in disagreement. It would never be over, India thought. She would always feel Jake's hands as they tore into her flesh and see his grotesquely huge erection poised to rip into her cringing body. It would never be over for as long as she lived.

After a few more moments the convulsive shuddering calmed and the sobbing faded to an occasional gasp and sniff. Still she had her face against his body and wouldn't lift her head to meet Christopher's eyes.

"Are you ready to go back to the ship?" Christopher asked gently.

India shook her head. She didn't want to meet Christopher's eyes. She didn't want to face Ian and Seamus after what they must have seen. His grasp relaxed slightly, and she pulled away, wiping at her swollen eyes with her hand.

"I've been such a fool!" she gasped.

"Well, that you have, sweetheart," Christopher agreed. "But I think this time you got more of a lesson than you deserved."

"Oh, God, Christopher! I was so stupid! I almost got Teddy killed, and you and Seamus and Ian, you had to risk your necks, come up here, and kill all these men."

She gasped for breath as the sobs threatened to burst forth once more. But she had to get it out. He had to know.

"That man, Christopher, that horrible man. He . . . he . . ."

"Yes, I know what he did," Christopher interrupted gently. "And I know what he was about to do. And if any of the others forced you before he got his turn, I won't even ask, because it doesn't matter as far as you and I are concerned, India. You're still the same person you were before they did this to you."

He brought her firmly into his embrace once again. She leaned against him and let the first hint of comfort slip into her battered soul.

"After all," he explained, gently rocking her as he would a hurt child, "they abused your body, it's true, but I've still got your heart right here safe with me, don't I?"

Troubled blue eyes looked up into his calm brown ones.

"You could say something like that after . . . after I . . ."

"After you what?" A smile quirked the corners of his mouth. "I've known from the first you were a pea-brained hellcat. Nothing has changed, as far as I can see."

She almost laughed, but it came out a sob instead.

"India." He shook her gently to prevent another sobbing spree. "India, you must know I love you, even though I haven't said it in so many words. I'm saying it now. I love you, and nothing here has changed that. I thought I was going to go out of my mind with fear when I learned you'd gone ashore and not returned. You've become my whole life, girl!"

She looked up into his now gentle face and tried to banish the ghastly visions that still clamored at her brain.

"I love you too, Christopher."

He smiled somewhat cockily. "Yes, I know. I've known that for some time."

She pulled back in indignation, ready with a sharp retort to wipe that arrogant assurance from his face. Then she stopped, noting the twinkle of merriment in his dark eyes.

"That's more like the India I know." He grinned.

She flushed in embarrassment. It appeared she didn't have many secrets, after all. But in the face of his declared love the sick despair was beginning to fade.

She moved away, avoiding looking at any of the three dead bodies in the room. She picked up her torn trousers—rather, Christopher's torn trousers—and pulled them on, tying up the ripped sections to keep them from falling down around her ankles.

"I see you even had the cheek to wear my clothes!" Christopher laughed.

"Teddy's beeches show too much," she answered simply.

"Indeed they do."

India took a breath for courage and moved with Christopher toward the door. She felt stiff, achy, and sweaty. Looking down at her bruised hands and wrists, still smeared with Jake's drying blood, she was sure that she looked even worse than she felt. The world seemed suddenly a very frightening place. In spite of Christopher's reassurances, she knew she was not quite the same girl who had so blithely dismissed danger and walked into New Providence the day before. Something of her had died in this room, had died when Jake had put his filthy hands on her. She didn't know what it was, but she didn't feel as whole or complete as she had just the day before as she'd explored the twisting paths of Nassau with Teddy.

"Christopher," she said softly as they reached the door. "I've been stupid, and selfish, and . . . and childish. And I've caused a lot of people a lot of trouble."

He stopped and looked at her curiously.

"Well, what I want to say is . . . is . . . I'm sorry. I was a stupid chit, and I'm sorry."

Christopher leaned forward and kissed her lightly on the forehead. "India, my love," he said quietly, "you just may be growing up."

As far back as she could recall, India never remembered ever before having said she was sorry.

CHAPTER TWENTY

India stood at her favorite place at the rail, enjoying the familiar rhythmic motion of the *Black Falcon* and watching the play of a school of dolphins as they cavorted in the bow wave. The warm breeze sifted through her hair, carrying the fresh, cool scent of salt and the sea. Everything was peaceful. She was once again suspended in the seemingly timeless, isolated world of a ship at sea, where the trouble and turmoil of the landbound passed by without touching. Blue sea, blue sky, and white, decorative clouds surrounded them day after day. One bright sunny day had followed another since they set sail from New Providence, with rainsqualls only frequent enough to cool the air and supplement their fresh-water supply. The white sails billowed with the warm, steady trade winds, and the *Black Falcon* was making good time toward the colder climes of Britain. The world was orderly and peaceful; everyone was content. So why, India wondered, was she so gloomy?

Standing hour after hour, day after day at her perch in the bow did not bring her the peace it had on the voyage out. India was a different girl from the one who had sailed into these tropical waters so many weeks ago. Then her problems had been relatively simple. She had been struggling with her newly discovered passion and fighting the deep attachment that was growing for her kidnapper, knowing that she could do very little about either. Now her problems were more complex, it seemed. She had admitted her love for Christopher. He had admitted his love for her. But their mutual declaration did very little to mend the problems between them. To him, she was still an investment in revenge. To her, he was still a man of frightening passions and violence, one who was capable of steeling his heart and using her for his own dark purposes. The love between them only made the conflict more painful.

But that problem could be suspended for a time, India told herself sternly. She had weeks before they would land in England, weeks in which they could enjoy each other without thought to the future. It seemed very little to ask, India thought bitterly—these few remaining weeks of happiness before his hatred and her loyalty to her father would inevitably draw them apart again. But now even this had become impossible.

The day had been bright two weeks ago when they set sail from New Providence. It had been so good to hear the familiar creaks and groans of the *Black Falcon* as the sails were unfurled to catch the trades, and the ship had wakened to life of its own. Even Christopher, withdrawn and irritable after three days of fruitless search for John Thomas and John Daughtery, looked happy to feel again the familiar sway of the deck beneath his feet. The crew had given a rousing cheer as the ship cleared the harbor and sailed under the silent guns of the outer island fortress. They had a lot to celebrate, for the sale of the *Navarre* and the *Lady Mary*, along with their cargo, had added considerably to each man's fortune. Added to the amount most of them had accumulated in their years of sailing with the notorious Christopher Barnett, many of the crew could now afford to live in considerable comfort for the rest of their days.

That first day at sea had been a happy one for India. Most of the three days in port after she had returned to the ship she had spent sleeping. She didn't venture abovedeck until the morning they set sail, preferring to think that Nassau might have dropped off the edge of the earth. Even the stink of New Providence, however, couldn't prevent her from being present when the sails were unfurled. As always, she was awed at seeing the great sails cascade down from the yards, fill with the breeze, and transform the ship from a floating conglomeration of planks, hemp, and spars to a graceful creature dancing with the sea and the wind.

India smiled as they cleared the harbor and the fresh sea breeze drove the last taint of New Providence from her skin and hair. Three days of healing sleep had done much to banish the goblins of that horrible night in Nassau from her mind. There was nothing on the ship to remind her of those fearful hours spent in the back of a tavern or of the ugly things that had happened there. Ian and Seamus treated her as though nothing had occurred. She'd hardly seen Christopher for three days, but he'd made it clear before they returned to the ship that what had happened that night made no difference in his feelings for her. India believed the whole revolting incident had been put behind her, where it belonged.

The first night at sea Christopher and India had enjoyed a leisurely dinner in the privacy of their cabin. For the better part of a week they'd been apart, India dead to the world in the cabin and Christopher catching only brief snatches of sleep in between long hours of searching the pirate colony for Thomas and Daughtery. Now at last they had time to relax together and enjoy each other's company. Both knew that this voyage was simply a peaceful prelude to the storm that would break when they once again had to face the harsh realities of the world. Both were willing to put aside their differences for these weeks and enjoy their love while they had the chance. Their feelings for each other might endure in their souls, but both knew the peace between them was unlikely to last when they returned to the cold shores of Britain.

Christopher poured them each a glass of after-dinner wine while India leaned against the window seat and stared out the stern windows, watching the silvery play of moonlight on the restless sea. How wonderful if we could always be like this, she mused, letting the peace of their evening together lull her into drowsy contentment. Christopher carefully placed a goblet of amber liquid in her hand, then gently encircled her waist with one arm and pulled her back against him, molding the soft contours of her body to his harder, more angular one. There was no doubt about his need. The hard bulge of his manhood pressed boldly into her lower back as he pressed her tightly against him.

"Want something?" she teased, rubbing lightly against him.

She was no longer afraid, as she once had been, of stirring his passions to greater heat.

"Mmmmmm," he replied, setting his wine on the shelf.

Deftly he unfastened the buttons of her muslin bodice and let his hand wander inside, cupping her breast and teasing the rosy nipple into tautness with his thumb. She let her head fall back against his shoulder as he slipped her chemise straps from her shoulders and sent it with her dress to fall in a heap around her ankles. His hands pressed against the bare skin of her breasts, then traveled slowly down across her stomach, hips, and thighs, brushing lightly, teasingly against the sensitive flesh between her legs. His touch seemed to trail a path of fire on her skin, and India could feel a tight aching begin in her loins and spread down her legs to make her knees turn to water. Christopher felt her sway slightly and laughed as he picked her up easily in his strong arms.

"You always were an impatient little witch." He grinned. "At least give me time to get my clothes off!"

"You call me impatient!" she teased, nuzzling his neck. "You didn't give me time to drink my wine."

"The wine be damned!"

He laid her gently on the bed and hurriedly removed boots, shirt, and breeches. Then he stood naked before her, letting his dark, hot gaze travel the length of her tender body, enjoying the anticipation of caressing her smooth skin with mouth and hands while burying himself in the soft moistness between her creamy thighs. Finally his desire, unsated for many days, grew to painful proportions. He could wait no longer, and moved to join her on the bed and cover her waiting body with his own.

India had enjoyed looking at him standing there, unconscious of the statuelike grace of his pose. The contours of his heavily muscled but lean body were detailed by the moonlight streaming in through the stern windows. His broad shoulders, narrow hips, and straight, thickly muscled legs could have been sculpted by an artist intent on portraying the ideal masculine form. Only the bandages that still protected his injured side marred the illusion of perfection. The fire of lust in Christopher's eyes was now tempered by love and his face softened by tenderness. His dark-eyed, darkly bearded face no longer seemed satanic, India realized, and the tight-jawed tension of desire in his face was no longer frightening.

India had no indication of trouble until her gaze slipped to the powerful physical manifestation of his arousal. The sight of his erect manhood triggered an unwanted tension, a stiffness in her body that only a moment ago had been pliant and eager to receive him. The heat in her veins turned to icy shards of fear as he lowered himself gently onto her and nudged her thighs apart with his knee. Her heart raced, but not with desire.

When Christopher's seeking mouth fastened on her own, her lips were stiff and unresponsive. The feel of his deft fingers caressing the velvety flesh between her legs suddenly made her cringe from his touch. A leering thick-lipped face flashed through her mind, then the unwelcome memory of Jake massaging his own engorged flesh while degrading her womanhood with his thick fingers.

Somewhere in the back of his mind Christopher registered

India's lack of response, but the demands of his own body had reached such a peak of urgency that to pause in his climb toward satisfaction was well-nigh impossible. He spread her legs wider and pushed himself slowly into her tight body, savoring the feel of her moist warmth against his demanding flesh. Then she screamed.

India screamed, and clawed, and kicked, catching him unawares and pushing away from the shaft that linked them. She was no longer on the *Black Falcon*, safely lying under Christopher's strong body; she was back in the shoddy, smelly store room of a Nassau tavern, pinned to the floor by the bulk of Jake's body while his putrid flesh sought entrance to her most intimate recesses. She clawed at his face, and tried to bring her knee up sharply into his groin, heaving desperately to rid herself of his loathsome weight. She screamed again as her hands were jerked above her head and held there.

Christopher stifled India's screams with his hand. He pinned her struggling body to the bed with his weight, breathing harder from frustrated desire than from the effort of subduing the slight figure that struggled beneath him. She wouldn't stop, though. Even securely held by his superior strength, she jerked and twisted, trying to free herself from his grip.

"India, for God's sake, stop!" Christopher commanded through clenched teeth. "Dammit! What has gotten into you?"

Then he looked into her wide, terrified eyes, and the answer dawned on him in a flash. The sound of his voice had brought India partway back home, and her struggles slowed. Her heart still raced and her body shivered with distress at the feel of his naked flesh against hers.

A tentative knock sounded on the door. Christopher groaned as Ian's voice called hesitantly from the corridor.

"Is everything all right in there? I thought I heard the lass screaming."

Thinking that this was a fine time for Ian to forget discretion, Christopher replied in as normal a voice as he could muster.

"Go back up where you belong, you daft Scotsman! India just had a nightmare."

"Aye, sir." Ian clumped off into the night.

India lay still beneath him now. Carefully, he released his grip on her hands and removed his hand from her lips. Then he rolled off her, watching carefully, his unsatisfied erection throbbing painfully at his groin.

"Better?" he asked softly.

India bit her lip nervously and nodded. The wildness in her eyes had faded. Christopher reached forward to brush her softly tousled hair from her face, but she cringed as though he meant to hit her. She looked at the naked length of his still-aroused body and swallowed hard, trying to control the urge to back into a corner and make herself as small as possible.

Christopher sighed and resigned himself to the fact that for tonight, at least, he was just going to have to cope with frustration. He couldn't really blame India. He had seen part of what went on in that room and could imagine most of the rest. It was understandable that a sensitive girl subjected to such trauma would have difficulty in accepting the intimate caresses even of a man she loved. But he had no intention of letting this come between them for long. He couldn't stand it.

Time dragged on, with India regarding Christopher warily from one edge of the bed.

"Come here, India," he finally said.

India drew herself into a tighter ball. "I can't," she whispered in a strained voice.

"Yes you can." Christopher's voice was soft, but firm.

"Oh, God, I'm sorry!" India sobbed into the pillow that she clutched against her. "I can't!" she repeated.

In one motion his long arms reached out and dragged her against him, molding her struggling body spoon-fashion to his and holding her firmly until her struggles ceased. India regained some control of herself and finally forced her body to relax against him.

"Better," he said.

"I'm sorry," India whispered.

Christopher sighed sadly. "It's all right, my love," he told her. "I understand, I think, but I've no intention of being cooped up in this cabin with you for this entire voyage and not making love to you. And I won't have you cringing away from my every touch."

India was silent. The tightness in Christopher's loins had not lessened in the least, and the feel of her silken thighs against his was not making matters better. He shifted uncomfortably, causing her to struggle for another moment of unreasoning panic when she felt the bold thrust of his manhood against the back of her thighs. His voice brought her back again, though, and she settled herself once more in wary quietude against him.

"I'm not Jake, India," he reminded her. "Jake is dead, killed by my own hand. He can't bother you anymore."

Jake was not dead, however. At least not for India. His ghost sprang to life in her mind each time Christopher tried to go beyond the very preliminary gestures of lovemaking. She tried to be reasonable, and failed. She tried to grit her teeth and force herself to at least lie still for him, but fear won out. India was miserable. Christopher was painfully frustrated and becoming increasingly angry with the whole situation. The tension between the two of them was growing to unbearable heights, until India took to avoiding him and Christopher attempted to work himself to exhaustion each day and fall into bed so late each night that India would be safely asleep.

So India stood at the bow rail and brooded gloomily, and Christopher stood on his quarterdeck and frowned his anger out at the world, not knowing how to solve the problem but knowing he would soon go crazy if things didn't change.

The mild weather and idle days at sea gave Christopher plenty of time to think, even though thinking brought him face to face with problems he was not prepared to deal with right then. India's frightened frigidity preyed on his mind. His acute physical frustration and the inevitable tension that resulted between them was making him as irritable as a wounded boar. But he knew that time was a great healer, and sooner or later India would welcome his embraces again, even if he had to help time along a bit with some action of his own. India's naturally passionate nature would rebound eventually. Other problems, however, would not be solved by time; they would just be brought to a head.

Christopher had no doubts that India's love for him was genuine, and he knew that, whether or not he had intended it, his heart had become inexorably intertwined with hers. He chuckled wryly, thinking of how his well-laid plans had backfired. He had single-mindedly pursued his goals, first to clear his own name and then to avenge himself on the man who'd judged him with more greed than justice. And now, not only had the man who could vindicate him slipped through his hands, but the slip of a girl he'd married for revenge had taken up permanent residence in his heart. For the first time since he'd lost his boyish innocence in those few days at Blenheim, he found himself confused as to what he meant to do.

Christopher had become a hard man after his sudden introduction to the unkind vagaries of fate. Time spent as a lowly seaman in His Majesty's Navy had hardened his soul as well as his body. His actions were always governed by coolheaded logic; he locked his emotions, all his hate, anger, fear, and despair, into the back of his mind, where they could occasionally be taken out and examined, or even freed to use if called for. But never had he let his feelings interfere with his life. Not until now, at least.

Love was something he'd not dealt with before. Perhaps, Christopher thought with chagrin, that was why it had taken him so unawares, with his guard lowered. Lust, passion, even mild affection—those were familiar enough. But this tenderness that held his heart in thrall where India was concerned was something else entirely. It threatened to disarm his anger and rob him of his thirst for vengeance.

And what did he get in return? Problems and more problems. Serves me right, Christopher despaired, for getting muddleheaded over a woman. There was no help for it now, though, because he wouldn't uproot India from his life even if he could. But she would never willingly be a true wife, share his life and bear his children, as long as her father suffered from her actions. Of course, that had been the whole point, in the beginning. He'd never expected her to be willing, just cowed into compliance. Now he wanted her willing and happy. He didn't want to hurt her any more than he already had. So what was he to do? He could let her go, deliver her back to her family, put her conscience at ease, and rob them both of any chance at happiness. Or he could keep her with him, force her to play the part of his wife, and watch her grieve over her father's suffering. I'm damned if I do and damned if I don't, Christopher thought. He was inescapably caught in the trap he'd so painstakingly laid for another. And he had no one but himself to blame.

As days passed into weeks the sea changed from the azure of the tropics to the deep, cold blue of the Atlantic. The mid-August sun warmed the air during the daylight hours, but the evenings and nights brought a definite chill. The little stove in the cabin was lit each evening as the sun set, and India spent most of the evening hours huddled close against it for warmth. The luxury of fresh-water washing had ended as the ship left the region of frequent rainsqualls, but an occasional steamy bath, even in salt water, was a comfort India wasn't prepared to forgo. A small brass tub had been rescued from the *Navarre* before she'd been sold, and India had it set up in one corner of the cabin. She herself would haul buckets of hot water from the galley and then soak herself until the water grew too cool for comfort. Soap was plentiful, and she used it unsparingly to scrub her skin and lather her hair. But no amount of scrubbing, she finally admitted, would wash away the poisons that Jake and his cronies had left in her soul.

Christopher interrupted her in the bath once. She had seen him so seldom these last several weeks that his entrance into their cabin was quite unexpected. He had raised a brow as he took in the scene before him, letting his unhurried gaze travel over the expanse of silken skin that was alternately hidden and exposed by the sudsy, oscillating water. His eyes then came to rest with seeming fascination where the water lapped at the smooth upper curves of her breasts. A muscle twitched in his jaw, and his whole body took on a coiled-

spring, ready-to-pounce look. The tense silence in the room
seemed to pulse in time with the fearful beating of India's
heart. She longed to duck beneath the sudsy water and hide
herself from view, but she could only sit where she was,
fearfully returning his gaze as the fire smoldered in his eyes.
Then the tension broke along with the silence.

"Pardon the intrusion," Christopher said with a slight
tone of sarcasm. "I can see you weren't expecting me."

"I . . . you. . . ." India stuttered.

"No matter," Christopher said. His face became an
impassive mask as he continued to regard her unveiled
charms. "I just came down to get a slicker. It's starting to
rain."

India attempted a smile. "You don't need to apologize.
It's your cabin, after all."

He smiled as though she'd said something funny, then
grabbed an oilcloth slicker and left the cabin without a
word.

Very late that same night she awakened from sleep to find
him lying beside her on the bed, regarding her with a gaze
that was frightening in its intensity. He reached out a hand
and ran it caressingly down her smooth, bare arm. She
jumped away like a small, startled rabbit, unable to control
the shudder that coursed through her body. He sighed
heavily and withdrew his hand. For a moment more he
regarded her with an enigmatic look on his face, then sighed
in resignation and lay back on the pillows. India continued
to watch him, like a doe rabbit unable to believe she'd
escaped the wolf's fangs. Finally she relaxed and turned to
face away from him, pulling the blankets up tightly under
her chin. She would have cried, but she felt empty of tears,
she'd cried so much in the past weeks. Twice since that first
dreadful night at sea Christopher had made attempts to make
love to her. Both times she'd been hysterical. She'd hoped
with time her fears would fade, but they were building on
themselves. Now his every touch made her quiver. The very
nearness of his lean, masculine body made her uneasy. She
was beginning to despair of ever again being able to accept
his embraces. Soon it would be too late. In just a few weeks

they'd be once again in British waters. His vengeance against her father would be renewed, and she would set herself against him to foil his plan any way she could. The time for truce, for enjoyment of the peace they'd found in each other's arms, would be at an end. It wasn't fair that the little time they had together should be taken from them like this. But she couldn't control the panic that descended every time Christopher laid a hand upon her. How ironic it was, India thought with a twisted smile, that Christopher had tried and failed to break her spirit for weeks after their hasty wedding. Jake had succeeded in breaking her in just one night.

CHAPTER TWENTY-ONE

Sleep eluded India for the next several nights. She lay in tense anticipation until the small hours of the morning, when Christopher would finally enter the cabin and drop down on the bed beside her. Then she huddled stiffly under the blankets, waiting for him to reach out to claim her. When he didn't, she was almost as disappointed as she was relieved.

Daylight hours were little better. India brooded at her perch at the bow rail while Christopher occupied himself with the ship, generally somewhere out of her sight. They no longer communicated. The wall between them grew hour by hour and day by day. Soon, India thought, it would be an indestructible, unbreachable barrier. She was driving him away, and who could blame him for shunning her.

"You look awful!" Helen had commented frankly on joining India at the rail to enjoy the bright, cool afternoon three weeks after lifting anchor at Nassau. "Are you sick?" she asked in worried concern.

"No," India replied gloomily.

"Well, then, is something wrong?" Helen pried.

"I don't want to talk about it." India stared sullenly out to sea and tried to ignore Helen's presence.

"Had a fight with Christopher, did you?" Helen continued, ignoring India's frown. "Must have been a good one. He's been going around snapping everybody's head off."

"We didn't have a fight." India sighed, realizing Helen wasn't going to take the unsubtle hint to leave her alone.

"Well," Helen insisted. "Something must be wrong to make the both of you act so snappish. I swear I haven't seen you two exchange a single word since we left that dreadful pirate island!"

India hesitated. "Everything's wrong," she finally said.

"That bad?" Helen sensed the depth of her friend's unhappiness. "Tell me about it," she urged. "Maybe I can help."

"Nobody can help," India replied softly.

"Nothing's that bad," Helen insisted. "I can't stand to see you so unhappy, India. Not now that I'm so happy with Seamus."

Helen permitted a dreamy smile to touch her face briefly, then returned her attention to her friend.

"Did Seamus tell you what happened on New Providence?" she asked hesitantly.

"He was very closemouthed about everything. All he said was that you were kidnapped by some ruffians who were involved with Daughtery, but that he and Christopher and Ian had brought you back."

"He didn't say anything more?" Bless Seamus for a true gentleman, India thought.

"No. Should he have?" Helen's eyes lit with curiosity. "Did I miss something interesting?"

India stared intently at the water swirling under the bow. "The men who kidnapped me," she said stoically, "one of them at least, he . . . he did some fairly awful things to me."

"Oooooh." Helen was all sympathy. "Did he rape you?"

"No." India's voice was a mere whisper. "He was going to, but Christopher killed him before he got that far. But it was awful just the same. He had some twisted ways of doing things," she said simply.

"Aaaah." Helen understood. Having herself been a poor girl without the protection of wealth or position, she had known a few Jakes in her time. "But that's over now, dear," she reasoned gently. "There's no sense in dwelling on it and letting it make you so unhappy."

"That's it, you see," India told her. "It's not really over. Every time Christopher touches me, I see that man again. I can't . . . I can't . . . I get hysterical when Christopher tries to make love to me." She blushed hotly. "I can hardly even be near him without cringing anymore."

Helen looked at India in surprise. "You mean Christopher is letting you get away with this?"

"What do you mean, letting me get away with it?" India was indignant. "I can't help it. I'm not doing it deliberately."

"I don't recall that Christopher ever before asked your permission to bed you." Helen chuckled.

India scowled. Helen wasn't being very sympathetic.

"This is different," she insisted. "He won't force me. He loves me."

"All the more reason he should throw you over his shoulder and carry you off to bed," Helen concluded.

"He knows I'm afraid."

"Oh, pooh!" Helen smiled. "That wouldn't last long. You've never been afraid of anything in your life, or if you have, you haven't let on. You're always the one who damned the consequences and went ahead with whatever you wanted to do. I can't believe you've let this thing get so out of hand."

"You're wrong!" India pouted. "I was scared to death of Christopher when I first met him. Now I'm scared again."

"That's different," Helen argued. "Every girl's afraid of being bedded the first time. But after you found out what he did to you wasn't going to kill you, you weren't afraid anymore. You were just angry. You just need to get on the horse again, that's all."

"What?" India looked at Helen in confusion.

"Don't you remember the time your father's stablemaster, old Billy Crow, caught you riding that devil black horse you weren't even supposed to go near?"

India frowned, not seeing the point.

"I was watching from a seat on the fence," Helen remembered, "and I squealed when I saw Billy come round the corner of the stables. That devil horse spooked and tossed you into the mud so hard you broke your arm."

"I remember," India said, grimacing at the memory.

"What did Billy do, after yelling at you for being a disobedient fool?"

India smiled. "He made me get back up on the fool horse, broken arm and all. He said even a girl shouldn't grow up afraid of horses."

Helen smiled smugly.

India brooded the rest of the afternoon alone, thinking on her conversation with Helen. Helen was wrong about one thing. She'd been afraid of many things in her life—her father's icy aloofness, Lady Carey's sharp tongue, that damned black horse when he threw her into the mud. But she'd never before let her fears take over her life. Always she'd been able to substitute defiance or anger when she was frightened. Even during those first days on board the *Black Falcon*, she hadn't let her fear of Christopher induce her to cower before him. Had she changed so much, that night in Nassau?

She ate dinner alone in the cabin. Teddy brought her a tray and, sensing her foul mood, scampered out of the room without saying a word. Even Thomas Cat pointedly left the cabin instead of staying to eye her dinner, as was his wont. She must be getting a reputation as a veritable dragon, India thought regretfully, glooming around the ship and snapping at everyone who dared talk to her. Surely things couldn't be allowed to continue this way!

Dinner was finished, the tray removed, and the evening dragged on. India restlessly paced back and forth, occasionally stopping by the small stove to warm her hands. The small noises of shipboard life, usually comforting, were now a source of irritation—the squeak of the lantern swaying on its brass hook, the creak of the hull straining under the pull of the sails, the whisper of water swirling softly under the stern windows.

India paced. She wished for company—Helen, Christopher, even Thomas Cat. She didn't want to be pacing this tiny cabin with only herself for company. Having to put up with oneself, she decided, isn't easy when you don't like yourself anymore. And she didn't much like herself right now. She'd lost control. She was being weak, and silly, and couldn't summon the courage to grab control of her life again.

She wandered away from the stove and toward the stern windows. Kneeling on the window seat, she stared at the swirling water below. A full moon rested low on the horizon, reflecting a milky trail across the surface of the sea. Flashes of white glimmered on the *Falcon*'s wake, spreading out in a wide vee behind the ship. The immensity of the vast Atlantic suddenly made her meager problems, her very existence, seem very small and unimportant. How many people would really care, she wondered, if she opened one of these windows and disappeared into the swirling black waters below? It would certainly solve her father's problem. And Christopher would grieve, perhaps, but in the long run it would make his life easier, also. Helen didn't need her any longer, being so happy with her new husband. Beyond those three people, no one else would ever notice she was gone.

Would it be terribly unpleasant to drown? she wondered. Would it hurt more than the daily pain of facing Christopher, of facing herself and her newfound cowardice? She faced a future of hating herself, of driving off the man she loved, of betraying the father whose affection and respect had always been her dearest, most unattainable dream. Why not? The sea was cold here. It wouldn't take long to die. She would probably be so cold she wouldn't even feel it.

She reached up and experimentally, tentatively touched the latch of the nearest window. It opened easily. She swung it open, letting the cold night air cut through her wool gown and send its icy fingers through her hair. Of course she wouldn't do it, but it was an interesting idea. The dark water below swirled invitingly. Fascinated, India pushed the window open just a bit wider. She watched, mesmerized, as the dark, clean cold of the Atlantic beckoned.

Suddenly a steel-fingered, painful grip closed around her arm.

"What in bloody hell do you think you're doing?"

She swung around so abruptly that she lost her balance and would have fallen had Christopher not braced her firmly with his arm. His eyes were dark with anger and his lips a tight line of fury.

"I . . . nothing! I wasn't doing anything!" She cringed from his rage. "I just . . . I . . ."

He looked out the window at the moonlit sea, then reached out a long arm to close and latch the window.

"I know damn well what you were doing, you little fool."

He pulled her away from the windows to the stove. It dawned on her suddenly that she had actually been toying with the idea of killing herself. She'd been about to throw herself into the sea because she found that life was a little tougher than she would like to believe, because some foul thing had crawled from the slime and dared sully her with its touch. She, India Catherine Carey, who always liked to believe herself so brave and strong, so free of the silly vapors that plagued her weaker sisters, she had looked life in the eye and then run away to cry, hide, and wallow in self-pity. She was a fool.

"I ought to turn you over my knee and let your bare little backside feel the weight of my hand! By God I should!"

Christopher's voice was colored with fear as well as anger. If he'd come in a minute later, would she have been here?

"Please, Christopher, you're hurting me!" India tried to wiggle out of his tight grip.

"You little idiot!" His eyes blazed at her. "I'll hurt you a lot more if you ever, ever try anything like that again!"

He shook her to drive home his point, and she watched in uneasy fascination the angry twitch of the muscle of his jaw.

Only one other time had she seen him this angry—when she had backhanded him after he berated her for flirting with Peter Reed. She remembered also what had happened in result. It came to her then what she had to do.

"Christopher, I want you to make love to me." She tumbled it out rapidly before she could think about what she was doing. "Please!" She closed her eyes and gritted her teeth, trying not to think about what she was asking.

He loosened his grip on her. The blaze of anger in his eyes faded slowly, then rekindled as another kind of fire.

"When have you ever had to beg me to make love to you?" he replied softly.

He ran his hand gently down her arm, and she backed away with a sob.

"What the . . ."

"I'm sorry!" she sobbed. "Just get it over with, please. Don't pay any mind to what I do. Just go ahead. I can't . . . I just can't . . ."

"Hush. I know," Christopher soothed, realizing finally what this was costing her.

He pulled her gently to him and cradled her against his broad chest, running his big hands soothingly over her dark tumbling curls and up and down her back. Finally he lowered his mouth to hers, brushing against her lightly with his lips, then forcing her mouth open and letting her taste the full depth of his hunger. She stood stiffly in his consuming embrace, fearing her courage would fail. When she felt the hardness of his manhood swell against her belly, her courage did fail. She pulled away, panting with fear as the all too familiar panic overwhelmed her senses.

"No!" she gasped. "I can't!"

"Too late," Christopher said huskily. He pulled her against him again and pressed gentle kisses to her eyelids, mouth, and throat while she struggled in his arms. As she felt his passion mount, her struggles increased, but that only served to inflame him further. He lowered his hands to the neckline of her bodice and ripped downward, freeing her breasts to his view. The throbbing in his groin increased to an unbearable pitch as he let his eyes feast on the dainty rounded mounds he'd felt so often beneath his seeking hands and caressing mouth. He'd been too long without a woman to ease his needs, and this particular woman had always driven him to frenzy without even trying.

India backed away and tried to cover herself with her hands. "I take it back!" she whispered in a frightened voice.

"You can't take it back, India. I should have done this in the very beginning, and you know it. I told you that same night I had no intention of being cooped up in this cabin without making love to you. I've waited long enough."

Christopher reached out and doused the lantern before he began to quickly divest himself of his clothing, remembering what the sight of his nakedness had done to her before.

India's heart thudded in the sudden darkness. She heard his boots hit the floor, followed by the soft rustle of sweater and breeches. She backed away fearfully and stumbled over the chair. His hands reached for her, steadied her, then moved to impatiently rip the remainder of her dress and shift from her quivering body. Ignoring flailing arms and legs, he picked her up and deposited her on the bed, trapping her there in the cage of his arms and legs when she tried to escape.

"I've never hurt you, India," he said hoarsely. "And I'm not going to start now. But I'm going to make love to you, whether or not you want me to. And I'm going to keep making love to you until you get those stupid notions out of your mind—until you realize that it's me on top of you and not that slobbering animal I killed for trespassing on my property!"

She lunged away from him in a panic, but he was on her in the blink of an eye, holding her gently but firmly with one arm while his free hand played a leisurely game on the soft contours of her breasts. He lowered his mouth to her rosy nipple and buried his face in the softness of her tender flesh.

"India," he groaned. "My God, but you're beautiful!"

India fought the images clamoring at her brain. Jake tore open her shirt, leering wet-mouthed at her exposed breasts while Dundee raked her body with his hot eyes. Jake reached down and squeezed painfully with his filthy hands. She heaved and jerked, but he laughed and held her down. Then Jake wasn't there any more. The pain was gone. Christopher was gently caressing the fullness of her breast while his thumb teased the pink-tinged nipple to alertness. In the soft darkness she felt his beard against her cheek and his lips close to her ear as he whispered soft reassurances.

"Christopher?" Her voice was barely audible.

"Yes, my love. It's only me."

He moved his mouth to cover hers as his hands slid smoothly down over her flat belly and into the soft triangle of curls between her legs. With great effort, he restrained his galloping desires and caressed her slowly, gently, in that most vulnerable area. She lay stiffly under his hands, unable to respond yet willing herself not to fight. He finally allowed his appetite full rein as his mouth plundered hers and his hands rediscovered the tender recesses of her sweet womanhood.

India's screams couldn't escape the gag as Dundee and Cory held her legs and Jake pushed his groping fingers into the most intimate folds of her body. He reached down to massage his own engorged flesh and then displayed himself before her terrified eyes.

"See what I have for you, slut?" he chortled evilly.

But she wasn't gagged, India suddenly realized. It was Christopher's insistently caressing mouth that stifled her screams as his skilled hand deftly massaged the tender flesh between her legs. She screamed.

"Dammit, India!" Christopher growled. "You're just not going to let me be gentle, are you?"

He stifled her scream with one hand and parted her thighs with the other.

"So be it, then, my love," he concluded.

As gently as possible, considering her writhing attempts to escape and the throbbing demands of his own body, he pressed the hard spear of his manhood deep into the soft recesses of her flesh. She was dry and tense, and he knew he caused her pain beyond whatever pain was haunting her mind. He settled his weight on her, pinning her to the bed with the length of him buried deep within her body.

"Be still, India," he whispered against her ear. The struggles slowed somewhat. "It's me, Christopher. I love you, little one. Don't fight me, India. Be still."

She opened her eyes to search the face above hers in the darkness. The wildness slowly faded from their blue depths, and sanity returned.

"Are you back, my lady?" he asked gently.

A tremulous smile pulled at her mouth, and he pressed a light kiss on her lips.

India gripped Christopher's arm and grimaced with pain when he started to move inside her. She felt as though she would be split asunder by the great, rock-hard shaft that penetrated deeper and deeper into her inner sanctum. Then the pain began to fade and the familiar fire kindled in her loins. Her blood throbbed in rhythm with his movements. Pain and fear were forgotten as her world gradually narrowed down to center on the hard, insistent flesh that filled her again and again. She thrust up to meet him, trying to take him even deeper inside her. Christopher felt her response and abandoned himself finally to the fires that he had denied for too long. He took her with merciless intensity, urged on by her soft cries of passion. The savagery of his lovemaking sent India to the peak of ecstasy time and time again, not letting her rest from one frenzy of fulfillment before driving her up toward the next. Finally, with a great shuddering groan, he found his release while she clung to him with arms and legs, sobbing out her love and passion.

Even then, it seemed, he wasn't through. He eased his weight from her body and rolled to his side, gathering her in his arms and pressing her close against him.

"Are you still with me, little one?" he murmured after a few minutes, pressing kisses into her tousled hair.

She nodded happily, drowsily content in the aftermath of their loving. She felt his callused hands slip down her back and press her more tightly against the length of his body. Then, as she squirmed to settle herself even closer, she felt the unmistakable evidence of his renewed desire. She looked up at him in surprise.

"Did you think I was finished with you, little wife?" He laughed softly. "I'm not half started yet, my love. It's been a long, long time!"

He gave her a disturbingly devilish smile as he turned her on her back and once more gently sheathed his hard length in the warm folds of her welcoming flesh.

India didn't wake until the bright midmorning sunlight streamed through the stern windows and fell on the bed, shifting back and forth across the pillows and teasing her from her sleep. She sighed and reached out a hand to the empty space beside her, groaning when her hand met cold, crumpled sheets instead of Christopher's warm, masculine body. Mumbling into her pillow, she pulled the blankets up under her chin and curled in a warm, contented ball to drift back to sleep, but the sunlight glared at her even through closed eyes.

"Blast!" she muttered to herself, reluctantly throwing off the covers and swinging her legs over the side.

Hastily she pulled on a wool gown and ran a brush through her tangled hair, then eyed the brass tub standing in the corner. It would be worth the work, she thought, to haul in the water for a good soak. She was sticky and uncomfortable with passion's leavings, and sore as a new bride the morning after.

The bath was indeed worth the work. India lay back in the steaming water with closed eyes, letting the heat ease all the tension of the last weeks from her body. The rhythmic motion of the ship and the comfort of the hot water had combined to lull her into a drowsy peacefulness when a spatter of hot salt water down her face ended her comfortable trance. She sputtered and splashed, opening her eyes to the sight of Christopher holding the sodden bath sponge above her, preparing to give her another dose.

"Blackguard!" she sputtered, wiping water and wet hair from her eyes. "Sneak! If I'd have heard you come in, I'd have been on my guard!"

Christopher grinned in good humor. "That's why we pirates have to be so light on our feet."

He lowered his long frame to the window seat, stretched his legs out in front of him, and contentedly watched the play of bath water against India's smooth skin.

"Some pirate!" India scoffed smilingly. "The only thing you've plundered lately is . . . is . . ." She thought better of her comment and blushed lightly.

But Christopher's face spread with a self-satisfied grin.

"Is you, right?" he finished for her. "And you enjoyed every minute of it . . . well, most of it, anyway."

India favored him with a warm smile. Her eyes lit with invitation.

"Don't look at me in that way, wench," he admonished her in mock indignation. "I've a ship to command. I can't be down here with you all day pounding a mattress! I just came down to see if you've hauled your lazy bones out of bed. Helen's been asking for you. Seems she's concerned about some commotion and muffled screams she heard last night."

His eyes wandered affectionately over the fine features of her face. He longed to reach out and smooth back the dark hair clinging in wet, curling tendrils to her forehead and cheeks.

"She didn't believe me when I assured her you were still in one piece. Are you?" He raised a mocking brow.

"As far as I can tell."

She gazed at him in wide-eyed innocence and slowly rose from the tub. Christopher's eyes widened and his breath caught unexpectedly in his chest as he looked at her standing there, the soapy water coursing in rivulets down the gentle curves of her young body.

She smiled sweetly at his discomfiture. "Hand me a towel, would you?"

"The towel be damned!" he growled as he rose like a stalking tiger from the window seat and effortlessly lifted her from the tub and set her on her feet to drip on the wool rug. "Shameless little hussy!" The twinkle of merriment in his eyes belied his chiding tone. "You certainly know how to tempt a man!"

His eyes caught fire as he slipped his hands around her slender waist and pulled her to him.

"Fie, sir!" she exclaimed lightly and slipped out of his grasp. "You have a ship to command! You can't afford to be down here pounding the mattress with the likes of me!"

He reached out and caught her in midflight, hauling her firmly but gently back against the rock-hard wall of his chest. His hands seemed to wander of their own accord to cup a firm young breast and caress the smooth curve of a creamy thigh, sending shivers of delight up and down her spine. She relaxed against him with a sigh.

"Someone should teach you not to be such a tease," he commented hoarsely, pressing a kiss on her bare, wet shoulder.

"You, perhaps?" she invited.

He turned her toward him and his mouth descended to possess hers in a deep and ravaging kiss. She melted against him as she felt his hands brush the sides of her breasts, then travel teasingly over her hips to finally cup her buttocks and press her against him in a compelling, sensuous rhythm. Then suddenly she was free. She blinked in surprise as he stood there with a knowing grin on his handsome face.

"Teasing, like revenge, can be a double-edged sword, my lady."

Her lips pursed in exasperated frustration as he wrapped the towel around her wet body and gave her an affectionate pat on the rear.

"Get dressed before you tempt me further from my duties, madam."

"You're impossible! Do you know that?" She slanted him a half-irritated, half-affectionate glance.

"So I've been told." He smiled. "Mostly by you."

"Someone needs to keep you humble." She grinned impishly. "Everyone else on this ship falls over backward in awe whenever you snap a command."

"Consider me properly humbled, my lady," he acceded lightly.

India pulled on a light blue wool gown that she'd made with material purchased in New Providence, undoubtedly taken off some hapless merchantman outbound from the Spanish colonies. A quilted silk underdress of contrasting dark blue peeked out from beneath the hem. Not the height of fashion, but certainly practical as they approached the cold northern seas. She turned to let Christopher fasten the back. He deftly closed the hooks of her bodice, letting his fingers linger a bit longer than needful on her bare skin.

India turned to him with a knowing smile. "In spite of the fact that I adore you, you're still the most arrogant blackguard I've ever met."

"Aye, my sweet." He grinned. "And you are the most impetuous, infuriating little minx I've ever had the misfortune to run across."

"Indeed?" She raised a mocking brow.

"Yes, indeed!" He ducked and headed toward the door as a pillow whizzed past his ear. "But India?" He turned with his hand on the latch.

"Yes?"

"I'm truly glad you're back, my love."

She smiled happily as he went out the door.

CHAPTER TWENTY-TWO

India watched the coastline slip slowly by as the *Black Falcon* glided majestically to her island anchorage off the Scottish mainland. The air on this early-September morning was damp and chill. The gray clouds were so low it seemed at any moment they would dip to join the sea. She shivered and wrapped herself more tightly in Christopher's thick woolen cloak. If she ever did get back to England, India thought wryly, she would certainly appreciate having once again a full and complete wardrobe of her own, instead of having to borrow Christopher's impossibly oversized clothing. The meager wardrobe she'd made for herself since her marriage was woefully inadequate for the variety of climates she'd been subjected to in these last months.

Christopher stepped up from behind and wrapped his arms around her slender body, adding his warmth to that of the thick cloak.

"Well, my love," he asked, "how do you like the Falcon's Nest?"

There was a note in his voice that betrayed his feelings on this homecoming. The feelings were echoed in the face of every crewman. Most had families here that they hadn't seen in months. One or two had grown up in this region, and all were grateful for the coming respite from endless days and nights at sea.

India leaned her head back on Christopher's hard chest.

"I can't see anything except water and fog and rocks," she complained. "Not very impressive, this hideaway of yours."

Christopher laughed gently. "You can't see the Lodge from here. It's on another inlet a few miles away, but this is a better cove for anchoring. The Lodge gets some high winds at times."

India shivered at the thought of cold winter winds howling around some rough-and-tumble structure that Christopher's band of smugglers called home.

"How will we get to this Lodge?" India asked gloomily.

"Horses. You can ride, can't you?"

"Of course I can ride!" India replied indignantly.

This was not precisely the homecoming India had imagined. She had some hazy picture of sailing back to a civilized English port and there confronting Christopher with the fact that she had no intention of sitting docilely by while he enjoyed the effect of their marriage on her unfortunate father. Instead, here they were anchoring at this little nameless island off the western Scottish coast. A wave of homesickness clutched at her heart as she thought of the green manicured countryside surrounding her beloved Hillcrest and compared it to the rocky, forbidding shore of the island the crew had dubbed the Falcon's Nest.

"Will we be here long?" she asked.

"Long enough, my love," Christopher replied. "This island is my home, India. As my wife you'll have to make it your home, too, at least until I can clear my name and persuade King George to restore what Queen Anne took away."

India watched the forbidding coastline in gloomy silence, unable to think of any fitting reply to the depressing picture he drew of her future.

"Don't be so sad, my love," he finally said, sensing her dismay. "You'll be quite comfortable here. We're not quite as primitive as you're imagining. And I'll be here much of the time. Now that I have you to think about I plan to cut down on the smuggling operations a bit."

"And what about my father?"

"What about your father, little one?" he asked gently.

India turned to him with a pleading look on her face. "Can't you give up this vengeance, Christopher? For my sake. Can't you send a message to my father saying you'll make no claims on the Carey estates and make no effort to besmirch his name? It would be so easy!"

His hard gaze forced her to lower her eyes, but then she plunged on with dogged determination. "You don't need the Carey holdings. If you succeed in clearing your name you'll have your own estates back."

"Not necessarily, India."

"If you don't clear your name you won't be able to claim the estates anyway!"

"My children will be able to claim them through you, however," he reminded her. "That's all I really require— that my descendants reap the precious heritage Sir William garnered for his own. That knowledge alone is enough, I'm sure, to rob him of peace of mind for the rest of his years."

India turned from him in a vain attempt to hide the trembling of her chin. It was hard to work up enough anger and indignation to wipe away her feelings of betrayal. The last few weeks at sea Christopher had been so loving. She'd felt protected and cherished as the both of them had explored each other's bodies and souls with an openness possible only between two people securely in love. As she had relearned to trust him with her body, she'd also learned to trust him with her feelings, discovering that beneath his granite-hard exterior was a reservoir of sensitivity and perceptiveness that she'd never suspected. And he'd held nothing back from her. Not his bitterness, his vulnerability, his hopes for the future—their future. He made no effort to hide his joy in her. Playing her like a fine-tuned instrument, with great skill he wove her emotional and physical desires into one fierce ache that could be satisfied only by him. One by one her inhibitions fell before his onslaught, until at last she had no qualms about his using her body any way he desired, knowing that he would never hurt her in spite of his strength, knowing that with every touch he was telling her of his love. She in turn learned what inflamed him to instant passion and how to kindle a slow burn that would culminate eventually in a conflagration of desire that would scorch them both with its intensity. And in their quiet moments, she glimpsed the deep-seated feelings he hid behind the fierce exterior he showed to the world.

In these last weeks, they had learned to trust each other as well as love each other, India thought. And yet now Christopher was callously reminding her that his primary use for her was to avenge himself on her father. She and any children she bore him would be instruments to make sure her father lost all he valued, and that Christopher won. The time for truce was over, it seemed. Her heart squeezed painfully. She'd laid herself open, and now he'd struck a blow deep into her core. She'd hoped that these days they'd shared so lovingly had mellowed his purpose, that for her sake, at least, he would consent to send reassurances to ease her father's mind. But no, his purpose was as firm as ever.

"I can't be a willing wife to you while my father suffers from our union," she finally said with a determined tilt of her head.

Christopher turned her to face him, and she hastily wiped the tear streaks from her face.

"You still believe your father is innocent of any wrongdoing, don't you?" he asked.

She lowered her eyes, then raised them to meet his openly.

"I don't for one minute believe that you did the horrible things he accused you of. Not anymore. He made a mistake, and it was an awful mistake, but you've no right to hound a man for making an honest error."

Christopher sighed. "He made a mistake, all right. But his mistake was to think he could make a hero out of himself by falsely condemning an innocent man, ruining my name, robbing me of my title and estates, and then escape punishment for the rest of his life. He's going to pay, and pay dearly."

"You're wrong," India insisted. "My father never did a dishonorable thing in his entire life."

A tear threatened to roll down her cheek, and she shook it away impatiently, ashamed to let him see how upset she was.

Christopher shook his head sadly. "My poor little love," he said softly. "You cling to your faith so stubbornly."

"How can you do this to me when you say you love me?" India demanded tearfully.

"I do love you," he countered gently. "You are dearer to me than life itself, and I would never willingly see you hurt. But this has been burning in me so long that it cannot be denied, India. How can you expect me to forget what he did to me?"

She refused to meet his eyes as he tilted her face up toward his.

"India," he continued, "you aren't responsible for what your father did to me, and you aren't responsible for what I do to him. It's out of your hands. Can't we just enjoy the fact that we're together, that we love each other, and that someday we will be back at Woodsford with a family that we both love, God willing, and all this will be cleared up?"

"Impossible!" She hid her face in her hands and let the

tears flow freely, but she didn't deny him when he pulled her to him and cradled her against his broad chest.

"Think of it this way, sweetheart," he finally said. "If I hadn't found you, then the minute my name was cleared— and it will be cleared, make no mistake about that, my darling—the minute my name was cleared I'd have sought your father out, challenged him to a duel, and killed him. So by being here with me you're actually saving his life."

"That's barbarian!" she said, pulling back from him. "He's an old man!"

"Nevertheless, my dear, I would've done it."

"You're a bloody monster!" Her face threatened to crumple again, and he pulled her back into the cradle of his arms.

"So you've told me many times, my love."

"How can I love you when you're such a cutthroat?"

He laughed softly. "You love me because I adore you, and because you know I'm not really a cutthroat. Someday you'll realize the truth that Sir William Carey is getting off lightly for the crime he committed."

India turned away in a temper. "You won't laugh, sir, when I find some way to foil your plans! I do love you. I'll probably always love you. But I have no intention of sitting by and letting you make my father suffer through me!"

"My fiery little India." In a gentle caress, Christopher lifted the heavy, dark curls from where they rested on her neck. She impatiently batted his hand away. "There's no way you can prevent me," he continued. "So give in, my love."

"I will escape you, if it's the last thing I do!" she vowed, trying to keep the tremor of grief from her voice.

"You can't escape," he reminded her with a smile. "You gave your word."

She turned and looked at him in amazement.

"Remember the duel." He raised a knowing brow.

"You would hold me to that now?" she demanded furiously.

"Most certainly," he assured her without hesitation. "I

will hold you to that forever. You not only promised to not escape, but to be my willing wife.''

''I didn't think I would lose,'' she explained. Even to herself, the excuse sounded silly.

''You did lose, most thoroughly!'' He grinned at the memory. ''And knowing you to be a woman of honor, who would not dream of breaking her given word, I suggest you prepare to settle down here on this cozy Scottish island and resign yourself to enjoying the most loving attentions of your husband.''

''Ooooooh, you swine!'' Her eyes flashed fire.

The unperturbed grin never left his face. ''You love me, though, don't you.''

His unassailable confidence infuriated her almost as much as his stubborn insistence on revenge.

''I do, you blackhearted bastard,'' she admitted. ''Though why, I'll never know. I wish you had left me on the *Sea Gull* that day. Better to drown than to spend the rest of my life in the arms of a blackguard like you!''

He chuckled as she swept away in a flurry of tossing curls and indignantly swirling skirts, favoring him with just one more angry, smoky-gray look before she descended stiff-backed to their cabin to pack.

Seamus Kennedy raised a quizzical brow when he joined Christopher on the quarterdeck a few moments later.

''Trouble in paradise?'' he inquired.

Christopher shrugged. ''Nothing that won't blow over eventually. I hope,'' he added as an afterthought.

''She upset about Sir William?''

Christopher raised a brow.

''Well,'' Seamus continued somewhat sheepishly, ''you two weren't exactly whispering, you know.''

''You're as nosy as an old woman, do you know that?'' Christopher accused.

''I like India.'' Seamus shrugged. ''I hate to see her get upset over that old bastard.''

Christopher looked at his friend in surprise. ''What do you know about India's father?''

''Just what Helen's told me. She despises the old guy.

Says he treated her like dirt from the day she came into the house. I guess he didn't treat India much better. Helen says he always let India know that as a daughter she was more trouble than she was worth. That's when he wasn't ignoring her."

"Well," Christopher mused, "I would guess she has his attention now."

"Not in the way she wants it, I expect."

"Aye, well, she still thinks he's a saint. When I catch up with John Thomas, maybe then she'll realize I'm telling her the truth. I suspect it was Sir William who conveniently got him out of the way before he could testify to the innocence of my conversation with Phillipe Duquesne that night."

Seamus stood in thoughtful silence as the *Falcon* slipped into a well-protected cove. A seaman in the forechains rhythmically sang out the water depths as the ship gracefully glided into the rocky inlet. Finally, Christopher gave the order to come about and drop anchor. The deck became a picture of well-organized activity as orders flew back and forth and seamen scrambled up the rigging to take in the topsail, the only sheet they'd used to maneuver into the tiny cove. The sail flapped and snapped rebelliously as the *Falcon* came across the wind and the seamen hauled in on the lines.

"Haven't seen the lads look so lively for weeks," Seamus commented.

Christopher nodded in agreement. "They're glad to be home. So am I, if the truth be known."

Seamus looked at him thoughtfully for a moment. "Why don't you give it up, Christopher?"

"Give what up?"

"This plan of revenge against Sir William," Seamus answered. "I know the man deserves anything you can give him, but is it worth hurting India to hurt him?"

Christopher paused for a long moment, ostensibly watching the seamen aloft.

"No," he finally said. "It isn't. I wouldn't hurt India for the world. But it isn't that simple."

"How not?"

"Sir William's greed. He's obsessed with his family's honor—and for him honor means money and land. When the king awarded the old toad my land, Sir William asked that the land never pass out of his family. And the king was only too happy to oblige the man who'd just unmasked a traitor. If Sir William dies without a male heir, the land goes to his eldest daughter, then to her eldest child. And the estate has to be kept intact. Oh, the heiress's husband would have to administer it for her, but he can't go selling off parcels of land. It would take an act of Parliament to overturn the arrangement, and Sir William doesn't have that sort of power."

"Seems like the inheritance wouldn't make that much difference to him," Seamus said. "After all, he'll be dead, and his grandchild will end up with the land."

Christopher laughed. "But his precious family blood will be tainted by that of his worst enemy. My child will one day own his lands. I can see only one way to prevent that. India would have to divorce me, and I certainly don't intend to let her try that. No, I'll sire the next generation of Sir William's family; that knowledge will be a worse punishment for him than if I slit him ear-to-ear with my knife."

"Aye, I'll take your word on it. But give me a good bloody fight any day over all this devious nonsense," Seamus concluded. "I can't see India sitting by while her father squirms for the rest of his life, especially if she thinks he's innocent as a lamb, as you say. She's a hardheaded girl, that wife of yours."

"She's hardheaded," Christopher admitted. "But she'll come around. I'm not planning on giving her a choice in the matter."

The Lodge was not what India expected. On first viewing it from atop the graceful little mare that had carried her the two miles from the anchorage to the neighboring cove, she thought the imposing gray-stone edifice looked more like a castle than a lodge. A huge, square, three-story building with a turret on one side, her new home seemed to grow naturally out of the rocky shore of a small, shallow inlet. A short distance from the thick stone walls of the house, a good-sized stream emptied into the cove. Its banks were shaded by birch and a few sturdy pines. Across the stream and separate from the main house and outbuildings, a group of cottages constructed from the same rough gray-stone as the main house huddled in the shelter of a birch grove. The whole scene, India thought, was reminiscent of a medieval castle standing guard over a tiny village.

"That doesn't look like any lodge to me!" India turned to Christopher, who had pulled up beside her on the great bay stallion he was riding.

"Ah, well," Christopher acknowledged. "We gave it that name because it's rather rough on the inside, more like a men's hunting lodge than a proper home. My officers live there, with their families, and so does Teddy. The crew live in those cottages in the grove, except for some who live in the fishing village on the other side of the island."

"Other people live on this island?" India asked in surprise.

"As I said, there's a village on the other side of the island, about five miles from here."

"Do they know they have an outlaw living in their midst?"

Christopher laughed. "Certainly they do."

"Aren't you afraid they'll bring the authorities down on your head?"

"This is Scotland, not England, little one," Christopher replied. "The Scots are not so fond of the English as to help them curb their wayward sons. Quite the opposite, in fact."

"Oh," she said.

"Cheer up, little one." He grinned. "You'll like it here."

She shot him a resentful glance as the bay stallion started down the rocky hill toward the main house, then nudged her mare to follow after.

India had to admit, though, that no matter how forbidding on the outside, the house was charming on the inside. The rooms were spacious, with huge fireplaces lending a cozy warmth that she wouldn't have believed possible in such a place. The stone floors were covered with rich oriental rugs, and colorful tapestries hung suspended in front of most walls. The furniture was rough-hewn but attractive. Much of it looked homemade, and India wondered who among Christopher's crew had the talent for some of the beautiful woodwork she saw displayed in some of the pieces. A few items were obviously imported, like the huge English oak desk in the study, and the beveled, full-length gilt mirror hanging in the entry hall.

"However did you get this place, Christopher?" India asked, warming herself in front of the main-room fireplace. She had to admit she was utterly charmed with the house, even though the atmosphere and furnishings were definitely masculine.

"The former owner was anxious to sell," Christopher told her with a wicked grin. "Seems there were rumors of smugglers and pirates operating in the area."

India's eyes widened a trifle. "You are a horrible rogue!"

Christopher smiled. "He got a fair price for it, and it suited my purposes ideally."

India moved away from the fire and ran an appreciative hand over the carved armrest of a large wooden rocker.

"Did someone here do this?" she asked. "I don't think I've ever seen anything like it before."

"My old ship's carpenter and I made most of the furniture. The carpenter's son Nate did the carving. He's got quite a talent, that boy."

"You can't mean old Tom Crowley!" India said in amazement, thinking of the crippled old ship's carpenter who'd lost a leg and an eye in Newgate prison after stealing bread to feed his family.

"No," Christopher replied. "This was George Dunbar. He and his wife and son are in England now, where young Nate is getting some schooling. George is doing quite well in London now, after spending two years with me aboard the *Black Falcon*."

"Is smuggling really that profitable, then?"

"It's made me a wealthy man, and most of my crew as well. I expect with the profits from the *Navarre* and *Lady*

Mary added to what they already have, most of the men will be wanting to settle down to a quieter life. I'll probably have to find the better part of a new crew before I set out again.''

"How wealthy are you, Christopher?'' India queried with a curious gleam in her eye.

He noted her interest with amusement.

"Very wealthy, my love. You don't have to worry about living in poverty here. Anything you want, I'll send someone to the mainland to get. If you want to make changes in the house so you'll be more comfortable here, we can do that. Money is of no concern. I just want you to be happy and comfortable.''

"There is only one thing you could do to make me happy here, Christopher, and you know what it is.''

India met his gaze with a level look of determination.

Christopher's face darkened. "That subject is closed. I want no more discussion on the matter.''

"You have all this wealth,'' she insisted. "Why should you want the Carey estates? Why should you even want to go back to Woodsford? You could buy something twice as grand!''

He regarded her with eyes gone dark with displeasure.

"You know my reasons, India. You just choose to ignore them.''

Their eyes locked in silent combat for long moments. Finally he moved to pick up his cloak where it was warming by the fire.

"I've got business to attend to aboard the *Falcon*, but I'll be back before dinner. I'll have Mrs. Toffler show you to our room.'' He put a slight emphasis on the word *our*, as if to let her know he expected their relationship to continue just as before. "I've asked her to engage a girl from the village to see to your personal needs, and she'll introduce you to the rest of the house staff. You're mistress of this house now, but Mrs. Toffler has been housekeeper here for quite some time, and I imagine she can be a help to you in learning how the place runs.''

India pointedly turned her back to him, angry that she

couldn't get him to budge from his determination to punish her only kin. He noticed the stubborn set of her shoulders, took two angry strides toward her, and roughly turned her around to face him.

"I've had enough of this, India!" he warned in a quiet, hard-edged voice. "What I feel about your father has nothing to do with how I feel about you, and I will not let you make this such an issue between us! What's done cannot be undone. By law your father's estate must pass to you on his death, and if it grieves him that I'll father his grandchildren, so much the better. The only way you can free your father, India, is by divorcing me, which would take an act of Parliament. And even if you could obtain a divorce, I don't believe that you truly want to leave me for the sake of a hypocritical old man who never gave you a scrap of affection in your life."

India looked up into his harsh face, that face that could be so tender and loving one moment and so grim the next, and she felt hot tears well into her eyes. If what he said was true, then she was baffled. She didn't know what to think or how to feel. She didn't struggle when he pulled her gently against his chest.

"I don't know what to think," she cried. "I feel so . . ."

"Well, isn't this a sweet scene!"

Both Christopher and India started at the feminine voice that interrupted them. India hastily pulled out of Christopher's embrace and wiped her eyes while a mingled look of surprise and dismay played across Christopher's features. A statuesque blond goddess lounged indolently in the doorway and regarded them with hooded and somewhat hostile eyes. India stiffened as the woman's gaze lingered briefly, appraisingly, on her, then seemed to dismiss her as unimportant and returned confidently to Christopher. She glided gracefully into the room.

"I can see you're surprised to see me, darling," the blonde purred at Christopher. "But I just couldn't resist welcoming you home. I knew you'd return to Falcon's Nest one of these weeks, so I just decided to move here for a short while. I knew you wouldn't object."

The woman swept Christopher with an intimate glance that set India's eyes to blazing. She realized now why Mrs. Toffler the housekeeper had looked so panic-stricken when Christopher had introduced her earlier. Now it was Christopher's turn to look slightly panicky. He regained his composure quickly, though, and fixed the silk-clad goddess with a wary frown.

"Sarah," he began, "may I present my wife, India Catherine. India, this is Mistress Sarah Perkins, an...old friend."

Sarah Perkins regarded India icily from under arched, finely drawn brows. She took in India's plain wool dress, loose, uncoiffed hair and damp, slightly bedraggled appearance and then fixed Christopher with an indignant gaze.

"Wife?" she inquired unbelievingly.

Christopher's tone was firm. "Yes, Sarah, India is my wife. We've been married almost half a year."

"You don't say!" The blonde's voice dripped acid.

Christopher sighed. Things were getting difficult.

India could have sworn she saw a look of pleading in Christopher's eyes when he turned to her.

"Why don't you go upstairs and rest a bit. Mrs. Toffler will show you our room."

India tapped her foot impatiently against the wool carpet. Old friend, indeed! And now he expected her to go upstairs and leave him down here to sport with this blond hussy. Never!

"I think I'd prefer to stay," she said sweetly.

"I insist," he returned mildly. But she saw the warning glint of steel in his eyes. "I'll join you in a few minutes."

"Yes, my dear," Sarah joined in. "You do look a bit worse for wear. The voyage must have been so arduous."

There was a look of triumph in her eyes.

India longed to mash the blonde's face against the nearest stone wall, but had to settle for tilting her little chin at a defiant angle and returning Sarah's challenging smile with a look of contempt. She swept out of the room with as haughty an air as she could manage, trying to hide the revealing tremble of her lips as she shut the door behind her.

"Damnation, Sarah!" The light of triumph faded in the blonde's eyes as Christopher turned the full force of his anger on her. "Since when have you started barging in where you're not invited!"

"I only thought to please you!" she insisted, drawing herself up to her full height and throwing back her shoulders to display her large breasts to full advantage. "How was I to know you'd drag back a mewling child bride with you! Really, Christopher, she's not your type at all!"

"Leave India out of this discussion!"

"I damn well will not leave her out of this discussion! I've been your mistress for three years, you bastard, and you have the nerve to drag home that snot-nosed child and parade her around as your wife. All the time you played with my affections and told me you didn't want to marry! You blackhearted scoundrel! You lying piece of—"

"Lower your voice, my dear," Christopher cut her off. "Unless you want the entire household to hear your shrieking."

"I don't care who hears!" she cried. "The whole island can hear, for all I care! You've made me a laughingstock!"

Christopher was unmoved. "You've made yourself a laughingstock, madam, by coming here uninvited. You presume too much on a casual relationship."

"Casual!" she gasped.

"Casual. It's true you've been my mistress off and on for several years, Sarah. But we both understood there were no obligations on either side. You know very well that I've had several mistresses during the years I've known you, and you've had more than one lover during that time. I'm sorry if India came as a shock to you, but you brought it on yourself by presuming on your welcome here."

Sarah turned away from him and composed her features. She was taking the wrong tack and getting nowhere fast. Somehow she had to salvage what she'd almost lost. The wife, and the obvious affection in Christopher's eyes when he looked at her, had been an extremely unpleasant surprise that had robbed her of her usual cool aplomb. She had been looking forward to sharing once again Christopher's bed and generosity. The widow's portion left to her by her late husband could hardly support one with her taste for high living, and Christopher had provided well for her while enjoying her favors in the past. She attempted a pathetic sniff and turned toward him once again.

"You're right, Christopher," she said in apologetic tones. "It was wrong of me to come here without your permission. But"—and here she allowed a tiny break in her voice to reveal the depth of her emotion—"I was so anxious to see you again, I just lost all sense of propriety."

Christopher suspected that Sarah's desire to see him again stemmed as much from the lightness of her purse as her fondness for his company.

"I admit your being married so suddenly came as a bit of a shock, my darling," Sarah continued in dulcet tones. "I apologize for my raving display of jealousy, but you've come to mean so much more to me than . . . than just a casual relationship. I can't bear the thought of losing you now, Christopher."

"You have lost me, Sarah. Rather, you never really had me," Christopher reminded her callously. "I think your memory has exaggerated the intensity of our involvement."

She stepped closer to him, positioning herself so that Christopher could see down her low-cut bodice. Perhaps the man had forgotten the delicacies she had to offer. She touched him almost shyly, rubbing her hand along his muscular arm, delighting in the feel of his hardness under her fingers. It had been such a long, long time since she'd been bedded by a man as skilled as this one. Memories sent little shivers up her spine.

"My involvement was very intense," she said huskily. "But I'm not a demanding woman, my love. I'll even forgive your marrying. We can just continue as before, anytime you want."

Christopher firmly set her hands from his body.

"No, Sarah," he said. "We can't continue just as before."

"But why not?" She arched her fine brows in amazement at his refusal.

"I have no desire to bed any woman other than my wife."

"How virtuous of you," Sarah commented in a disbelieving

tone. "I've never known you to be overcome by virtue before, my dear, and you can't tell me that that little chit can satisfy a stud like you in bed!"

Christopher's eyes glinted dangerously.

"Sarah, you're trying my patience. I want you out of here by dinner tonight."

Sarah looked at him in shock. This couldn't be happening. It simply wasn't possible that she, with all her bountiful charms, could lose Christopher to the whey-faced little stray kitten of a wife he'd picked up who knows where and who knows why. She needed time to regroup. A strategic retreat was called for at this point.

"By dinner!" she laughed. "Impossible, my dear! I've been here for two months! I can't possibly be packed and out in under two weeks' time!"

Christopher sighed. Women!

"A week. That's all I'll give you, Sarah. And if you upset my wife during the time that you remain here, I'll confine you to your rooms; I swear I will!"

Sarah watched him climb the stairs to his room with a catch in her throat. Lord, he was magnificent, the way he moved with the sinuous grace of a hunting panther. She remembered only too well the feel of that hard body possessing hers. A week was a short time, but she'd think of something to regain her position in his bed. She certainly didn't intend to give up without a fight, so that skinny little wife of his better watch her every step.

CHAPTER TWENTY-THREE

"Old friend?" India greeted Christopher with a sarcastically lifted brow as he stepped through the door into the master suite.

"Ex-mistress," he explained calmly, not at all taken aback by India's dangerously glinting eyes.

"You admit it?" India stood with hands on her slim hips, regarding him with more than a little irritation.

Christopher took in her indignant stance and chuckled.

"Of course I admit it. Why shouldn't I?"

India was nonplussed. She'd expected a hot denial, protestations of innocence, apologies, anything but a calm admission that the blond overripe trollop had been his lover.

Christopher saw her confusion and smiled tolerantly.

"Don't be a prude, India," he said. "Do you think I lived like a monk before I pulled you off the *Sea Gull*?"

His eyes were gleaming mischievously.

"Well . . . no," she admitted. "But I didn't expect to be living in the same house with your whore, either!"

"Sarah's not a whore," he countered levelly. "She's a respectable . . . well, near-respectable . . . widow from Edinburgh. Kin to Ian by marriage, as a matter of fact."

"I don't care who she is, Christopher. I won't stand by and be insulted by that overblown cow while she waves her udders at me!"

"Um," Christopher said noncommittally, noting with mischievous pleasure the hot flush that rose to India's face as his eyes raked over her slim figure as if to compare it to Sarah's voluptuous contours. India was so angry that she missed the sparkle of merriment in his eyes.

"Oooooooh! You impossible, arrogant, strutting peacock! You're enjoying this!"

He smiled.

"Why, that woman looked ready to pull off her clothes and jump on you right from the moment she walked into that room. And you loved every moment of it, you insufferable male animal you!"

Christopher lolled indolently against one post of the bed and watched while India fumed.

"You're jealous," he finally pronounced.

"Jealous?" she cried indignantly. "I most certainly am

not! If you've such a taste for overstuffed pillows, you can just go ahead and . . . and . . . and I hope you choke on all that overripe flesh when you do!''

Christopher chuckled. "If I'm going to enjoy anyone's flesh; my sweet, I'm afraid it will have to be yours. I told Sarah to pack her things and leave.''

"Really?" India's voice immediately took on a happier note.

"Really," he confirmed. "I gave her a week to gather up her fripperies, and then out. I'm no longer interested in what she has to offer.''

"Oh," India said somewhat sheepishly. "I guess I am a bit jealous, after all," she admitted.

Christopher reached out and pulled her to him. "I recognize the disease because I have it myself," he said. "Remember?"

"Mmm, yes, now that you mention it." India wrapped her arms around his lean waist and tilted her head up to look at him.

"You're really not the least bit interested in her anymore?" she asked searchingly. "She is awfully . . ."

She groped to find an appropriate word to describe Sarah's impressive proportions, but nothing came.

"Yes, she is, isn't she." Christopher chuckled appreciatively, knowing very well what India meant.

"You lecher!" India smiled up at him, knowing this time that he was teasing.

"Guilty," he admitted. "But you've no reason to be jealous, my love. Why should I need a mistress when my wife is so wonderfully bedable.''

India blushed and smiled briefly, but when she pulled out of his embrace she turned away with a look of distress clouding her face. Christopher sighed. Women! With all his experience with the fairer sex, he thought he understood them fairly well. But every time he thought he understood his wife, she baffled him again. What could be bothering her now? He sighed in resignation.

"Well"—he started to take his leave—"I've got business on the *Falcon*, but I should be home before dinner. The crew will be bringing our chest up later today, and you can ask Mrs. Toffler to help you in the unpacking.''

She turned to him with a smile he knew was a sham, and he wondered what she was hiding. He pressed a light kiss to her lips and another to the tip of her nose.

''I'll see you later, then,'' he said as he walked out the door.

India stood at the window and watched as Christopher mounted the bay stallion and cantered down the rocky path. He sat a horse as gracefully as he bestrode a tossing deck, India noted. She continued watching until long after he was out of sight.

The master suite had a magnificent view of the cove and its entrance into the sea; at least it would be a magnificent view on a fair day. When the air was exceptionally clear, Mrs. Toffler had informed her with pride, one could look out the window of the master suite and sometimes see clear across the water to the much larger island of Skye. The view today, however, suited India's mood very well, with the low-scudding clouds dipping down almost to touch the gray sea and the cold fog curling around the gray-stone walls of the house as if searching for ways to invade the interior.

India sighed and dropped the heavy curtain back into place. Would Christopher think she was still bedable, as he'd called it, when she was swollen with his child? She walked over to the full-length mirror that hung from one wall, pressing a hand to her flat stomach and regarding herself in profile. There were no outward signs yet, but she was positive she carried Christopher's child. Her occasional nausea and dizziness during the last few weeks at sea she'd excused as seasickness, and if Christopher thought it strange that she'd developed seasickness after so much time at sea, he hadn't mentioned it. But after she'd missed her monthly flow for the second time, India could no longer fool herself as to the cause of her nausea, her sore and swollen breasts, and her unreasonable fits of depression. She was most definitely pregnant.

Christopher would be delighted, no doubt, that she was

going to present him with a child who would assure his revenge on William Carey. That had been his purpose, after all, to strike at his enemy by presenting him with a legitimate grandchild sprung from Christopher's loins, a grandchild who would carry on the precious Carey tradition and safeguard the vaunted Carey honor, sired by a man William Carey had called traitorous scum and condemned to the gallows. Her father would be apoplectic, India thought, if he knew. And she was sure Christopher would see to it that he knew.

But what of herself? Now that Christopher had accomplished his purpose on her, would he turn to Sarah, or someone like her, to enjoy her bountiful charms while India grew swollen and awkward? Christopher enjoyed bedsport too much to want to sleep with a misshapen cow, India thought bitterly. She scowled at herself in the mirror, trying to imagine how she would look six months hence. Would Christopher still love her when she looked more like a pear than a woman? Would he still cherish her now that his vengeance was accomplished—now that he had won? India's scowl grew deeper as she realized she no longer wanted to escape her husband, even if there were a way out of the trap he'd sprung. And there really was no way out. Annulment was out of the question, since she was carrying a child. Divorce was almost as impossible, as he'd pointed out earlier. And here she was, India thought miserably, grieving not over her father's anger, her family's disgrace, but over the thought that she might even temporarily lose the attentions of the man she'd come to love, rogue though he was.

Christopher did not return in time for dinner, as he'd promised. Instead, he sent a message with a crewman, saying that he'd been detained and to serve the meal without him. So India had the doubtful pleasure of dining alone with Sarah Perkins.

Sarah did not pass up the opportunity to show Christopher's upstart wife just what she was up against. She dressed carefully, having her maid Lisa, who'd come with her from Edinburgh, pile her silver-blond hair high in a fashionable coiffure while she applied just enough color to her cheeks, lips, and around her eyes to enhance her natural charms. Her gown of emerald-green damask set off her coloring to perfection and displayed a vast expanse of impressive bosom above the low-cut bodice. She wished only that Christopher were present to appreciate the effect. Sarah's effect on India, however, was most satisfying to the voluptuous widow.

It was all India could do to keep from fleeing back up to her room when Sarah made her appearance at the dinner table. It was obvious that the older woman had declared war, and her appearance left no doubt as to the potency of her weapons. India felt like a drab little wren in her plain wool gown with no flounces or furbelows, not even a fashionable number of petticoats or hoops. The day of unpacking sea chests and touring the kitchens, storage cellars, and gardens with Mrs. Toffler had not left her refreshed and in a mood for feminine battle this evening. She cursed Christopher for not being there to defend her, then on second thought was grateful he was not present to appreciate Sarah's display of her charms.

"Good evening, Mistress Barnett," Sarah began politely. "Or may I presume to call you India?"

She had to be careful, Sarah knew. If she gave the chit anything concrete to complain about, Christopher would have her out on her ear, packed or not.

India tried not to stare in awe at the stunning effect of the green damask combined with Sarah's green eyes and silver-blond hair.

"You may call me India, if you wish," she finally answered.

The soup was served before the battle began in earnest.

"Where did you meet Christopher, my dear?" Sarah asked with saccharine sweetness. "Yours must have been a very sudden marriage. Certainly none of Christopher's friends knew he had plans to wed." Her smile dripped acid.

India hesitated over a spoonful of chowder. Had Christopher told the woman about the circumstances of their marriage? If not, she'd be damned if she'd let the overstuffed trollop know that Christopher had married her out of revenge and not out of love. But again, maybe she already knew and was simply trying to embarrass her by asking.

"Christopher rescued a friend and me from a shipwreck off St. Albans Head early last spring," India said with as much poise as she could muster. She wished desperately that Helen had come to the house instead of staying with Seamus on the ship. Helen's sharp tongue would have set this hussy back on her heels!

"My, you must have been married very soon after that to have been married almost half a year, as Christopher said."

A light of suspicion gleamed in Sarah's green eyes.

"Yes, we were," India replied noncommittally.

The look in Sarah's eyes made her uneasy.

"How interesting," Sarah persisted. "Christopher has always been such a rogue where women are concerned. How did you ever get him to marry you?"

"Actually," said India, glad to be able to stick to the truth, "he was the one who was eager to be wed."

Sarah shot her a look of disbelief as the soup was cleared away, but refrained from saying anything more for a few moments.

The second attack was aimed in a different direction.

"My dear," Sarah started again with a look of sympathy in her eyes, "you really should make Christopher treat you better. Why, you look like you haven't visited a civilized port since your shipwreck. I'm surprised that Christopher would let his wife go around dressed like a serving maid. He usually is so appreciative of a woman's appearance."

India stiffened. That barb had hit home.

"My wardrobe was lost in the shipwreck," she explained.

"I can't imagine why Christopher hasn't bought you a new one, dear." Sarah's eyes were alight with malice now. "He knows all the best dressmakers in Edinburgh. London, too. Why, just last autumn he ordered this dress made exclusively for me by Madame Blanche in Edinburgh. He said no other woman he knew could complement a gown the way I can."

India regarded Sarah icily. "He has good taste in clothes, at least, I'll have to admit."

Sarah stiffened at the thinly veiled insult. So the bedraggled little kitten had claws, did she!

A platter of lamb was placed on the table, complemented with fresh garden vegetables and a golden-brown loaf of freshly baked bread, still warm from the oven. India looked at the platter of meat and gravy with distaste, though normally she enjoyed lamb. Why couldn't morning sickness confine itself to mornings!

"You really should eat, dear," Sarah said solicitously. "You're so thin, you could almost pass as a boy. A little more flesh might possibly make you look more like a woman."

India smiled wickedly. "The truth is that youth, and not lack of appetite, is responsible for my slenderness, Sarah. But I imagine when I reach your age I will begin to round out. I've been told that women over thirty do tend to put on weight."

Sarah's eyes narrowed to slits, but she could find no reply. Round three was over. The rest of the meal was eaten in hostile silence.

India did not hear Christopher return during the night, but when she awoke in the gray dawn of morning, he lay beside her with his hard-muscled arm flung possessively over her breasts. She lay still, not wanting to rouse him, and gazed lovingly at his face, as though to memorize every detail for recall at some later time when she might no longer have him. He didn't look nearly so fierce in his sleep, she noted. With thick, dark lashes resting against his cheeks and his well-molded, sensuous mouth relaxed in the dark beard, he looked more vulnerable than frightening. It had been quite a while, India realized, since she'd really been afraid of him. She wondered now at what point she'd discovered that he wasn't as tigerish as he seemed, at least where she was concerned. When had she finally realized that Christopher never really intended to hurt her?

India let her eyes travel from his face, down the muscular column of his neck, and across his powerful shoulders and back to where his hips disappeared beneath the sheets. He had a certain grace and power even lying there asleep, India thought. Suddenly an unwelcome vision of Christopher's powerful body straining on top of the well-padded curves of Sarah Perkins flashed through her mind, and her stomach churned. In fact, India realized, her stomach had been uneasy since first awakening, and was now reaching an uncomfortable climax of nausea. The memory of the gravy-laden lamb she'd picked at the night before danced unbidden before her eyes. She groaned and pulled away from Christopher's heavy arm, waking him with her movements. He felt her slip toward the edge of the bed and tightened his grip, pulling her back toward him.

"Don't go," he murmured sleepily.

India struggled to hold back the insistent nausea.

"Let me go, Christopher! I'm sick!"

"What?" he mumbled.

She broke his hold, swung her legs over the edge of the bed, and dashed behind the screen to the chamber pot, getting there just in time. In moments, Christopher was beside her, holding her head firmly while she lost the meager contents of her stomach into the pot.

"My God, India!" he exclaimed, fully awake now. "What's wrong? Are you ill?"

He dipped a towel in the basin of water on the dresser and sponged off her forehead and face, frowning with concern.

"No, really, I'm much better now." She took the cup of water he handed her, rinsed out her mouth, then sat back down on the bed in relief. "The dinner last night just didn't sit very well with me, that's all." She smiled a bit shakily. "I'm quite all right now."

He sat down beside her on the bed. Now that he was awake and his wife was sitting here beside him, quite enticingly naked, his mind was beginning to turn to other things.

"You're sure you're all right?"

"Quite sure," she confirmed, hoping he wouldn't put two and two together and come up with four. She hadn't yet gathered the courage to tell him about the baby.

"Well, in that case . . ." He shot her a devilish grin. "It's much too early to wake the household, so perhaps we should just go back to bed.''

He pressed a kiss on her shoulder, then wandered slowly down until his mouth caught firm but gentle hold of her already taut nipple. India sighed contentedly as he pushed her back into the pillows and slipped his hand between her thighs. She wanted to be mad at him for leaving her undefended against Sarah Perkins last night, but as usual his touch banished all thought but the longing to have his body possess hers. She gave a little moan as his deft fingers found their way inside her, tantalizing her skillfully as she arched her hips up to meet his hand. She buried her fingers in his dark hair and lifted his head from her breast, bringing his mouth down to meet hers in a hungry kiss.

"I see you are feeling better." He chuckled softly.

He kissed her again deeply, almost savagely, as he felt her hand drift down his chest to his hips and then close over his erect manhood, urging him to accomplish the union that both bodies craved. He smiled down at her, then kissed her eyelids, the tip of her nose, her chin, and again possessed her mouth.

"Ah, wench," he mocked. "When will you learn patience?" He captured both her wandering hands and pinned them above her head. "I think this time we'll take our own sweet time," he murmured, and lowered his mouth to play a leisurely game with her breast while his unoccupied hand lovingly stroked the silken skin of her belly, hips, and thighs. She squirmed with desire as his skillful caresses sent shivers of delight coursing up her spine. Her body thirsted for the fulfillment that he tantalizingly withheld.

"Christopher, please!" she whispered as he continued to pin her helpless to the bed while his hands and mouth took their pleasure.

A wicked laugh sounded in his throat. "Easy, my love," he advised. "Relax. You'll get everything you want in good time."

His mouth wandered lower, tracing a path of fire across her flat belly, pausing to tease at her navel and then even lower as he buried his face between her firm thighs. As his tongue tasted the sweetness of her womanhood, India felt her body take fire. His hands held her hips still and pressed her more tightly against his plundering mouth as she squirmed in delight. His tongue and lips drove her again and again toward the peak of fulfillment, only to hold her back just short of that sought-after release. Finally, after an eternity tossed in the flames of passion, he sought her mouth again. Then in one swift motion he draped her legs over his broad shoulders and buried his aching, swollen shaft deep within the folds of her woman's body. She cried out her welcome as she felt his hot flesh fill her again and again, seemingly trying to flood her whole body with his, to engulf her very soul with his own. His mighty thrusts were slow and deliberate, and he held her to the rhythm of his choosing, then slowly increasing as the frenzied urgency of their joining could no longer be denied. The world exploded in a kaleidoscope of joy as he possessed her with a final mighty thrust and found his pulsing release inside her body. Her cry of joy was muffled as she buried her face in the hollow of his shoulder, not feeling the pain of his intense embrace as his powerful arms locked her tightly against his straining body. Blackness threatened to overwhelm her as her passion approached the limit. She relaxed in his arms, giving herself completely to the drives of their united bodies. Slowly, ever so slowly, the fire died and they drifted pleasantly back to earth, still joined together, arms and legs intertwined. When he withdrew his body from hers, India knew, part of his soul would be left behind to rest with hers. It was as if they had, for that period of time, truly been welded into one being. If he ever left her, some part of his spirit would still be hers.

The rest of the day did not pass so pleasantly. Christopher left early with Seamus and Ian, who had come up to the house late the night before. Saying they wouldn't be back before dinner, the men left Helen and India to get acquainted with Bess, Ian's wife, who had just arrived from her family's home in the fishing village on the other side of the island.

Bess was a sturdy young girl with hair almost as red as Ian's and blue eyes that twinkled with good humor. India had noted with amusement how Ian, formidable as he was on board the *Black Falcon*, deferred to this girl who was half his age and half his size. Her down-to-earth, no nonsense attitude made even Seamus and Christopher sit up and pay attention. India wished with more than a little envy that she could develop the easy camaraderie with the men that seemed second nature to this pretty fisherman's daughter.

The three women spent the better part of the morning getting acquainted. In spite of their vastly different backgrounds, they soon were chatting like old friends. Bess was delighted that both Christopher and Seamus had married, declaring that at last she would have the company of someone besides men in the big house. Helen then dismayed both the others by announcing that she and Seamus planned to leave for his home in Ireland within a month.

"So soon?" India asked with surprise. "I'd hoped you'd be here at least through the winter."

It bothered her more than she cared to admit to think of bidding farewell to this girl who'd been her companion for so long.

"Now that Seamus has decided to leave," Helen explained, "he's eager to go. But don't worry, we'll be back to visit. Seamus says he may buy his own ship. So it's not like I'll be stuck in Ireland with no way to get around. He's not going to leave me at home while he sails off and has all the fun!"

India quailed at the thought of facing the long winter and her pregnancy without Helen's support. Bess's sharp eyes were quick to perceive India's sense of loss.

"Well, it'll be fine," she said in her thick Scots brogue, "to be having another woman in the house. Always before I've had to put up with those braw lads without another lass to keep me company, except for Mrs. Toffler, who's seventy if she's a day."

India chuckled, somewhat comforted for Helen's impending loss by Bess's open offer of friendship.

"From what the ship's boy has told me, I would've thought Christopher had a virtual parade of women through this house."

Bess chuckled. "So that scamp's been informing on his captain, has he?" The Scots girl looked at India carefully, as if to gauge her reaction. "Well, there's some truth in what he says. There's been women in and out, occupying the captain's bed and lording it over the household. But there's never been one I cared to be friends with." She laughed softly. "If the truth be known, I don't think there's been one the captain was really friends with either."

As if on cue, the doors to the main room opened to admit a languorous Sarah Perkins dressed in a fetching morning gown of silk brocade.

Bess's face froze in stunned surprise.

"What are you doing in this house?" she demanded of Sarah indignantly.

"Stop gaping, dear," Sarah returned. "I've been here waiting for Christopher for two months while you've been living in the village cleaning fish."

Bess looked confused.

"It's all right, Bess," India said, sensing her new friend's embarrassment at the presence of Christopher's former mistress. "Mistress Perkins and I have met. She will only be with us a short while." She arched a significant brow toward Sarah. "A week, in fact, is what my husband gave her to be packed and out. Now only six days, I believe."

Sarah favored India with an enigmatic smile.

"That was yesterday though, of course."

"And things are no different today," India said.

"Mmm." Sarah smiled knowingly, as though savoring a secret.

India's irritation was growing by leaps and bounds at the other woman's unexplainable smugness.

"I know very well you haven't talked to Christopher this morning, because he left early, and you obviously didn't rise until just now!"

Sarah arched one delicately drawn brow. "You should know by now, my dear, that one needn't rise from bed to entertain a gentleman."

India gasped at Sarah's brazen implication. It wasn't possible. Christopher couldn't have jumped from her bed to Sarah's this morning, not after making such intense love to her. No, even Christopher wasn't capable of such a thing. Last night, then? Could he have eased his needs on the widow's willing body before coming to her bed to sleep the rest of the night? He wouldn't have done such a thing—not after telling her just hours earlier that he was no longer interested in what Sarah had to offer! Christopher had never lied to her before. But then, he'd never had reason before. Did he now?

"You lie!" she finally said, wishing Sarah didn't look so damned confident.

"Lie?" Sarah smiled. "Lie about what? I haven't said a thing."

"But you've implied a lot!" India's eyes flashed ice-blue anger. "All of which is untrue."

"Of course it's untrue, my dear, whatever your suspicious little mind is obviously thinking. You wouldn't expect me to tell you if Christopher had actually slept with me, would you?"

Sarah's answer only exacerbated India's irritation. She rose from her chair and faced the green-eyed beauty, arms akimbo and dainty foot tapping impatiently on the floor. She felt disconcertingly like a puny brown mouse facing a golden eagle.

"Now see here, Mistress Perkins!" she began bravely. "My husband"—and she put a heavy emphasis on *husband*— "has given you a week to pack your things and gracefully exit from our lives. I personally think that's about six days too long. Unless I see you doing some actual packing, instead of floating around making snide insinuations about your relationship with Christopher, I'll see to it that you and your bustle are booted out so hard you won't be able to sit on that padded posterior for a month!"

Sarah regarded India in mild surprise. "You really are a

little termagant, aren't you, dear? It's little wonder Christopher shows so little preference for your company!''

India opened her mouth for a stinging retort, but before it could be delivered, Sarah had swept regally out of the room, leaving only a trace of perfume behind. Left without a target for her rebuttal, India sat down in a huff. Bess looked at her with sympathetic concern.

"Don't let that woman bother you, India," she said reassuringly. "I'm sure there's not a shred of truth in what she's implying. She's just horribly jealous over losing Christopher. I believe she always thought that one day she'd talk him into marrying her.''

"She's very beautiful," India said thoughtfully.

"Aye," Bess agreed. "But she's got the personality of a viper."

India was silent, wondering how much it mattered to a man like Christopher if a beautiful, seductive body had a poisonous personality hidden inside. Bess might not have dismissed Sarah's words with such confidence if she knew Christopher's real reasons for marrying her.

But Christopher said he loved her. He told her that awful night in Nassau that he loved her. But perhaps he'd said the same words to others—to Sarah Perkins, for instance. Perhaps he'd told Sarah those very same words last night, or this morning.

"I don't feel very well," India finally said. "I think I'll go lie down for a while."

In truth, the conflict with Sarah had upset her stomach once again, and she felt a distinct need for the chamber pot.

Helen looked at her suspiciously. It wasn't like India to become ill over a little spat like this. She'd always weathered her frequent shouting matches with her father with astounding aplomb.

"You do look a bit green, India," Helen noted with surprise. "Are you sure you're not taking seriously ill? Seems you've been feeling poorly quite a bit lately."

"Nothing," India assured her. "It's really nothing."

Nevertheless, she made considerable haste up to her room.

Sarah Perkins stood in the entrance hall and noted with great satisfaction the look on India's face as she ascended the stairway toward her chamber. The war was barely begun, and already the first victory was hers.

CHAPTER TWENTY-FOUR

The men did not return to the Lodge until late at night. India woke when Christopher came to their chamber, noting how the deeply etched lines around his mouth and eyes reflected his exhaustion. Her questions about his day met with non-committal grunts. When he had stripped, washed, and climbed into the big bed, his lovemaking was distracted and perfunctory, leaving India physically replete but emotionally dissatisfied. She couldn't help but wonder if he was exhausted from his day refitting the *Black Falcon* or worn out from an encounter with the willing widow Perkins. Mentally cursing herself for her lack of faith, she tossed for an hour before finally drifting into a restless sleep.

Christopher left before the sun made its appearance the next morning. India was glad of his absence several hours later as she bent over the chamber pot, wracked with spasms of nausea and retching. Unknown to her, however, her midmorning miseries were not unnoticed. Passing by the door of the master suite on her way to the stairway, Sarah Perkins, awake at an hour much earlier than her habit, stopped in her tracks as she perceived the telltale sounds issuing from the master chamber. Her finely drawn brows puckered into a frown over thoughtful green eyes as she remembered other signs of physical distress in Christopher's troublesome wife. The obvious conclusion was disconcerting. The chit was with child. The sounds of retching stopped. A low moan was followed by silence. The delicate frown clouding Sarah's face increased to a scowl as she moved back toward her chamber. This was an unexpected development that required a slight alteration of her plans. Things would not be so easy now. If Christopher knew that whey-faced little urchin was carrying his babe he would never give her up to return to the more lush playground she herself could offer. But something was not quite right here. Why hadn't Christopher mentioned his wife's condition? Hadn't the silly girl told him? In India's place, Sarah would have broadcast her condition to the world, making sure that Christopher knew his ties to her were now unbreakable, especially if her position was threatened by an ex-lover who was trying her best to become a current lover. So why hadn't she told him? Perhaps the stupid child didn't know herself. Or maybe, just maybe, there was some reason for hiding her condition. Could the silly chit be worried that Christopher's affections might stray when that pert little shape of hers started to round out? If that was what the ignorant child believed, then very possibly India's uncertainties could be turned to Sarah's advantage.

Thirty minutes later Sarah emerged from her room, dressed, coiffed, and with a bright smile on her face. She passed Mrs. Toffler on her way down the stairs and informed her that she would not return until the evening meal. The housekeeper scowled disapprovingly at Sarah's back as she swept out the door.

India heard a light tapping on her chamber door as she stood in front of the glass, making sure that no signs of her pregnancy could yet be detected on her still-slim body. It seemed to her that her breasts were enlarging, and they were certainly sore to the touch. How long could she keep the news from Christopher? She sighed and closed her dressing gown, one left here by a former occupant of the master suite and large enough to wrap twice around her slim waist.

"Come in," she called.

Mrs. Toffler stepped into the room and put a tray down on a side table.

"When you weren't downstairs earlier this morning I

thought you might not be feeling well, so I brought you a tray."

She tried to keep the sympathy from being too obvious in her voice, but she couldn't help but notice the faint shadows under India's eyes and the signs of strain around her mouth. She wondered if there were some trouble between the captain and his pretty young wife, or if the girl simply had a delicate constitution that was prone to illness.

India certainly had no interest in the fruit and biscuits on the tray right at this moment, but she smiled and thanked the housekeeper courteously, saying she would be down shortly. Mrs. Toffler eyed her with motherly concern, but stifled her impulse to stay and make sure India ate. She turned with her hand on the doorlatch, however, and noted sadly how the smile had disappeared from the girl's face the minute she had turned away.

"I've engaged a young woman from the village to attend to your needs, Mistress Barnett," she said. "Her name is Mary Jane, and she should be arriving here this morning. I think you'll find her quite suitable. She was in service in Edinburgh and returned to the island to tend to her mother who passed away three weeks ago. She says she'd rather come up here to the Lodge than return to the city."

"Thank you," India murmured. "I'm sure she'll do just fine."

"Oh, yes," the housekeeper continued. "The captain left me a message that he'd sent for a lady from the mainland, a dressmaker who just retired from her business in Glasgow. She should arrive in a couple of weeks, so there's no need for you and Bess to go on stitching on those plain fabrics you brought over from the ship. I'm sure Mistress Douglass will bring much finer material with her."

"Oh," India commented. She wondered wryly if Mistress Douglass's talents included designing gowns that could expand with her expanding waistline. She smiled at Mrs. Toffler. "That was very thoughtful of Christopher."

Mrs. Toffler thought India didn't look nearly happy enough for a young woman who'd just learned she was to have an entire new wardrobe. Either she was completely accustomed to such luxury or something was distressing her very much indeed.

India's nausea passed sufficiently for her to eat the food and bread from the tray Mrs. Toffler had brought. She felt much improved with some food in her stomach. She felt better still when she learned that Sarah expected to be gone the entire day, and even the uneasy feeling that Christopher's ex-mistress was up to no good was not sufficient to spoil her relief at spending the entire day without her lurking in the background.

Mary Jane Cameron arrived in the late morning, and immediately charmed India with her cheerful smile and good-natured ways. She and Bess knew each other quite well, as might be expected, and they teamed up together with Helen to shake India from her doldrums, which had begun to show through her cheerful facade. Since it was a fine day, the three of them insisted on packing a late lunch and dragging India on a picnic to the island's one lake. Not heeding her protests, they bustled her into a warm cloak, bullied the young stableboy into saddling four horses, and set off across the brush-covered hills to a secluded pond surrounded by birch and pine.

When they arrived at the pond, India was grateful they'd come. Though the scenery was far different, the picnic spot reminded her somewhat of her private meadow at Hillcrest, the spot she'd always sought out whenever she was troubled or felt like being alone. Private, at least, until her father and Lord Marlowe had discovered her there that awful morning, dressed in grass-stained and mud-spattered breeches. She sighed when she thought of the chain of events that one innocent escapade had triggered. She realized somewhat guiltily that, even with all her doubts and worries, she would truly rather be on this island with Christopher than safe back in England as the pampered wife of the insufferable Lord Marlowe.

Her three companions didn't let India brood for long, though, and soon all four of them were alternately talking and stuffing themselves with the baked chicken, bean salad, fruit, and tarts that the cook had provided them for lunch.

How strange, India thought, to be enjoying female company again. For so many months she and Helen had been surrounded by nothing but male voices, male laughter, male bodies, and male needs. Suddenly the men were gone or, at the most, present only a very few hours of the day, and she was thrown back into the world of women. It was refreshing to hear the soft trills of feminine laughter and to banter and chatter with these new friends, but in a way it made her lonely for the sound of Christopher's deep voice and the secure feeling his presence always gave her. If only her life weren't so complex. If only Sarah weren't here, her father didn't exist, and she could give herself wholeheartedly to Christopher as she wished.

A fit of giggles from her companions interrupted India's wishful thinking. Mary Jane was telling a story of a young man of her acquaintance in Edinburgh, where she'd been in service to a wealthy family before returning to tend her mother six months before. She ended by bemoaning her chances of finding a worthwhile husband if she stayed on the island.

"Oh, you never know what will happen." Bess smiled gently. "So don't give up yet. After all, you went to Edinburgh in hopes of finding a husband. And while you were gone, I stayed right here on the island and married Ian."

"Aye, so you did!" Mary Jane laughed. "But I want some sweet lad for a husband, not someone like that ferocious hulk you married!"

Bess smiled, thinking affectionately of her husband.

"He's as gentle as a lamb, really. You judge too much of the man by his appearance, Mary Jane," Bess told her.

"Ian really is a gentle sort," India agreed, thinking of the big redhead's fatherly attitude toward her during those tumultuous months with Christopher. "But I'll agree he looks fearsome if you don't know him well. I was quite frightened of him the first time I saw him."

She admitted to herself, though, that she'd been much more frightened of Christopher than of Ian, in spite of Ian's appearance.

"How did you ever get acquainted with a person like Ian, Bess?" Helen asked. "He hardly seems the sort your parents would encourage to call!"

Bess laughed and willingly related the story of how, eighteen months past, she'd been approaching her twentieth birthday and was fast becoming regarded by the entire village of Glenmuir as an old maid. None of the available men, fishermen's sons or widowed fishermen, tempted her in the least, and she seemed to be faced with the choice of following Mary Jane to Edinburgh or remaining an old maid the rest of her life. Then one fine afternoon when her household chores were all done, she decided to take a walk. She let her curiosity get the better of her and walked the five miles across the island to sneak a look at the gray-stone manor house that was known to be a hideaway of smugglers and pirates. She stood on the rise above the Lodge and noted with some disappointment that the house looked very innocent, rather like the dwelling of any other wealthy lord. There was no sign of cutthroats or the illicit booty one might expect in such a den of thieves. Emboldened by the apparent lack of activity, she started down the rise for a closer look, concentrating so closely on the rough, uncertain footing that she was taken totally by surprise when she ran straight into the towering, husky frame of Ian McCann, who was on his way from the Lodge to the *Black Falcon*'s anchorage.

Bess stood frozen in her tracks, her heart bouncing frantically around the inside of her chest. She was terrified by the sight before her, the burly flame-haired man with impossibly wide shoulders and a frown thundering across his face. Ian, after recovering from the shock of being run into headlong by a pint-sized girl with hair almost as red as his, reacted with the caution of one who had lived long outside the law. He reached out with both ham-sized hands to keep the intruder from fleeing while he figured out what she was doing here in the first place. His grip goaded Bess to panic, and in the struggle that ensued, Ian became very aware of the firm but yielding female flesh struggling in his arms. So he did what any self-respecting pirate would do.

He forced her head back and kissed her, soundly and thoroughly. And then, discovering that he was enjoying himself hugely, he kissed her again, this time making an effort to be gentle enough to elicit a response from the girl pinioned in his arms.

Bess had never been kissed before. At first she was shocked and terrified at the intimate invasion of her mouth. But then, when his mouth became more gentle and caressing on hers, she began to feel a warm tingle brush over her body. She shocked herself by relaxing in the stranger's arms and accepting the insistent pressure of his mouth, and then responding instinctively to his kiss. When he set her back on her feet, her skin turned the same color as her hair, and in an agony of shame and confusion, she slapped his face as hard as she possibly could, then cringed, awaiting the expected retaliation.

But Ian just laughed. He deserved the slap, he knew, for this was no light piece of tail that a man could trifle with casually. But it had been well worth it, because he'd never before gotten such a jolt from a woman's flesh being next to his. Whatever had brought the lass to this spot on this particular afternoon, Ian vowed he would not let such an opportunity pass him by. He firmly steered her down to the main house, using the excuse that interlopers on Captain Christopher Barnett's property were not sent on their way without the captain's knowing why they were there to begin with.

Once in the house, she had been even more thoroughly frightened by confronting both Christopher and Seamus at the same time, as they were leaving to follow Ian to the ship. Christopher had right away detected the twinkle in Ian's eye and declared the lass should be held for further investigation and that Ian should see to the details. Ian had promptly installed her in the room next to his own, declared that no one could see her except himself, and then locked her securely in while he figured out a plan to win her for himself. Not knowing who she was or where she came from, Ian admitted to himself that in the space of an hour he'd fallen in love.

Bess laughed as she recounted the ways Ian had tried to win her to him, for she'd been onto what he was doing from the first day after he'd brought her to the house. She quickly decided that this burly Highlander was not nearly as fearsome as he seemed and that a woman could do far worse than spend her life in the protection of his arms. She led him a merry chase, though, and caused him many a night sleepless from worry, in punishment for his high-handed abduction of her.

India smiled at the affection in Bess's voice when she spoke of her husband. She'd grown genuinely fond of Ian, and in fact had become quite close to the big Scot during their mutual fight for Christopher's life after the boar attack. She was glad that Ian's wife was such a sweet girl and that they seemed to have a loving relationship. Her own relationship with Christopher, however, continued to plague her on the ride back to the house.

The women arrived back at the Lodge just as the sun was setting over the hill behind the house, washing the sky with shades of orange and rose. Mary Jane swept India up the stairs, declaring that no true lady would be seen at the dinner table without spending at least an hour at her toilette, whether or not the men were present. India thought ruefully how far she'd come from being a lady in the last months, but allowed Mary Jane to prepare a bath in the brass tub that had been delivered from the *Falcon*. Mary Jane was horrified that India had no oils or perfumed soaps, but India demurred when she rummaged through the dressing table and triumphantly uncovered a vial of scented oil left behind by a former occupant. She couldn't bear the thought of smelling like one of Christopher's former mistresses when her husband finally made his way home and into her bed.

In contrast to what India was expecting, dinner that night was quite pleasant. She sat and chatted amiably with Bess and Helen while waiting for the gibes from Sarah to begin. Sarah was in quite a pleasant mood, though, and the gibes never came. She looked seductive, as usual, in a dark blue gown that contrasted stunningly with the silver-blond of her hair, and beside her, as usual, India felt like a drab brown mouse. Sarah's usual acidity was absent, though, and her mood even approached friendly at times as she amused her table companions with a few rather risqué anecdotes from her colorful past. Listening to her gay chatter, India understood how any man could be charmed by her combination of spectacular looks and bright wit. She was suspicious, though, of this sudden change in Sarah's attitude. Where had she gone and what had she done today to make her so happy and at ease? India began to think she was more comfortable with Sarah's hostility.

It wasn't until several hours later that India discovered the reason for Sarah's satisfaction. The men were not expected back until very late, as usual, and India was propped up in her lonely bed, reading from a book of poetry. She was too restless to sleep, but too tired to really enjoy her reading, and soon the book fell unheeded onto her lap and her head fell wearily back onto the pillows. She had almost dozed off when she was startled by a light tap on the chamber door.

"Come in," India said, frowning.

The door opened and admitted Sarah Perkins, dressed alluringly in a silk dressing robe that accentuated the lush curves of her body. India raised a brow in surprise.

"I hope I didn't wake you, dear," Sarah smiled silkily. "But I believe it's time we have a talk."

India was both suspicious and confused. "A talk?"

"Yes," the blonde replied. She moved into the room and settled into a large damask-covered chair, looking like a queen about to grant audience. "To start with, I do want to apologize for the way I've treated you. I had no inkling of your awkward situation, and I really did let my tongue get away from me."

"Awkward situation?" India wondered what the woman knew and felt her heart begin to sink.

"Yes." Sarah's friendly, sympathetic smile didn't quite reach her eyes. "I did some investigating among the *Black Falcon*'s crew today. Some of those fellows I've known for quite a while, you understand. In any case, my dear, I know now that you were forced into this marriage, and several of the crew told me Christopher treated you quite ruthlessly during this voyage. You really do have my sympathy, India. I know how savage he can be at times. I've been with him quite a while, you know.''

India looked at her in amazement, unable to think of anything to say. Sarah took her silence as confirmation of the story, though she would have felt easier about her plans had she been able to find out the reason behind Christopher's strange behavior.

''You understand, dear, how I felt,'' she went on. ''Christopher had promised to marry me, and naturally I was hostile when presented with you as his bride. But now that I understand the situation, I see that we should be helping each other instead of fighting.''

India looked at the voluptuous widow in disbelief.

''You and Christopher were promised? He didn't tell me.''

''Of course he didn't. I'm sure there is much he hasn't told you! Do you imagine that I would've moved into his home like I did if we were not betrothed? I do have some sense of morality, my dear!''

India doubted it. She also doubted that Christopher had ever promised to marry this woman, no matter how appealing he'd found her in bed.

''I'm sorry to have played a part in your disappointment, Sarah,'' India finally said. ''But what's done is done, and there's nothing either of us can do about it now.''

Sarah frowned impatiently, but inside she exulted. The naive child was falling right into her trap.

''But of course there is!'' she said with a convincing tone of sympathetic friendliness. ''By helping you I help myself, you see.''

''I don't understand.'' India frowned.

''It's very easy,'' Sarah explained, hoping desperately that India would rise to the bait. ''I will help you get away from here. It will take some doing, but I can arrange it. You will be safe back in the bosom of your family, and I will have Christopher to myself again. We both benefit, you see.''

Sarah's eyes narrowed almost imperceptibly as she looked for India's reaction.

Four months ago, India knew, she would have jumped at this chance. Now, no matter how distraught her conscience was for her father, her heart would not allow her to leave. In any case, it would serve no purpose; the damage had been done. Their marriage was legal, and Christopher would have his heir, whether it was delivered here or at Hillcrest.

"I have no desire to leave Christopher," she said quietly. "No matter how our marriage was begun, it is a true marriage now."

Sarah raised her delicate brows in surprise, attempting to hide her disappointment and hatred behind a mocking smile. She unsheathed her second weapon.

"Why, then, haven't you told him you carry his child?"

India turned a shade paler and regarded Sarah with consternation.

"Oh"—Sarah pounced on India's obvious distress—"your condition is obvious to anyone who is the least bit observant. You certainly won't be able to hide it from Christopher much longer. I'm simply trying to save you a great deal of pain."

"What do you mean?" India asked, feeling suddenly that this conversation was rapidly getting out of control.

"You apparently don't know your husband as well as I do, my dear. Remember, I've been with him for a long time."

"I don't understand."

India wasn't sure that she wanted to understand.

"Christopher has left me many times," Sarah explained, her voice dulcet with kindness and sympathy. "But he always returns. I'll admit that ours has been a very on-and-off affair. He's gone off with new bedmates from time to time, but then he tires of them and always makes his way back to me. What do you think he'll do when you become bloated with his child? He'll be married to you, it's true, but he will be mine in reality. And once he discovers your pregnancy, he'll never let you escape, at least not until after the child is born. Then he may let you go, but he'll never let you take his child."

India's eyes widened as she perceived the possibility of truth in Sarah's words. Her assertions echoed her own fears.

"Poor dear! I see you've come to love Christopher," Sarah said understandingly. "And I know how easy that is, for he's certainly an attractive rogue. I believe he could charm my sainted grandmother out of her virtue if he tried. But if you think he'll honor you as his wife once he's tired of your body, my girl, then you're sadly mistaken. Others have believed they've held his heart in their hands, for he has a way of making a woman feel loved when he's using her for his pleasure. But he's always returned to me in the end. And he always will."

India desperately didn't want to believe Sarah's words. The trollop's motives were obvious, she told herself. Sarah wanted Christopher back, and the easiest way to do that was to get rid of the unwelcome wife. But that thought couldn't keep at bay the uncertainties that had hounded her these past days and now threatened to beat down the fragile walls of good sense.

"I would think," Sarah said quietly, "that you would want to spare yourself the pain of being forced to stay and wait for his rejection. You can escape now and keep your child with you. You might escape later, but if you did, you would leave alone."

Sarah watched with satisfaction the play of emotions across India's face. She'd even halfway convinced herself with her performance.

"If you want," she urged, "I could arrange to have you out of here in two days' time. Christopher would never dare to pursue you once you've reached the safety of your home. In time, you may even be able to obtain a divorce and remarry, begin your life anew."

"No," India whispered. "Divorce is out of the question. The scandal would be unbearable to my family."

"Well, whatever," Sarah conceded. "Legalities are of no interest to me, my dear. I'm simply offering you a way to resolve this situation to everyone's benefit."

India felt a numbness steal over her heart. She didn't for one moment believe that Sarah had anyone's interest at heart but her own, but just the same, the woman's words were in frightening concordance with her own fears. Would Christopher find her unattractive while she grew heavy with the child he'd planted within her body? Would he turn to Sarah or some other sleek female who caught his fancy to satisfy his masculine needs? Such a thing was common enough even among the society gentlemen at home in Hampshire. How could she expect a self-acknowledged rogue such as Christopher to behave differently?

"Well?" Sarah prompted.

India frowned at her. "I'm thinking over what you've said, Sarah."

She regarded the older woman coldly. She was beautiful, India admitted. But the sight of her turned India's stomach. And the thought of giving up Christopher to that blond overripe trollop was unthinkable. What Sarah was saying might be true, or it might not. But in spite of her uncertainties, she couldn't give up the fight so easily. She couldn't run like a frightened rabbit just because this viciously clever hussy knew how to play on her innermost fears. She was stronger than that. She had to have faith in Christopher's love.

India gave Sarah a sweetly venomous smile. Her clear blue eyes glinted icily. "There might be truth in what you say, Sarah."

Sarah felt her exultation swell, and was unsuccessful in keeping it from her face.

"Then again . . ." India savored the sudden tightening of Sarah's exultant features. "Then again, there might not be."

India schooled her face to a blank, impassive mask as she tried to hide her still-clamoring uncertainties from the other woman. The blue depths of her eyes, however, couldn't quite hide a flash of anger as she continued.

"Fie, Sarah. You must truly take me for a brainless twit. Do you think I'd flee like a silly ninny and leave Christopher to your overblown charms? I carry Christopher's child, it's true—a child Christopher wants very much. Do you think you have a chance with him while I'm about to give him what he wants most in the world?'' India assumed an expression of cool confidence to match her brave words. She wished she felt as certain as she sounded.

Sarah rose sensuously from her chair, her face white with anger. ''You stupid fool! I offer you a way to escape what awaits you, but I see I shouldn't have taken the trouble!''

India smiled sweetly into Sarah's sneering face, enjoying the woman's anger.

''See if you're still smiling when he discards you!'' Sarah spit venomously. ''Do you think a man like Christopher can long be held by a skinny little child's body like yours? You'll regret you didn't take advantage of my generosity when you could!''

She stalked toward the door like a sleek, indignant cat. She paused with her hand on the doorlatch and looked back at India, whose infuriating clear blue eyes still regarded her with disdain. ''You're a fool!'' she repeated.

''We'll see, won't we?'' India answered with false cheerfulness as Sarah huffed out the door. ''We'll see.''

When Sarah passed out of sight, India allowed her face to fall and the insistent hot tears to pour from her eyes.

Sarah paused outside the door of India's chamber and clenched her teeth in helpless rage. The stupid little slut! How dare she challenge her in such a way, thinking she could hold Christopher to her in the face of Sarah's far superior charms! India would regret this, Sarah swore silently. She would pay. Oh, how she would pay!

CHAPTER TWENTY-FIVE

The next two days were an agony of uncertainty for India. But the agony was made more bearable by Christopher's decision to take a holiday and stay home with his wife the very next day.

After Sarah had angrily exited her bedchamber the night before, India had released all her pent-up misery in a fury of weeping, finally crying herself into an exhausted slumber. She didn't wake when Christopher returned in the small hours of the morning. She didn't wake, in fact, until the sun suffused the chamber with its pale early-morning light. Reluctantly opening her eyes to the new day, she found, somewhat to her surprise, that she was pinned down by the weight of Christopher's arm across her chest. Her shifting had awakened him, and he propped himself on an elbow, looking at her out of eyes that made her heart turn over in love.

"What are you doing here?" she asked, trying hard for a normal voice.

"I live here." He smiled down at her. "Remember?"

"I mean . . ." she started uneasily. "Aren't you supposed to be refitting the ship or something?"

He raised a hand and gently traced the line of her cheek, neck, and bare shoulder. Her willful body shivered at his touch, anticipating more pleasure to come, and he smiled in satisfaction at her response.

"I decided to take the day off and get reacquainted with my wife. I've been neglecting you, little one."

"No, you haven't," India objected. "I know you have work to get done."

"Mmm," he acknowledged.

His eyes took on a distracted look as his hand wandered from her shoulder to her breast, gently cupping its fullness in his palm while his thumb teased the dark rose nipple to alertness.

"Have I ever told you what beautiful breasts you have?" he murmured.

India welcomed the warm rush of passion that invaded her body at the feel of his callused hand brushing the sensitive skin of her breast. His gentleness and the light of affection in his eyes as he caressed her made her forget all her tortured imaginings of the past few days.

Christopher has a way of making a woman feel loved, Sarah had said, while he's using her for his pleasure. Perhaps that was true, but India chose to believe that Christopher truly loved her. It was easy to believe when he was here with her, lying beside her, flooding her with aching passion. Surely he would love her even more when he learned of their child. Wouldn't he?

He lowered his head to nuzzle at her breasts while his hands ran tantalizingly down her hips and thighs. She fought the urge to surrender completely to the wave of pleasure.

"Christopher?"

"Mmm," he said.

His hard-muscled thigh nudged her knees apart and rubbed teasingly against the vulnerable flesh of her womanhood. She gasped at the startling contact.

"Would you love me if I were ugly . . . or fat?" she persisted through a thickening haze of desire.

He raised his head from her breast and regarded her with a puzzled frown. Then he laughed.

"What peculiar notions do you have in your head this morning?"

"I just want to know"—she pursed her lips stubbornly—"if you would still love me if I was fat."

"What difference does it make?" he asked impatiently, anxious to get back to the business at hand. "You're not fat."

"Supposing I became fat?" she persisted.

"Then I'd starve you until you were your tempting little self again." He smiled winningly. "And you are oh so tempting!"

He nuzzled her neck and pressed against her insistently with his hard thigh.

"Let's discuss this at another time."

His hands slipped under her and grasped her firm buttocks, pressing her close against his lean body.

"You think I'm being silly," she accused, trying to keep her mind off the primitive rhythm that was beginning to pound in her blood.

"Yes," he agreed. "But oh how I ache for you, my silly little love! So be quiet and let me make love to you."

His hands moved to push her thighs wider apart, and she felt the hard tip of his manhood poised at her entrance. Finally surrendering helplessly to the urgent demands of her body, she arched against him, encouraging him to accomplish his aim. He chuckled low against her as her hands sought his buttocks to push him to her. Then with one mighty thrust he made them one. She gasped in pleasure as the hard, thick length of him spread her and filled her with his hard-thrusting invasion. Their shared passion wiped all other concerns from her mind. The sole point of her existence was the demanding male body that moved on her, over her, in her, and subjugated her very being to his urgent desires. Again and again the spasms of ultimate joy gripped and shook her, and she cried out her delight, but still he drove into her, impaling her again and again on the shaft of his passion, worshipping her body in a frenzy of desire. Finally he allowed his own release, straining over her pliant form as he pumped the fruit of his desire deep into her womb. But even in this moment of ultimate ecstasy, the niggling thought wormed its way through to India's mind. Would he have bothered making her the object of his passion this morning had he known his seed fell on already planted ground?

The tension in Christopher's body eased as his passion turned to a warm glow of satisfaction. Still joined to his wife's body, he gathered her into his arms and rolled to his side to relieve her of his weight. She rolled with him, clasping him with her slender legs as if she would never let him go. Now would be the perfect time to tell him, India thought as she buried her face contentedly in the warm hollow of his shoulder. She should tell him and end all these silly imaginings. But she couldn't find the courage.

"Now," Christopher said softly, "what were you saying to try to divert me from delving into your precious treasures?"

"It was nothing," she murmured into his shoulder.

Christopher sighed and held her closer, wondering if he would ever understand his wife's turbulent emotions.

She allowed herself to relax against him and enjoy the feel of his arms holding her secure and close.

"Christopher?"

"Yes?"

"I love you."

He chuckled. "I know," he said, running his hands down to where her legs clasped him, still holding him firmly within her.

"No," she said softly. "Not just that way. I love . . . all of you. Everything."

He smiled gently. "I know, India. You're not a woman who could love any other way."

His eyes were warm as he looked down at her.

She remembered with poignant amusement the first time she'd seen those eyes, that face, looking down at her when she'd regained consciousness on the deck of the *Sea Gull*. She'd thought him the Devil, come to carry her to hell as her strict cousin Prudence had predicted, but he'd not inspired her with fear in his guise as the Prince of Darkness. In fact, it had occurred to her still-muddled mind that spending time in hell with him might even prove entertaining. It wasn't until she found out how very human he was that she'd begun to be afraid. But if he'd truly been a demon, he could have cast his spell no more effectively. Whether here or at Hillcrest, far from his touch, she was his forever. What torture it would be if Sarah was right! What pain it would be to watch him turn to another woman if he ever tired of her.

"I just wanted you to know," she whispered, disappointed that he'd not reaffirmed his love in return. She snuggled more closely against him, forced her fears into the very back of her mind, and allowed herself to drift back into the peacefulness of sleep.

The rest of the day passed too quickly for India. After a late, leisurely breakfast, they rode out together to enjoy the island. First they crossed to the secluded cove where the *Black Falcon* was anchored. India was surprised at how glad she was to see the little brigantine. In less than a week off the ship she missed the feel of the polished decks under her feet and the familiar motion of the sea. She understood how a man could become so attached to seagoing life that he could feel displaced on dry land.

From the anchorage cove they followed the curving, rocky shore line, most of the time walking their horses in companionable silence. Occasionally, when the rocks and wave-worn cobbles gave way to stretches of sand, they would race through the shallow surf, the horses' hooves kicking up fountains of sand and spray. After two races that left her far behind Christopher's powerful bay, India begged to trade mounts, if only for a few minutes. Christopher looked doubtful.

"He needs a firm hand, India." He frowned. "Besides, I'm riding bareback. You wouldn't even have the security of a saddle."

India put on her best pout.

"Please, Christopher! He's such a magnificent animal. I've wanted to ride him since our first day on the island."

She thought of her spirited chestnut mare, Brandywine, back in Hillcrest's stables, wondering if she were still there waiting for her mistress to return.

Christopher went against his better judgment and gave in to the pleading of her deep blue eyes.

"All right," he smiled. "But just down to that headland. The country gets rough after that."

"Oh, thank you!" India leapt down from the patient mare she was riding and hitched her skirt up, tying the back hem securely into the front waistband so she could ride astride. She gave brief thought to the child she carried, but concluded that this early in her pregnancy a few minutes astride a horse wasn't going to hurt anything. Placing her knee in Christopher's interlaced hands, she vaulted lightly onto his back. The stallion's muscles bunched between her bare legs as the horse tensed at the feel of an unfamiliar rider on his back, but she ran her hand soothingly along the powerfully arched neck and crooned. He relaxed, then tensed again and sidestepped as she picked up the reins and squeezed lightly with her legs. India's delighted laughter mingled with the splash of the surf.

"He's wonderful," she crowed.

As if in answer, the bay kicked up his rear legs and twisted in a rebellious buck, then snorted in disgust as the unfamiliar rider didn't sail off his back as planned. Christopher leapt off the mare, ready to subdue the stallion, but then stopped and looked on in amused wonder as it became obvious that India was more than a match for the big bay. The stallion finally settled under her sure hands and legs.

"Race?" India's eyes sparkled with deviltry.

Christopher's mouth quirked in a smile as he remounted the mare.

"I'll even give you a head start," India offered. "That's more than you ever gave me!"

"Foolish woman!" Christopher grinned.

He was off in a flash of hooves and sand, and India had to rein in hard to keep the big bay from plunging off in pursuit. She waited until they were a hundred feet down the beach, then gave the stallion his head, thumping her heels against his sides. The distance closed as though the mare was standing still. The wind raced through India's hair and the stallion's mane whipped back to sting her face. India reveled in the surge of pure power beneath her as the stallion stretched out in full stride, passing the mare in a shower of spray and sand. She locked her hands in his mane and leaned low over his neck, letting the big horse set his own pace down the beach. The rhythmic thundering of his hooves and bunching of the muscles under her legs sparked a joy in her blood that she'd almost forgotten. It had been so long since she'd ridden Brandywine across the Hampshire countryside, jumping hedges, ditches, and walls, and racing full speed across rocky meadows.

Finally the headland approached, and India sat up and drew back on the reins. Somewhat to her surprise, the stallion responded to the pressure on the bit, slowing to a steady canter, then to a sedate trot. She turned to watch Christopher and the mare galloping far behind, Christopher sitting awkwardly astride the mare's sidesaddle.

"Where did you learn to ride like that, you little hellion?" Christopher asked as he drew abreast of her. She could tell from his tone that he was more amazed than mad.

India regarded him from under raised brows. "I haven't spent my entire life sitting in the parlor stitching samplers, you know!"

"Apparently not!" he acknowledged. "Are you ready to give me back my horse?"

"Not really." She grimaced. "But if you insist."

"Next time we ride," Christopher conceded, "I'll make sure you're given a horse more suited to your talents."

"You do that, sir!"

India's smile faded somewhat as she wondered if such happiness could really last. And how dare she be happy at her father's expense, at the price of her family honor! She slid off the stallion and patted his neck affectionately. He was hardly even sweating. Christopher wondered at the smoky-gray shadow of sadness in her eyes as she smiled and handed him the reins.

From the headland they struck inland for a few minutes until they came out at a bay that sheltered a small village in the curve of one arm.

"Glenmuir," Christopher said as they stood looking down at the little settlement. They picked their way down the slope, then rode along the one main lane that paralleled the curve of the bay. The fishing boats were out to sea and the village was quiet, with only the occasional bark of a dog or wail of a baby to break the peace. Christopher pulled up at the village's one tavern, near the end of the lane where it exited the town.

"I could use a pint to quench my thirst." He smiled up at her, warming her to the very innermost regions of her heart. "How about you?"

She hesitated. "I've never drunk ale before."

"A situation we should remedy right now." He laughed.

She marveled at his attitude. He was treating her more like a friend than a reluctant and troublesome wife. Her heart ached as she wished they had met under different circumstances, in a saner world.

"If you say so," she returned lightly, and dismounted, handing her reins to a grimy urchin to whom Christopher had tossed a coin.

Ale, she discovered, was heavy and bitter, and how anyone could regard it as refreshing was beyond her understanding. She finished only a quarter of her mug, and Christopher willingly quaffed the remainder. She asked the tavernkeeper for water to wash the dust from her throat and the taste of ale from her mouth.

They rode from the village in midafternoon and made their way to the lake where the women had picnicked the day before. The pond was prettier than she remembered even, with the birch leaves turning the yellow of autumn and shimmering green-and-gold in the light breeze. Christopher dismounted and expertly hobbled both mounts with a rope tied to India's saddle. Then he spread a blanket on the ground and smilingly pulled India down beside him.

"This is what I've been waiting for all afternoon," he said as he deftly unfastened the buttons of her bodice and slipped his hand inside.

"You are a satyr," she complained mockingly.

He slipped the dress off her shoulders and pulled it down over her hips, then quickly divested himself of his own garments.

"Aren't you ever satisfied?" She smiled as she admired the play of afternoon shadows on his strongly muscled body.

"No," he admitted. "With you, never!"

He made gentle love to her under the birch trees as the afternoon sun sank lower in the sky. The frenzied urgency of the morning was gone, leaving room for a tenderness that almost broke her heart. How could hands that wielded sword and knife with such deadly ferocity be so gentle in coaxing her body to fulfillment? She still hadn't found the answer in her mind as she allowed herself to doze off in the circle of his arms. Not until the sun sank below the hill and the air took on a chill did they untwine their limbs and don their clothing. All in all, India thought as they trotted slowly away from the little lake, the day had been one of the most perfect in her life with Christopher Barnett-Armstrong. But her mood was dampened as Sarah's words pushed their unwelcome way into her mind. If that woman had her way, India suspected, the day would be a perfect ending to her life with Christopher.

It wasn't until late that evening that the spell of the pleasant day was broken. Christopher was in the library with Ian, discussing plans for altering the armament of the *Falcon*. Everyone else in the house had retired, but India was reluctant to give up even a few minutes of Christopher's company, so she stayed up to wait for him before retiring. She was reading in an intricately carved chair by the fireplace when the door to the main room opened and Sarah floated into the room in a cloud of diaphanous material that left very little to the imagination. Her smile was feline. In fact, India thought without amusement, the expression on Sarah's face reminded her very much of Thomas Cat after snitching a biscuit from some unwary person's plate. The voluptuous widow wasted no time in coming to the point.

"Well, dear"—she smirked—"did you tell our lord and master the good news yet?"

India fixed her with a gaze cold as ice. "If it's Christopher you're referring to, he's not *our* lord and master. He's *my* husband. And you only have a few days left before he's going to show you to the door." She smiled wickedly. "I hope you're getting on well with your packing."

Sarah refused to be ruffled. "Touchy little witch, aren't you?" She arched a knowing brow. "From your mood I would guess you haven't told him. He'll find out sooner or later, you know."

India scowled blackly, irritated with herself for letting Sarah get under her skin when the woman was so obvious. "Not that it's your affair, Sarah, but it's as I told you before. Christopher will be very happy when I tell him about the child. I have no doubts about that."

Sarah's green eyes rested appraisingly on India's trim form bathed in the warm glow of the fireplace. Her breast filled with acid as she noted how at home she looked in the place Sarah wanted to call her own.

"I have no doubts either." She smiled condescendingly.

"Christopher will be delighted to hear he's about to become a father. But I wonder how pleased he will be that his little wife is going to turn into a pumpkin."

India lifted her chin and met Sarah's laughing green eyes with a level gaze. "One can hardly carry a man's babe without becoming somewhat awkward."

"How sad," Sarah replied venomously, "that men have never come to accept that. They sow their seed, then when the fruit begins to ripen they're off to plow some other fertile field."

India sighed wearily. She was rapidly growing tired of this mutual baiting. "Haven't we been through this once before?"

"La, my dear." Sarah laughed with saccharine sweetness. "I was simply concerned for your feelings, finding you sitting so lonely by the fire here. I might still be persuaded to make arrangements for you to go home."

India fixed her with a clear blue gaze that she hoped was cool and confident. Would the overstuffed she-bitch ever tire of this game? "Four more days, Sarah," she reminded her. "Or is it only three now? If I were you, I'd be anxious to leave and find some other unfortunate man to trap with your overripe charms. Because if Christopher ever does tire of me, it certainly won't be you he turns to."

Sarah's sensuous lips curved into a knowing smile. "The play is not yet over, little child-bride. We'll see who wins in the end."

Sarah floated gracefully toward the door, then turned as another thought struck her. "I think perhaps I've been too concerned for your feelings, India—too fair-minded, too soft. Perhaps it's time I stopped being a lady and showed you just how much your precious Christopher loves you when his feelings are really put to the test."

She exited with another satisfied-cat smile, leaving India to wonder what the trollop was planning for her next move.

The next day passed in agonizing slowness for India. Christopher left early again to resume work on the *Falcon*, so she was deprived of his reassuring presence. Seamus and Helen rode to the village to arrange for the first leg of their trip to Ireland. Bess was with Mrs. Toffler, inventorying preserved foodstuffs in storage for the winter. India made a halfhearted attempt to help them, but finally gave up, pleading a headache for an excuse to go to her room. Even there, however, she was not left to the privacy of her own thoughts, for as soon as she had curled up in the chair next to the window, gazing in melancholy fascination at the gray mists that blanketed the somber sea, Mary Jane appeared at the chamber door with a look of determined cheerfulness on her face. India was quick to forestall Mary Jane's attempt to improve her mood, however, by telling her to take the rest of the day off. The patient girl had too often borne the brunt of India's moodiness these past few days. India guessed she could use a break, and her absence would give India the solitude she longed for.

So India spent much of the day curled in her chair, a blanket pulled tightly up to her chin to ward off the chill in the room, staring moodily at the gray scene out the window. She sat alone with her thoughts, musing over the events of the past months, examining her feelings and motives, trying to rid herself of the burden of guilt and uncertainty that plagued her situation. There had to be a way, she told herself, to resolve her problem so that her happiness would not bring suffering and disgrace on her father.

Occasionally voices cut through her thoughts—Mrs. Toffler and Bess discussing household affairs as they walked down the hall, Sarah berating Lisa, her maid, for an imagined flaw in the hem of her new gown, Lisa complaining to one of the household help about her mistress's temper.

India grimaced whenever Sarah's voice floated through the chamber door to interrupt her thoughts. The woman's words of the night before gnawed tenaciously at the back of her mind, creating an uneasy feeling that Sarah had tricks up her silk sleeves that were going to mean trouble. In a few more days, India comforted herself, the voluptuous widow would be gone. If she wasn't gone by then, Christopher would boot her, bustle and baggage, out into the cold, or so he'd promised. The only thing India wanted from that overstuffed man-trap was her absence. Perhaps with her

gone, with her ceaseless baiting no longer a constant distur-
bance to her peace of mind, India could settle down and
convince Christopher to make some compromises about her
father.

And then there was the problem of her pregnancy. Not
that the baby was a real problem, India told herself. A little
uncertainty was only natural, especially in her situation.
And, of course, Sarah with her insinuations had been no
help. Christopher loved her, India told herself firmly. And
when she was big as a cow he would love her every bit as
much. She'd been letting her fears run away with her
common sense. Now was the time to end all this silliness.
Tonight, when the household was retired, when they were
alone together wrapped in the privacy of their love—that
was when she would tell him he was going to be a father.
She pictured him reassuring her of his unending devotion,
making love to her until the sun burned through the morning
mist. Then she carried her fantasy even further, imagining
how Christopher would give up all plans of vengeance in his
joy at being a prospective father. All her fears would be
squelched once and for all. Tonight would be the night. She
would be securely wrapped in Christopher's love and content to be his devoted wife for the rest of her years.

Dinner came and went. Much to India's surprise, the men
had returned from the ship in the late afternoon, and after
dinner they were appearing to settle in for a long evening of
companionship with their wives. Teddy had come back to
the Lodge with the men, and after stuffing himself with the
heavy lamb stew that Cook had provided, was trying valiantly
to stay awake to listen to the adult conversation. India
wished desperately that she could get Christopher to retire
early with her to their chamber, but he was engrossed in
conversation with Seamus and paid little mind to her subtle
hints.

As the evening threatened to drag into the late hours,
India pleaded another headache and excused herself to
retire. Christopher escorted her to the stairway, a concerned
frown darkening his features. He placed a gentle kiss on her

brow, brushed her pale cheek with a finger, and told her to take better care of herself.

"Do you want me to come with you?" he offered.

India opened her mouth to say yes, then stopped herself, knowing he really wanted to return to his conversation about ships and cannon and rigging. "No." She smiled. "You come up when you're ready. I'll wait up for you."

"You're sure?" He hesitated. "You look awfully pale. Why don't you go on to sleep?" A slightly wicked grin tugged at his lips. "I'll wake you when I come up. Never fear."

She smiled in reply and gave him a quick kiss on the lips, a promise of things to come, she hoped.

India climbed to the master suite, wearily shed her clothing, and collapsed into the big bed, the bed she'd shared these past nights with her husband. She snuggled down into the warm softness and waited. An hour passed, then two. One by one she heard footsteps of people retiring for the night. She waited tensely for the sound of Christopher's step coming toward the door, rehearsing in her mind the words she would use to tell him about their child, imagining the loving pledges he would give in return. He didn't come. The hour grew late. The heaviness of her eyelids became irresistible. Try as she would, she couldn't keep her eyes open. Finally, she slept.

A light scratching at her door brought India to sleepy awareness. When her eyes fell on the stub of the candle still burning by the bedside, she started awake. It must be the wee hours of the morning, and still no sign of Christopher. In a flash of irritation she threw back the bedcovers and bounced out of the bed, padding barefoot across the room to extinguish the oil lamps and add another log to the fire. Her bare skin was sprouting goosebumps as she hurried back toward the warmth of the big bed.

The scratching came again. India frowned. Who would bother anyone at this hour of the night?

"A moment," she called softly as she wrapped a dressing gown around her nakedness and made her way to the door. She opened it a crack and peered out.

"It's me, mum," a timid voice said. "Lisa."

"Lisa?" whispered a surprised India. "What are you doing here?"

Lisa slipped in the door as India relit a lamp she'd just extinguished. Sarah's serving girl cleared her throat uneasily, uncomfortable with this role her mistress had bade her play.

"Begging your pardon, mum, for disturbing you like this. 'Tis late, I know, but . . ."

"Go on," India told her. The girl was obviously scared to death. What in heaven was going on?

"But, well," Lisa continued, her voice beginning to tremble, "I thought you should know what was happening. You been nice to me, mum, and I didn't think it was fair, them carryin' on with you not around and all. So I thought I'd tell you."

Lisa frowned at the floor. India had been nice to her, and she felt bad about all this. She knew Miss Sarah was using unfair means to rid herself of her competition, and Lisa hated to see India become the victim of her mistress's conniving. But still, if she didn't do exactly as Sarah had instructed her, she'd get a beating and be out on her ear, as well.

India stared at the girl, her heart sinking in her chest. Very slowly she drew in a shaky breath. "Just what exactly are you telling me, Lisa?"

When Lisa looked up, her eyes swam in unshed tears. "The captain and Miss Sarah . . . they were laughing and drinking down in the library. Then I saw them go up the stairs together, to Miss Sarah's room . . . and . . . and I just thought you oughta know, that's all."

India didn't believe it. Christopher wouldn't betray her, he just wouldn't. This was some sort of scheme of Sarah's to get him to return to her, but Sarah wouldn't succeed. Just the same, her heart squeezed painfully in her chest.

"Thank you, Lisa," India said quietly. "I know you think you're doing the right thing."

Lisa curtsied and slipped out the door, seeming anxious to go. India grabbed the bedpost and swayed for a moment as she closed her eyes against the pain that gripped her heart. Fool! she told herself. You're getting upset over nothing. She would go to Sarah's room and see for herself that everything was as it should be. Sarah had probably gotten tipsy. Christopher had been polite enough to help her up the stairs to her chamber and was probably now reading a book in front of the library fire.

She fastened her robe more tightly around her and picked up the candle burning at the bedside. Silently she slipped out the door into the dark hallway.

CHAPTER TWENTY-SIX

Sarah had had very little trouble gaining Christopher's attention after India left the room. She had been at her most charming all evening. Her low-cut green gown emphasized the luminous emerald of her eyes and set off the silver-gold of her hair. Its simple, clinging lines dramatized the voluptuous contours of her figure.

When Christopher excused himself from the rest of the group in the main room and entered the library, she followed. He was perusing the bookshelf when she entered, and turned with a look of irritation on his face. Untroubled by his black scowl, Sarah moved to the cupboard and took out a bottle of his favorite brandy.

"Why don't we have a drink for old times' sake," she suggested with a smile.

"Why don't we not, Sarah?" he snapped. "I came in here for some privacy, if you don't mind."

"Such a grouch!" she complained, but nevertheless turned her back and poured two brandies, covertly slipping a white powder into one of the glasses. In spite of what she'd told her rival, there were times when a man needed a nudge in the right direction.

Sarah turned and walked to where Christopher was glowering by the bookshelves.

"Come now, Christopher," she pleaded prettily, handing him a glass of amber liquid. "I just want to show I can be a good loser. India is a . . . a charming girl, and I'm sure you'll be very happy together."

The words threatened to stick in her throat, but she managed a gracious smile just the same.

Christopher arched a brow in surprise. "Well, Sarah, I'm happy to see you in such good spirits, and being such a good sport."

He took a sip of the brandy and set the glass on the desk. A slight frown puckered the fine line of Sarah's brows. He had to drink more, or her plan would never succeed. She smiled and struck a pose she knew to be seductive.

"I'll be leaving very soon, and I thought I'd take this opportunity to have a last drink with an old . . . friend." She lifted her glass in salute. "We did have some fine times, didn't we, Christopher."

Christopher smiled tolerantly and lifted his glass in return.

"We did have some good times, Sarah, and I'm glad there are no hard feelings."

The blonde watched with satisfaction as he took another swallow. She waited several moments until she detected a faint telltale flush on his face, then moved slowly closer, presenting him with a view of the heavy swell of her breasts above her décolletage. He cleared his throat uncomfortably. His hand moved to loosen the top button of his shirt, then the second.

"Hot in here, isn't it?"

His breathing quickened to a rapid rate as his eyes

seemed to fasten of their own accord on the tempting vista offered by Sarah's neckline.

"It is warm," she agreed.

Christopher felt an almost uncontrollable wave of desire surge over him as he looked down at the plush curves of Sarah's almost completely exposed breasts. He felt dizzy for a moment, from the heat, or the brandy, or both. Then all he could think of was how it would feel to reach out, push down that precarious bodice, and take those ripe orbs into his hands. What was wrong with him? He hadn't felt a need for Sarah in a very long while. He tried to push the thought from his mind, pulled his eyes away from the tempting view, and took another swallow of brandy.

"I don't want you to think, Christopher, that I'm happy to lose your attentions." She moved in front of him again, seemingly by accident brushing against his arm. "And if you ever have needs that your little child-bride can't satisfy, you know where I live."

Her smile was temptation itself.

The room was spinning slowly. The brush of Sarah's arm against his set Christopher on fire. His judgment was rapidly being submerged in the flames of drug-induced lust. He looked at her standing in front of him, so inviting—the finely molded lips, the lush swell of her breasts, the indentation of her waist above sensuously flaring hips. He remembered those hips, yes, and the smooth white thighs, and the moist, eager, plump flesh that lay between them. He knew her body well, had possessed it innumerable times. Why not once more? She wanted him, and he was burning for her. In fact, burning was a mild word. He felt like a boar in rut. He wanted to leap, to tear the garments from her body and bury himself in the soft, white flesh that he knew lay under all that silk.

Sarah reveled in the sweet glow of triumph as she saw a film of sweat break out on Christopher's forehead and upper lip. The animal lust that gleamed in his eyes testified to the efficacy of her methods. He belonged to her now, and she didn't intend to let him stray again. She laughed, a low, throaty sound of triumph.

"I see a familiar spark in your eyes, my love," she purred. "Perhaps we should retire to my room, where we can say good-bye more . . . appropriately."

She rested her hand on his chest, then casually let it slip down to brush provocatively against the swelling between his legs.

"Why delay?" she purred, rubbing against him lightly. "That group in there will never miss us."

Christopher's brain exploded in a white-hot conflagration of desire at her skilled touch. It was all he could do to keep from pushing her down on the library floor, raising her silk skirts, and taking her right then and there. She sensed his intention and pushed teasingly away, retaining a grip on his hand and pulling him toward the door.

"Upstairs, my love," she urged.

Christopher followed.

The hallway seemed very dark and cold as India closed her chamber door behind her. Her candle's flickering glow was barely enough to see by as she made her way toward Sarah's chamber, her bare toes curling in objection to the cold wood floor.

India paused in front of Sarah's door. The stunned disbelief that had kept despair at bay was beginning to recede, leaving a heart-pounding dread in its place. Sarah's chamber door stood invitingly ajar, almost, India thought fleetingly, as if the woman wanted to be interrupted. India pushed the door open and stood looking into the room.

No need for her candle here. The chamber was brightly lit by the oil lamps, revealing every damning detail to India's view. But only one thing caught her gaze and held it. Everything else blurred.

Christopher lay in Sarah's rumpled bed, snoring inelegantly, his naked body brown against the sun-bleached sheets. Sarah reclined beside him, bare as the day she was born, regarding India with laughing green eyes. Christopher's muscle-corded leg was thrust between Sarah's milky thighs.

The room was musky with the odor of their lovemaking, leaving no doubt as to what had transpired. A slow, languorous smile of victory spread across Sarah's features as India took in the full import of the scene.

For a stunned moment, India just stood in the doorway, her eyes unwillingly riveted on the pair of them lying there still intimately entwined. The pain of it seemed in that moment to be unbearable. Then a spark of anger ignited deep within her and grew quickly to a conflagration. It rose, cutting through her pain, and surfaced, blazing in her eyes.

"You amoral slut!" she said with deceptive quietness. "You overripe piece of rotten meat! How dare you sport with my husband under my very eyes!"

Sarah's smile of victory just grew wider, but it faded rapidly as India stepped forward and picked up the wine bottle that sat empty on the table. She scrambled out of bed as India advanced, bottle in hand.

"Oversexed cow!" India's voice trembled as she hurled the empty bottle in Sarah's direction, sending it crashing against the wall behind her.

Sarah screeched. She hadn't thought the little ninny had enough spirit to become violent.

India grabbed a china jewelry box and sent it after the bottle. Two brooches, a diamond necklace, and a string of pearls clattered to the floor as the box splintered against the wall, missing Sarah's head by only inches. Before Sarah could recover, India had bent down and picked up a broken shard of wine bottle, holding it in front of her as she advanced on the now wide-eyed, terrified, naked woman.

"I ought to cut you so no man would ever look at you again, you lowborn trollop!"

Sarah gasped. This scene wasn't being played out quite the way she'd pictured.

India pushed her back toward the window, still threatening with the broken glass. Then her eye was drawn to the chamber pot as it came into view behind the privacy curtain. She grinned.

"I think this needs emptying, Sarah," she said casually, dropping the glass shard and grabbing up the hefty pot.

Before Sarah could react, India poured the contents over her shrinking flesh, dousing her from head to toe. Sarah stood in stunned horror.

"I wonder how irresistible he would find you now!" India laughed, but there was no humor in the laugh. She looked at the still-snoring Christopher splayed out on the rumpled sheets. His arm still stretched out to where Sarah had been lying, and an unwelcome picture of Christopher fondling Sarah's big breasts, stroking her milk-white thighs, and pressing his lean body down upon her pillowy softness flashed through her mind, making her stomach heave threateningly.

"Damn you both!" she cursed. "You deserve each other!"

With one more look at the dripping Sarah, now retching over the empty chamber pot, India marched toward the chamber door with as much dignity as she could muster. She walked to her room in a daze, closed the door behind her, and crumpled onto the bed as tears streamed down her face and her entire body shivered in a fit of trembling.

Fool! she berated herself. Stupid, naive, gullible fool! Where was her faith now? Where was her love? Trampled under Christopher's heel or, perhaps more appropriately, under his heaving body as he wallowed in that blond hussy's well-padded flesh. Her stomach threatened to heave again as her body shook with reaction.

Shakily she rose from the bed and wiped the tears from her eyes. She couldn't stay here. She had to get away, impossible as that seemed. She didn't care what happened to her, as long as she didn't have to stay and face Sarah's smug gloating and Christopher's lying excuses, assuming he would even bother giving excuses. She stuffed the wool and muslin gowns she'd made on shipboard into two tight balls, then wrapped them in Christopher's wool cloak, tying a belt around the awkward bundle to serve as a handle. Then she doused the lamps and stepped silently out into the hall, wondering if she dared sneak into the library on her way out to take some of the gold pieces she knew Christopher had stashed there. She decided to risk it, not wanting to face the long journey to Hampshire with no funds at all.

Every floorboard seemed to creak loudly as she made her way down the stairs and into the library, but no one roused to question her. She quickly located the coins in Christopher's desk and backtracked into the main room, remembering the ornate set of dueling pistols hanging over the fireplace. She knew nothing about firing such a weapon, but thought just the same one might come in handy. She had almost reached the fireplace when her silently treading feet bumped against something pliant—something pliant that moved and made noise.

"Ow! Owoowow!" Teddy howled as India's toe came in painful contact with the small of his back. "What the bloody hell?"

India uttered a small gasp of dismay.

"Huh?" Teddy sat up, rubbed the sleep out of his eyes, and squinted through the dark at the slim figure backing away from him. "Oh! Miss India! What are you doing down here? Is it morning?"

India shushed him with a hiss. "It's not morning," she whispered. "And I might ask what you're doing down here. Don't you have a bed to sleep in?"

"Yah," Teddy acknowledged, ignoring India's gestures to keep his voice down. "But it's cold up there and warm down here by the fire." He gestured to the few embers that still glowed in the fireplace. "I don't mind sleepin' on the floor." He looked at her curiously. "What's the matter? Can't sleep?" Then he noticed the bundle that hung from the belt in her hand. His eyes narrowed suspiciously. "What're you doin', Miss India?"

India collapsed wearily in a chair. "I'm leaving." She sighed. She was so tired that almost all feeling was numbed. Even life itself hardly seemed important right now.

"Leavin'?" he whispered, now caught up in what promised to be an adventure. "Where you goin'?"

India's head dropped to her hands. "Oh, I don't know." She sniffed forlornly. "Home, I guess."

"Home?" Teddy echoed. "This is home."

"No," she replied bitterly. "This isn't my home. Hampshire is my home. I'm going there."

"Ooooooh!" Teddy was impressed. This was adventure, indeed! "The cap'n'll thrash you if he finds out!"

"The captain be damned!" India whispered hotly.

Teddy smirked with worldly-wise condescension. "Had a fight, did ya?"

"No!" India hissed. "We did not have a fight. Right now he's lying up there . . . up there with . . . Well, never mind. Just trust me that I have good reason to leave." India's eyes lit with an idea. This might be a God-sent opportunity. "You can help me, Teddy. You can help me get away from here."

Teddy regarded India as though she'd suddenly taken leave of her senses. "Are you kiddin'? The cap'n'd have me hide, he would! Even if I thought you oughta leave, which I don't. Why'd you want to leave the cap'n? He's rich! And he loves you!"

"Teddy," India pleaded. The tears she'd thought were all shed out came again to wet her lashes. "Teddy, you're my friend. Help me. I need you. Christopher will never know you helped. How could he know, if you're back here when morning comes and I'm nowhere to be found?"

"Well . . ." Teddy hesitated. India, with tears in her eyes and a catch in her sweet voice, was hard for his adolescent sensibilities to resist.

"Please."

"Well, all right. But I think you're daft!" But already his mind was spinning with schemes.

"Thank you, Teddy. My good friend. I knew I could count on you." She got up eagerly. "Do you know someplace on this island I can hide, just until I can make arrangements to get to England?"

Teddy grinned. "I can do better than that, Miss India! I got friends around here, you know. Maybe I can get you off the island tonight. We'll have to walk to the village is all. Can you do that? In the dark?"

"Of course I can do that." The tears were flowing freely again, and India wondered if she would ever in her life stop crying. "Let's go. Let's get out of here."

*   *   *

The walk to the village was a long five miles. The damp vegetation caught at India's skirts and soaked her shoes as they followed the well-worn path up the hill away from the Lodge. The night was moonless and dark, and their progress along the path was slow. Buried roots and jutting stones seemed to leap out of the path to trip her, and she had to squint carefully ahead in the dark to avoid cold puddles of rainwater and occasional piles of horse manure. The utter silence of the dark woods was frightening, but the occasional rustling, twig-cracking, and chittering by the side of the path was even more alarming. Her heart jumped into her throat when a rabbit shot out of the brush and leapt across the path.

After three long hours of misery they finally came out onto the narrow lane that led into the fishing village. Teddy led India toward the tavern, which she remembered was at the end of town. The village was silent and dark. Fog enveloped the little bay and sent tendrils of mist to swirl and eddy around the wharves, storage houses, and cottages. India felt almost as though she were walking through a dream, a bad dream, trudging up the lane through the ghostly, mist-shrouded little town. By the time they reached the other end of the village, the fog was so thick that she would have missed the tavern completely had it not been for Teddy, who grabbed her arm and tugged her toward a dark shadow in the gray mist. India shivered in the eerie swirls of fog, her imagination running wild. Christopher's demon magic at work? she wondered wryly as she allowed Teddy to pull her toward the tavern. Bending nature to his will to foil her escape? Somehow, in the midst of this ghostly dreamscape, her earlier fantasies seemed to take on the life of reality. The tavern was dim when they finally stepped through the door. A single lantern burned behind the bar, its light barely reaching into the taproom. Other than two drunks snoring loudly at a table in the back, the room appeared deserted.

India cleared her throat nervously. She hoped Teddy knew what he was about. "Is anybody here?"

No answer.

"Is anybody here?" she repeated, louder this time.

"Eh?" came the answer. The unshaven face of a man about fifty rose from behind the bar. "Who wants ta know?"

India regarded the man with a pounding heart. He wasn't a very appealing sight to a young woman alone in the night with only an undergrown boy for company. His features were rough, his hair graying and greasy and sticking out at odd angles from under his knitted fisherman's cap.

"We're lookin' for Walter," Teddy told the man, confidently taking charge. "Is he here tonight?"

"Where else would he be?" the man mumbled. "He's in the back." He called in a rough voice through a door to a back room. His voice, India thought with a grimace, could wake the very dead!

A few moments passed before a man emerged from the back room, his eyes puffy with sleep and his graying sandy hair plastered to one side of his head.

"Whazzis?" he mumbled, spotting India sitting demurely at the bar.

"Walter!" Teddy called, stepping out from India's side.

"Umph!" Walter grunted as he recognized the boy. "What you doin' here, boy? You should be sleepin' somewhere, not botherin' decent folk who work all day for a living and need their sleep at night."

India was beginning to have serious doubts about Teddy's whole scheme as Walter's eyes roved over her curiously.

"Walter," Teddy continued, "I need a favor."

Walter's eyes swung back to the boy. "A favor, is it?" he snorted. "In the middle of the night? Come back when normal folk are up and about, and leave me to my sleep."

"I need it now," Teddy persisted.

Walter grunted in derision and turned as if to return to his pallet.

"Walter! You owe me." Teddy wasn't about to give up.

"Remember when you stole old Mattie's goat? Didn't I tell Mattie that Ian took it?"

Walter turned reluctantly. "Aye, that you did, boy."

"And didn't Ian thrash me so hard I hobbled like an old dame for a week?" Teddy grimaced in memory. He'd figured old Mattie couldn't do a thing to Ian, but a destitute Walter, whom Teddy thought of as friend, had needed that goat to provide milk for an ailing babe. Ian had been fit to be tied when the old bat had come around, accusing him of swiping the old nanny. He'd beat him good, he had, for telling that lie. But he hadn't let on who had the goat, bless him.

"Well, now"—Teddy fixed Walter with a smug gaze— "I'm callin' in the debt."

"Now?" Walter sighed.

"Now."

"All right, boy. What's this favor you must have?"

Teddy cleared his throat self-importantly. "This lady needs a way off the island. I figured you could take her over to Skye in *Penelope*."

"Oh you did, did you?" He spared a glance for India, taking in her bedraggled appearance with interest.

"Aye." Teddy interrupted his perusal. "Little enough to ask for the beating I took to keep you from trouble."

"And I don't suppose either of you has the coin to pay for this."

"Did you pay for that nanny goat?"

"Hmm." Walter did not look happy.

"You'll be paid." India decided it was time for her to take the reins. "My father is wealthy. He'll send you a goodly reward. I promise."

"Will he, now?" The lass had an honest look about her, Walter decided, and the shadows beneath her eyes and slight trembling of her chin when she spoke testified to her need.

"It's the truth, Walter," Teddy chimed in, grateful that India had come to his rescue. "Her father's a quality gentleman, with a title besides. He's got a bundle, he has!"

Mention of reward gave Walter pause. Such a bad year it had been, with hard luck pounding him from all sides. Now his wife and bairns must live with her mother on Skye, and he was here scrabbling for a bare living, unable to hire an adequate crew for his boat, sleeping in the back of a tavern, getting poorer every week that passed. A reward could change all that. Still, he was a suspicious man.

"Who be your father, lass, that he can afford the gold to line me pockets?" When India hesitated, he continued. "And which one of those pirates are you runnin' from?" He nodded his head in the direction of the Lodge.

The silence continued as neither Teddy nor India answered.

Walter sighed. "Well, no matter, I suppose, lassie, as long as I get that reward you've promised."

India smiled, and Teddy looked extremely proud of himself.

"This cancels our debt, boy." Walter shook a warning finger at Teddy. "And then some! I won't steal no more goats, and you don't steal no more ladies in distress, you hear?"

He turned to India. "We'll sail before the dawn, with the morning tide. So if you truly want to go, you'd best be sayin' your good-byes now. And you, boy, best be off before that redheaded giant catches you again, and gives you another thrashin'. This time I think you're lookin' to get us both in trouble."

India's good-byes to Teddy were tearful, and much to Teddy's chagrin, she actually put her arms around him and cried. He wondered what the cap'n had done to make her so sad. When he realized he wasn't likely to see her again, he tried hard to remain manly and stalwart, but couldn't prevent a boyish tear from trickling down his cheek.

"I'll never forget you, Teddy," India assured him through her sobs. "You're a true friend. One of the very best."

"You take care of yourself, Miss India." He wiped his nose on his sleeve, stifling a forlorn sniff. "I wish . . . I wish you could stay."

"No," India said quietly.

In silence they looked at each other, remembering the last months of companionship.

"Say good-bye to Thomas Cat for me."

Teddy hung his head, then launched himself toward her for a last hug.

An hour later, Walter showed India to the cramped, cold, fishy-smelling cabin below the deck of the little sloop that was his only possession. When he left her alone, she sat down on a wooden crate and wrapped her cloak tightly around her to ward off the chill. She tried to doze, but visions of Christopher with Sarah kept flashing through her mind, alternating with fears that he'd discovered her absence and at any moment would come bursting through the cabin door. Finally she drifted off. A short time later she was wakened by the pitching of the sloop as it headed out into the bay. She clutched her damp cloak around her and ascended the ladder to the hatch. Peeking out, she saw the little village was slipping rapidly behind them, fading fast in the gray predawn. She opened the hatch and stepped out on deck, feeling the cold morning air drive the cobwebs from her brain. Walter's callused hand was there to assist her.

"You're safe, now, lassie," he said with a smile. "No need to worry anymore."

India smiled at him and thought how much less sinister he looked in the gathering light of the dawn. Just a simple fisherman, after all, rough but good-hearted. She went to the rail and stared out at the water. The still-present fog paled the light of the rising sun, and the water was becoming rough as they approached the open sea. Her heart lay like a heavy, dead burden in her chest as she realized she'd finally pulled herself irrevocably free from Christopher's embrace. Cold salt spray misted her face as the little boat pitched and rolled through the waves, running down her cheeks and mingling with her salt tears as she wept silently for the love she was leaving behind.

The morning sun struck a cruel spear of light through Christopher's head as he opened his eyes to face the new day. His heart thudded dully in his chest, his mouth was fuzzed over with a vile-tasting film, and his whole body felt as if it had been keelhauled in a North Atlantic storm. He groaned and raised himself on one elbow, squinting as the bright daylight set his head to pounding painfully. Slowly, the memory of the night before returned.

"Oh, God!" he groaned. "A pox on all females. Wait'll I get my hands on that bitch!"

India would wake without him and guess the worst, he knew, and then he'd be in for a time of it. Why did he have to backslide now, of all times? He must have been drugged. Even Sarah with her lush body couldn't get a man as hot as he'd been last night. Still, that excuse wasn't going to hold water when India discovered him stumbling from another woman's bed, exhausted from the night's exertions and coated with the leavings of his own lust. No excuse in the world was going to save him from the consequences of his own stupidity.

He swung his legs over the edge of the bed and grimaced as a lance of fire speared through his brain.

"Damnation!" he mumbled. "I'll be lucky to make it to my own room alive!"

He did make it to the master suite alive, though in imminent danger of losing the contents of his stomach. Rushing past the bed to the screened chamber pot, he didn't at first notice the emptiness of the room. But after the rebellious heavings of his stomach calmed, he looked around the room with a puzzled, woozy frown. The bed showed no evidence of having been slept in. The wardrobe gaped wide and empty without the presence of India's few garments.

"What the hell?" He slammed the wardrobe shut, kicked the bedpost, and shouted in a hoarse voice. "India!"

The sick guilt over the night before was fading before a gnawing certainty that the unthinkable had occurred. India had left him.

"India!" he shouted again, and strode from the room, slamming the door behind him.

Helen looked up uneasily as Christopher bounded down the stairs, taking three at a time. She'd lost her fear of this big man months ago, but this morning he looked like a beast not to be trifled with.

"Where's India?" he demanded.

"I . . . I haven't seen her yet this morning," Helen admitted hesitantly. "I thought she was with you."

Sarah appeared, posing seductively at the top of the stairway in a diaphanous robe. The look she gave Christopher was blatantly possessive.

"The girl could hardly have been with Christopher, Helen, dear. He was with me all night." She glowed with triumph, having already wormed the story of India's flight from a repentant Teddy.

Helen looked at Sarah, then at Christopher, with a puzzled frown. Her face turned sour with disapproval.

"Well, I haven't seen her. Maybe something was bothering her and she left to take a ride," she said, looking at Christopher significantly.

Fear was beginning to clear the cobwebs from Christopher's brain. As he looked up at Sarah the sudden knowledge in his eyes made her confident smile fade. He started up the stairs toward her, and before she could back away his hands grabbed her arms in a painful grip.

"You had something to do with this, bitch!" he said in a voice that was all the more frightening for its level coldness.

"I don't know what you mean!" she countered. "How should I know where the silly chit has taken herself? You know where I was all last night!" she declared innocently.

"Yes," he continued in the same frightening voice. "Thanks to you and your tricks I was playing stud for you the entire night. Could there have been a purpose to that, other than the obvious one?"

"Don't be ridiculous!"

"Tell me the truth, Sarah," he urged fiercely. "Or I swear to God I'll beat it out of you! Nothing would give me more pleasure!"

He gave her a shake that rattled the teeth in her head.

"Tell me!" He slammed her up against the wall and drew back his hand to strike her when Helen's plump little hand grasped hold of his arm to restrain him.

"Christopher, stop!" she cried. "You're going to hurt her!"

Christopher calmed somewhat at Helen's touch, but he still held Sarah in a painful, unbreakable grip.

"Indeed I will hurt her!" he promised grimly through clenched teeth. "Unless she tells me what she knows about India's disappearance."

An idea occurred to him then. "Helen," he ordered. "Go find Mary Jane. And Lisa, too. Find out if they know anything about this."

Helen took her hand from his arm, somewhat frightened of the violence she witnessed in his eyes.

"Mary Jane had the night off last night," she told him. "She came back about two hours ago and said India wasn't in her room. I thought maybe she'd gone with you to the ship. All the rest of the men and Teddy left early this morning. Lisa left early, too, to go into Glenmuir."

Christopher sighed, then turned back to Sarah, who saw her fate in his eyes. How could she have so misjudged the man, believing he would simply turn to her as soon as she had eliminated her rival? She perceived suddenly, with an awful sinking of her stomach, that Christopher was capable of doing her serious injury if he thought she had in some way been responsible for India coming to grief.

"Well, Sarah?" His tone was ominous.

Sarah took a shaky breath. "I'm sure she's safe, Christopher. She saw us together last night and threw an absolute childish fit. Teddy told me early this morning that she persuaded him to arrange for a fisherman to take her across to Skye. She should be well on her way by now."

He released her with an ungentle shove.

"And I suppose you made sure she broke in on us last night at just the right moment?"

She shrugged gracefully. "She saw enough to bring out her vixen's temper." She shuddered delicately, remembering how hard she'd had to scrub to rid herself of that noxious odor. "You should be grateful she's gone, Christopher. Her type's not for you." Her green eyes held an invitation, hoping against the odds that her plan might yet succeed. But he only looked at her with contempt, his hands itching to close around her throat.

"You'll be out of here by noon, Sarah," he said in a voice heavy with loathing. "You can arrange the same kind of passage for yourself that Teddy did for my wife. And heaven help you if you and I should ever meet again."

Sarah's lip tightened into a grim line of frustration. All her careful planning gone for naught! All because of that simpleton girl! Well, she wished Christopher joy of her. Sarah hoped the little hellcat would give him the same treatment, when he caught up with her, that she'd given her the night before. With a final look of wounded pride and injured dignity, she turned away from the twin spears of anger shooting from Christopher's eyes and retreated gracefully to her room.

Christopher watched her go, then turned and almost collided with Helen, who had a distressed Mary Jane in tow.

"Oh, Captain. Is it true?" she gasped. "Has Miss India disappeared?"

"When did you last see your mistress?" he asked impatiently.

Mary Jane cringed from the intensity in his face.

"Why, I saw her yesterday, Captain. She gave me the whole day off, and the night, too." Mary Jane thought for a moment. "She's been acting rather strange, but who knew she'd do something like this!"

"You didn't see her at all when you returned this morning?" he prompted, hoping against all evidence that Sarah had been lying.

"No, sir," she confirmed. "And I came back right early. She wasna' in her room. Though I just barely peeked in, I could see she wasna' there."

"All right." He sighed. "Mary Jane, go out and tell the stableboy to saddle the bay stallion, and the black mare as well, with a sidesaddle." He turned to Helen. "Will you ride the mare to the anchorage and tell Ian and Seamus I want to see them back here two hours from now? And tell them to lock Teddy in my cabin. I have a score to settle with that scamp!"

"What are you going to do, Christopher?" Helen's plump, pretty face clouded with concern.

"I'm going down to the village to find out if Sarah was telling the truth. Maybe that fisherman didn't leave yet. It looks pretty foggy out there."

"Oh, it is!" Mary Jane confirmed. "Foggy and cold, too. And the bay was rough when I left this morning. Did she leave in a boat, do you think?"

"Yes," Christopher answered shortly. "It appears so."

"Oh, poor Miss India," Mary Jane wailed softly. "She shouldna' be bouncing around in a little boat in her condition."

"Condition?" Christopher snapped, all his attention suddenly riveted on his wife's maid.

The unfortunate girl stammered in confusion, seeing those hot black eyes turn on her. "I . . . I thought . . . I assumed you knew."

"Knew what?" Christopher demanded.

"Well . . . she never exactly told me, Captain sir. Not right out, I mean. But I know the signs," she asserted. "Being the oldest of seven, I ought to know the signs of a woman being with child."

Christopher looked at her, stupefied. Then the reaction began to set in.

"Damnation!" he shouted, furious with both himself and the whole world. "Son of a bitch! Why am I always the last one to know about anything around this house?"

Both women cringed in the face of his tirade. He slammed his fist against the wall in a fury of temper, then grimaced as his knuckles spouted crimson. Still cursing angrily, he turned and stomped down the stairs and out the main door.

Forty-five minutes later, Christopher stood at the village wharf, looking out at the bay. The fishing fleet was gone, the *Penelope* and India with it. The loss tore at his heart in a way that he would not have believed possible six months ago.

Inquiries at the tavern had revealed the truth of Sarah's story, at least part of it. The local drunk had said that, yes, he did vaguely remember a young woman and boy stumbling into the tavern during the hours of darkness, though just when he didn't recall, being far gone in drink. Yes, it did seem that the lass left with Walter Simmons, a rough but honest man who'd had a bad year of it, with his catch not being all that good and his children taking ill.

The fog was finally lifting, letting the watery sunlight filter down to the choppy gray water of the bay. It would have been a rough crossing, he thought, especially for a girl feeling ill with her first pregnancy.

Christopher's facial muscles tensed with anger as he looked toward the gray horizon. He cursed India for her waywardness, he cursed Teddy for his complicity, and he cursed Sarah for her deviousness. But most of all he cursed himself for his stupidity in letting himself be lured away from India's side and allowing her to flee from him.

Just two days ago she'd been so loving, so radiant, responding to his every touch with a hunger that matched his own. Why hadn't she told him about the child? Surely she knew he would be delighted at the news. Why did she flee? Why not stay and berate him for his unfaithfulness? She must know he loved her, and only her, and that he would have done anything to mend her tattered heart. Running away in the dark of the night was not like the India he knew.

Christopher turned and walked back to his horse. India was gone, fled from his grasp like a doe from the wolf. He realized now how empty his life had been before she'd come into it so unexpectedly that day in March. He'd lived for the excitement of reckless adventure, with the dark goal of revenge and the possibility of vindication his only holds on the future. Now all his priorities had been turned inside out by a slip of a girl with blue eyes and black hair. The only thing of real meaning in his life had fled into the early-morning fog, and he was stuck with a half-dismantled ship and no way to pursue.

Christopher vaulted to the stallion's back and wheeled him around toward the lane leading out of the quiet village.

"Damn!" he shouted into the teeth of the wind. "Damn

all women! And damn all men stupid enough to fall into their soft little traps!''

He set spurs to the stallion as they pounded down the lane toward the Lodge. Christopher smiled grimly to himself. If Ian could round up the crew and they could set to work on the *Falcon* immediately, he might be in Hampshire in a month, maybe a little longer. But he'd get there. For sure he'd get there.

"When I get my hands on that little minx," he told the horse, and the wind, and the world, "I'll make her sorry she ever even thought about leaving!"

CHAPTER TWENTY-SEVEN

India sat in the bright sunroom of the great house trying in a desultory fashion to concentrate on her needlework. She looked for all the world like the young girl who had sat in that very room more than a year ago, stitching on her trousseau and complaining to Helen Atkins about her coming marriage to an unwanted suitor. The dark, glossy head was the same, bent industriously over her work. The graceful, slender fingers even seemed to ply the needle with similar impatient energy.

She was not the same, though. The girl who'd railed against her father's edicts was no more, and a woman grown sat in her place. For India there were no more shouting matches with her father and no more escapades in the meadows surrounding the great estates. Those who had called at Hillcrest since her return a month ago remarked on the change in William Carey's unfortunate daughter. The rebellious hellion had become, it seemed, a woman devoid of spirit, with smoky-gray wisps of sadness seeming to cloud the deep blue of her eyes.

India muttered a curse that would have made any other young woman of breeding swoon on the spot. She laid aside her needlework and sucked at her finger. The silk of her fashionable afternoon gown rustled as she rose from her seat and went to the window overlooking the gardens, frowning out at the riot of October colors that surrounded the estate. The day should be gray and cold, she thought, to match her mood. She wondered is she would ever lose the feeling that, for her at least, the world would never be bright again.

She had hoped with the passing of a few weeks, thoughts of Christopher would fade. Instead, as the Hampshire summer turned to autumn, her heartbroken flight, which had seemed so necessary in the grief of the moment, was beginning to appear the height of foolishness. How had she been so stupid? Why hadn't she stayed and fought to keep the man she loved, instead of letting Sarah and her own insecurities drive her to flee?

Her gloomy thoughts were interrupted by the light scuff of a footstep behind her. She turned to see gray-haired Mollie waiting to be noticed. The India that had returned a month ago was not the bright-eyed, mischievous girl Mollie had left with a year past to travel to France, nor the frightened but rebellious maid she'd left on the *Black Falcon* so many months ago. In fact, she didn't know this strange India who'd finally returned to them, and that made her sad. Where was the naughty but spirited child she'd raised from a babe? Aye, India and her sweet mother, as well. Both of them she'd nurtured with all the love in her heart; she'd been privy to all their secrets, nursed all their hurts, large and small. And now she felt helpless to mend the hurt gnawing at India's heart. The poor child just sat and pined for that big man who'd carried her off so abruptly. And Mollie could only stand by and watch as the girl's heart died a little more every day.

"Yes, Mollie?" India prompted.

"Oh, yes . . . uh . . . will you take your tea in here, Miss India?"

"Yes, that would be fine," India replied without interest.

"Oh, and one other thing," Mollie continued. "Sir James Thornton left his card about an hour ago, miss. And he asked me to tell you he'd call at the same time tomorrow if you'd care to step out for some air in his new coach and six."

India snorted. "Coach and six, indeed! He's done very well for himself since I saw him last!"

Mollie pursed her thin lips in disapproval. "Yes, well," she said, "you'll pardon my repeating gossip, miss, but the word is that Sir James has been winning very heavily at the tables in London. The way he spends it, though, he's sure not going to hang on to that money very long!"

India smiled at her maid's acerbic comments. "Well, Mollie dear, you needn't worry that I'll give in to that gentleman's advances. He needs to be reminded that I'm a married woman."

Mollie harrumphed her disapproval of India's married state and left the room. India smiled bitterly. She wondered if Mollie would be quite so disapproving of her being a married woman if she knew that the waistlines of most of her gowns had just been let out to make room for the child that was rapidly growing in her womb. She sighed and turned back to the window.

When she'd first arrived home, exhausted from many days of travel and emotionally drained, she'd spent a week in near-seclusion, most of it lying in bed. Her father's welcome had been nonexistent. His attitude made it clear that she should have had the good taste to kill herself rather than return home and subject her family to scandal. She'd not seen Sir William at all during that first week, other than when she'd first entered the house on her return. Since leaving the seclusion of her room, she'd seen little more of him than was absolutely necessary. His attitude, India reflected, had become even more stiffly autocratic since she'd left. Perhaps the death of Lady Carey, miscarrying the babe he'd spawned in hopes of replacing her as his heir, had embittered him beyond redemption. India had remembered him as a hard man, but the harsh and unforgiving autocrat she had found on her return had seemed like a stranger. Was this the man whose affection she had craved all these years? Was this the man whose grief she agonized over as she lay awake so many nights these past months with Christopher? She'd been a fool, India realized. Perhaps now she was really seeing her father for the first time. She was ashamed to be sprung from a man whose soul knew no kindness or compassion. In her disillusionment, her convictions were beginning to change. Perhaps this man who was her father was indeed capable of the base acts Christopher accused him of.

If her father's welcome had been bitterly disappointing, the local gentry's reaction to her return was simply what she'd expected. Speculation on her adventures and misfortunes provided ample entertainment for every group of gossiping matrons, giggling schoolgirls, and avidly curious men. At the few social functions she attended, she found herself the target of indignant stares from the matrons, contemptuous glances from their marriageable daughters, and speculative, often inviting looks from many of the gentlemen. It seemed that as a woman of "experience" she was fair game for the advances of any man with a mind to give her a try. Even at church she was subjected to unwanted attentions. The local eligible bachelors would accost her in a manner they wouldn't dare have used with a chaste unmarried girl, and the attentions from some of the married men, though much more subtle, were even more offensive. India's friends, the young people that she'd grown up with, were all sympathy to her face. How horrible, the girls exclaimed, to be kidnapped by a pirate and then forced to wed the scoundrel. How brave she was to have survived it all! But in their eyes India read the same contempt that everyone else felt for her. She became resigned to the fact that in society's view, when a woman is victimized, the disgrace is her own and not her assailant's. Only the fact that she was legally married kept her from being ousted completely from the local Hampshire society. The attitude of her former friends, however, soon discouraged her from leaving Hillcrest except to attend church. She sat in the sunroom day after day, working disinterestedly on her needlework and staring out into the autumn-hued formal gardens.

Depressing as this existence was, India admitted, life was going to get worse before it got better. Soon she would have to tell her father of her pregnancy. She couldn't hide it much longer by simply letting out her dresses to accommodate her expanding waistline. Her condition was going to become obvious to anyone with eyes in a very short time. She'd best get it over with, India knew, instead of sitting around brooding about it.

But it was fully a week later before India gathered the courage to confront her father. A glimpse of her profile in the mirror that morning convinced her she could wait no longer, so she informed her father at breakfast that she would like to speak to him in private. His impatient, disapproving frown didn't make her task any easier. He intensely disliked any association with his daughter and didn't bother to hide his feelings. Nevertheless, at India's insistence, he consented to meet her in his library after the noon meal.

The interview went badly from the very first. Sir William sat at his desk and regarded India morosely as she entered the room. He didn't offer her a seat, so she stood uneasily before him, cursing herself for still being afraid of this man after all that she'd survived in the past months.

"Well?" he growled impatiently. "What was so important that you must interrupt my day for a private audience?"

His fingers drummed on the top of the desk, sounding eerily loud in the quiet of the library.

India had always hated this room, with its dark, heavy drapes cutting out any trace of sunlight and its dusky atmosphere of studious gloom. The room weighed down her spirit, making the thought of Sir William's certain displeasure even harder to face. But there was no way around what had to be done. She cleared her throat and attempted to fix her father with a level, calm gaze.

"Well?" he repeated brusquely.

"I am with child," India blurted out. There was no sense, she decided, in mincing words.

Sir William's face went stonily blank. Only the tightening of his thin, aristocratic lips and the stain of heightened color revealed his agitation.

"And the father?" He sneered. "I suppose it is that scum who calls himself your husband?"

"Yes."

Sir William rose from his seat and began to pace the room, striding back and forth before the bookcases for such a long time that India was beginning to believe he'd forgotten her presence. But then he stopped and fixed her with a look of such contempt that she almost cringed.

"Slut!" he accused.

His voice was icy, coldly tinged with the fury that was roiling inside him. His eyes were like shards of splintered ice as they bored into her, paralyzing and pinning her to the spot where she stood.

"You dare to return here and present me with the whelp that scum planted in your belly? Did I raise my only daughter to be a whore, that she spreads herself for the use of a scoundrel such as Christopher Armstrong, then carries his leavings home to ruin her family? Have you no sense of honor, no shred of decency? Better you had killed yourself!"

His voice had risen to a shout, and droplets of spittle flew from his mouth as he ranted.

A cold center of fury was beginning to push away India's fear. He had no right to speak to her so, to call her a whore with no shred of decency. How could he think her very life was less important than his precious family honor? Her blue eyes shot sparks as she lifted her chin and faced down her father's fury.

"Do not lay the ruin of your dynastic ambitions at my feet, sir! I didn't go willingly with your enemy, but after living with him for a time I discovered him to be a good and honorable man in his own fashion, a man who had been gravely wronged by you! If not for your hasty, ill-conceived action at Blenheim, none of this would have happened. If you want to lay the blame for this situation at someone's door, try your own!"

Sir William turned purple with rage. "How dare you speak to me in such a manner, you impertinent trollop!"

India looked at her father with contempt. How had she ever worshiped this man?

"If you wish me to play the part of dutiful daughter," she said calmly, "perhaps you should try being a dutiful father."

He looked at her in amazement. Where was the girl he could cow with a mere glance, the girl who indulged in ridiculous pranks to gain his attention? He almost didn't recognize the young woman standing before him fending off his fury with a wall of her own cold wrath.

"I'm not afraid of you any longer, Father," India said.

"Well, you should be!" Sir William countered. "I can throw you out of here without a penny to your name. See how defiant you are then!"

"You won't, though." India smiled knowingly. "Think of the scandal it would cause."

An idea suddenly sparked in India's brain. She went on rapidly.

"The best way to save a scandal at this point, Father, even if not your own pride, is to locate John Thomas, clear Christopher's name, acknowledge him as your legitimate son-in-law, and admit that he has won."

"You must be mad!"

"No," India replied calmly. "Just practical. My marriage to Christopher is legal under English law. This estate is entailed. There's no way you can prevent these lands from going to Christopher through me, and then on to his children."

Sir William fixed his daughter with a look of such hatred that it almost daunted her newfound courage.

"Christopher Armstrong will never have my estates! If I see to nothing else before I die, I will see to that!"

India took in the acid of her father's words and finally understood the depth of his feelings.

"You hated him even before Blenheim, didn't you?" she asked.

Sir William sneered. "I did. And he deserved it."

He stared unseeingly at his daughter, his face full of bitter memories.

"He was an arrogant young whelp, merely the second son of a minor earl. Twenty years old, and the troops followed him more willingly than they followed me. His every victory made me look bad. The whole situation was unjust. Marlborough was actually paying more attention to that boy's opinion than to mine. Then his father and brother were killed. The haughty young pup was actually going to come into a title. Everything came so easily to him . . ." He trailed off, lost in the bitterness of thirteen years past.

India was almost afraid to ask. "Did you deliberately condemn an innocent man?"

"Innocent? Bah! He was guilty as sin!"

"He was innocent!" India insisted.

"What do you know of happenings so long ago? Nothing!"

"I know more than you think," India said. "What of John Thomas? He could have cleared Christopher at the trial."

"He disappeared," Sir William said with satisfaction. "I wouldn't be surprised if Armstrong had him murdered so Thomas couldn't testify against him."

India turned away in disgust. She was ashamed suddenly that this man was her father. How could she have been fooled by him these many years?

"I know for a fact that Christopher Armstrong is innocent of the crime you condemned him of," she asserted in a level voice. "I suggest you help clear his name or the fine Carey tradition which you value so highly will be maintained by the children of a condemned man."

Sir William's lip curled in a sneer of contempt.

"No child of that scum will ever lay claim to the Carey estates!"

"There's no way you can prevent it, Father," India insisted.

He regarded her coldly. "How naive you are, India. Of course I can prevent it. Do you think I would allow myself to be outsmarted by the renegade who dares to call himself my son-in-law?"

India felt the first flutter of uneasiness invade her mind.

"You, my disloyal daughter, will leave as soon as practi-

cal for France,'' Sir William continued, ''to stay with
Prudence until the child is delivered.''

He thought silently that if fortune was truly with him,
both India and the child would die in childbirth, freeing him
to name an heir of his choice.

''I'm sure a home can be arranged for the child, somewhere where he will never learn his identity and therefore
will be no bother to us.''

A coldness began to creep into India's soul.

''And as for the rogue who calls himself your husband,''
Sir William continued, ''I will have him tracked down and
hanged like the dog he is.''

''You'll never find him,'' India said tensely. ''You don't
even know the name he uses.''

''But you do, and so does old Mollie, though she claims
she doesn't.'' Her father smiled unpleasantly. ''And you
should also know where he takes himself when not out
flouting our good English laws.''

''I won't betray him,'' India said quietly.

''You betrayed me easily enough!'' Sir William snapped.

''I never betrayed you willingly,'' India asserted. ''And I
won't be a part of a plot to trap a man you wrongfully
condemned. It wouldn't do you any good, in any case,
because I have no intention of giving up my baby.''

Sir William regarded her sternly, his confidence returned
now that he'd thought of a way to handle the situation.
''You'll do as you're told, miss, and let there be no mistake
about that.''

''I won't give up my baby,'' India repeated, holding his
eyes with a level gaze of determination.

''You'll find yourself out on your own, with no one to
help you,'' he threatened.

''That won't do you a bit of good. I'll still be your heir.
Christopher's child will inherit through me.''

''You overestimate your own ability to survive without
someone to support you,'' Sir William said with deadly
calm.

''I think not!'' India countered. ''I'm tougher than you
believe. Besides, if you cast me out, your own daughter,

and me heavy with my husband's child, you would have such a scandal on your hands that you'd never be able to hold up your head in society again!''

Their eyes held in silent combat, both determined not to yield. A sudden knock on the door sounded like a thunderclap in the silence of the room. The butler cleared his throat uneasily as he opened the door and perceived the tension between father and daughter.

"Excuse me, sir," he ventured in a discreet voice. "There is a . . . uh . . . gentleman awaiting you in the small parlor." His tone indicated that he considered the visitor to be somewhat below his exacting standards for the title *gentleman.* "He insists that he must see you right away."

"Who is it?" Sir William snapped impatiently.

"He wouldn't give his name, sir," the butler stated calmly, accustomed to his employer's sharp manner. "But he was most insistent."

Sir William sighed. "His business damn well better be important. Tell him I'll be there momentarily."

When the butler left, he scowled blackly at his daughter's still defiant face.

"We will finish this another time, India," he said. "You are fooling yourself with all sorts of stupidities, but I've heard that temporary unbalances are common in pregnant women. Eventually, you will come round to my way of thinking."

There was an unspoken menace in his tone that was somehow more frightening than all the threats that went before.

India paced the library once her father had left the room. It was tempting to give in to the urge to cry, to release the flood of hot tears that were pressing for an outlet. But there was no time for that. She had to think, and think fast, of a way to halt her father's plans.

She left the library, closing the door softly behind her, and headed for the stairway, intending to go to her room. Then on second thought she turned and walked toward the main door. She wanted someplace to be alone, someplace that her father wouldn't think to look for her when he decided to resume their dispute. She didn't feel up to facing him twice in the same day.

She slipped silently past the small parlor, where she heard Sir William's voice raised in sharp discussion. One of the double doors was slightly ajar, affording her a brief glimpse of the room's occupants. One brief glimpse, however, was more than enough to send her heart racing in her chest. For a moment she was stunned into immobility, then she flattened herself against the wall next to the door, where she could hear but not be seen.

There was no way in the world she could mistake the ravaged face of the man talking to her father, but she could scarcely believe her eyes. What was John Daughtery, erstwhile boatswain on the *Black Falcon*, perpetrator of the vile kidnapping and murder attempt on New Providence, doing in the parlor talking to her father? Her pulse raced as she strained to catch the words being spoken by the two men.

"This is madness!" Sir William was saying heatedly. "You dare to come back, after all this time, and make these demands! Absurd!"

"No, sir!" Daughtery insisted. "I'm just asking my due. I've kept quiet all these years, and now the debt comes due!"

"You were paid your due years ago!" Sir William retorted angrily. "And now you've the gall to come back and demand more!"

"You paid me little enough!" Daughtery objected. "That was before I realized how hard it is to make a living in this world."

"Seems to me you've done all right for yourself!" Sir William's voice was colored with contempt. "You're better dressed than most gentlemen of my acquaintance."

"I did all right for a while," Daughtery conceded. "I pirated in the Caribbean for a time, then sailed with Armstrong for a couple of years and made a fair amount in prize money and smuggling. But I've had a bellyful of pirating and smuggling. When that girl of yours came aboard I knew my time was up. All I needed to do was let slip one thing to let her recognize me. She would've told Armstrong and my life would've become right unpleasant. The man's not the same callow boy you framed at Blenheim."

"So I gather!" Sir William snorted. "But I can't think

you were in any danger from India. Good Lord, man, your own mother wouldn't recognize that face of yours!''

"Whether I was or wasn't, I prefer not to take the risk. I'm through with all that, and it occurs to me that you owe me a living.''

"Like hell I do!''

India pressed back against the wall and closed her eyes, trying to calm her racing pulse. Surely the sound of her heart pounding so loudly could be heard by the men in the parlor! She could scarcely credit what she was hearing. The man Christopher had searched for all this time, the man who could set him free of his infamy, had been right under his nose, protected by the disguise of his ruined features. That was why Daughtery—no, Thomas, John Thomas—had tried to eliminate her in New Providence. He had feared she would somehow recognize him through the mass of scar tissue. But what was all the talk of payment? She pressed her ear to the door once more.

"You can protest all you want, Sir William,'' Daughtery's voice was saying. "But you can't change the fact that besides you, I'm the only person alive who knows the truth of what happened that night.''

There was a long pause. India strained to hear as her father mumbled something indistinct. Then Daughtery's voice continued.

"I'd think again if I was you. What I'm asking is a pittance. Not nearly what you could afford to pay. Be grateful that I'm not a greedy man.''

"Not greedy!'' Sir William practically shouted. "My God, man, do you think I'm made of money?''

Daughtery chuckled. Not a pleasant sound. "I'd think you'd rather part with a few shillings than have it broadcast by an eyewitness that you were really the one that Frenchie came to meet that night. And don't think I won't carry out my threat, Sir William, because I will. I'll be real careful to carry out all my promises, one way or the other.''

The tone of his voice made India shudder.

"Scoundrel!'' Sir William spat.

"Call me what you will,'' Daughtery returned. "But I

wouldn't be too long about sending the money. I'm staying at the Hare and Hounds down the road.''

"Get out!" Sir William ordered.

Numb with the shock of what she'd heard, India fled out the main door and toward the stable, which had been her original destination. She had to get out of the house before Thomas-Daughtery saw her and realized she'd been eavesdropping.

The stable door gave a rusty creak as she opened it, making India jump in startled fright. But the soft amber light and warm animal smell of the interior was welcoming and silent. No one was there.

Brandywine whickered a welcome as she opened the stall door and slipped inside. For a moment she buried her face against the mare's satiny neck. Finally the tears flowed—tears for Christopher, who'd been justified all along in his hatred; tears for her father, whose villainies had finally come back to haunt him; and most of all, tears for herself, who had nowhere to turn and no one to help her face the consequences of what she had just learned.

On the spacious porch of the great house, Sir William watched as his former valet rode down the long curving drive. Eyes of splintered ice followed the man and horse as they disappeared around the curve. Then his face twisted into a sneer of contempt.

"Blackmailer!" he spat venomously. "We'll see what stories you tell with your throat split ear to ear!"

His sneer relaxed into a smile of grim satisfaction as he turned and disappeared into the house.

CHAPTER TWENTY-EIGHT

India sat in a corner of Brandywine's stall and let the aroma of warm straw envelop her. She was exhausted from her mind's turmoil, and the urge to escape her problems through sleep was almost irresistible. Her head had fallen back against the rough planking behind her and her eyes had drooped when a nudge from the chestnut mare brought her to attention once more. She pushed the velvety nose aside.

"I know, I know!" she complained as the mare whuffed in her face. "I've got to think. I've got to find the answers to this mess." She looked into the liquid brown eyes above her. "But what if there are no answers?"

She slumped back into the corner, grimacing as the rough boards sent a splinter through her bodice. Her world was coming apart. In the space of two hours she had discovered that her perception of reality was all wrong. Christopher was not quite the scoundrel she had thought him, and her father was a vile traitor who'd plotted to send an innocent man to the gallows in his place. On top of everything else, she was threatened with either losing her child or being cast out to bear it in a ditch or gutter. India sighed. This was too much turmoil for such a short space of time.

Could she somehow let Christopher know that Daughtery was the man he sought and Sir William was the contact whom the Frenchman had come to meet that night? Perhaps she could send a message, or even contrive to go herself. But supposing Christopher wasn't at the Falcon's Nest anymore? Or supposing Daughtery dropped out of sight in the meanwhile? And further, if she informed Christopher of the turn of events, she would be condemning her father to a traitor's death. No doubt he richly deserved the fate, but he was still her father, her own flesh and blood. The thought of playing even an indirect part in his being condemned sickened her. On the other hand, India knew, if she didn't somehow contrive to get a message to Christopher, she might well be condemning him, an innocent man, the man she loved and the father of her child, to be branded a traitor the rest of his life. And his life wouldn't be long if her father carried out his threat to hunt him down. Doubtless Daughtery had offered the location of the Lodge as well as Christopher's assumed name as part of his foul bargain.

India groaned and rested her forehead on her bent knees. In the final analysis, the problem came down to a simple choice between her family and Christopher. In reality that was no choice at all. Christopher won hands down. But how would she get him the message, short of returning herself to the little island? And where would she get funds for fare on the public coach?

She rose and brushed the straw from her skirts. "This is going to take a bit of doing, my friend," she told the mare.

Then the idea struck her. She wouldn't need fare for the coach if she rode Brandywine. All she would need was enough to pay for food and lodging along the way, and something to purchase a boat ride out to Glenmuir. Of course, it was unheard of for a young woman of quality to travel unchaperoned on the dangerous roads of England and Scotland, especially on horseback, and especially in India's condition. But perhaps this problem called for unheard-of measures! India laughed to herself. If not for the too obvious rounding of her belly, she could disguise herself as a lad for the trip. What a lark that would be! Her spirits soared from the pit of gloom where they'd been resting as she resolved to carry out her decision. The thought that she would see Christopher again, even if only for a short time, made her feel life was worth living. She gave Brandywine a final pat and had turned to open the stall door when the creak of a rusty hinge signaled the stable door was opening. India quickly ducked out of sight behind the stall partition.

Bright sunlight flooded the dusky gloom of the stable as the door creaked open. Voices sounded outside, and though India strained to hear the words spoken, they came through to her ears as only indistinct mumblings. Then the door opened wider. Peering through a crack, India saw Walt the stableboy lead in two unfamiliar horses. She waited until the boy disappeared down the opposite corridor before slipping out of Brandywine's stall. She peered around cautiously as she opened the stable door barely wide enough to allow her slim body to pass through. No one was in the stableyard.

The men had disappeared along the path that led to the great house. She followed, suspicious now of everything that was happening in this place that used to be her secure, beloved home.

The front door opened quietly as she slipped into the entrance hall. Voices issued from behind the closed doors of the small parlor. One of the voices was her father's. She flattened herself against the wall to listen, just as she had to overhear Daughtery's threats.

"I'm becoming quite a little sneak," India told herself silently. She thought ruefully that she must have inherited the tendency from her father. Then her thoughts turned to the conversation within.

"You pay well for a simple job, Sir William," one of the voices was saying.

"I want to be sure the job is done right," Sir William replied.

A deeper voice chuckled. "For this amount of money you can be sure it's done right."

Her father still sounded uneasy. "Just make sure you don't make any mistakes. This fellow's a tough one. He's been living outside the law for a long time."

"Don't worry," another voice said. "He won't give us any trouble. Just tell us how to find him."

"He's staying at the Hare and Hounds down the road," Sir William told them. Then he chuckled unpleasantly. "There's no way you can mistake him. His whole face is one hideous mass of burn scars. He looks like a ghoul in a man's clothing."

"All right, sir," the deep voice said, accompanied by the chink of a purse of coins being thrown and caught. "The job'll be done before the night is out."

"Good enough," her father concluded. "Just remember I want this to look like an ordinary robbery and murder; and don't leave him with anything that might identify him."

"Whatever you say," the first voice agreed.

Footsteps came toward the door. India picked up her skirts and fled toward the stairway. She'd just barely disappeared around the corner of the hallway when the first man emerged from the parlor. As the door closed behind the strangers, India forced herself to walk sedately down the hall to her room, not glancing around when she heard Sir William come out of the small parlor at the foot of the stairs. Her mind was whirling, but she couldn't give her father, who was now in plain sight, the least hint that she'd heard his plotting. Finally she was safely in her chamber with the door securely closed behind her.

She took a deep breath to calm herself, then hurried to her small writing desk and whipped out a sheet of vellum. As much as she feared and despised Daughtery, she couldn't allow him to be removed from the scene right now. He was the only man who could completely clear Christopher and bear witness to her father's duplicity. She rapidly penned an anonymous warning to the ex-valet of what was intended for him, praying that he would take heed. Then she folded the paper and hurriedly stuffed it into a blank envelope, pouring wax on the closure to seal it but not imprinting the family seal. She hurried out of the house and down the path toward the stable, intending to send the message with the stableboy, who, for a shilling, could be persuaded to keep quiet about his errand. Unfortunately, Walt was nowhere in sight.

"Damn!" India cursed under her breath. "Where is that boy?"

She walked impatiently down both corridors, looking into every stall, then in the tack room and the hay loft. Still no sign of the stableboy. For a brief moment, she considered taking the message herself, and getting someone in the inn to deliver it while she was safely hidden. But she quickly dismissed the idea as being too risky. No telling what Daughtery would do if he sighted her. She walked anxiously back to the house and went around to the kitchens in the rear. Hurrying through the door, she almost collided with a buxom, motherly looking woman with a huge bowl of washed vegetables in her arms.

"Oh, Miss India!" the woman exclaimed. "What are you doing back here? You almost toppled me the way you ran through that door!"

"Edith!" India gasped. "You're just the person I wanted to see."

"Well, that's fine." Edith bustled impatiently. "Now you've found me, why don't you sit before you die of apoplexy. What's gotten into you, girl?"

Edith used the same chiding tone that she'd used when India was a child and prone to filching tarts and sweets before they were served to the rest of the household. But India was no more daunted by her scolding now than she had been as a child.

"Where's that young scamp of a nephew of yours who masquerades as a stableboy?" she asked sourly. "Have you seen him?"

"Oh, Lord!" Edith moaned. "What's the boy done now?"

"He hasn't done anything. I just need him to run an errand. Right now."

"Well." Edith chuckled. "He was here just a moment ago, filching sweets, just like you used to do. He probably took the roundabout way back to work. He generally does, the young layabout! He going to be gone long?" she added as an afterthought. "I wanted him to fetch me in some wood."

"No," India replied. "Just to the inn down the road. He'll be back in a flash."

India sighed and headed back to the stable. She found Walt in the tack room, oiling her father's saddle. He was jubilant when India handed him the message, anxious to escape from the dreary tasks set for him by the stablemaster. His elation knew no bounds when India handed him a shilling.

"Now, remember," India warned him. "Not a word to anybody about this. I mean it!"

"Me lips is sealed, mum!" the boy promised.

He grabbed his jacket and cap and took off down the lane without a backward glance. India frowned after him, hoping desperately that the message would arrive in time.

Sir William stood at the parlor window and watched as the small boy ran down the long curving drive that led from the great house. A puzzled frown marred the aristocratic lines of his face. Then a spark of suspicion flared in his brain. He turned to the butler, who was arranging the tea service on the sidetable behind him.

"Do you know where young Walt is going in such a hurry?"

The butler's expression indicated it was not his job to keep track of mischievous stableboys. "I've no idea, sir."

"Well, find out!" Sir William snapped.

"Very well, sir," the butler said with slightly raised brows.

Five minutes later he returned. "Edith in the kitchen says her nephew was sent to the Hare and Hounds on some errand for Miss India, sir. She didn't know what the errand was."

Sir William's face suffused with anger. The spark of suspicion flared into a conflagration.

"I can guess what the errand was!" he muttered as he strode angrily out of the parlor toward the staircase. "Damn well I can!"

India jumped at the pounding on her bedroom door.

"India!" her father's voice shouted through the door.

Her heart gave a lurch. That tone always meant trouble. She tried to compose her features into a mask of calm as she admitted him.

"What is it, Father?"

Sir William fixed her with a murderous glare. His deadly anger took her somewhat by surprise. Could he have found out about her plans?

"Why did you send Walt down to the Hare and Hounds?" he demanded.

India's face went pale. She groped desperately for a plausible lie, and didn't find one.

"I . . . I . . ."

"Don't lie to me, girl!" her father warned.

"I . . ."

"Do you know about Daughtery?" His eyes were wide with accusation. "Do you know who he is? Do you?"

India stiffened her spine before his onslaught. Could she

brazen out the truth, she wondered desperately? She had to say something!

"I know," she admitted.

"How much do you know!" Sir William's face darkened with anger and despair.

"I know you accused Christopher of a crime you committed yourself, and that you've plotted to murder John Thomas so he can't betray you."

"So you sent Walt to warn my intended victim, eh? You must think you're very clever."

India was silent.

"Don't look so self-righteous, miss," Sir William finally said. "Everything I've done I did to preserve our family fortune and honor."

India snorted in disgust. "Our family has no honor!"

Livid color was creeping into Sir William's face, but India ignored the warning signs. She was so outraged that she no longer cared for the consequences of her words.

"You've betrayed every principle you profess to hold dear!" she accused. "I'm ashamed to be your daughter!"

His blow took her by surprise, sending her staggering back against the bedpost and thence onto the floor. Her head rang with the force of his fist against her cheek, and a thin trickle of blood appeared at the corner of her mouth. Sir William raised his arm for another blow, but an unexpected voice stayed his hand.

"You'll not be layin' another hand on that girl, Sir William!"

Sir William turned in surprise. Neither of them had noticed Mollie's silent entrance into the room. She stood with arms folded across her ample bosom, regarding the pair of them with stern eyes.

"What the hell?" Sir William advanced toward Mollie threateningly. "How dare you interfere, old woman! Begone before I take my fist to you as well."

"Not before I've had my say," Mollie replied in a calm voice. "Lord knows I should've spoken up long ago, but I didn't, and more's the burden I must bear now."

India rose shakily from the floor, grasping the bedpost for

support. She feared the expression on her father's face, feared for the faithful Mollie, not for herself.

"Mollie," she pleaded. "Do as my father says. You cannot help."

Mollie only took a firmer stance, as if daring Sir William to remove her by force.

"I'll say what I came to say, Miss India. All these years I've watched his Lordship here mistreat you, ignore you, and tear at your tender young heart with his coldness. Still I've held my peace. I promised your mother, my sweet Lucille, that I'd keep a still tongue in my head for your sake, but I've done you no service, that I haven't!"

"What are you babbling about, you old hag?" Sir William rasped. "Get out of here before my patience wears thinner than it is already!"

Mollie shot him a look of contempt. "I'm too old to fear your bellowing, my Lord. You can't do anything to these old bones that the years aren't doing already. You'll listen to what I have to say, that you will."

"Mollie," India was feeling steadier now. "What is it?"

Mollie turned to India and her gaze softened. "Miss India, how'll you forgive me for not telling you all these years? Lord help me! When I think of how unhappy you've been! When I think of all you've suffered because of his high and mightiness here. When I heard him shouting at you, and saw him hit you— Well now, I can be still no longer." She turned to Sir William, who was regarding her as one might a madwoman. "You've no reason to take out your frustrations on Miss India, my Lord, for she's none of yours, and never was."

"What are you saying?" Sir William sneered.

"What I'm saying is this, and well you should listen. Miss India's not your daughter. My sweet Lucille, my darling girl whose heart you broke with your cold and cruel ways, she found her comfort in a man who loved her well. 'Tis this man, a far better man than you, sir, who got my Lucille with child."

"Impossible!" Sir William snorted.

Mollie chuckled. "Impossible, you say. Look at her!

How can you believe her yours. She's the image of her father with her black hair and blue eyes.''

Sir William's face paled as his eyes were drawn against his will to India's face. India stood dumbly, feeling as though another blow had been delivered to her head.

"This can't be true!" she whispered.

"True enough, my pet," Mollie assured her. "Your sweet mother swore me to silence, and not a word have I said until now. She thought you'd be better off with Sir William, poor trusting baby that she was. Even when that pirate took you and made you suffer because you were your father's daughter— even then I held my peace. Who knows what he would've done with us all had you no value to him? Lord knows, a pretty maid like you, he wouldn't have let you go before he'd had his fill of you. At least, thinking to have revenge on Sir William, he guarded your virtue with a wedding, such as it was.''

"But who . . . but who, then, is my real father?''

"Long dead and gone he is, my sweet. But his family are good and honorable people, and once they see you they'll have no doubt whose child you are. They'll not refuse you help if you ask. You needn't stay and suffer this tyrant any longer.'' She spared a glance for Sir William, whose bloodless face was devoid of expression.

India leaned up against the bedpost. She didn't know whether to laugh or to weep. All her suffering, all of Christopher's carefully laid plans, all her father's—no, not her father, Sir William's—scheming, all gone for naught. All her concepts of who she was and what was her place and duty in life—all shattered by a single, calmly uttered sentence. Her almost hysterical train of thought was interrupted by a humorless laugh from Sir William.

"So Lucille has her trollop's revenge.'' He regarded India with scorn. "She saddles me with a useless daughter to feed and clothe for these many years, and now that I've put up with the nuisance for all this time, I find that you're a damned bastard, not even good for continuing on the family line.'' His voice was dangerously quiet, making India more afraid than his shouting. "After all these generations, my line is at an end. Thanks to that slut Lucille, my plans are undone.''

India's only recollections of her mother were hazy, a kind and smiling face and warm enfolding hugs. The idea of that mostly unknown but much beloved lady having to endure the heartlessness of this man she'd thought of as her father sparked a cold fury inside her breast.

''Don't call my mother a slut! If she had to seek comfort and affection outside her home, it was because her husband lacked even the pretense of a heart. You are a monster, sir, and I will not stay here one day more!''

''Monster?'' His brows arched cynically. ''For feeding and clothing my wife's bastard for eighteen years?''

He regarded both India and Mollie with icy thoughtfulness for a moment, then stepped toward the door, laying his hand on the latch and looking back at India's still bleeding face. Her cheek was beginning to color a bluish purple.

''It would've been better for all of us had you kept your silence, old woman,'' he told Mollie tonelessly. ''Now I must alter my plans, and you will pay for your deception all these years. And you.'' He fixed India with an icy glare. ''You will pay dearly for all the attention I have lavished on you, thinking you were the last of my line,'' he told her levelly. ''Blood kin or no, you will remain in this house and under my guardianship as my acknowledged daughter. I will have no scandal on my head, and I won't have my neighbors and acquaintances laughing at me for being made cuckold. You, if you're wise, will think better of letting anyone know of the less than acceptable nature of your birth. Something might yet be retrieved from this mess. I've several distant cousins I could marry you off to. Better the estate go to a remote branch of the family than none at all.''

India's face didn't change from its stubborn set. ''No, father . . . Sir William. I'll have none of your schemes. You've no hold on me now. I've suffered enough because of you.''

Sir William's face twisted into a sneer. ''We'll see about that. If you don't behave to my satisfaction you'll discover what suffering really is." He chuckled unpleasantly as Mollie took up a protective stance beside her charge.

Both women maintained a frozen silence as the door closed softly behind Sir William. Then India slowly raised a hand to touch her bruised and swollen cheek.

"What you said is the truth?" she asked softly.

"Every word, my love. I swear on my immortal soul. May my sweet Lucille forgive me for breaking my solemn vow, but, Lord smite me, I thought if he knew the truth he'd want no more to do with you. I thought we'd go to your father's family in London and start a new life."

India sat down on the bed. She wanted to laugh. At the same time, she wanted to cry, but the tears wouldn't come. Surely this was a nightmare, not a reality that threatened to take over her entire life.

"Who was my father, then?"

Mollie clucked sympathetically. "Long dead he is. But he was a good and honest man, though not as high as your blessed mother. A rich London merchant, handsome as a pagan god, he was. And so kind to my poor baby. When he learned about you he begged her to leave Sir William and come to him. But she thought you'd have a better life as Sir William's daughter. So she stayed, stayed and died still young, my poor girl. Sir William wasn't home much then, you see, being with the Duke's army. Your poor mother didn't know the depths of the man."

India lowered her head to her hands, confused, disoriented, and weary of spirit. "We must find a way to leave, and soon," she told Mollie.

"That we must," the old woman agreed heartily.

The sound of hoofbeats brought India to her feet. She hurried to the window in time to watch Sir William cantering away from the house, doubtless intent on stopping Walt before he could reach the inn.

"Dammit!" India cursed, some of her spirit returning as she remembered Daughtery, Christopher's only hope, waiting to be slaughtered at the Hare and Hounds.

"He's gone to stop Walt. I've got to carry the warning myself."

Mollie cried objection as India grabbed a cloak and headed for the door, but the door wouldn't budge.

"It's bolted!" She let loose with a string of epithets she'd learned from the pirates. "Curse him for a villain!" she said finally. "He'll not get the best of me!"

She ran to the window and flung it wide, letting in a blast of cold air. Glad now for her hoyden days when she'd often escaped Miss Adams tutelage by this route, she swung her legs over the sill and dropped the short distance to the veranda roof.

"Miss India!" Mollie wailed, hanging out the window. "You'll kill yourself!"

India waved reassuringly when she reached the ground. Then she turned and raced toward the stables.

Not waiting to summon a stablehand, she grabbed her sidesaddle and swung it to Brandywine's back. The mare snorted an objection to this hasty intrusion into her afternoon somnolence, but nevertheless willingly accepted the bit as India fastened the bridle over her head.

"Come on, my sweet," India crooned as she swung into the saddle. "We've got work to do."

India knew if she cut through the meadows instead of following the road, she could arrive at the Hare and Hounds without passing Sir William. Perhaps once she had warned Daughtery, she could convince him to seek out Christopher as his best hope for protection from Sir William's designs. If not, then she would seek out Christopher herself. Her own future was uncertain. Staying at Hillcrest, once her beloved home, was unthinkable. But now was no time to brood on her own fate.

She headed Brandywine off the road and through a small stand of trees, urging her to a gallop. The mare flew over a ditch, then immediately over a broad hedge that stood in their path. In spite of the turmoil in her mind and spirit, India was exhilarated by the rhythm and speed of the mare's pace. How often in the past they had flown over the countryside together, taking all obstacles as if they were placed there solely for their sport. The mare settled into a steady canter, launching herself over walls, ditches, and fences with a grace that allowed her rider to sit the saddle without effort. India stroked her neck fondly as she pulled her up to a trot, then a walk, as they neared the inn courtyard. As the ostler stepped forward to help her dismount, his face revealed his surprise at seeing an unescorted lady on horseback, but the coin she pressed into his hand forestalled any comment he was thinking to make.

"I'll only be a few minutes," India said, patting the mare. "But you might give her a bit of water."

The interior of the inn glowed with the tapers that had just been lit against the gathering dusk. The room was practically deserted, the dinner hour having not yet arrived. Only one customer sat in the corner by the fireplace, leaning back on his chair as though dozing, long legs stretched out in front of him and a battered hat over his face. India gave him a glance when she entered, ascertained that he wasn't the man she sought, then turned to the innkeeper, who had hurried toward her the minute she stepped through the door.

"Ah . . . Miss Carey." He was somewhat taken aback by seeing her in the taproom unaccompanied, but he put on his best innkeeper's manner just the same. "How can I serve you, my lady?"

"I'm looking for a man who I believe has taken lodging with you. He's a fellow with scar tissue covering his face. Do you recall him?"

The innkeeper suppressed a shudder. Indeed he did remember the man! He'd sent a shiver down his spine when he first came in, not only for his disfigurement but for his cold-eyed manner. He couldn't guess what a sweet young lady like India Carey would want with such a creature, but he'd learned long ago not to mess into other people's business.

"I remember the man you speak of," the innkeeper said. "He came in late last night, and I've barely seen him since. Would you like me to see if he's in his room?"

"Yes, please." India tried to control the shaking that threatened to invade her limbs. The last man in the world that she wanted to face was John Thomas, alias John Daughtery, but this had to be done.

"Would you please tell him that Miss India Carey would like to see him in the taproom on an urgent matter?"

When the innkeeper came back down the stairway he had a slightly disapproving look on his face.

"Mr. Daughtery will be down momentarily, mistress," he confirmed. "Would you care for some refreshment while you wait?"

"No, thank you," India declined, giving the man a polite smile.

She sat herself in the corner opposite the taproom's one customer, who hadn't moved since she entered. An occasional snore emerged from beneath the hat, and he didn't move when the innkeeper's wife cleared away the two empty glasses from his table, shaking her head as she did so. India thought there was something hauntingly familiar about the man, but she put it from her mind when she noticed Daughtery coming down the stairs.

He walked over to her warily, as if thinking she had henchmen lurking behind her chair. No expression could be read from the near inhuman face, and his cold eyes glittered suspiciously.

"Miss India," he greeted her in a flat voice. "I didn't know you'd returned to your home."

His manner was noncommittal. India guessed that he was unsure of how much she knew about his role in the New Providence kidnapping and about his true identity.

"Sit down," she said, glancing around the room to make sure no one was in earshot.

He sat, still eyeing her warily.

"I won't mince words," India started. "I know who you are, I know why you're here, I even know you tried to have me killed in Nassau so I wouldn't recognize you by chance and destroy your little game with Christopher."

The slit of his mouth tightened almost imperceptibly.

"The reason I've come to this inn is to warn you that Sir William has hired two men to murder you before the night is out."

He sat in silence for a moment, digesting her news.

"Why would you warn me?" he finally asked.

"I'd like to see you stay alive long enough to clear Christopher Armstrong of the crime he didn't commit."

Daughtery's snort of disgust brought a flush of anger into India's face.

"You're a fool," she said calmly. "You're a fool to come to Sir William for money. You should've known he'd rather have you killed than be paying you the rest of his life. Your only chance is to go to Christopher and tell the truth."

Daughtery spat, making the innkeeper's wife look up in dismay.

"I may be a fool, lady, but I'm not that big of a fool. Christopher Armstrong's not a man I care to see riled. I don't want to be in his reach when he finds out I took a bribe to keep my mouth shut about what happened that night."

"He needs you alive," India insisted. "You can't help him if you're dead!"

"True," he admitted. "But there's no reason for him to let me live after I've done what he wants, now, is there?"

India shot him a level stare of contempt. She found she no longer feared this man.

"How you stay alive is your business," she said. "But I guarantee you won't live long if you stay many more hours in this place. And let me add that Christopher might be more inclined to be merciful if you seek him out than if he has to search for you."

Daughtery spat again. "He'll never find me."

"I wouldn't count on that," India gave it one last try as she rose from her chair. "You're going to be running from both Sir William and Christopher for the rest of your life unless you take my advice."

Daughtery followed her out into the courtyard. Dusk had become darkness, and the lanterns that lit the yard cast eerie, flickering shadows against the enclosing walls. She felt uneasy with Daughtery at her back and looked anxiously for the ostler to fetch her horse, but the courtyard was silent with no one in sight.

Suddenly, two figures materialized from the shadows.

They moved silently toward them, menace in every stride they took.

India voiced an unintentional cry of fear and moved back toward the door, but it was closed and latched behind her. She hadn't seen the taproom's sleeping customer rise and follow them out when they left, securely latching the door behind him. He stood now in the black shadows, watching unseen as the duo of assassins approached.

"What the hell?" Daughtery cursed and drew his knife, the only weapon he had on his person. Then his long arm snaked out and caught India around the waist, drawing her in front of him to act as a shield.

One of the assassins, the one with the deep voice India remembered from the parlor, chuckled.

"Let the girl go, matey. I don't really care if I have to skewer her to get to you, but you might as well give yourself a chance to fight. Be more fun that way."

Daughtery cursed again and pushed India aside, shoving her with such force that she landed on the rough cobbles.

The deep-voiced one raised his sword and chuckled again.

"Deal with the girl," he ordered his comrade. "We don't want no witnesses to this. The old man wouldn't be pleased."

India scrambled up from the cobbles and started to run. Before she got three steps, a hand snatched roughly at her hair and dragged her backward. She managed to scream before her mouth was covered, but no help was forthcoming. Where was the ostler, she thought desperately, or the innkeeper? Surely he could hear the struggle that was going on right outside his door!

India's assailant dragged her back against him in spite of her frantic kicking and flailing. He pinned her to him. His rough stubble of beard scratched against India's cheek as he pressed against her, groping at her tender breasts with his rough hands.

"Oh," he sighed wetly. "You are a right pretty thing! Too bad we're in a hurry. No time to stay and play with you, girlie."

India almost gagged from the smell of his breath. She

dimly heard the sound of fighting a few feet away, the ring of steel on steel as Daughtery tried to defend himself with a knife. Then her whole attention was riveted on her own struggle as her attacker took one hand from her breast and groped for his knife. He raised it in front of her, a glittering, sharp-edged lance of destruction eerily catching the glow of the flickering lanterns. Trying to hold the man's knife arm with her hand, she gazed in sick fascination at the horror poised above her. She didn't notice that the other sounds of fighting had ceased.

"We'll make this nice and clean, little dollie!" the man grunted in her face.

"I wouldn't if I were you." The voice was calm, but steel edged and deadly.

The assassin started in surprise as cold steel came to rest against his throat. India twisted her head to look at the newcomer, but he was in the shadows and she could make out neither face nor form. But the voice! The voice was unmistakable.

"Christopher!" she breathed in relief.

"The very same," the answer came in that achingly familiar voice.

Christopher moved from the shadows. India couldn't twist far enough to see him, but her assailant, with Christopher's foil still at his throat, could, and apparently he didn't like what he saw. He released India and drew back, trying to avoid the deadly steel.

"At least give a fellow a fighting chance!" the man whined as he made a cautious attempt to draw his own sword.

Christopher had him backed against a wall now. A tiny nudge with his point and a crimson droplet appeared at the assassin's throat.

"Were you going to give the lady a fighting chance?" he asked in a level, icy voice.

India moved back, not wanting to get in the way of the struggle she knew was coming. It was then she noticed the deep-voiced assassin lying in a pool of his own blood several yards away. Daughtery lay beside him, trussed in his own shirt, alive and looking very apprehensive.

Her attacker's squeal brought her attention back.

"No!" he shouted, as he read deadly intent on Christopher's face. "I wasn't going to harm the little lady! Honest, I wasn't! I was just fooling around!"

"Like hell!" Christopher said. "Go ahead and draw your weapon." A grim smile touched his face. "We'll see how good the paid killers of London are."

The battle was short but decisive. India's skin crawled at the death's-head grin on Christopher's face. She had forgotten, in their weeks of lazy, loving peace, how very deadly he could be when the need arose. When he finally wiped his blade on his opponent's vest and turned to her, she involuntarily backed away a step.

He looked her up and down, the old enigmatic expression on his face. Then his eyes came to rest on the swelling of her abdomen, which could no longer be completely hidden by her altered skirts.

"You broke your word," he stated levelly. His face was impassive.

"Yes," she admitted.

She longed to run to him and feel his arms gather her close to his comforting warmth. But she didn't. An unwelcome image of him making love to Sarah intruded its way into her mind, igniting a small spark of anger deep within her. She ignored it—for now.

"How can you think of such a trivial thing when . . . when . . . do you know who he really is?" she asked, pointing to the bound Daughtery.

"I know who he is." He spared Daughtery a scornful glance. "I had a chat with his cousin before I came here, the one who sent us on that useless chase to New Providence." A wolfish grin spread across his face. "He was persuaded to tell all. It seems Daughtery thought he'd be safe if he kept me running in circles after some phantom who didn't exist."

India sighed and shivered as the October chill began to penetrate her cloak.

"It was him you came to find," she said in a small voice.

For one short moment, when she'd first heard Christopher's voice come out of the darkness, she'd thought he'd come for her, and her heart had soared with unexpected joy. But of course he'd really come for Daughtery, and to complete his vengeance on her father, who wasn't her father, and who seemed to deserve anything Christopher cared to dish out. Suddenly she was very tired.

"No," Christopher replied softly. "It was you I came to find."

It was true. He hadn't realized, until she was gone, that his carefully laid plans, his vengeance, even his hopes for clearing his name and regaining his rightful title, meant nothing if she weren't beside him. It had been mere chance that he'd run into Daughtery's cousin in Portsmouth, where they docked. His only thoughts had been to find India and take her back to Falcon's Nest.

India gazed at him in confused disbelief. She couldn't imagine Christopher sailing all the way from Scotland just in search of her, not when he had the willing Sarah Perkins to comfort him for her loss. He saw the doubt in her face and sighed.

Just then a rectangle of yellow light fell on the cobblestones as the inn door slowly opened. The innkeeper's head peered cautiously around the edge to view the courtyard.

"What's going on out here?" he asked.

Christopher laughed cynically. "You're a bit late to join in the action, innkeeper."

The portly little man doubtfully regarded the scene before him—the three bodies, two obviously dead and the third trussed and glaring ominously, as well as this tall, bearded stranger who had the definite look of a predator about him.

"I try to stay out of other people's business," the innkeeper explained.

From the look of things, the tall man hadn't needed any help. He held a sword as though he were born with one in his hand.

"Well, in any case," Christopher said amiably, "you can clean up the leavings. Call someone to haul those bodies

away and then find a secure place to stash this one." He
prodded Daughtery with his toe, eliciting a series of mumbled curses. "And this lady and I will require a room for the
night."

India looked at him in surprise. She opened her mouth to
voice a protest, but at a warning glance from Christopher
her mouth snapped shut with objections unvoiced.

The warmth radiating from the fireplace in the spacious
room to which the innkeeper showed them was more than
welcome. India took off her damp cloak and spread it on a
chair to dry, then turned to face Christopher's questioning
eyes.

"Now, madam," he said, "we can finish our conversation. Why did you leave Falcon's Nest?"

India sighed and turned toward the fire, spreading her
hands in front of her to absorb the warmth.

"Do you really not know why I left?" She slanted him an
irritated glance, one shapely brow arched in question.

Christopher scowled and turned toward the fire, resting
his hands on the carved mantel. "I suppose I do," he
admitted.

India turned and looked at him. She had thought never to
see him again, and there he was, standing not ten feet from
her. She wanted to fly into his arms, bury her face against
the hardness of his chest, and cry out her love. But anger
and hurt held her back. She couldn't forget the last image of
him she held in her mind, snoring and satiated in Sarah's
rumpled bed. The thought of him there spurred her anger to
fiery life.

"I saw you, you know." Her voice was quiet, but it
trembled with remembering. "I saw you lying in her bed,
dead to the world, exhausted from servicing that oversexed
cow—still stinking from your passion!"

Christopher opened his mouth to reply, but India angrily
waved him to silence as she turned back to stare moodily
into the fire. Somewhat to his own surprise, he obeyed her
and held his peace.

"Did you think I would sit meekly by and let you parade
your mistresses before my eyes, all the while I grew heavy

with your child?'' Her chin trembled as she fought for control, remembering again the painful fears and uncertainties of those days. ''I was going to tell you that night about our baby. I had the words all planned out to say to you when we were alone together. I waited and waited, lying awake wondering if you would still find me attractive when I was round with your child. But you never came.'' Her face tightened. ''Lisa came instead, came to tell me my husband had crawled into bed with her mistress. So I went to see myself, not believing it could be the truth. And I saw...'' Her voice faltered. ''So I left.''

''You ran away.''

''Do you blame me? Do you think I have no pride? No feelings?''

Christopher sighed wearily. The hurt on India's face was from a wound still fresh, and he had no knowledge of how to mend her heart or salve her feelings. He had done what she accused him of doing. There was no defense against the facts. The circumstances were not quite what she believed, but in matters of the heart women seldom listened to reason. He could but try.

''India,'' he started, ''I will tell you what happened that night.'' She opened her mouth for a sharp retort, but he shut the angry words back in her throat by a finger placed on her lips. ''You've had your say. Now let me have mine.''

India leaned back against the stone of the fireplace, arms folded over her chest, to listen to him in skeptical silence. He paused to gather the right words and gain the courage to say them.

''I was unfaithful to you that night you speak of. There's no denying what you saw with your own eyes.'' He shook his head in warning as she frowned and started to speak. ''I was unfaithful to you, I admit it freely, but Sarah had to drug me to get me to her bed. Elsewise I'd not have gone. I'd no desire to bed her, or to bed anyone other than my wife, before Sarah slipped a potion in my brandy.''

India's expression was a trifle less forbidding when he looked at her again.

''I tell you the truth, India. And this is the truth also. A

man's a man, and when his passions run amok it doesn't
matter who the female is that serves as relief. It has nothing
to do with love, or even affection.''

The expression on India's face tightened again to anger,
but this time the anger wasn't directed against Christopher.
''The witch! Her charms weren't sufficient to lure you, so
she drugged you. Then no doubt she arranged for Lisa to
bear the news to me, hoping I would behave as I did. What
a stupid twit I was, acting out the part she assigned me!''

Christopher chuckled sadly. ''You were not the only one
who lacked a full measure of sense that night. I played into
her hands like a raw boy.''

He moved to where India stood, and grasping her little
chin gently in his big hand, forced her eyes to where they
were trapped by his. ''India, I'll tell you now I'm sorry and
ask your forgiveness.'' His eyes never wavered from hers,
nor let hers stray. ''Then I'd like it buried, forgotten, and
gone. The memory of that night is no more pleasant for me
than for you. I wouldn't have it come between us again.''

India looked up at him, unable to escape from his gaze. A
twitch of a smile on her lips warred with the sadness still
lingering in her eyes. ''I'll forgive your stupidity if you'll
forgive mine.'' She finally smiled. ''I should've stayed to
confront you instead of playing the coward and running
away. And,'' she added vengefully, ''I should've beaten
Sarah senseless after emptying the chamber pot over her
head! How dare she do that to the man I love!''

Christopher's full-throated laugh was bursting with relief.
''India, my little hellcat, what would I do without you?''

India backed off when he made to pull her into his
embrace. There were still issues unresolved.

''Leave me be, Christopher. There's still much I have to
tell you. And you may find your temper sorely tried when
you hear what I have to say.''

He took in the seriousness of her face. ''All right, tell me.
What is so important that it should delay me making love to
my wife?'' His eyes twinkled with mischief, but he couldn't
lure her into a better humor.

India looked into his face, the face whose every plane and

curve she'd memorized with love. She feared what he would do on learning the truth about Sir William, and the truth about her birth, but just the same she had no choice. Better the story should come from her than someone else.

She began to speak, slowly and carefully, leaving out no detail. Christopher held his silence during her tale, not saying a word when she told him of Sir William's treason—how he had been the Frenchman's contact all along, and how he had seized on Christopher's conversation with the spy to protect himself, win the Queen's gratitude, and satisfy his own rancor by seeing Christopher destroyed. He held his silence still when she told him of Mollie's revelations of just hours before, that he had married not the daughter and heir of his enemy, but the bastard daughter of a London merchant, a bastard who could now call nothing in the world her own. He didn't need her, India insisted, refusing to meet his eyes with her troubled ones. She would understand if, under the circumstances, he wished to put her aside.

Her story finished, India waited tensely in the silence that followed. Her face was taut with strain as she awaited his reaction.

He shook his head sadly and she suspected the worst. In her distress, she missed the spark of humor that gleamed in his dark eyes.

"So all my plans are laid to waste, after all, though now with the truth revealed I've little need of Sir William's daughter to assure my vengeance. Still, it's a shame to see all my carefully planned villainy gone for naught."

When India turned away from him, trying to hide the beginnings of tears misting her eyes, he grabbed her arm and swung her gently around, immediately regretting his attempt at humor.

"I've truly married a foolish little twit." He sighed, but his mouth curved into the beginning of a grin. He pulled her into the warm circle of his arms, ignoring her protests. "India! Sweet India! Not need you? You're my love—no, more than my love. You're my very life. Now that I know you truly love me I'll never let you go. Besides," he continued, pausing to steal a quick kiss, "the crew told me not to come back without you. There's one youngster in particular who's mighty tired of being on my blacklist. Teddy thinks you should come back and rescue him."

"Oh, Christopher!" India cried in dismay. "You didn't punish him!"

Christopher grinned. "Of course I punished him." He brushed away a tear that had escaped India's eye. "But not too much. After all, I know what it's like to be caught in the web of your charms."

"What about Sir William?" she asked after a long, warm silence.

Christopher smiled and placed a light kiss on India's brow. "His treatment of you is one more thing I should pay him back for, but I seem to have lost my taste for vengeance," he admitted. "I think I'll just let John Thomas spill his story to the magistrate and let the law take care of Sir William."

India propped her chin against his chest and looked up at him, smiling her gratitude. She was glad that Christopher at least would not be personally involved in whatever happened to the man she'd thought of as her father all these years.

"I wonder what my real father was like?" She sighed.

"To have a daughter like you, he must've been one hell of a man. I'm sorry I'll never get to meet him. I'd like to tell him how much I love his daughter."

India grinned up at him.

"Are you sorry, India," Christopher continued in a more serious vein, "that you're not Sir William's daughter?"

"No." India sighed. "I suppose not. All these years I tried so hard to win a father's affection, doing the most outrageous things to get his attention. But I think now perhaps I have enough love to last me for a lifetime."

Christopher gazed at her for a long moment, his heart in his eyes. Then he lowered his mouth to take the kiss he'd been able only to dream of during this last month of separation.

CHAPTER TWENTY-NINE

The heir to the Earldom of Woodsford came forth into the world, squalling, on the third of March, 1717. For long hours Christopher Armstrong, now Earl of Woodsford with all rights and privileges restored by King George I, had been at his wife's side, bathing her brow with cool water, holding her hand when she was wracked with pain, and diverting her with stories from his notorious past while she lay waiting for the pain to build again. During the last minutes, when India's screams had resounded off the walls and Bess McCann had tried her best to chase him from the room, Christopher refused to be budged, claiming the unheard-of privilege of being present when his babe was born. Bess gave up and turned her attention to the expectant mother, knowing that someone twice her size would have difficulty forcing Christopher to do something he didn't want to do. She settled for snappishly instructing him to stay out of the way.

But India was glad to have him stay, believing that it was only right that since they'd made the child together, they should be together in the culmination of that act of love. He calmed her with soothing words and allowed her to grip and twist painfully at his hands. His face floated above hers in a haze of pain, and his calm encouragements kept the blackness at bay when her body seemed to be splitting into pieces. The final wrenching moment came; then the pain diminished. Christopher turned to Bess questioningly. He turned back to India with a grin threatening to split his face. The lusty squall of an infant filled the room.

"We have a son, my love," Christopher told her.

India smiled tiredly, and a flood of satisfaction and

exquisite love filled her. She looked up at her husband and raised a hand to trace the lines of tiredness etched in his chiseled face.

"You look as exhausted as I feel," she commented with a mischievous grin. "Did I work you so hard?"

"Hard enough," he laughed softly. "If I'd known it was such work to birth a babe, perhaps I would've refrained from making love to you."

"Like hell you would've!"

Christopher laughed out loud. "Watch your language around my son, madam. You'll have him growing up sounding like a scoundrel of the worst sort."

The smiling face of Bess swam into India's view, and in her arms was a wrinkled red mite of humanity waving his tiny fists and making soft sounds of indignation at his precipitous entrance into the cold, raw world. India held out her arms and Bess laid the babe gently on her breast.

"He's perfect in every way," Bess crowed, "down to the last fingernail."

From the expression on her face one would've guessed that Bess had birthed the babe herself. She could barely tear herself away to go downstairs to tell the news to Ian, Seamus, and Helen, who had all gathered for the great event.

"Oh," India cried softly. "He's beautiful! Oh, my little Robert, you are the most beautiful baby in the world!"

They'd agreed earlier to name the child after Christopher's late brother. Both were so sure of the babe's gender they'd not bothered to choose a girl's name.

Christopher looked down at his new son gurgling in his mother's arms. Personally, he didn't see anything beautiful about the wrinkled little old-man face gazing in his direction with unfocused eyes, but he felt himself swelling with pride just the same. This was the son who would inherit the title he'd fought for for so long, who would someday profit from the shipping business—legitimate shipping this time—that he'd started to keep himself from growing fat and lazy living the good life of a country gentleman and peer of the realm. He began to understand Sir William Carey's obsession with family tradition and honor. Too bad the old man couldn't live up to the standards he set for others. In the end it had cost him his life, taken by his own hand when he realized the certainty of the ignominious fate before him.

India's touch brought his attention back to his little family.

"Don't you think he's beautiful?" she asked, a slightly worried frown creasing her brow.

Christopher smiled proudly. "He is!" he declared, then looked at the babe carefully. "I don't see any horns, though."

India frowned. "Horns?"

Christopher's eyes sparkled impishly. "You asked me once if I was the Devil. Remember?"

A soft shade of pink colored her face. "I did?"

"Yes, indeed." Christopher smiled. "You were very drunk at the time, if I remember correctly. The first night on Pig Island."

India's blush grew deeper.

Christopher gently ran his big hand over the soft fuzz covering his son's head.

"No horns," he repeated. "Guess I'm not the Devil after all."

"Oh, Christopher." India laughed softly. "You're making fun of me. You shouldn't make fun of the woman who's just given you such a beautiful son."

He grinned and lowered his mouth to take hers in a gentle yet deep kiss that told her all she needed to know about his feelings for her.

"I remember," she said, "the first time I saw you on the *Sea Gull*. I truly thought you were the Devil come to fetch me to hell. My cousin Prudence had told me often enough that it would happen if I didn't mend my ways." She smiled at the memory. "Even then, I would have gone with you willingly. I think I fell in love with you the first time I saw you. I just didn't recognize the feeling until much later. I was so afraid that you didn't love me in return."

Christopher smiled and took her hand in his.

"Believe me, India, you never have to worry about being

loved. I intend to love you for all the days and years to come, and have many more babies just like this one. Who knows, maybe we'll have a whole crew of those little ones!''

India laughed. ''If that is your intention, sir, I suggest we switch places. Next time you can birth the babe and I will hold your hand!''

''With that absurd statement I declare you need some rest.'' When she grabbed his hand, not wanting him to go, he shook his head. ''Sleep,'' he ordered. ''I'll send in Bess to tend to the babe.''

He turned as he reached the door to see her already drifting into exhausted slumber, their child still held securely in her arms. As he looked at his wife, her black hair splashed against the pillow and the color just beginning to return to her pale, creamy skin, he wondered at the twists of fate that had made him abandon all his relentless plans for the sake of her love and then handed him everything he'd wanted to begin with. In those last weeks away from her, he hadn't cared about finding John Thomas, and he'd forgotten his yearning for vengeance against William Carey. He'd only wanted to find India and win her back. India. His sweet India, who'd turned his life from darkness to light, as if he'd been the very Devil she'd thought him on that day many months ago. As he looked at her, sleeping peacefully with their child in her arms, he saw the road of their future, filled with love and joy and endless happiness, stretching far down the years to the end of their days. He smiled as he closed the door behind him, a smile of peaceful contentment that was echoed on the sleeping face of his wife.